SWORD READIED, LARSON WHIPPED AROUND THE FINAL CORNER. . . .

Bolverkr stood three quarters of the way to the opposite side of the rampart, his back to Larson. Beyond him, Taziar stood braced before Astryd, sword bared, while the sorceress shaped a spindle of orange light between her fingers.

Even as Astryd shaped her spell, a white starburst of magic flashed in Bolverkr's hands, dwarfing Astryd's power. She shouted. Her arm snapped out. Her sorceries arched toward Bolverkr.

The sorcerer hurled his own spell. Orange met white in a wild splash of sparks. The darker winked out, the white sputtering a savage backlash in the trail of Astryd's spell. For an instant, the sorceress seemed bathed in milky light. Suddenly, she went limp, collapsing from the ramparts like a rag doll.

Taziar screamed in anguish and rage. Sword raised, he rushed Bolverkr even as Larson charged the sorcerer from behind. . . .

Be sure to read all five novels
in Mickey Zucker Reichert's
magnificent DAW fantasy saga
of the eternal war between
LAW and CHAOS—

THE BIFROST GUARDIANS:

GODSLAYER (#1)

SHADOW CLIMBER (#2)

DRAGONRANK MASTER (#3)

SHADOW'S REALM (#4)

BY CHAOS CURSED (#5)

MICKEY ZUCKER REICHERT
THE BIFROST GUARDIANS #5

D A W   B O O K S ,   I N C .

DONALD A. WOLLHEIM, FOUNDER

375 Hudson Street, New York, NY 10014

ELIZABETH R. WOLLHEIM

SHEILA E. GILBERT

PUBLISHERS

First Printing, June 1991
1 2 3 4 5 6 7 8 9

To Nigel Ray,
for a lot

ACKNOWLEDGMENTS

Special thanks to the following people for their help with difficult, frustrating, and bizarre research (the facts are theirs, the mistakes my own): Police Captain Donald Strand, Meyer and Florine Elkin (New Yorkers), Chris Mortika (magician), Arthur Bailey-Murray (SCA), Rockwell Williams (VA psychologist), SPC Ted Meyer, John Stitely (lawyer, martial artist), several unnameable thieves and a gang of New York street montes, who taught me to cheat at cards.

I would also like to thank the rest of "the group": Eleanor, Susan, the Lauras, Beth, Roxanne. Bill, Wendy, and Anastasia for teaching me to like Mondays.

And, as always, to Dave Hartlage, Sheila Gilbert, Jonathan Matson, and Richard Hescox for their repeated help and contributions.

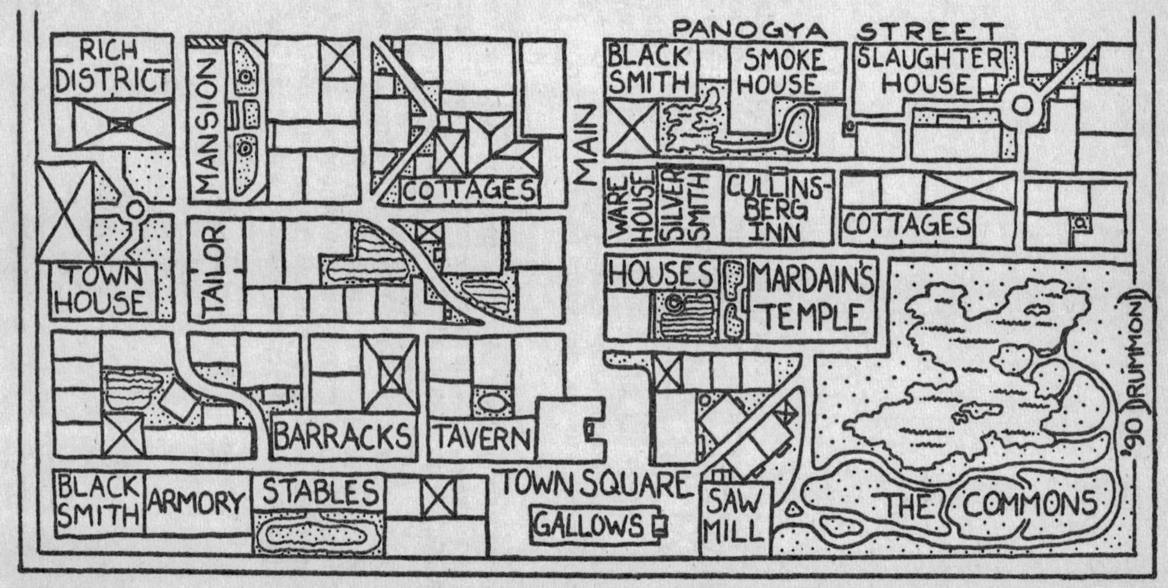

PANOGYA STREET
RICH DISTRICT
MANSION
COTTAGES
MAIN
BLACK SMITH
SMOKE HOUSE
SLAUGHTER HOUSE
WARE HOUSE
SILVER SMITH
CULLINS-BERG INN
COTTAGES
TAILOR
TOWN HOUSE
HOUSES
MARDAIN'S TEMPLE
BARRACKS
TAVERN
BLACK SMITH
ARMORY
STABLES
TOWN SQUARE
GALLOWS
SAW MILL
THE COMMONS
'90 DRUMMOND

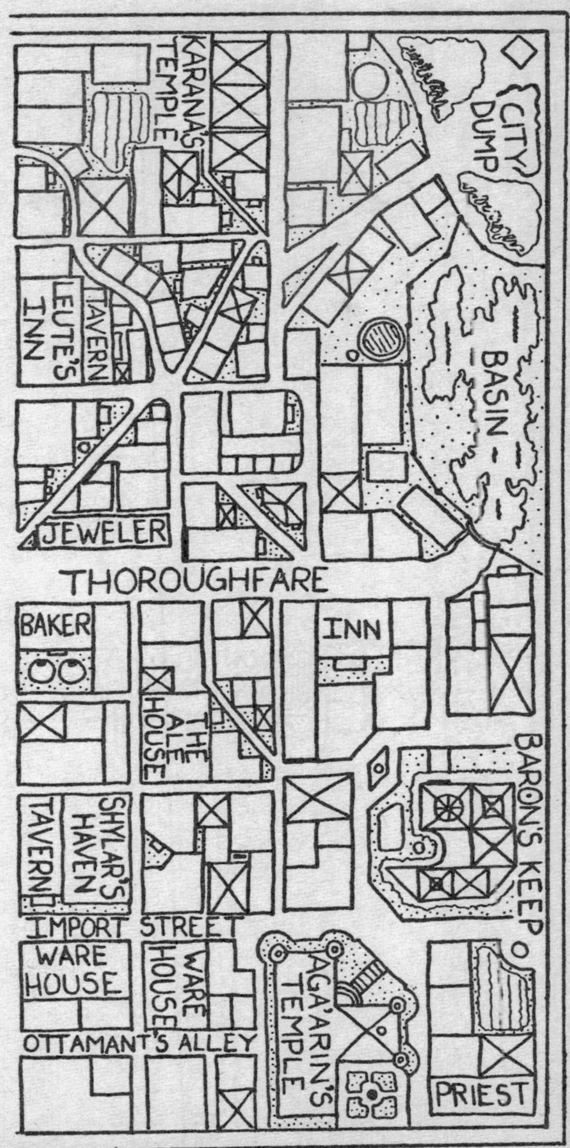

CITY DUMP
KARANA'S TEMPLE
LEUTE'S INN
TAVERN
JEWELER
BASIN
THOROUGHFARE
BAKER
INN
THE ALE HOUSE
SHYLAR'S HAVEN
TAVERN
BARON'S KEEP
IMPORT STREET
WARE HOUSE
WARE HOUSE
AGA'ARIN'S TEMPLE
PRIEST
OTTAMANT'S ALLEY

CONTENTS

PROLOGUE

Vidarr ambled across a meadow on the god-world of Asgard, pleased by the way the omnipresent sun sparkled off each grass blade as if from a plain of emerald knives. Yet, sharp as the highlights made them seem, the blades tickled harmlessly between the bindings of the sandal on Vidarr's left foot. Constructed from the mismatched scraps of a thousand mortal cobblers, the boot on Vidarr's right foot crushed ovals in the grassland, the blades springing back to attention as he moved. A breeze ruffled golden hair twisted into war braids. His face was fair, handsome, and timeless in the near-perfect way only the gods could achieve. His cloak shimmered, interwoven with silver threads.

Unhurriedly, Vidarr continued his walk, far from the gates of Valhalla, the Bifrost Bridge, and the citadels of his colleagues. Taciturn in the extreme, Vidarr had learned to radiate his emotions in lieu of words, but he preferred the more complete silence that could only come with solitude. Let the other gods argue over the quality of the wine or who deserved the honor of sitting beside beautiful Freyja. A seeker of wisdom and truth could speak with Vidarr's father, Odin. For tales of strength and courage, no one could match Vidarr's brother, Thor; and, for polite and attractive company, Vidarr's other brother, Baldur, recently raised from Hel's underworld, was the ideal. For scintillating conversation, a god could do worse than seek out Freyja's brother, Freyr. Still, it was not bitterness that sent the Silent God tramping the fields of Asgard. Quiet, demure Vidarr simply preferred to be alone.

A patch of aqua and gold wildflowers seized Vidarr's attention, and he swerved toward it. Two long-legged strides brought him to a patch of singed foliage before the flower bed. He froze, suddenly assailed by memory. He recalled a day nearly a year ago, an eye blink to the time sense of a god. Deeply etched remembrance rose, painful in its clarity. Vidarr recalled marching across this same field. Then, he had had a companion. Radiant as a new bride and nearly as handsome as Baldur, Loki the Trickster had matched Vidarr stride for stride, verbally goading the Silent One to interest in the new sword at his hip.

Aware Loki would one day betray the gods, Vidarr cared little for his walking mate. As did all the gods, he knew Loki's destiny was to lead the giants and the souls of the dead against them in a bloody war, called Ragnarok, which would kill all but a handful of the Norse deities. But Vidarr also believed he had nothing to fear. The time for war had not come yet, and, of them all, Vidarr was to be the war's hero, the only god every legend named certain to survive the Ragnarok.

As vividly as if it had been yesterday, light slashed Vidarr's vision, and the explosion of Loki's magics thundered through his ears. Pain slammed his chest with the force of a galloping stallion. Bowled to the ground, he was caught in a whirling vortex of sorcery that stole all sense of time, place, and existence. The recognition of flesh and self disappeared, replaced by a perfect prison of cold, solid iron. Vidarr vaguely recalled the high-pitched fear of his own scream ringing across his hearing through an eternity of otherwise unbroken, silent darkness.

Now, Vidarr shivered at the thought. Trapped within a block of metal, he had fought for a glimpse of light, a whisper of sound, a taste or a touch. As one eternity seemed to pass to the next, he came to believe himself forgotten, lost in an endless void of imprisonment. No external battle gained him so much as a flash of sight, so he strove for a madness that would not come. In this, mankind had surpassed the gods. The knowledge of their own mortality gave men a bent toward insanity that allowed them to surrender to it when other options seemed worse. Vidarr simply suffered, never knowing how hard Freyr tried to reach him through the iron nor how the god of elves and the sun had the dark elves craft Vidarr's prison into a sword.

Freyr had then searched the world for a man without the natural mental barriers that prevented gods and sorcerers from intruding on people's thoughts and dreams or warping their perceptions. Finding no one, Freyr had turned to alternative times, the magic involved costing him volumes in time, health, and valuables. And the answer had come in the finding that future civilizations had no sorcerers and no Balance of Law and Chaos. Unused and unneeded, the mental barriers had evolved away, and Freyr had found his hero/victim in the person of an American soldier in Vietnam, a twenty-year-old private named Al Larson who, against all propriety of his era, called upon Freyr himself as the enemies' machine guns took his life.

The details of the transfer went beyond Vidarr's knowledge. The other gods made only distant mention of the permanent damage to Freyr's magic and his mental stability. Larson had lost his human body, replaced by that of an elf follower of Freyr.

And Vidarr's first glimpse of reality had come through the eyes of his wielder, perceptions warped by battle fatigue, flashbacks, confusion, and gross ignorance. Struggling to sort reality from madness, Vidarr had forged a bond with his human wielder stronger than any ties to the gods. With the help of Larson's Freyr-chosen companions, a powerful Dragonrank sorceress named Silme and her ronin bodyguard, Kensei Gaelinar, Vidarr finally pieced together the means to break Loki's spell, a solution that had required the death, and ultimately the complete destruction, of Loki and the Chaos he harbored. In the process, Vidarr learned details about human nature he could never have guessed.

Now, before the hole of brown, curled grasses burned by Loki's magic, a smile twitched across Vidarr's lips. Unlike the humans of this era who fawned and groveled at the feet of the pantheon, Larson had little respect for anyone or anything. Through him, Vidarr learned that mortality made humans' existence more, not less, precious than the gods'. Each day held the value of a deity's decade. Lives so short and death so complete gave honor and glory to any life voluntarily sacrificed for the good of others. And Vidarr learned one thing more.

Intolerant of untruths, even among themselves, a god's word was always held to be inviolate, unquestionable authority on man's world of Midgard. Morality used to seem simple to Vidarr. What was right was simply right. But mankind, and especially Al Larson, knew a spectrum of behavior in shades of gray that Vidarr would never have hypothesized or understood without having tangled himself so deeply in a mortal's mind. It was Al Larson who taught Vidarr to lie and to deceive and, appropriately, Al Larson who was the victim of that betrayal.

Killed centuries earlier by Loki's treachery, Vidarr's brother, Baldur, had spent his time in the dank, dark, malodorous halls of Hel, comforted by the knowledge that he was destined to live again after the Ragnarok. But Loki's death meant that Ragnarok would never occur. Concerned for his brother, Vidarr had used trickery to commit Larson, Gaelinar, and a quick-witted thief named Taziar the Shadow Climber to a quest long considered impossible. As a result, they were forced to battle unmatched volumes of Chaos-energy in its natural form: as a dragon. The quest had cost Gaelinar his life, but it had brought enough Chaos into the world to balance the resurrections of two powerful keepers of Law, Baldur and Silme, and to replace the permanent loss of Loki.

The reminiscence roused Vidarr's curiosity. Larson had come out of that quest gut-shot by a rifle as out of time as himself and clinging to the meticulously-crafted katana that had belonged to his beloved and respected Kensei swordmaster. Aware that Taziar's Dragonrank girlfriend, Astryd, had some knowledge of magical healing, Vidarr had left Larson, Taziar,

Silme, and Astryd to their own devices. *I wonder how they're doing?* Vidarr considered. Larson had made it clear that he resented the gods' intrusions into his mind. Through effort, the elf had learned to wall trespassers into pockets of memory. Vidarr had learned the danger of that tactic when Larson had trapped him and an enemy in the Vietnamese jungles, their only escape, back through Larson's mind, neatly blocked by its owner.

Still, Larson had never found a means to detect the presence of a gentle probe. Through it, Vidarr could communicate and read the elf-man's superficial thoughts. *I'll read his mood without him ever knowing I was there. If he's relaxed, I'll say my hellos. So long as I don't play with his thoughts, he shouldn't mind.* With that idea, Vidarr thrust a probe for Larson's mind.

Vidarr's search met nothing. Shocked, he withdrew and tried again. Once again, he met only darkness.

Vidarr slid to the grass, sitting cross-legged, his fingers to his temples. Never before had it cost energy or effort to explore Larson's mind. Vidarr lowered his head, putting his full concentration into the task. Again, his mental probe met no resistance. *Dead? He's dead?* Surprise and concern sharpened his focus. Gradually, words, images, and the snarl of looping thought pathways took shape, black against near-black, like the outline of sun glazed through thunderheads, viewed as much from his knowledge of its necessary presence as reality. *Not dead,* Vidarr realized, gaining little solace from the realization. *But nearly so. How?* For now, the reason did not matter. Vidarr rooted through the darkness for a single spark of life.

For some time, the search frustrated Vidarr. Apparently Al Larson still lived, otherwise he would have no memories at all, not even the vague, smeared images obscured by the hovering fog of death. Vidarr drew fully into Larson's mind, forcing himself to evaluate the quality of each shadow, following a subtle and scattered trail that was more ''less dark'' than light.

Gradually, he discovered a single, cold pinpoint of light, rapidly fading.

A thought struck through Vidarr. *If he dies before I get out of here, we're both dead.* Gently, he fanned the glow. It sputtered, frayed like ancient string. For an instant, Vidarr thought he had blown it out. Fear gripped him as the spark sputtered, then grew ever so slightly. He felt a survival instinct shift, erratic as a rusted hinge, then cringe back into hiding from pain.

You bastard! Since when has pain ever stopped you from doing anything? He kicked the wire-thin pathway that housed the instinct. Agony sparked through Larson's mind, but this time the survival instinct hovered, uncertain, tenuous.

Vidarr held his breath.

In Larson's head, a hand clamped onto Vidarr's shoulder.

Shock wrenched a gasp from Vidarr, the strength of the emotion splashing insight through Larson's mind. Heart pounding, Vidarr snapped back to Asgard. He could feel the other presence flash out with him.

After the crushing darkness of Larson's mind, the hovering fire of Asgard's sun blinded Vidarr. He whirled, slashing an arm up instinctively. His forearm crashed against a wrist, breaking the grip, and he found himself facing Freyr.

Freyr stood with arms crossed in judgment, and his pale eyes shone like the sun that was his charge. "What are you doing?"

Vidarr rarely used words. Over time, he had become adept at communication only by radiating his primary emotions. Now, as surprised waned, he stared dispassionately at Freyr.

"Allerum." Freyr used the name Larson had won through an inadvertent spell of stuttering during his original introduction to his friends. "You were healing Allerum."

That being self-evident, Vidarr mimicked Freyr's outraged stance without a reply.

"You can't do that." Freyr made a brisk gesture

with his arm that set his clothes shimmering color-fully.

Still, Vidarr waited, not bothering to contradict an obvious fallacy. Freyr's commanding manner was starting to annoy the Silent God, but he kept the first stirrings of irritation from his disclosure and his manner.

Apparently recognizing the ludicrousness of his own claim, Freyr amended. "Well, of course, I suppose you can heal Allerum, but you shouldn't. Vidarr, it would be bad."

Vidarr cocked his brows, demanding explanation. If not for Al Larson's courage and his willingness to fight against Loki, Vidarr knew he would still be trapped within a lightless, soundless void. Loki would still live to lead the hordes of Hel and giants against the gods and men. Without Vidarr to slay the Fenris Wolf, the beast would have survived to aid its loathsome father, Loki. Instead of the prophesied Ragnarok that would have ended with a few gods and men still intact, Loki and his followers would have torn the worlds asunder with a limitless Chaos of slaughter. Wives killing husbands. Fathers raping daughters.

The images wound through Vidarr's mind, bringing a chill that the sun-filled Asgard meadow could not touch. *Averted, all averted, thanks to Allerum. I owe him my life as do all the gods. And he paid a price we should never have asked of anyone.* Vidarr cringed, recalling how moments before the sword stroke that took Loki's life, the Evil One had reminded Larson that destroying him would prevent Ragnarok. Without the war, the Norse gods would reign through eternity, never replaced by the Christian religion Larson embraced. Larson, his family, his friends, and his world would never exist.

Freyr's voice became fatherly. Apparently partially guessing Vidarr's concern, he rationalized. "I know you think you owe something to Allerum, but you don't. Men are pawns, meant to serve us. The opportunity to do so is all the reward they deserve."

"I used to believe that," said Vidarr quietly, his voice a mellow tenor.

Caught off-guard by Vidarr's switch to speech, Freyr stared.

"Before I spent so much time in Allerum's head."

Freyr recovered with a snort. "You can't judge all men by Allerum. He was addled by a war without glory, and he's a product of his time and place. His god chooses to fade into the background, leaving men to make their own decisions and mistakes. I passed over hundreds of loud-mouthed, disrespectful future Americans before I discovered Allerum."

Vidarr did not bother to argue. Natural mind barriers prevented the gods from reading the thoughts and intentions of mortals, so neither side of the discussion could be corroborated by fact. Vidarr extrapolated from the only model he could access: Al Larson. And, having learned how sincerely humans voiced their lies, he had to guess that most of the gods' pawns hid their grudging acceptance of the position behind an artificial enthusiasm. Vidarr let impatience sift through his facade, making it clear he considered Larson's life more important than a discussion on human motivation.

Accepting the cue, Freyr came to the heart of his explanation. "You are familiar with the Balance." It was a statement, not a question.

Vidarr nodded. The Balance between Law and Chaos was eternal, since long before the gods entered the nine worlds. The natural forces seemed to keep themselves in line without need for a guardian. Minor inequalities had no effect upon the worlds and their inhabitants. The deaths of strong proponents of one side were always naturally compensated by equal deaths for the opposite cause.

"Then," Freyr continued, "you must also know the effect Allerum has had on that Balance."

Vidarr lowered his head, feeling responsible. Freed from his imprisonment, joy had made him careless. He had left Loki's corpse where it had collapsed near Hvergelmir's waterfall, never guessing Larson would hurl the body into the cascade that destroyed all things. Annihilated, body and soul, Loki's harbored Chaos disappeared, leaving a gap no one could fill. *Chaos.* Vidarr shook his head. *The stuff of life.* It seemed odd that the very substance defining existence also poisoned it, so that corruption naturally accompanied power. The world's only mortal sorcerers, the Dragonrank, drew their powers from tapping their own internal chaos known as life force. Therefore, those who served Chaos were always more powerful than their counterparts, and there were always larger numbers of Law abiding souls in the world to compensate.

"Allerum destroyed Loki," Freyr explained anyway. "Then he raised Silme from the dead, balancing her resurrection with an equally powerful servant of Chaos. . . ."

Vidarr nodded smugly, but this perfect example of Larson's concern for the Balance was crushed by Freyr's next description.

". . . whom Allerum later killed, thereby skewing the Balance dangerously further in the direction of Law." Freyr sat in the grass, hugging his knees to his chest. Thin, white-blond hair tumbled about his shoulders. "Then there was that Geirmagnus' rod quest. . . ."

"That's not fair!" Vidarr interrupted. "It wasn't Allerum's idea. In fact, he fought against it so hard I had to lie and cheat to make him finish it. My father forced me to send Allerum on that quest. He couldn't bear the thought of his most beautiful and gracious son rotting in Hel for eternity. . . ."

Freyr raised his hand to stop Vidarr's uncharacteristic flow of words. "I never said it was Allerum's idea, only that no one else could have succeeded. As it was, Allerum, Taziar, and the Kensei resurrected Baldur." Freyr added quickly, "Don't misunderstand. I'm as glad to have Baldur back as anyone. But the rift in the Balance would have been enough to destroy the world. If not for the dragon."

Vidarr nodded. He had seen the beast through Larson's eyes, a towering manifestation of raw Chaos energy imprisoned by the first leader of the Dragonrank sorcerers at a time when the Balance had tipped dangerously in the other direction. Again, he saw the house-sized creature bank and glide on its leathery wings, maneuverable as a falcon. He knew Larson's fear as teeth long and sharp as daggers gashed his arm, and Vidarr also knew the tearing depth of grief when Kensei Gaelinar goaded the beast through a coil of razor wire, sacrificing his own life in the process. Dragons were conglomerates of unmastered Chaos-force; slaying it dispersed rather than destroyed its power. Here, Vidarr believed, was how the Balance had been put right.

But the expression of outrage on Freyr's face cued Vidarr to the fact that there was knowledge he did not yet have. Freyr cleared his throat. "You have no idea how Allerum came to be as near to death as he is. Do you?"

Vidarr shook his head, hoping the gesture made it clear it did not matter. Regardless of the cause, he owed Larson his loyalty. *Don't I?* Doubt seeped silently into his awareness. Feeling weak, he sat beside Freyr.

The lord of elves plucked at grass spears, avoiding Vidarr's stare. "Raw Chaos can't be destroyed, only disbanded. To destroy it, you must destroy its host."

Vidarr waited, aware Freyr had started with the obvious in order to make a more serious point.

"Chaos-force is nonintelligent, geared only toward survival and the Balance. It knows only that it must find a strong host, one capable of surviving its transfer and its demands for cruelty, mayhem, and disorder. Once freed from dragon form, that raw Chaos-energy raged across the Kattegat to a farm town called Wilsberg. There, it struck with a storm that slaughtered every citizen *except its new master.*"

Freyr's words stunned Vidarr into an awed silence. *All of that Chaos into one man?* The thought was madness. Until now, he had assumed the Chaos would disseminate, that every man, woman, and child in Midgard would become a trace more evil. *No one could have survived the transfer of so much Chaos energy.*

"A Dragonrank sorcerer named Bolverkr." Freyr answered the unspoken question. "He came from the earliest days of the Dragonrank when the mages drew reams of raw Chaos to themselves rather than using life energy, ignorant of the cost to the Balance." Freyr paused, leaving time for the words to sink in, waiting to see whether Vidarr would make the obvious connection without further hints.

Vidarr remained stunned.

Freyr met and held Vidarr's gaze. "Chaos hunted out the strongest possible master on the nine worlds."

Suddenly, understanding radiated from Vidarr. *It went to Bolverkr, not me or Freyr or Odin.* The natural conclusion was too enormous to contemplate. *This Bolverkr apparently wields more power than any single god.* He shuddered at the observation.

Freyr concurred. "Frightening, isn't it?"

Vidarr nodded.

Freyr rose, brushing pollen and grass spears from his leggings. "Bolverkr knows Allerum and Taziar loosed the Chaos that destroyed the town and the people he loved, his pregnant wife and his fortress, and turned him into a puppet of Chaos, contaminated beyond redemption. He's sworn to be avenged, but he isn't stupid, either. He knows Allerum and Taziar have already defeated the Chaos-force that is his power, and now they have the Dragonmages, Silme and Astryd, as partners in love and war. He's playing it careful and well. Allerum's current condition demonstrates Bolverkr's skill." Again, Freyr held Vidarr's pale gaze. "And now I think you understand why you can't rouse Allerum."

Vidarr beetled his brows, missing the connection.

Seeing Vidarr's confusion, Freyr explained. "Allerum is an anachronism and Silme, by all rights, should still be dead. Taziar and Astryd are small enough in power that their deaths would not severely affect the balance. But, should Bolverkr die, wielding as much Chaos-force as he does, the Balance would overturn. The world might be destroyed, all men, elves, and gods with it. Or, perhaps, his death would need to be matched with equal amounts of supporters of Law. All the mortal followers of Law might not prove enough. Gods would die, Vidarr. Perhaps you and I? Odin? Thor and Baldur? For the sake of the world, Allerum and his companions must lose this feud. You'll have to undo anything you've done and *let Allerum die.*"

Vidarr bit his lip, pained by Freyr's words. He understood the necessity. The Balance and the lives of gods had to take precedence over one soldier, no matter how much good he had done for Vidarr. The idea of leaving Allerum to his own devices seemed difficult enough. *But what's done is done. To snuff the slight spark I encouraged would be murder.*

Freyr tried to soften his command. "You have to remember, Allerum was as good as dead when I plucked him from the battlefield. We gave him life, if only for a few extra months. If not for me, he'd be a bloody corpse lying in an empty riverbed in Vietnam."

Vidarr said nothing.

Freyr sighed. He clasped Vidarr's shoulder comfortingly. "Do what you have to do." Without further encouragement, Freyr started back across the meadow, his boots crushing foliage in huge patches, his eight foot frame still visible against the sun long after he passed beyond hearing distance of Vidarr.

For some time, Vidarr remained seated without moving. Then, dreading the inevitable, he maneuvered a probe into Larson's mind.

This time, Vidarr met a diffuse grayness that revealed the tangled tapestry of Larson's thoughts as vague sculptures in shadow. He thrust farther, drawing himself directly into Larson's mind. Pain assailed him, wholly Larson's, and the god focused instead on the ring of companions whose words wafted clearly to Larson.

Taziar was speaking, "Everything's impossible until

someone accomplishes it. They said no one could escape the baron's dungeon, but I've done it. Twice . . .''

The words droned on, reaching a crescendo, but Vidarr lost his thoughts in a different conversation. He recalled a time when the Fenris Wolf had penetrated Larson's mind, intending to torture the elf with manipulation of his memories. Then, Vidarr's sudden appearance in Larson's mind had startled the Wolf into leaving.

Later, facing Larson's anger rather than gratitude, Vidarr remembered his own words and the frustration that had suffused him at Larson's stubbornness. ''. . . And you seem to have forgotten that Freyr rescued you from death to bring you here, at no small risk to his own life . . . Freyr pulled you from a hellish war . . .''

Parts of Larson's reply returned clearly. ''. . . to place me into another hellish war. Into Hel itself even! I'm supposed to feel grateful that Freyr ripped me from a world of technological miracles and dumped me into the body of a ninety-eight pound weakling?''

''Technological miracles or not. You were dead.''

''Dead or not, I was free. I'm no slave. If I am to serve gods, I shall do so willingly or not at all. Otherwise, you can kill me right now.''

The memory slipped from Vidarr's thoughts, driven away by the growing light of Larson's mind as the dying elf responded to Taziar's rallying speech.

Vidarr cursed, groping for the flaring glow of life before it could fill Larson's being. He seized its stalk, aware he would need to retreat as he cut or else die along with Larson. Beneath his grip, he could feel Larson fighting aside the hovering numbness and peace that death offered. Some subconscious portion of Larson's mind must have sensed Vidarr's presence because his thoughts brought another memory vividly to life:

Larson lay, again near death, on the grounds of Geirmagnus' estate, trying to keep Vidarr's telepathic words in focus.

''. . . I always knew any or all of you might die, but I had no other choice . . . I care for Baldur very deeply. I did not enjoy the deception any more than you, but I saw no other way. I plead the cause of brotherly love and hope you can find it in yourself to forgive me.''

Then, Larson had fallen unconscious before he could delve an answer. Now, Vidarr could see that Larson had added an addendum to the memory, a selfless acceptance of the apology and an offer of friendship.

Vidarr stared, not daring to believe what he saw. His fingers slipped from the stalk. Larson's will flared, sparking thoughts throughout his mind, and Vidarr withdrew.

If Allerum is to die, let him do so honestly and by his own doing. I won't have a hand in his murder.

In the vast meadow of Asgard, a songbird twittered in a minor key.

CHAPTER 1:

Chaos Madness

Chaos of thought and passion, all confused;
Still by himself abused, or disabused;
Created half to rise, and half to fall;
Great lord of all things, yet a prey to all;
Sole judge of truth, in endless error hurled;
The glory, jest, and riddle of the world.
—Alexander Pope, *An Essay on Man*

A sliver of moon hovered over the Barony of Cullinsberg, revealing the rows of buildings along Panogya Street as familiar blocks of shadow. Taziar Medakan, the Shadow Climber, had chosen the moon's phase from habit; years of work beneath crescents that shed only enough light to etch landmarks had given him cause to call this phase the "thieves' moon" and to consider it a friend. The cobbled roadway felt familiar through the thin, flexible soles of his boots. More times than he cared to remember, he had stalked the thoroughfares and alleyways of Cullinsberg dressed, as now, in tough, black linens. A comma of hair as dark as his clothing spilled from beneath his hood and into his eyes, a familiar annoyance he could not seem to avoid no matter how carefully he cut the straight, fine locks.

As a child, Taziar had memorized every corner of Cullinsberg in order to survive. Later, unable to pass up any task labeled impossible, he had learned the intricacies that came with detailed study of the city's most magnificent defenses, most of which he had thwarted simply for the challenge. But tonight Taziar had no interest in Cullinsberg's secrets and challenges. Beyond the imposing stone walls of the baron's city, Taziar knew a Dragonrank sorcerer named Bolverkr plotted torture and cruel deaths for Taziar and his closest friends. And the Shadow Climber was determined to assess this enemy with his own eyes, to ascertain just how imminently the coming battle loomed.

Taziar caught handholds in the stone and mortar wall of the slaughterhouse and shinnied to its rooftop with the ease that had earned him his alias. He crouched, though even upright he stood half a head shorter than an average woman. Sounds wafted to him, a dull mixture of high-pitched insect shrills, a fox call, distantly answered, the rasp of garbage blowing through an alleyway, and the creak of wood in perfect rhythm with the wind. Taziar sifted through the routine medley of city night. Beneath it all, he heard the steady thump of footsteps, strong and competent, unlike the intermittent shuffle and halt of street people hunting food or the quiet caution of orphan gangs or thieves.

Guards. Taziar verified his guess by a cautious peek into Panogya Street. A half dozen soldiers in the barony's red and black uniforms paced toward the town's central thoroughfare. During the fifteen and a half years that Taziar's father had served as their captain, the patrols had filled young Taziar with pride. But that respect had withered to loathing the day the baron hanged Taziar's father based on evidence contrived by a crooked politician. Taziar's own capture and torture at the hands of sadistic, corrupt guardsmen had destroyed any vestige of deference toward Cullinsberg's defenders.

Taziar lowered himself flat to the roof tiles, intent on the patrol. Usually, the guardsmen prowled in groups of twos and threes. The baron would only have doubled his night watches for a purpose. And, since Taziar had masterminded and commanded Cullinsberg's only prison break just three days earlier, freeing the seven key leaders of the Underground, he had every reason to believe the baron wanted him.

Concerned for Al Larson, barely rescued from the

brink of death; for Larson's pregnant, sorceress wife, Silme; and for his own girlfriend, Astryd, who spent her days draining her life energy casting spells to enhance and hasten Larson's healing, Taziar had found his attention singularly focused on the Chaos-driven Dragonrank sorcerer who had sworn vengeance against them. In the shadow of Bolverkr's power, Cullinsberg's guard force had paled to an insignificant threat unworthy of Taziar's worry. Yet, now Taziar realized that if he was run through by a guardsman's spear, sword, or crossbow bolt, he would be as dead as if Bolverkr's magics had done the deed.

Taziar smiled, intrigued by the mundane challenge offered by Cullinsberg's guardsmen. Days without the rush of natural stimulants his body produced in times of stress had made him as twitchy as an addict. Sleep had become impossible. Restlessness had driven him to sneak away from his friends, where they hid and recovered in Shylar's whorehouse, in the care of the best comforters and providers the Underground could offer. Taziar knew Larson, Silme, and Astryd would chide him for not acting like what Larson called a "team player." The twentieth century English phrase seemed ridiculously out of place in Taziar's thoughts. But to ignore an enemy as powerful and competent as Bolverkr, trusting luck to hold him at bay until they became strong enough to strike back was insanity, not a strategy.

Days ago, Bolverkr had captured Silme. Attempting to jettison some of the Chaos that warped him, he had tricked her into opening a link to the source of his Chaos-power. Silme had managed to break that contact, freeing the Chaos he had shared with her and causing it to backlash to its master. Silme seemed to believe the shock force of that rebound would keep Bolverkr busy rebuilding his sense of self and his keep, but Taziar felt less certain of Silme's reassurance and more confident of Bolverkr's strength. *I have to see for myself just how badly the Chaos injured Bolverkr and his fortress. And I have to delay his next attack a little longer if I can.*

Taziar watched the gloom swallow the patrol as their footsteps receded to clicks, then disappeared. *But first, I have to get past the sentries.* Taziar rose to a crouch, skittered across the slaughterhouse roof and into a zigzagging series of alleyways. *Which means I need to get a feel for the new patterns of the watch.* Skirting scattered scraps of wood, cloth and food, feasting rats and rotting crates, Taziar crossed the thready branchways without a sound. His keen, blue eyes measured the depth of every silhouette and shadow, guiding him always to the ones that hid him best. His walks and sprints were steady, sinuous as a cat's, without the jerky impetuousness that draws the attention of predators: hunters, soldiers, and thieves.

Padding southward, Taziar came to Mardain's temple, a towering, seven-story structure of mortared stone. Aside from the baron's keep and Aga'arin's church, both closely guarded even in the most peaceful times, Mardain's temple stood taller than any building in Cullinsberg. Acutely aware of the lack of handholds in its smoothly-chinked lower story, Taziar sprinted down the byway, fingers scraping the temple's masonry. Nearly at the far corner, he hurled himself toward the wall. Momentum carried him to the second story where he ferreted out the familiar handholds and clambered to the rooftop.

The sky spread above Taziar, stars gleaming silver like scales in a fisherman's net. Below him stretched the familiar patterns of the city of Cullinsberg. Safe in his domain high above the citizenry, Taziar felt like a king surveying his realm. To the south, Cullinsberg's gates lay open, as always. Though too distant to discern, Taziar knew guards paced the walls. Usually, people could enter and exit the town without challenge, but Taziar guessed the guards now questioned anyone passing out through the gates, especially at night.

The looming shape of the gallows in the town square unnerved Taziar, so he chose to look another way. To the west, a dozen guards huddled in conference on the main thoroughfare. As he watched, they split into three equal groups, one marching down Panogya Street and each of the others tramping a parallel route in the alleyways on either side.

Taziar held his breath, aware that a few moments earlier that maneuver might have seen him surrounded. *Of course, I still could have escaped by climbing.* He considered this flaw in the guards' tactics. Taziar's capture months ago had lost him the cover of his alias. *They know who I am and that I climb buildings.* The last was gross understatement. Taziar had scaled heights and surfaces that mountaineers would have dismissed as impossible. Though he had never been given the opportunity, he believed he could climb a vertical pane of ice, and those who had seen him in action never challenged the claim.

Intrigued by the guards' formation, Taziar watched the closest set of men as they passed between the smokehouse and Cullinsberg's inn. The sentries wove through the alley. One always stayed in the lead, apparently watching for movement. Two bobbed their heads, following the sweep of each wall to its ceiling. The last glanced behind rain barrels and garbage, using a torch to peer into any crack large enough to fit a rat.

It seemed only natural for Taziar to anticipate his reactions had the guards, in fact, intercepted him in the alleyway. *I would have slipped ahead and climbed.* He tracked his potential route to a series of shops and cottages closest to the eastern wall enclosing the city. His eyes narrowed suspiciously. *They must have some strategy in mind. Why would they flush me toward the wall? They know I could scale it. Then I'd be free.* Squinting, he studied the eastern wall, wondering if the baron had packed it with sentries. If so, it seemed a foolish mistake that would require him to skimp on guardsmen for the other three walls. *Why short defenses on three sides of the city for one? What would make him that certain I'd go eastward?*

Darkness glazed the outer wall to a blur. Taziar blinked, for the first time cursing the limits of vision imposed by the "thieves' moon." He tensed for a better look, and his movement brought a glint of metal to view. *Too near to be from the catwalk.* Taziar froze, staring. The object flashed away. *Too high to be from a sentry on the ground. Has to be some sort of steel fitting or object on a rooftop.* Discomfort jangled within Taziar, its source not quite able to slip from instinct to understanding. Taziar considered, twisting his head until he found the glitter of metal again. This time, the answer came. *It disappeared even though I didn't move.* Since the moon could not have shifted that abruptly, it had to be the metal that had changed position.

Taziar contemplated the significance of his observation. *Either it's a loose edge of something being blown by wind, or someone is on that rooftop.* The second possibility would have seemed ludicrous under ordinary circumstances, but the guardsmen's behavior in the alleyway clinched it. *The baron stationed sentries on the rooftops for me?* Taziar followed the natural extensions of the strategy. *The patrols weren't trying to drive me eastward, just toward any wall at all. They probably figured I'd know to dodge sentries on the walls, but I'd run right into the ones hiding on the roofs.*

Now the baron's scheme made perfect sense, and Taziar tried to rework it to his advantage. *I can't go through the main gate. I have no choice but to climb the walls.* One alternative presented itself to Taziar. When he had escaped the baron's dungeons months ago, he and his barbarian companion had crept from the city through the sewer system. Now, that option appealed less to Taziar than battling through the guards, though he carried no sword. If not for Moonbear's strength, they would never have hammered free the grating that kept attackers from using the same means to enter the city. *A grating that may have been replaced,* Taziar realized, remembering that Moonbear's quick reflexes had also kept the Climber from drowning when he fell into a depression in the riverbed. *Forget the sewers. I'm just going to have to avoid the outer circle of rooftops and slip over the wall be-

tween sentries. Decision made, Taziar waited until the patrol again turned westward, then clambered down the east side of Mardain's temple, dropping from the second story into the alley.

Back pressed to the wall, Taziar glanced into a connecting east-west roadway. The backs of three retreating guardsmen loomed to the west. Eastward, the path lay open. Quietly, huddled in pooled darkness, he rushed toward the eastern wall and freedom. Flitting past a row of cottages, he slowed as he approached a well-known crosswalk leading to a statue-crowned basin where much of the populace drew its drinking water. Edging forward, Taziar peered around the corner.

He found himself face-to-face with a guardsman urinating on the stone and sod of the candle maker's shop.

Taziar back-stepped.

The guard's expression went from startled to urgent. Without bothering to fix his britches, he lunged for a spear leaning against the wall. "Here! Shadow Climber. Southeast. Candle maker's!"

Taziar groaned at the crisp efficiency of the signal; evidently, the guards had organized precisely for the cause of his capture. Spared only the moment it took the guard to jab his spear, Taziar reacted from long habit. Seizing handholds in the wall, he scurried to the roof. Too late, he realized his mistake. As his head came over the ledge, he caught a split-second glimpse of guardsmen rushing toward him and cold steel whipping for his face.

Momentum overrode Taziar's instinct to duck. Instead, he flung himself to the rooftop. The sentry's sword tore the hood from his head, close enough to ruffle a breeze across his scalp. The backswing caught the Climber nearly at the hilt, a clouting stroke that sent him reeling across the tiles. Head ringing, he dropped to one knee, twisting to face his attackers. One rushed him, catching a tenuous grip on Taziar's sleeve. Taziar jerked backward, and a more solid pair of hands seized him from the opposite side.

"I had him first." A knife flashed in the first guard's hand.

The second recoiled with a gasp of pain. "You bastard!" Blood splashed Taziar's cheek.

The words slurred through Taziar's spinning consciousness. Reflex had him up and halfway to the northern edge of the roof, tearing free of the fingers entwined in his sleeve, before logic took over. He judged the gap between buildings; a leap across a narrow alley would take him onto a cottage roof. He had tensed to spring before sense seeped fully back into his numbed mind, and he recognized the shapes on the reinforced thatch roof as guardsmen with drawn bows. *Karana's hell.* Taziar flinched back, hoping his nearness to the other guards would force the bowmen to hold their fire.

The twang of bowstrings sounded almost simultaneously. Taziar ducked and rolled. Steel heads clattered to the tiles. One guardsman cried out, apparently pierced by a companion's arrow. Others swore, scrabbling for cover. In the confusion, Taziar sprang from the rooftop toward the now empty alley where he had stumbled upon the indisposed guard. He skimmed his fingers and toes along the wall to slow his descent without bothering to catch secure holds. Baron Dietrich's mistake seemed obvious; apparently, the baron had offered an individual reward or bonus to the guard who killed the Shadow Climber. While it encouraged alertness, morale, and healthy competition, it also stretched the already marginal cooperativeness of the guards.

Perhaps, Taziar thought as he crossed the byway and hauled himself up a warehouse wall to a slated, second-story rooftop that came to a central point, *the baron doesn't care how many men he loses, so long as he gets me.* The idea seemed morbid, but not beneath the morality of a leader whose control by Aga'arin's priests had driven him to hang his faithful captain. *If the bowmen aren't afraid to kill their own, how can I possibly survive their barrages?*

Taziar dodged to the northern side of the roof, boots scrabbling on the slanted surface. Arrows thunked into sod or tile; more clicked or snapped against stone.

Other noises wafted to him beneath the muffled shouts and curses: scraping, the hollow clunk of wood hitting wood, and the louder impact as heavy objects struck tile. The roof shook beneath his hold. *What?* Needing to understand this new threat, Taziar risked craning his neck around the corner.

The bowmen on the cottage roof had abandoned their attack to place a sturdy board from the lip of their rooftop to Taziar's, spanning the byway the Climber had run across. Farther south, the swordsmen on the neighboring roof had placed a similar passage to the row of cottages next to Taziar's current location.

Taziar jerked his head back around. *They're prepared this time. Those makeshift bridges can get them across roadways too wide for me to jump.* Taziar worked his way to the western side of his roof, considering in which situations the guards' preparation gave them the advantage and how he might turn it against them. *The boards will slow them down. So long as I stay on buildings set closely enough for me to jump across them, I'll be faster.* Taziar frowned, listening to the pound of footsteps as the guards crossed the bridges. *They'll expect me to stay high. That's my style. So, at some point, I'll have to go to the streets.* Taziar leapt from the slanted rooftop, over a narrow alley, to the flower shop, gathering momentum from the story of difference in height. *I need to draw them away from the rooftops near the outer wall.*

Disguising his voice, Taziar shouted, ''Here! Shadow Climber. Southeast. Slant-roofed warehouse!'' He was rewarded by the clatter of moment as guardsmen on-high all along the eastern wall joined the chase. *All right. I've got them away from the wall. Now how am I going to get them away from me?* No ready answers came.

The patrol on the cottages rounded the slant-roofed warehouse. Atop the warehouse itself, the archers swore. Tile pattered down the slope and into the street. One screamed as his footing tore free, and he toppled to the packed dirt road below.

Taziar shinnied into the street. Ignoring the moaning guardsman, he sprinted across the roadway and scrambled to the roof of the L-shaped cobbler shop. Behind him, he could hear the scratch of wood dragged along tile. Footsteps thundered across the slaughterhouse roof.

Taziar measured the distance to the smokehouse, then sneaked a peek in the direction of the pursuing guardsmen. It would be a race to the smokehouse. *If I don't leap across, they'll meet me.* The space between buildings gaped. Not daring to contemplate it for too long, Taziar sprinted across the long limb of the L-shaped roof and dove for the smokehouse. He hit with his shoulder, rolling in a crooked arc that saved his life. Arrows rebounded from sun-baked stone and tile, every one taking the straighter path he should have taken.

Once on the smokehouse roof, Taziar wasted no time. He half-leapt, half-climbed into Panogya Street. He twisted his head as he fell, gaining a momentary semicircle of view. Guardsmen clustered on the cottages west of the slant-roofed warehouse, the cobbler shop, smokehouse, slaughterhouse, and the roof of Shylar's whorehouse. Quick as a squirrel, Taziar whisked up the wall of the butcher's shop even as soldiers in black and red uniforms slapped boards into place from Shylar's whorehouse.

Too close. Taziar's heart pounded. His lungs felt as if their linings had been gasped away, leaving them raw and bleeding. *Think. Have to think. A trick.* He knew this side of town well; as a young teen, he had spent much of his time here, filching food for himself and his friends through the baker's third-story window. Running westward, he sprang the short gap between the butcher's shop and the cooper's, then leapt down into the cross street, grabbing a handful of stones from the roadway as he ran.

"Shadow Climber!" someone yelled behind him. "Northeast. Cobbler's!"

Taziar jammed his fingers into cracks of the building that housed the baker's huge ovens. The stone felt warm beneath his hands, and he clambered toward the top without glancing back. He kept himself tightened into the smallest target possible, feeling the wary prickle that came with known enemies at his back. But, apparently, the guardsmen were preoccupied with angling their boards from the single story of the cobbler's shop to the three-story structure that housed the baker's ovens.

Taziar darted across the oven building to the attached baker's shop. There, he paused, his fingers on the westernmost ledge of the baker's shop, overlooking the main thoroughfare, waiting for the guardsmen to come back into sight.

As the first guardsman appeared, Taziar swung down over the side, clinging to the lip of the rooftop as if to drop into the main thoroughfare. At the last moment, he swung his legs and hooked through the baker's window. He landed silently on the floor, turned and hurled the stones he had gathered through the window and into the main street, hoping the mild thump of their landing simulated a small man rolling onto the cobbles with enough accuracy to fool the sentries. Drawing back into the darkness of the baker's shop, Taziar waited.

Shortly, a cry broke the night. "Shadow Climber just entered the northwest quad. Jeweler."

Taziar smiled. The main market thoroughfare onto which the front gates opened ran north and south while Cullinsberg's second largest street, Panogya, ran east and west, dividing the city into four sections. The sentry's misidentification revealed that they believed the Climber had crossed the main thoroughfare.

Cautiously, Taziar avoided the tables, ledges, and tray racks that, before sunup, would hold cooling cakes, pies, and breads. Not wanting to risk waking the baker and his family on the second floor, Taziar padded down both flights of steps to the shop level. Ignoring the front exit onto the main street, he pushed open the heavier, unlocked panel leading into the oven building. Finding the hearth cold, he ducked into the chimney, braced his back and feet against the stone, and edged upward.

Dirt coated Taziar's limbs and face. Soot wedged beneath his fingernails and blackened the tips. He choked on ash, hating the taste, suppressing a cough with effort. At length, he came to the roof. Peering out, he saw no evidence of guards. Relieved, Taziar pulled himself to the tiles. *Ought to charge the baker for the chimney sweeping.* Taziar could not raise a grin for his feeble joke. *Maybe that'll pay him back for some of the bread I stole as a child.* Lowering himself over the ledge, he climbed back into Panogya Street.

In the wake of the guards' chase, the city seemed eerily quiet. Taziar slunk with a graceful speed that brought him swiftly to the eastern side of the outer wall. He waited until the soft slap of footsteps on the upper walk wafted clearly to him. Then, as the sound receded, he shinnied up the stone, scuttled across the top, and lowered himself to the fire-cleared plain that surrounded the city of Cullinsberg. *Done.* Excitement ebbed, replaced by the cold sweat with which Taziar had become all too familiar. The euphoria inspired by action had disappeared, yet the feeling of satisfaction that accompanied outwitting the baron's guardsmen felt twice as sweet for the period of idleness that had preceded it. *It's not over yet. I still have to find out what Bolverkr's doing. And sneak back in.*

Taziar knew the latter would prove simple enough. Once the guards realized he had outwitted them, they would believe he had escaped the city. There was no reason to expect him to return, so the patrols would likely become lax. The last time the baron had sent soldiers beyond the city limits in pursuit of Taziar, he had lost a strong faction of his army, a captain, and a prime minister in a fiasco that nearly reignited the Barbarian Wars. Taziar doubted the baron would risk his men that way again.

Taziar darted across the open stretch of ground to the woodlands that enclosed most of northern Europe. Born and raised a city boy, Taziar had not cared much for forests with their lack of roads, sudden dead ends, and crisp leaves and sticks that revealed his location with every step. But during his several months' stay among Moonbear's barbarian tribe in Sweden, Taziar had learned to anticipate and circle deadfalls and areas of thickest brush. They had taught him to sweep through copses and branches and over the natural carpeting with almost as little noise as on cobbled roadways or tiled rooftops.

Hidden among the trees, Taziar turned southward. Silme had told him that Bolerkr's fortress perched on a hill in the ruins of the town of Wilsberg. The Shadow Climber moved quickly, needing to return to Cullinsberg before daylight. Without the "thieves' moon" to hide him, his black climbing outfit would look conspicuous amid the brighter colors worn by Cullinsberg's townsfolk.

Once encased in forest, Taziar fell into a pattern of cautious movement. No matter how seriously injured Bolverkr was, he still wielded enough Chaos-energy to keep his defenses raised against enemies. Taziar recalled the teachings of a Dragonrank sorcerer who had mistaken him for a low level mage the day Taziar sneaked into the Dragonrank school, defying its "impenetrable" defenses: "The wards become visible if you don't look directly at them." Taziar had gotten his share of practice at finding wards that day, including the one he had accidentally triggered to an explosion that seared his arm and chest, sapping him of consciousness. Now, in the forests south of Cullinsberg, Taziar winced at the memory, focusing on Astryd's explanation: "Magic, by its nature, functions best against creations and users of magic. The ward which harmed you might have killed a low rank Dragonmage. And most of our spells work only when used for or against sorcerers."

I'm the best one to spy on Bolverkr's fortifications. Any defenses Bolverkr created will prove far more dangerous to Silme and Astryd, and possibly to Allerum, too, since elves might be considered creations of magic. Taziar considered this new thought, wondering why he was rationalizing a scouting mission that needed no justification. *Because I know my friends will be furious when they find out I left without telling them.* He continued through the woodlands. *And they'll be right. I'd be mad if one of them went off alone, too.* Taziar shook the black strands from his eyes. *This is stupid. Of course I'd be mad at them. I'm the only one who knows Cullinsberg, and scouting is what I do.*

Still, Taziar could not banish guilt. In his days as the Shadow Climber, his feats had put no one but himself in danger. Since he had climbed the Bifrost Bridge on a dare and accidentally loosed the Fenrir Wolf on a world unequipped to handle it, his love for impossible tasks had placed others in jeopardy as well. *Mostly Allerum, Astryd, and Silme, the people I care about.* He considered how Bolverkr had drawn him and his companions to Cullinsberg by threatening to destroy Shylar, the Underground, the street orphans and beggars, the men and women Taziar had helped establish and learned to love. *Maybe it's time to stop accepting every impossible task for the challenge and start considering consequences. I am, after all, a "team player" now.*

Taziar's first warning that something might be amiss came in the form of three dead rabbits and a sparrow. He stopped, head cocked, gaze perpendicular to the line created by the corpses. His off-center glance gave him a perfect view of magics twisted into shimmering, parallel bands that arched into the woods as far as he could see. The lowest braid hovered at ankle level. Nine higher ones rose in increments, the upper one at twice Taziar's meager height. They were spaced widely enough that Taziar considered trying to slip between them. He traced the lines with his vision, suspecting each made a perfect ring. A walk around the perimeter confirmed his guess.

Whether or not I can slip through here, I know Silme and Allerum don't have a chance. Silme was tall for a woman and, though still slim this early in her pregnancy, carried a third again Taziar's weight. Larson stood a half head taller than his wife, and Astryd, though a bit smaller than Taziar, had little experience wriggling through tight spaces. No matter how lightly, touching the wards meant triggering them, and Bolverkr wielded more than enough power to make his sorceries fatal.

Choosing a sturdy oak with branches that overhung Bolverkr's defense, Taziar climbed. Seated in the V formed by trunk and branch, he examined the magics again. His aerial view allowed him to see something missed on first inspection, a second row of wards circling within the first. He nodded at the genius of Bolverkr's arrangement. Had Taziar used any less caution, he might have slipped through or over the outer wards and skidded or fallen into the inner ones. Cued, Taziar scanned for a third ring of magics. Seeing none, he edged out onto the branch. Passing over and beyond the wards, he sprang to the ground, thoughts on his companions. He imagined they could all jump from the tree without injury, though he made a mental note to bring rope just in case.

Now on Bolverkr's territory, Taziar discovered a random array of protective wards. He moved slowly, twisting his head in all directions before each step, zigzagging his way toward the center of the circle where he expected to find Bolverkr's citadel. Though abundant, the spells gave Taziar little difficulty. Wiry and agile, he slipped between magics that Bolverkr needed to place to accommodate his own larger frame and bolder gait. Certainly, no one ignorant of the ways of viewing magic could take more than a few steps without triggering one of the wards. But, as soon as Larson was taught the trick of indirect sighting, Taziar believed all of his companions would have the necessary training and dexterity to maneuver past Bolverkr's obstacle course. *So long as we don't have to do it too fast.*

When Taziar judged he had crossed half the radius of Bolverkr's circle, he paused to climb a tree. The "thieves' moon" drew a glittering line along Bolverkr's catwalk. Leering gargoyles lined the outer wall of the keep, meticulously cleaned though the castle they protected lay in a state of disrepair. Jagged breaks gashed three corners, and crumbled piles of stone, once towers, lay at the base. The fourth tower pointed arrow-straight at the sky, though rubble on the ground below it revealed that it had once been destroyed as well. The design confused Taziar. It seemed odd that Bolverkr had taken the time to completely renovate one full tower while the others gaped open, admitting rain. Glancing at shattered stonework before the outer wall to the keep, Taziar realized Bolverkr had also chosen to repair the decorative masonry and statuettes before working on the major structures of the castle.

As Taziar stared, a figure emerged onto the wall. Moonlight revealed fine, white hair that had once been blond and a slate gray tunic and breeks covered by a darkly-colored cloak. Tall and slender to the point of frailness, the man paced the stones with a brash, solid tread that belied the apparent fragility of his frame.

Bolverkr? Taziar watched, intrigued, certain this could be no one else.

Yet, the way the man on the wall moved seemed somehow alien. On the streets, Taziar had obtained much of his food money through con games, pick-pocketing, and entertaining the masses. His survival had depended upon his ability to read wealth, moti-vation, and intention through word and action. Bol-verkr's movements, though fluid, fit no human pattern Taziar could define. It inspired the same deep discom-fort that he felt in the presence of the most unstable lunatics, from the type who might stand in a state of statuelike quiet and stillness one moment then lash out in violent frenzy the next, to those who slaughtered in the name of imaginary voices, or the kind who mut-tered half-interpretable nonsense while violating every social convention.

Suddenly, Bolverkr froze. He whirled to face a gar-goyle that rose to the height of his knee and shouted a garbled word, unrecognizable to Taziar.

The gargoyle jumped, torn from its granite founda-tion, then shattered in a fountain of chips. Stone frag-ments rained into the courtyard.

Bolverkr resumed pacing as if nothing had hap-pened.

Taziar stiffened, wrung through with chills. The sorcerer's casual power shocked him, and he could not help imagining himself in the gargoyle's place.

"Who am I?" Pain tainted Bolverkr's shout, but it still rang with power.

Taziar was so caught up in the display that Bolverkr's voice startled him. He stiffened, slipping sideways on the limb. An abrupt grab spared him a fall, and he clutched the branch tightly enough to gouge bark into his palms. Balance regained, he watched in awe as Bolverkr stilled, head tipped to catch the echoes, as though he expected them to give him an answer.

The Dragonrank mage lowered his head. His hands twitched, as if he carried on a conversation with himself, but Taziar's perch was too far away for him to see if the sorcerer's lips were moving.

Taziar gauged the distance between himself and the sorcerer, wondering if he could kill Bolverkr with a well-placed arrow. *Assuming I had a bow. Or knew how to use it.* Taziar had become a mediocre swordsman only because teaching Taz swordplay had seemed so important to his father. Pleased enough to get his tiny son practicing any weapon at all, the elder Medakan had never pressed him to learn to shoot, and the thought of doing so on his own had never occurred to Taziar. *Bad enough killing a man who can defend himself. What need do I have to learn long-distance slaughter?* Taziar shivered at the thought. Grief-mad after her husband's hanging, Taziar's mother had forced her only son to assist in her suicide. The experience had so crippled Taziar's conscience that he had found himself unable to take a life, even to save his own. Circumstances had forced him to overcome this limitation enough to kill enemies in defense of innocents or friends, but only at times of grave necessity.

Bolverkr raised his face heavenward. The wind whipped his locks to an ivory tangle. "Who . . . am . . . I?"

Each syllable shocked dread through Taziar. There was something eerily inhuman about the call, though the words emerged plainly enough in the language of

Cullinsberg's barony and colored by a clipped Wilsberg accent. The urge to leave as quickly as possible seized Taziar. Studying the ground for glints of magic, he descended with caution, creeping silently back toward the northern forest.

Bolverkr's laughter shuddered between the trunks.

CHAPTER 2:

Chaos Dreams

Deep into that darkness peering, long I stood
   there wondering, fearing,
Doubting, dreaming dreams no mortal ever dared
   to dream before.

—Edgar Allen Poe
The Raven

The dream assailed Silme in the deepest part of her sleeping cycle; yet it seemed distant, the trickling backwash of another's nightmare borne on a thread of shared Chaos. Sated with health and life power, she paced the walled defenses of a fortress. But the life aura she had always known as a friend, an integral part of herself, had became a stranger, an enemy crushing, tearing, and stripping her of identity. A scream cycled through her mind: "Who am I?" No answer came but echoes. Still, the reverberation of her familiar voice soothed, bringing snatches of memory. She knew a humble childhood as the third son of a farmer, the dusty, green perfume of new-mown hay, the milk-breath of spotted cows, and the tickle of piled straw while roughhousing in the barn before the cows trooped inside. A brother's laughter rang in her ears.

As each remembrance blossomed, Chaos rose to meet it, battering it to pale outline. Anguish hammered Silme, and she twisted in her sleep, unable to comprehend life energy revolting against its master nor why she would fight the chaos defining her own life. Again, the cry cut above the struggle: "Who am I?" New memories whisked by, veiled in white, now of

Dragonrank training beneath the original master, Geirmagnus. She remembered, too, a wife named Magan and a fetus destroyed in the Chaos-storm. She felt the cold bite of winds carrying thatch, stone, and corpses, its swish as cruel and mocking as laughter.

A fetus. Silme anchored her reason on her own growing baby. Always before, she had received only a hint of its presence; its tiny life aura became blended and lost in the vastness of her own chaos. Now, she felt a strong sense of its aliveness within her. It seemed to have tripled in power overnight. Its energy wove intimately into her own: vital, hovering, waiting. Conscious of the changes within her, Silme slid toward waking far enough to realize that the remembrances of farm and storm and training were never her own. Now removed from the struggle between lord and Chaos, she explored both sides with a clarity of thought that could only come with impartiality.

Still ensconced in sleep, Silme saw only a man battling his own life aura, a war he could never win. Without knowledge of the vision's source, she somehow understood that if it bested him, he would lose whatever identity he still clung to, the snatches of memory Silme had just shared in dream. But to destroy his own life aura, the stuff of life itself, could bring only death.

Silme had dedicated her life to helping the innocent. Sleep stole logic and caution in the same manner as drink. The oddity of their link obscured any recognition of the man, and Silme's dream-state did not leave room for suspicion or questioning. Concerned for this stranger, Silme did not know him as Bolverkr, a sorcerer more than two centuries old, the man who had ordered her friends and husband killed and nearly succeeded at both. She did not identify the Dragonrank mage who had declared vengeance against Larson and promised to share reams of Chaos with Silme through a contact she had created in ignorance. She saw only a creature in agony, trapped and aching from a battle with a Chaos it did not yet recognize as self. And she tended him like a mother with an injured child.

Silme reached out to help, certain she would meet a physical or mental barrier. But her words slipped effortlessly through the contact. Gently, she reassured him that the Chaos was a part of himself, that he should welcome it without fighting and let it serve him as a life aura must. She felt him soften at her words. The fiery rage within him died, and the Chaos, too, gave up its struggles, settling within him, gradually poisoning Bolverkr's last vestiges of self with its presence. Complacency seeped through the contact, drawing Silme deeper into her slumber. At first, she followed it, every muscle falling into perfect laxity, a comfort beyond any she had ever known. Then, a more primitive portion of her mind kicked in, warning of imminent danger. Suddenly fully awake, Silme sprang to her feet, bashing her head on the shelves above the headboard.

An avalanche of books and fruit thundered to the floor. A bowl shattered, and shards of pottery skittered across the wood.

Startled from his sickbed, Al Larson dove beneath the frame in a tangle of blankets. "Incoming!" he screamed.

Then the room fell silent.

Silme reoriented quickly. She sat on a straw-ticked mattress mounted on a metal frame. A half dozen books lay scattered at her feet amid bruised fruit that had once sat in a bowl whose pieces decorated the floorboards in colored triangles. Across the room and nearer the door, Astryd slept despite the noise, alone in the bed she normally shared with Taziar. Propped against the footboard leaned the familiar dragonstaff that identified Astryd as garnet-rank, a smoothly-sanded pole tipped with a faceted, red stone clamped between four black-nailed, wooden claws. Between her and Silme, the room's single window stood ajar. Autumn breezes stirred the gauzy blue curtains. Beneath it, a dresser held their belongings.

Larson's angular, elf face peered from beneath his bed. His pale eyes swept the room, and he seemed to take time to get his bearing.

"I'm sorry," Silme said, her voice loud in the silence.

Astryd continued to sleep.

Larson hauled himself from beneath the bed. "What happened?"

"Bad dream." It sounded like understatement to Silme, so she qualified. "*Very* bad dream."

Larson frowned, apparently thinking about the nightmares that had beset him since Freyr had dragged him to a Norway centuries before his birth and into the guise of an elf. It had turned out his were not dreams at all but sorcerers and gods entering his thoughts through the openings left by his lack of mind barriers. But they both knew no one could penetrate Silme's mental barriers.

Or could they? Doubt trickled through Silme's thoughts. *I opened my mind barriers to Bolverkr's Chaos before. Could he have manipulated that weakness?* Silme grimaced. She had walled off that contact with defenses Chaos should not have been able to breach. Yet, it seemed to have done so with an ease that could only come of an invitation. *As if some part of me accepted Chaos willingly.*

The idea frightened Silme, suggesting that, deep down, she supported Chaos' evil or, worse, coveted the power it promised. Again, she clutched the baby's aura to her absently, felt the fullness of life energy that had seemed trivial days ago. And the answer accompanied that touch. *The baby is taking the Chaos-energy offered by Bolverkr.* Fear shuddered through Silme at the realization. She knew the child was not capable of thought, that it was simply being a normal fetus, taking whatever nourishment it could, oblivious to the source. *It needs to grow. Yet, the volume of Chaos-energy to which it's become exposed is immeasurable.* The possible consequences seemed so staggering, Silme dared not consider them yet. She buried her face in her hands.

Apparently attributing Silme's discomfort to her dream, Larson limped to her side and caught her into an embrace. "What happened? Tell me about this nightmare."

Silme wrapped her arms around Larson, feeling him wince as the pressure ignited healing bruises and scars. "It's nothing to worry about." She tried to soothe, but her uncertainty sabotaged the effort. "It's not the dream itself. There's something we need to discuss as a group. Why don't I wake up Astryd and . . ." She trailed off as the realization of what she had seen earlier finally seeped into her consciousness.

Larson's gaze went naturally to his friends' bed where Astryd sprawled alone, a petite, curly-haired blonde nearly lost in a twist of blankets.

"Shadow's gone." Silme stated the obvious needlessly. Larson's attention had already shifted to the open window.

"That stupid, little . . ."

Taziar's head and shoulders appeared over the ledge. ". . . son-of-a-bitch," he finished in English, simulating Larson's Bronx accent. He scurried inside, closing the window behind him.

Larson had unconsciously grasped the finely-crafted Japanese longsword that had belonged to Kensei Gaelinar. He glared. "That's not what I was going to say."

Taziar made a vague gesture to indicate Larson should speak freely.

"I was going to say 'obnoxious, fucking *asshole* son-of-a-bitch.' "

Taziar bowed his head. "I stand corrected," he said with mock seriousness.

"And," Larson pulled free of Silme, slipping easily into the facetious manner of his companion. "I speak your language fluently. How come the only things you've bothered to learn in mine are swear words?"

It was an unfair question. Some effect of Freyr's transporting magic had given Larson the ability to speak the period languages naturally, while Taziar could only glean English phrases from the rare times Larson used them, usually in annoyance or anger. Still, the Shadow Climber found an answer. "Swear words, are they? I was starting to wonder why the only things with names in your language were excrement, sex, and animal relatives.''

Larson chuckled.

''Actually, though, I have learned a few other words.'' Taziar sat on the edge of the bed, turning his head to watch Astryd roll to a sitting position, the blankets clutched to her chest.

Silme frowned, recognizing Taziar's attempt to turn the conversation away from his recent absence.

'' 'Jerk' and 'creep' are mild insults.''

''Terms of endearment,'' Larson interrupted with a smile.

''Right.'' Taziar placed a hand on Astryd's covered knee. '' 'Mac' is a casual thing you call a stranger, 'sir' a more formal one.'' Taziar rolled his eyes in consideration. ''There's places: 'New York,' 'America,' 'Vietnam.' Then, I know 'excuse me' and 'team player.' 'Buddy' means a trusted friend who holds your life in his hands. 'Gun' describes an object I've seen once and never want to come up against again. A 'Buick' is an object large things are compared to in size.'' He paused. ''Oh, and I've heard 'follow that car.' ''

''Great.'' Larson winked at Silme, apparently oblivious to her displeasure, and stretched his legs in front of him. ''You're all set if you ever want to take a transcontinental cab ride in an American-made car.''

''Enough!'' Silme said, bothered by the men's playful banter. ''Stop it, both of you!''

All eyes flicked suddenly to Silme, the expression on every face one of befuddled surprise. Never before had the sorceress become angered by a harmless exchange of gibes.

Silme addressed Larson directly. ''I understand that you sometimes use humor to release tension, but this isn't the time.''

Larson stared, looking hurt. ''I was only . . .''

Silme cut him off, fixing her hard, gray eyes on Taziar. ''Where were you, Shadow?''

Taziar shifted uncomfortably. His lips framed a feeble smile. ''Would you believe enjoying the night air?''

He used a small voice that made it clear he was stalling.

Silme's glower deepened, etching wrinkles into her artistically-perfect features. She realized she was acting harsh beyond her nature, perhaps due to the concerns her dream had raised, yet the brusqueness seemed justified. "I'm not kidding, Shadow. Where were you?"

Taziar stared at his feet. "I couldn't sleep. I went scouting."

"You went to Bolverkr's fortress." Silme knew Taziar well enough to guess. "Didn't you?"

Astryd's and Larson's attention whipped to the Shadow Climber.

Taziar nodded grimly. "I found out some information that . . ."

Silme did not allow him to change the subject. "This is all a big game to you, isn't it?"

Taziar went silent. The comma of black hair sagged into his eyes, giving him the look of an unruly child.

"This isn't some interesting challenge someone handed you for fun. Bolverkr commands the largest volume of Chaos-force ever assembled. He's the most powerful creature in existence. Ever. And he wants us dead."

"I'm sorry." Taziar sounded sincere. "I wasn't trying to belittle Bolverkr's power. I was trying to assess it. Know the enemy. It's just good strategy."

Taziar's defensive reply fueled Silme's rage. "You don't even understand what you did wrong! How could you go off alone in the night without telling anyone? If we can stand against Bolverkr, and I'm not at all certain we can, it's going to take all of us working together and at our best. Did it occur to you that you might disturb Bolverkr? Alone, you don't have a chance against him. He could have killed you without bothering to stand. Then, enraged by your interference, he might have come after us. He'd have found us asleep because we had no idea one of our companions had run off recklessly, *stupidly*, into a lion's den."

Larson stroked Silme's long golden locks, trying to

appease her. Usually, he respected Silme as the voice of reason, but apparently even he believed she had gone too far. "Shadow made a mistake. He's apologized. No harm done. I think that dream's got you upset. Maybe you should talk about it."

Silme knocked away Larson's caress with the back of her hand. "Don't patronize me, Allerum. I've been fighting Chaos and sorcerers since long before you heard of either." Her fists clenched, her memory gliding back over more than a decade spent protecting innocents from the cruelties of her half-brother, Bramin. Then she had required the aid and protection of the world's greatest swordsman, Kensei Gaelinar. She missed the old ronin's loyalty, his single-minded, predictable code of honor, and the seriousness with which he viewed the world and his role in it. Though crippling at times, Larson's guileless morality had attracted Silme in the same way Taziar's impetuous good intentions had charmed Astryd; but, faced with the most powerful enemy in her life, Silme would have traded man and elf for the Kensei's humorless efficiency. "This isn't the first time Shadow's run off alone without thinking, but it's damned well going to be the last. I'm not going to have my baby, husband, and apprentice endangered by . . ."

Several rapid taps at the door interrupted Silme's tirade.

Larson sighed in relief, rolling his eyes to the ceiling as if to thank some unnamed god.

"Come in," Taziar said, his voice a soft parody of his normal carefree tone and harsh Cullinsberg accent.

Unaccustomed to berating friends, Silme felt a pang of remorse.

The door swung ajar on silent hinges, and Asril the Procurer stood framed in the doorway, backlit by a candle in the hallway. A mop of mouse brown hair crowned knife-scarred cheeks, and his strange, violet gaze swept the room, taking in every sight from long habit. The son of a free-lance prostitute, Asril had won his education and his wounds on the wildest streets of Cullinsberg. Of the seven leaders Taziar had broken out of prison, Asril was the only one who had weathered the guards' tortures well enough to help Larson and Taziar battle Bolverkr's henchman, Harriman, and his berserker bodyguards. "Ah, what a glorious morning and a joy to wake up to friends quibbling. Pressure getting too intense? I don't suppose this means you'll let me help against Bolverkr now?" He bowed with feigned deference. "Lords, ladies, my sword arm is at your service." He winked at Taziar. "I owe you the favor, partner. Won't you let me repay it?"

Silme knew Taziar's caution with his friends' lives would force him to refuse the offer, so it surprised her when he looked to her for guidance before answering. She tightened her lips to a blanched line, shaking her head vigorously. *Our survival is tenuous enough. No need to involve anyone else in our affairs.*

Apparently, Silme had given the response Taziar wanted because his features mellowed with relief. "Shylar and the Underground need you here. Since when have I ever needed help to do anything?" Taziar winced. He had obviously meant the words to assuage Asril, then realized they might provoke Silme as well.

Asril the Procurer's interruption had given Silme time to think, and guilt assailed her. *I shouldn't have scolded Shadow so hard. Stupid as his decision seemed to me, he meant well.* Naturally calm and gentle by nature, as well as competent in her judgments, Silme rarely found herself in a position calling for apology. Now she tried to express her regret to Taziar, but the words seemed to die on her tongue. Emotion lumped within her, nameless irritation, smothered excitement, sorrow, and fear, their sources too vague for her to trace. She knew other feelings as well, a protectiveness toward her forming child and the friends she would give her own life to spare, and a distant, veiled realization that some of the sentiments she felt were not consistent with the self she knew.

Oblivious to Silme's turmoil, Asril shrugged. "If you change your mind, my offer of help stands." He closed long lashes over his violet eyes, then opened them slowly, his full attention on Taziar. "So, how did the enemy seem last night?"

Asril's voice jarred Silme from the brink of an important revelation. The recognition of the alienness of her current mind-set slipped beyond her grasp, and she did not notice the insidious, almost nonexistent trickle of Chaos seeping through the contact with Bolverkr.

In response to Asril's question, Taziar stiffened. He rolled his gaze toward Silme, awaiting reprimand. When none came, he replied softly. "How would I know that?" He made a brisk gesture to silence Asril.

The violet-eyed thief ignored Taziar's apparent discomfort. "When I saw you trying to get over the walls, I just assumed you went to check on Bolverkr."

Taziar spoke hesitantly, as if trying to hide his surprise. "You . . . saw . . . me?"

Larson frowned, Astryd stared at Taziar, and Silme glowered at the realization that the Climber had not only run off alone but had done so sloppily enough to get noticed by friends and potentially by enemies as well.

Asril closed the door and draped his frame casually against it. "Didn't actually see you, but it's hard to miss a hundred clomping guardsmen. And what purpose would they have on the rooftops besides chasing the Shadow Climber?"

Taziar cringed.

Asril grinned, revealing straight rows of yellowed teeth. "I'd have thought the Climber more careful, though that was before I knew he was reckless Taz."

Taziar made an abrupt quieting gesture, far less subtle than the first.

Silme bit her lip, reminding herself that the reprimands had already been spoken. Compared to the risk of facing Bolverkr alone, Taziar's confrontation with Cullinsberg's town guardsmen seemed trivial.

Asril laughed. Pushing off the door with a foot, he approached Taziar, his voice softer but still discernible to Silme. "Clever ruse, whatever it was you did on the baker's roof. I'm relieved to realize you didn't know you put the whole pack of wolves on my tail.''

Taziar looked stricken. "I had no idea. I'm sorry."

Asril shrugged off the apology. "It worked out fine. Gave you time to get away. The guards were so busy worrying about you, they didn't even recognize me. Snarled a few words about being out after curfew, then went back after you." He chuckled. "By then, you were long gone, of course."

"Of course," Larson repeated thoughtfully.

Having failed to silence his friend, Taziar tried changing the subject. "I did discover something important about Bolverkr, though. I think he's gone completely insane."

Larson lay back on the mattress, supported by his elbows with his body curled around Silme's stiffly-seated figure. "What do you mean? Chasing down strangers to torture and kill them never seemed all that sane to me to begin with."

Taziar drew his knees to his chest. "He's not just irrationally vengeful anymore. I found him pacing his wall, wasting his magic on statues and rocks, jabbering about not knowing who he is."

The similarity to her dream struck Silme. No longer able to deny the reality of her connection with Bolverkr, she fidgeted.

No one seemed to notice Silme's new uneasiness. Taziar continued. "Mind you, I don't have any experience with Chaos-madness. I don't know how long it'll last." Taziar squirmed, obviously concerned about the suggestion he was about to make. "So far, we've let Bolverkr do all the attacking while we handled his minions and tried to get a feel for his power. Based on the information Silme and I gathered, I think it's time we took the initiative. We need to strike while he's alone and too crazed to think clearly."

Larson nodded soberly. "Good battle strategy. I think I'm feeling up to . . ."

Realizing she might have accidentally helped stabilize Bolverkr in her sleep, Silme blurted, "We'll need to move as quickly as possible."

The impulsive interruption seemed so unlike Silme that her companions went silent and stared in surprise.

Feeling obligated to clarify, the sorceress continued. "Chaos or power generally comes to people in tiny doses based on the balance of the world and life events. For them, the corruption of personality comes gradually. Bolverkr was forced to contain, in seconds, enough Chaos to help offset Loki's destruction and the resurrection of a god." Absorbed in her narration, Silme sat ramrod straight, her hands clenched in her lap. Though Bolverkr had proved himself a bitter and dangerous enemy, she could not help feeling a twinge of sorrow for him. The Bolverkr whose memories she had shared was a sweet-tempered and gentle victim of circumstance. "Forced to cope with a sudden, drastic change in character, Bolverkr's fighting the Chaos, trying to find the self he used to be."

Larson traced a wrinkle in Silme's gown with his finger. "You mean he might be able to shake this Chaos? Deep down, the dirty scum who ordered Shadow's friends killed, me tortured, the baby destroyed, and you raped is really a nice guy? Forgive me while I laugh hysterically. I find that a bit hard to swallow."

Larson's effortless interplay between English slang and the barony's tongue made his words difficult to understand, but Silme managed to follow his main point. "Essentially."

More attentive to Larson's native language, Taziar deciphered and replied more directly. "Are you suggesting Bolverkr might overcome this Chaos? We might not have to kill him?"

"No. I don't mean that at all." Silme's back muscles began to cramp in protest of Silme's sitting "at attention" for far too long. She sagged, absently massaging her lower spine with a fist. "The Chaos is far too great and strong for Bolverkr to fight. His only choice is to give in to it, to incorporate it into himself as part of his life energy. Any other decision would be folly."

Taziar and Astryd both raised their brows, though neither spoke aloud.

Silme answered the unspoken question. "Because even Bolverkr isn't powerful enough to win a battle against renegade Chaos of that magnitude. Remember, embodied Chaos, the chaos inside of a person, is his life force; it dies when its master is killed. But if a host to renegade Chaos is destroyed, that Chaos would be free to hunt for another host. Along the way, it would destroy anything in its path: people, animals, forests, entire cities." Silme repositioned herself, crossing her legs on the pallet. "Since this particular massing of Chaos chose to go to Bolverkr first, it's probable he was the most likely to survive its linking. If Bolverkr was killed before he merged with his new Chaos, it would try to find another lord. Most probably, no one else could survive the merger. It would kill its next host, and each subsequent attempt would bring it against weaker and weaker hosts. It wouldn't quit until every sentient creature in the world was killed." Silme shivered at the impact of her own words.

Taziar twisted his fine features in thought, brushing the hair from his forehead. "So we have to time this carefully. The only way to destroy this Chaos is to wait for Bolverkr to completely assimilate it, taking it as his life force. Then we kill him." Taziar shook his head, obviously displeased with the concept.

Silme knew Taziar well enough to understand that he cared little for killing, especially pawns. The method did not appeal to her either, but she could see beyond murder to the practical necessity. Bolverkr was too dangerous to everyone to live. "The timing doesn't matter any more. If Bolverkr's still alive when we reach his keep, he'll have certainly surrendered to Chaos. He's at too critical a juncture not to have made the decision last night. We should strike as soon as possible, before he gets a firm grasp on what he can do with his new-found power."

Larson rubbed at the sore spot on Silme's back. "You're sure?"

"Of course I'm sure," she said, irritability rising from a source she did not bother to name. She wanted to detail her dream, to explain that she knew Bolverkr's struggle had reached its climax because she had shared it with him, knew he had surrendered to Chaos because she had pressed him to the concession. But a part of her understood the wrongness of admitting to such a thing. It led her to believe detailing her dream would accomplish nothing except to undermine her companions' morale, and, though her silence seemed as wrong as Taziar's impetuous spying, she clung to it. "Shadow described the situation accurately. Are you well enough to fight today?"

"I'm not at my best," Larson admitted honestly. "But if it's urgent, what choice do I have?" His hand fell away from Silme and to the brocaded hilt of Gaelinar's katana. He smiled. "I'll be fine."

Silme knew Larson gained courage from touching his teacher's katana. In the way of the samurai, the Kensei had always considered his swords an extension of his spirit. As such, he had treated them with more respect than any person, letting his own wounds gape and bleed until he had cleaned, sheathed, and accorded the blades their proper respect. Composed of joined layers of hard and soft steel folded hundreds of times, the katana could cut through armor as if it did not exist or cleanly decapitate a man with a single stroke.

Astryd raised a practical issue in her usual soft-spoken, deferential manner. "I'm years and multiple ranks below you in training, Silme, so you know things I don't. But doesn't the death of a powerful creature of Chaos have to be balanced by one of Law?"

Taziar seized on Astryd's question. "Like Fenrir?"

The reference confused Silme. "Fenrir? The Great Wolf?"

"Right." Taziar went on excitedly, his gaze probing Larson. "Remember back before we fought the Chaos dragon, when Fenrir was our most dangerous enemy. He said we couldn't possibly kill him because it would upset the balance of the world."

Larson remembered. "We never did kill him, either. We captured him." He stroked his hairless, elven chin, following the conversation to its natural, if unnerving, conclusion. "Are you saying it might be literally impossible to kill Bolverkr?"

Astryd shrugged, and Larson touched Silme's thigh to turn the question back to the more experienced, sapphire-rank sorceress.

"I don't know. Nothing like this has ever happened before, as far as I'm aware." Silme inclined her head toward Taziar. "Since I met Shadow, impossible doesn't have a lot of meaning for me anymore. If someone had asked me a year ago, I would have said destroying Loki was impossible. Certainly, killing Bolverkr will be the most difficult challenge any of us has ever faced. Impossible? Maybe. I don't know."

Taziar still clung to the chance of a peaceful solution. "Silme, is there any way to siphon off Chaos from Bolverkr and distribute it around in small, harmless parcels?"

Silme considered. Taziar's idea had not occurred to her before. "By reopening the connection Bolverkr allowed me to create between us, theoretically, yes. I could take Chaos from him. In practice, I don't see how it could work. First, Bolverkr might oppose me. Then we'd have to fight under less than ideal circumstances, on his terms. Second, there's a near certain possibility that I might misjudge and become corrupted myself. Third, in order to spread the Chaos thin enough not to seriously poison each new host, I'd need hundreds or, more likely, thousands of willing volunteers. Each one would need to fight down his mind barriers for me to make the transfer."

Larson finished sarcastically. "By the time you finished, Bolverkr would have died of old age."

Silme shrugged. The only survivor of the original Dragonrank sorcerers, Bolverkr had had access to the earlier, more powerful spells, before the mages had learned the danger of summoning renegade Chaos. Already two hundred and seventeen years old, Bolverkr still seemed spry and agile to Silme, and she had no way to judge his potential life span. Still, Larson's point regarding time seemed valid. "Bolverkr's certain to confront us long before I could muster the necessary volunteers, assuming I could even find people inclined to let me infuse them with Chaos. Having dedicated my life to protecting innocents from Chaos, I don't feel comfortable with the idea, either.''

Asril the Procurer rested a sandaled foot on the edge of Astryd's bed, near the garnet-tipped dragonstaff. "So it's settled. You have to kill Bolverkr, and the sooner the better.''

"One other thing.'' Larson glanced at Astryd and Taziar for support, raising a topic they had apparently already discussed in Silme's absence. "You're not coming with us.'' He caressed Silme's side as he spoke.

Silme twisted toward Larson in disbelief. "You'd better be talking to Asril.''

"I'm talking,'' Larson said firmly, "to you.''

Outrage welled within Silme, quickly snuffed by knowledge. *It's not me they're overprotecting, it's the baby.* Instinctively, she clutched the tiny aura to her, felt the edges of its life energy blur into her own. She could not separate the two. Any spell she threw would sap its life force as well as hers, and, once emptied of chaos, the child would die. Thoughts of the coming battle and the risks to the baby had haunted Silme throughout Larson's recovery. When the war against Bolverkr had seemed a distant threat, the decision had come easily. Now, the lives of her friends and husband had to take precedence over that of an unborn child. "That's nonsense, Allerum. You won't have a chance against Bolverkr without a Dragonrank mage.'' As she spoke, memories tortured Silme. She recalled the hands of Bolverkr's minion tearing at her clothes and person while she wrestled with the realization that Larson, Taziar, and Astryd battled dozens of prison guards, though a few simple spells and a dead fetus could rescue them all from humiliation and death.

"We'll have Astryd.'' Taziar gave Larson his full support, unaware Silme's thoughts had wandered far beyond her protest. "With you or not, we're not going to be able to best Bolverkr with magic. He's too powerful. It's going to have to be by surprise and luck.''

Astryd spoke next, as if to demonstrate that she had thought the subject through as well. "Of us all, you're the only one Bolverkr won't hunt down. We have nothing to lose by fighting him. If we don't, he'll kill us anyway. But you, he'll let live. And the baby." Astryd's loyalty to and excitement about the baby had been unwavering since its conception. Though a mediocre sorceress compared with Silme, she had taken over the magical needs of the group. When Bolverkr's sorcery had trapped Silme in an alternate dimension, escapable only by magic, Astryd had allowed Silme to tap her life aura, a rare process that had nearly resulted in Astryd's death. "By killing Loki, Allerum assured that our Norse gods would endure through eternity. The White Christ will never come, and Allerum's friends and family, his entire world, will never come about. This baby is the only proof that the nine worlds will ever have that Lord Allerum the Godslayer ever existed."

Silme closed her eyes, allowing Astryd's words to seep into her soul, dragging the burden of grief with it. Though not directly spoken, Astryd's words brought home the realization that the task her companions were going to undertake this day was nearly or completely impossible and almost certainly fatal. To die with them was folly. Yet she could not shake the fact that, even though far weaker than Bolverkr, she could add power to her friends' attack. The understanding that she had inadvertently stabilized Bolverkr in her dream, losing her friends the days or weeks they might otherwise have had to prepare, saturated the realization with guilt. "At least let me come along. I'll only use magic if the situation becomes desperate."

"No!" Larson sat up and pounded a fist onto the shelf hard enough to send the last few books tumbling to the floor. "The situation is desperate already. The last time you helped me fight a Dragonrank Master, you forced me to kill you. I won't do it again. I swear it, Silme. I'll let Bolverkr destroy me and everyone else in the world before I'll take your life again.''

Silme remembered as vividly as if it had happened the previous day. Before Larson had fought Loki, he had had to face her half brother, Bramin. In order to neutralize Bramin's magic, Silme had linked her life aura to his, and Larson's sword had killed them both. To restore Silme's life, Larson and Gaelinar had been forced to barter with the goddess Hel, an insane task that had made them enemies among the gods and had ultimately resulted in Bolverkr's tragedy and crazed hunt for vengeance. ''But even without magic, I could distract . . .'' she began.

Larson interrupted with a crisp wave of dismissal. ''The only person you're going to distract is me. You and the baby would be just one more thing to occupy my mind when all I should be thinking about is killing Bolverkr. I don't want you there, and you're not going to be there. Case closed.''

Anger boiled up inside Silme, but she bit it back. In her mind, the case was far from closed, but the time for arguing had ended. She saw no need to aggravate Larson just before what might well prove the final battle for them all.

Larson sprang to his feet. ''Let's get this over with.'' He strode toward the door.

Taziar intercepted Larson, hooking his sleeve with a finger. ''Not so fast, *buddy.*'' His harsh, German accent mangled the American slang. ''Don't be in such a hurry to die. We can't fight Bolverkr unless we can make it to Bolverkr.''

Larson studied Taziar blankly.

''The baron's guards think I escaped. They probably won't be quite so alert and numerous as before, but they do know you came to Cullinsberg with me. The baron's offered a generous enough bounty to make the guards willing to slaughter one another. They're not going to let you walk through the front gates without a thorough questioning.'' Taziar placed the emphasis on the last few words, obviously intending the expression as a euphemism for torture.

Asril the Procurer laughed. Rising, he stretched like a cat, then leapt lightly between Larson and the door. "You concentrate on Bolverkr and leave the baron's imbeciles to me. With the help of a few dozen thieves, con men, and street gangs, I'm sure I can divert Cullinsberg's red and black long enough for you to get over the south wall. Deal?"

Silme's gaze went naturally to Taziar. She saw the familiar sparkle in his blue eyes that accompanied the opportunity to work against impossible odds. Yet the dullness of his other features belied the excitement. Beneath it all, Taziar knew he no longer belonged in the city of his birth, the place he had called home for all but the last half year. And it pained him.

A deep silence ensued.

A moment later, Silme found herself enwrapped in Larson's arms. His fine white hair felt like silk against her cheeks, smelling pleasantly of soap. His elven frame appeared delicate, but there was nothing fragile about the arms that crushed her to him.

Tears filled Silme's eyes, and she knew with grim certainty that the only man she had ever loved enough to marry would almost certainly be lost to her forever.

CHAPTER 3:

Chaos War

A still small voice spake unto me,
"Thou art so full of misery,
Were it not better not to be?"
—Alfred, Lord Tennyson
The Two Voices

The pine and hickory forest beyond the walls of Cullinsberg seemed to close in on Al Larson. He trailed Taziar in silence, trying to focus his thoughts on Bolverkr. But other concerns crowded in, unable to be banished. The tight, damp foliage dragged up memories of suffocating Vietnamese jungles, the reek of blood, gasoline, and excrement, death screams, the echoing shrieks of macaws, and the distant chop of helicopter blades. Through it all, he could not shake a feeling of enemies prowling silently behind him. Every few steps, he stopped abruptly, straining his hearing for the rustle of movement at his back. Occasionally, the rattle of brush or a twig snap answered his efforts, increasing his discomfort though he knew the noise had to come from Taziar, Astryd, or his own hyperactive imagination.

"Here. Stop." Taziar whispered suddenly. Though soft, his voice shattered a long and oppressive quiet.

Larson pushed past Astryd to Taziar's side.

Taziar halted Larson with an extended hand. "Remember what I told you about seeing magic?"

Larson nodded, staring ahead indirectly as the others had shown him. Now he could see the braid of Bolverkr's ward, as tangled and forbidding as a perimeter of concertina wire. "I see it." His voice sounded strained, even to his own ears. Only then did he realize he was gripping Gaelinar's hilt so tightly that his hand had blanched and the brocade had left impressions in his palm. Bothered by his paranoia, he freed his hand and shook it to restore the circulation.

"There's another circle of magic just inside the first." Taziar rested a palm against the trunk of a sturdy oak with several jutting branches. "Careful now. Follow me." He shinnied to a high limb with an ease and quickness Larson could never hope to copy.

"Yeah, right," Larson mumbled. Turning, he motioned Astryd over to the base. Cupping his hands, he created a step for her. "Put your foot here. I'll give you a boost."

Astryd looked doubtfully from Larson's fingers to the wards while Taziar watched with nervous expectation. Dutifully, Astryd passed her dragonstaff to Taziar, then placed her booted foot on Larson's hands.

Short even compared with Taziar's five foot nothing, Astryd seemed nearly weightless to Larson. He hoisted her without difficulty, waiting until she caught a solid grip on a higher branch before lowering his hands. Though agile, Astryd looked as awkward as a growing adolescent compared with Taziar's practiced grace. Sighing, Larson seized the trunk and followed her, the rough bark scratching his hands.

Taziar waited only until Larson had reached the branch on which he and Astryd perched before tossing the garnet dragonstaff safely over the wards. He leapt in a gentle arc to the ground, then signaled for Astryd to jump.

Astryd hesitated while Larson waited, clinging to the branch with one hand, the other braced against the trunk. She lowered herself over the limb, dangling by her hands to lessen the distance to the ground, then let go. She plummeted dangerously close to the wards. Larson held his breath, scrambling to a position that might allow him to make a desperate dive for her. Before he could leap, Taziar stepped between Astryd and the barrier, catching a slender arm and hauling her to safety.

Larson clambered to the branch, heaving a sigh of relief. He waved Astryd and Taziar out of his way, not liking the distance of the jump. In junior high school, a lesser fall had broken Larson's arm. Edging to the end of the branch, he sprang to the ground, hit, and rolled to his feet, unharmed.

"That's the hardest part," Taziar said. "The rest is just dodging around wards. Take your time, don't get sloppy, and you should do fine."

Larson clapped dirt from his palms. He took little solace from Taziar's words. Accustomed to judging obstacles by his own ability to surmount them, Taziar's idea of "sloppy" rarely gibed with Larson's. A high school soccer player, weight lifter, and college boxer, Larson had always considered himself fit, but Taziar's nimbleness made the American feel clumsy. Worse, thrown into an unfamiliar body, Larson had been forced to relearn coordination, a competence rapidly acquired and sorely tested by Gaelinar's sword lessons as well as Bramin's and Loki's attacks.

Without further warning, Taziar headed off, soundlessly weaving through the brush. Astryd followed. Larson darted glances in all directions, locating the splayed pattern of magical glints, memorizing positions and trying to trace Astryd's footsteps. Yearly deer hunts in the New Hampshire forests had accustomed Larson to pine forests and moving quietly over twigs and brush, and months in Vietnamese jungle had made him oversensitive to the sounds of rustling foliage. Again, he thought he heard a distant noise behind them. His palms went slick, and sweat dampened the leather-wrapped hilt of Gaelinar's katana. Larson cursed himself. *Keep your mind on the wards. There's nothing behind you. And even if there is, it can't possibly be as dangerous as what's ahead.*

The uppermost branches of oak caught the dawn light, silhouetting the autumn leaves red and gold against pink. Taziar frowned, and Larson understood his discomfort. Accustomed to working in near darkness, night gave the little Climber an advantage. Daylight would turn the odds even further in Bolverkr's favor.

At length, Taziar stopped, motioning to Larson and Astryd to stand in place. Without turning to see if they had complied, Taziar went on alone. Within seconds, he had disappeared between the trees.

Wind shivered through the branches, sending the pines into a bowing dance. Larson lowered his head. In a safe position between the wards, he went deathly still. Something brushed his hand, and he glanced up at Astryd. She held a stance of defiance, yet fear glazed her eyes. Larson took her hand, squeezing encouragingly. He had faced death enough times to know that the trick to succeeding at a suicide mission was to concentrate wholly on the goal and forget the consequences. To think about a future without himself, Taziar, and Astryd, to know fear instead of certainty, even for a moment, might jeopardize the success of their attempt. So Larson pushed failure out of his mind.

But Astryd had lived her first fifteen years as a shipbuilder's daughter and the last six protected and isolated from the world on the grounds of the Dragonrank school. She had not yet learned to accept her own death. Larson pitied her, sympathizing with her struggle against innocence, yet he knew he could do nothing except understand.

Taziar returned, dodging through the wards once again. "Bolverkr's still pacing the curtain wall. Any suggestions?"

Larson stated the obvious strategy. "We need to hit him fast and hard, preferably from more than one side. Our only chance is to catch him by surprise and strike before he can retaliate."

Taziar nodded in agreement. "I can get us onto the ramparts." He patted his side to indicate a coil of rope he carried beneath his cloak.

Larson frowned, wondering why Taziar had not produced the rope when they'd been maneuvering over Bolverkr's magical perimeter. *Apparently, he didn't see the need. Or he didn't think we could spare the time.* Larson found it difficult to fault a tactic that had worked. *We made it over. That's all that matters.*

Apparently recognizing Astryd's discomfort, Taziar took her other hand. "The wards get thicker the closer we get to the keep. Pay attention. Don't get too eager or distracted. Insane or not, Bolverkr's not stupid. The only safe path to the wall is on the side where he's pacing."

Larson dropped Astryd's hand, leaving her solace to Taziar. They all knew Bolverkr's retribution was aimed specifically against the men who had loosed Chaos against him; if Larson and Taziar were killed, Bolverkr had no further need of Astryd. They had already discussed the contingency; if their attack failed, the Dragonrank sorceress was to use any means at her disposal to return to Silme, accepting the men's deaths without consideration of revenge.

Alert to the urgency of time and the necessity for quiet, Taziar gave Astryd a fond but quick embrace unaccompanied by verbal explanations or platitudes. Pulling away, he knelt, seized a fallen twig amid the underbrush, and cleared a patch of dirt. Using the tip of the branch as a stylus, he drew a series of curved and tangled lines on the ground. "This is the pattern through the wards from the edge of the forest to the curtain wall. We may have to run through it. Can you do that?" He glanced up at his companions.

Larson frowned, uncertain. He had experience with obstacle courses, but none so hair-trigger deadly as a Dragonrank sorcerer's magic.

Apparently, Taziar intended his last question to remain rhetorical, because he did not wait for an answer before pushing silently through the brush.

Astryd and Larson trailed Taziar. Branches parted before them, leaves brushing quietly against linen and leather. Larson kept his head tilted, his concentration fully on the glittering traces of sorcery, though he could see them only indirectly. Taziar's words haunted him. The idea of racing, almost blindly, through a mine field brought memories of a corporal named

Steve, severed at the waist by a V.C. trap, still breathing as his life's blood colored the jungle clay a deeper red. A chill rushed through Larson, and it took an effort of will to keep from seizing Astryd and heading home.

The trees thinned, granting Larson distant glimpses of wall through ragged, dawn-gray holes in the brush. Taziar stopped, allowing his companions to draw up to his side as closely as the tightly bunched wards allowed. He pointed ahead.

Larson shifted until he found a gap wide enough to accord him an unobstructed view of what had once been a farming village called Wilsberg. Shattered stone littered land that rose gradually to a central hill, the carnage interspersed with an occasional jutting foundation of a cottage or fountain. Magics of varying hues reflected the twilight in wild patterns, their otherworldliness enhanced by the need to view them from the corners of his vision. It seemed only natural to Larson to glean details by direct focusing, and the disappearance of the wards whenever he tried to study them drove him into fits of silent but vicious swearing.

On the summit of the hill, Bolverkr's ten foot curtain wall rose squarely around a crumbled ruin of a keep. A man marched along the closest rampart. Though tall and slender, Bolverkr walked with a stomping gait, his fists clenched, his white hair streaming behind him in a snarled mane. He seemed to take no notice of the three hidden spies in his forest, to Larson's intense relief. He traced Bolverkr's straight path across the top of the wall to its farthest corner. There, the sorcerer paused. His hands snapped to chest level, and light blossomed into a ball between his fingers.

''Now,'' Taziar whispered. He sprinted toward the wall, dodging through the narrow ribbon of safe pathway surrounded by Bolverkr's wards.

Astryd chased Taziar.

Riveted on the sorcerer, Larson all but missed the signal. He raced after Astryd, taking the first several steps by mimicking the location of her footfalls before he remembered the method to seeing wards. The procedure required him to lose sight of the enemy above him, a lapse that sent his survival instinct jangling and wound his nerves to knots.

Larson heard an explosive crash, followed by a woody crack that reverberated from the forest canopy. He stumbled, dropping flat to the ground from habit, his head jerking toward the noise. His left arm scraped a ward, and the magic burned a slash from wrist to elbow. Pain drove a scream from his lungs. He chocked it back into a gasp, aware that drawing Bolverkr's attention would be sure suicide, gaining strength from the memory of a young private with his chest flayed by a grenade who had managed to bite back the moans of agony that would have revealed his companions. *I'm not hurt that badly.*

Taziar stood with his back pressed tightly to the base of the curtain wall, directly beneath Bolverkr's line of vision. Even through dawn's copper-pink and gray, Larson could see the concerned expression on the Climber's face. Astryd had nearly reached Taziar. Bolverkr still stood at the farthest end of his walkway, his back toward Larson. On the ground before him, an oak lay beside its smoking, splintered stump. Leaves whipped and tumbled in a multicolored wash. Bolverkr started to turn.

Larson scrambled to his feet, aware he had to cover the three yards to Taziar and Astryd before Bolverkr completed his about-face. *Shit!* Larson sprang for safety.

Astryd gasped.

Larson jerked his head toward her, and a ward appeared in vivid relief, directly before him at waist level. He jolted backward in midair, all but grazing it as he landed.

Taziar cringed, gaze whipping to Bolverkr.

No time to get fancy. Larson hurled himself over the ward. Landing on his shoulder, he rolled to Taziar's feet, then scuttled in a wild crawl to the base of the curtain wall. He rose and pressed against the wall. The granite felt cold and solid through the sweat-dampened fabric of his tunic. His heart hammered, and his skin itched with a sense of imminent peril. He could almost feel the tear of Bolverkr's magic through his flesh. His injured arm dangled, throbbing without mercy, and he drew some solace from the realization that the injury from Bolverkr's sorcery could have proved far more critical. *It could have killed me. I was lucky. It was weak or old, or perhaps I only grazed it.*

Beside Larson, Astryd stood still as a statue, her back crushed to the wall. Overhead, Bolverkr's bootfalls grew louder as he approached.

Larson held his breath, praying to any god who might listen that Bolverkr had not seen him.

The footsteps stopped for several moments, directly overhead. Larson suppressed the urge to look up. If Bolverkr had seen him, it was already too late; movement could only draw the Dragonrank sorcerer's attention.

The silence dragged into an eternity. Larson's lungs ached, and his muscles cramped. Each second seemed too long, and he forced himself through every one individually, trying not to contemplate the next.

Bolverkr's pacing resumed.

Cued by the sorcerer's footfalls, Taziar began a hunched run, his spine just shy of the curtain wall, drawing himself into as narrow a target as possible. Astryd sidled after him.

Gaze off-centered on the wards, Larson understood the Climber's caution. The wards closed in on the wall, hopelessly intertwined, leaving them only a narrow lane around the granite to maneuver.

A series of side steps brought Taziar, Astryd, and Larson around the first corner of the curtain wall. Now, Larson released his pent up breath, allowing himself several deep inhalations of damp, autumn air. It seemed impossible that a sorcerer of Bolverkr's power had not seen the intruders near his citadel. Yet magic often seemed illogical to Larson. Spells he would have considered simple, like disguises or locating people and objects, often proved difficult; thought readings and illusions were impossible. Others that seemed grandiose, like Astryd's dragon summonings and wards that burned flesh, required far less life energy.

As Larson inched around the surrounding wall, following in Astryd's footsteps, he viewed the town from varying angles. Dawn light reflected from scattered and jagged stone in bloody highlights. Strands of thatch fluttered from between wedged granite. All other evidence that these structures had once been cottages had dispersed to the winds. Over the carnage, spells glinted in tortuous bands, like the webs of a thousand spiders, adding madness to the art of Chaos' destruction.

Larson turned the second corner. Now against the south wall and directly opposite Bolverkr, Taziar drew halfway along its length before stopping. He turned, studying the granite for some time with his head cocked at varying angles. Apparently satisfied, he jammed his fingers between stones that looked seamless to Larson's untrained eyes and clambered to the top. From there, Taziar gazed into the courtyard for a time before scrambling down the far side of the wall and out of Larson's sight.

Uncertain of Taziar's motive, Larson looked to Astryd, who shrugged her ignorance. Kensei Gaelinar had often claimed that a warrior decided his strategies in the instant between sword strokes, but Larson had still not grown accustomed to fighting enemies without making a coherent plan in advance.

Shortly, Taziar reappeared at the top of the wall and tossed the end of a rope over the side. He gestured at his companions to join him.

Now Taziar's intentions became clear to Larson. *He must have secured the other end to something stable in the courtyard.* Larson watched Astryd brace her feet against the granite. Using the rope for support, she clambered to the top of the wall. Larson waited until Taziar helped her to the ramparts before following.

Once the three companions were perched safely on the ramparts, Taziar whispered. "You go that way." He indicated the clockwise direction. "Astryd and I will come around the other. We'll try to surprise Bolverkr from both sides.'' Taziar trotted off in the opposite direction without pausing for a reply or sign of agreement.

Astryd followed.

Turning on his heel, Larson started around the other way. Alone except for the almost inaudible scrape of his boots against granite, he felt like a child playing army on a real battlefield. *Surely Bolverkr won't fall prey to a simple flanking maneuver.* Yet Larson failed to find a flaw in Taziar's plan. *Often the simplest tactic works the best, and Bolverkr seems ignorant of our presence so far.* The idea that the Dragonrank sorcerer might know they were there and not care seized Larson with frightening abruptness. His step faltered. Concerned the hesitation might throw off his timing from Astryd's and Taziar's, Larson dragged onward, forcing the thought aside. *If our presence means that little to Bolverkr, there's no sense worrying about it. We've just got to do the best we can.*

Larson rounded the first corner and started along the western wall. Bolverkr's single, fully standing tower blocked Larson's view of the north wall completely. Ignorance of Bolverkr's position made him wary, though he gained solace from the realization that the tower would obstruct Bolverkr's view of his own approach as well. He continued on, straining his hearing for some evidence that the Chaos-racked sorcerer still paced his curtain wall.

As the final corner came into sight, Larson drew Gaelinar's katana from its scabbard. The haft filled his grip, already warm from an unconscious series of touches to its hilt. A sense of calmness accompanied the unsheathing. Time seemed to strip away. For a moment, Kensei Gaelinar crouched beside his only student, his every movement crisply precise, each sword stroke flawless in its arc and timing. Competence radiated from him like physical light. His casual confidence remained, a reassuring constant in Larson's mind. He could still hear the Kensei's guttural voice suggesting that they travel to Hel to retrieve Silme's soul, speaking of the impossible as if it were trivial, suggesting Larson defy Vidarr because the Silent One was, "after all, just another god." A weight lifted from Larson's shoulders. The battle with Bolverkr seemed like just another task, scarcely different than the ones before. With Gaelinar at his side, he could do anything.

Sword readied, Larson whipped around the final corner, taking in the situation at a glance. Bolverkr stood three quarters of the way to the opposite side of the rampart, his back to Larson. Beyond him, Taziar stood braced before Astryd, sword bared, while the sorceress shaped a spindle of orange light between her fingers.

Even as Astryd shaped her spell, a white starburst of magic flashed in Bolverkr's hands, dwarfing Astryd's power. She shouted. Her arm snapped out. Her sorceries arched toward Bolverkr.

The sorcerer hurled his own spell. Orange met white in a wild splash of sparks. The darker winked out, the white sputtering a savage backlash in the trail of Astryd's spell. For an instant, the sorceress seemed bathed in milky light. Suddenly, she went limp, collapsing from the ramparts like a rag doll.

Taziar screamed in anguish and rage. Sword raised, he rushed Bolverkr.

Larson charged from behind.

A single laugh rumbled from Bolverkr's throat, rich with ancient evil, a sound so primitive it raised the hair on the nape of Larson's neck. The sorcerer flicked a hand. Lightning flashed from a cloudless sky, lancing toward Taziar like a blue-white arrow.

No! Larson all but shrieked aloud.

Less than half a second elapsed between the time Bolverkr moved and his deadly bolt struck. Electricity crackled against stone. Light flared, wrung through with a thunderclap that set Larson's ears ringing. Blinded and deafened, Larson did not pause to mourn his companions. The katana rose, then crashed down on the spot where Larson last recalled Bolverkr standing. The blade met resistance. Razor-honed, it bit into

Bolverkr's shoulder, sheared through his ribs and into his abdomen.

Bolverkr loosed a single cry, as eerie and high-pitched as the scream of a dying rabbit, then collapsed to the ramparts.

Larson tore his sword free, knowing with perfect certainty that the blow he had dealt was fatal. As his vision returned, he caught a glimpse of bone, lung, and heart through the cut; that sight and the odor of blood made his stomach heave. Stepping over Bolverkr, he dropped to his knees, vomiting into the courtyard. He staggered to his feet and threw up again, a thin bile. Horror and grief trembled through him. It required an effort of will to shuffle the last few steps to where he had last seen Taziar. Once there, he stared at Gaelinar's katana, mesmerized, trying to gather the strength to see how little of the Climber remained.

Ozone gorged Larson's nose, overpowering the stench of blood. Static sizzled the air. A circle of burnt stone met his glance. Beside it, something moved.

Larson shifted his gaze in shocked disbelief. Taziar lay prone on the ramparts, his head raised, eyes blinking rapidly as if to clear his vision.

Joy thrilled through Larson. Apparently, the little Climber's quick reflexes had allowed him to backpedal before the lightning hit. Larson harbored no doubt a direct blast would have killed him.

"Shadow." Larson caught Taziar by both arms and hefted the smaller man to his feet. "Are you all right?"

Taziar nodded, floundering as Larson allowed him to handle some of his own weight. The blue eyes flicked open, then widened in horror at some sight over Larson's shoulder. "Allerum! Look out!"

Larson whirled, dropping Taziar, who fell to one knee.

Steeped in blood, Bolverkr again stood upon the ramparts. The unequivocally-lethal wound Larson had inflicted had disappeared as if it never existed.

Holy shit! Shock froze Larson. *How?*

Light blazed to life between Bolverkr's hands.

Mobilized, Larson charged, katana raised for another death blow. *This time, I take off his fucking head!*

Larson managed only a single step before Bolverkr's magic burst in a spray of multicolored pinpoints. Larson crouched as he ran. Bits of magic rained across his back, every speck as hot as molten lead. Pain all but incapacitated him. Days in a sickbed had taken their toll on his endurance, but his will to survive remained strong. He sprang forward.

A blast of magic caught Larson squarely in the chest, dashing the breath from his lungs. He toppled over backward. The katana crashed against stone. Struck from the opposite side by sorceries as solid as the granite, the blade snapped. Its tip gashed Larson's wrist. Stone sheered skin from his arms and side. A sideways view of grass filled his vision as he teetered on the edge of the catwalk. Rolling, he scrambled to his hands and knees, catching the katana's hilt in his grip. A hand's length of cleanly fractured blade jutted from it.

Horror tore through Larson with a violence that made him scream. The agony of his wounds faded beneath a savage avalanche of grief. *Gaelinar!*

Bolverkr towered, regal as a king before a groveling subject, but Larson's vision failed him. He saw only the aging, Oriental features of his teacher, dark eyes glazing in death. Larson felt the Kensei's touch, the thrust of the katana's hilt into his own scarred hand. The old man's final, whispered words echoed in Larson's ears, "It begins again. Carry on," then faded to an ominous and permanent silence. Now, on Bolverkr's ramparts, something died within Larson. He felt weak and flaccid, unprepared to face even the simplest of challenges. He clenched the hilt to his chest, feeling the leather-wrapped steel gouge painfully into his breastbone. *Astryd's dead. In a moment, Taziar and I will join her. It's over.*

Bolverkr chuckled joyously, his triumph beyond that of simply winning a battle.

The Dragonrank sorcerer's laughter stung Larson. Sorrow parted before a deep courage that had lain dormant since he had charged a circle of AK-47s, Freyr's name on his lips and his buddies' deaths haunting his mind. *If I'm going to die again, it won't be crawling.* Determination spiraled through Larson. Lurching to his feet, he brandished the damaged sword and rushed down on Bolverkr.

A snort escaped Bolverkr. He made an effortless gesture of contempt, and a stone from a shattered gargoyle rolled beneath Larson's feet.

The granite caught Larson across the shins. He tripped, sailing over the boulder. Twisting, he landed on his side, suppressing the urge to roll before it sent him tumbling over the ramparts. His hand tightened on the haft violently; brocade scored his palm. Tears of frustration blurred his vision as Bolverkr stole his chance to at least die with dignity. Anger flared. Larson clambered to his feet, swearing, and raced toward Bolverkr once more.

Again, Bolverkr's arm raised. A sliver of magic glittered in his palm. Suddenly, with a sound like thunder, it erupted to a blood-red ball that seemed to throb in Bolverkr's hand. Back light washed the creased cheeks, making him seem like an evil parody of a grandfather. He tensed to throw.

Larson sprang forward, realizing as he did that he could never hope to beat Bolverkr's spell.

From the grounds beyond the keep, a stone shot through the air. It crashed against Bolverkr's ear, staggering him. Surprise crossed the pale features. His sorceries exploded in his fist. Sparks splattered to the granite, fizzling onto stone. Bolverkr whirled to face this new threat, just as a second stone whisked through air and slammed into his cheek.

Larson bounded forward, whipping the broken katana for Bolverkr's neck. The sorcerer dodged, slipped, and toppled into his courtyard.

Larson's blow cut air. Momentum sent him tumbling after Bolverkr.

"Allerum!" Taziar shouted in alarm, running to his friend's aid.

Desperately, Larson twisted, flailing. One hand

raked granite. He clamped his fist onto the ledge. His fall jarred to an abrupt halt that strained the muscles of his forearm and shot pain through a partially healed tear in his shoulder. Blood soaked his sleeve. He flexed against the agony, clawing for a grip with his other hand.

Taziar's small fingers surrounded Larson's wrist, supporting his mad scramble to the wall top. Once there, the elf glanced down at Bolverkr.

Apparently dazed and injured by the fall, the sorcerer had barely managed to stagger far enough to get beyond range of heavy objects shoved from the ramparts. Light flickered around the sorcerer.

Enraged, Larson flung the remains of Gaelinar's katana at Bolverkr's head. His aim was true, but, inches from its target, the haft bounced from an invisible shield and pitched into the grass. Larson swore, grabbing for Taziar's sword. "Run. I'll finish the bastard right now!"

But Taziar caught Larson's hand, jamming the blade into its sheath instead. "He's too strong. Let's go. Fast!" Taziar bounded from the ramparts, hauling Larson with him.

Dragged into another fall, Larson was forced to concentrate on landing. He touched down feet first. Taziar jerked Larson's arm then let go, sending the elf into a roll. Unhurt, Larson spun to his feet. He glanced first at the wall. Seeing no one on the ramparts, his attention shifted naturally to the direction from which the rocks had come. Silme stood partway up the hillside, another stone clasped in a hand white with strain.

Silme? Larson took a protective step toward her. Then, concerned for Taziar and Astryd, he turned back toward the keep.

Taziar had hefted Astryd. She lay draped across his arms, her limbs dangling and her head lolling. Yet Taziar's expression mingled relief with concern.

She's alive, Larson guessed. *Thank God.* Rushing to Taziar's side, he grasped Astryd's limp figure and hauled it over one shoulder.

Taziar hefted Astryd's dragonstaff, looking distressed. Whether Taziar's unhappiness came from fear for Astryd or disappointment that his slight stature made help necessary, Larson did not bother to consider.

"You lead." Larson gestured at the ruins. "Get Silme away as fast as you can. I won't have as much chance to locate magics, so I'll try to follow in your steps."

Taziar drew his sword and handed it to Larson. Without explanation, he ran toward Wilsberg, maneuvering the maze of wards with deft shifts in direction. Silme whirled and headed away from the keep, to Larson's relief.

Larson followed more ponderously, tracing Taziar's footsteps without wasting time identifying wards. The idea of leaving an enemy at his back pained him, yet Larson understood the necessity of a strategic retreat. His body felt as if it was on fire, every sinew tensed in anticipation of an exploding ward or a spell hurled from behind. Death hovered, drawing in on him, tightening until he scarcely dared to breathe. The feeling had grown familiar since the day his plane had touched down in Vietnam, and he had only managed to shake it a month ago. Now, it returned, a hyperalertness that would preclude dreamless sleep, that made him certain an enemy hovered behind every rock and tree.

Memories pressed Larson, quick glimpses of a past he thought he had suppressed. Vivid as reality, he watched his friend, Bill Charnin, flip an NVA body, watched the "corpse" empty a pistol clip into the G.I.'s face before Larson could think to shout a warning. He remembered how, forced to tend half a dozen NVA prisoners, Charnin had bound them using detonation cord. Again, the explosion rang through Larson's ears along with Charnin's growled explanation. "Now *that* is how you take prisoners."

Larson continued dodging between the wards, memorizing Taziar's path with meticulous devotion to detail. *Not now. Please, God, no flashbacks now.* He forced memory away using the control he had only recently learned with Vidarr's aid. Remembrance faded, leaving only one set of words to haunt Larson as he ran: "It begins again."

CHAPTER 4:

Chaos Link

The sick are the greatest danger for the healthy;
it is not from the strongest that harm comes to
the strong, but from the weakest.
—Friedrich Wilhelm Nietzsche
Genealogy of Morals

The Dragonmage, Bolverkr, banished pain with a muttered word and a broad sweep of directed Chaos. Once the agony had faded enough for him to concentrate, he mentally explored his body for damage. He discovered a fractured left hip and arm as well as a ruptured spleen and a bruise that ran the length of his side. Calmly, he tapped his life energy, performing the sequence of mental exercises that healed each injury. The glow of his aura faded from its usual fiery white to pewter. Curative spells cost dearly, and he had already tapped considerable life force for a gaping wound, inflicted by Larson's sword, that would have killed a lesser man.

Bolverkr rose, drawing another sliver of the Chaos-energy that raged within him for a transport spell. The effort brought him to his lookout perch on the main curtain wall. From there, he watched Al Larson maneuver the familiar pattern of wards, Astryd's limp body bouncing on his shoulder. Ahead, the black-clothed shape of Taziar Medakan dodged along the trail with an effortlessness that made it look like child's play, the garnet on Astryd's staff bobbing like a tiny, red sun above his head. Nearly at the forest's edge, Silme ran in the lead. Her fine blue dress flapped about perfect curves. Her hair streamed in a soft fan, reflecting the sun in highlights that glittered golden through the yellow. Bolverkr filled in the details from memory: high cheekbones chiseled about a straight, aristocratic nose, vast blue eyes and firm ample breasts.

Desire burned through Bolverkr, grown far beyond simple lust. Silme's flawlessness went deeper than beauty. Though sorely outmatched, she had once faced Bolverkr with no weapon except her own defiance. Unable to cast spells without harming her developing baby, she had resorted to wit to incapacitate him. *Strong, intelligent, competent, and beautiful. What more could a man want?* Yet there was one more thing. The most powerful living Dragonrank sorceress, Silme had already proven herself capable of understanding and sympathizing with Bolverkr's situation, if only in her dreams. She could comprehend the loneliness that came of being one of the rare mages in a world where most men believed in sorcerers only as mother's stories to scare children or as demon spawn to be reviled or feared.

Bolverkr gathered power to him, reveling in the energy roiling through his veins; a Chaos that had once attacked him as an enemy and had now become an integral part of himself. A paralyzing spell came to mind, forming so quickly it might have shaped itself. He aimed it for Larson's bounding figure. Once stilled, Larson and Astryd could be killed at Bolverkr's leisure. He knew from past experience that Taziar would come to his friends' aid, opening himself to any slaying spell Bolverkr might choose.

Yet Bolverkr hesitated, the paralyzation magics locked in limbo. It was not mercy that froze him. Mercy, like belief in the sanctity of life, was an arbitrary construct of man and Law. What stopped Bolverkr was the realization that, to slaughter Larson, Astryd, and Taziar now, while Silme still believed she loved them, would ingrain a hatred so profound even Chaos might not overcome it. *They're running. I can't claim self-defense any longer.* Curiosity goaded him to check the slow leak of Chaos between himself and Silme, but he resisted. To draw her attention to its presence might spark her to struggle against its influence. *The unborn baby Silme's friends insist on protecting will become the means of Silme's betrayal and their own destruction.*

Bolverkr chuckled, releasing his spell and letting his quarry reach the sanctity of the forest without persecution. Once, concern for the foursome's power had made him cautious. Now he knew they could never stand against him. *They attacked me while I was surprised and crazed, and still I bested them.* He thought of Larson's broken sword, the beautiful randomness of its destruction, the symbolic slaying of Gaelinar's soul and the splintering of Larson's morale. "I am all powerful! I am king!" He had not intended to speak aloud, yet his words knifed through Wilsberg's ruins, reverberating mournfully back from the huddled forest.

And Bolverkr's own Chaos rose to answer. *To kill you would annihilate too much Chaos for the Balance to remain. It would destroy the nine worlds and every living creature in them. The Fates, the gods, eternity will work to keep you alive. You are invincible!*

Despite having drained a relative avalanche of life energy, enough to have killed him three times over before the Chaos-bond, Bolverkr felt vigor shift through him, as restless and powerful as the tides. He felt giddy, seized by a desire to shape the world to his needs. The creatures of Law served the gods and mankind, but Bolverkr served the older, more primitive power of nature. He knew an elegance that only the finest artists learned, that beauty breeds not from order but from its lack. Chaos' asymmetry and unpredictability inspired Bolverkr to its tenets: hatred, destruction, pain, and subversion. He knew the pleasure that accompanied a scattered array of fragmented rock and corpses, the music inherent in a panicked scream.

Bolverkr stared out over the ruins of Wilsberg, entwined in a raw blaze of wards. Selecting a tree at the edge of the forest, he called down a blast of lightning from the sky's only cloud. The bolt lanced from the heavens and slammed into the trunk. A crack filled the air, soft but impending as a snake's rattle. Split near the base, the tree toppled, its limbs raking through its neighbors in a chorus of swishes and rattles. Branches and smaller trees broke beneath its weight, adding a wild series of snaps to the cacophony. Leaves billowed out in all directions, still floating long after the noise died to silence. Gradually, the odor of charred bark and ozone drifted to Bolverkr's nostrils, a perfume that bore the name Chaos.

Surrounded by his art, Bolverkr laughed, wondering why he had ever bothered to fight the Chaos within him.

Once beyond the outer circle of Bolverkr's wards, Larson followed his companions blindly between trunks, and through brush and deadfalls. His shoulder cramped beneath Astryd's weight, and his brain had gone equally numb. He felt as if the world had crushed in on him, stealing everything worthwhile, revealing Al Larson to be a hopeless incompetent. *What possessed me to think I could take the place of the world's greatest swordsman? That I deserved Silme's love or Astryd's and Taziar's trust?* Larson straggled onward, accepting the pain of his burden as appropriate punishment for his stupidity.

Deep in an unfamiliar part of the woodlands, Taziar called the retreat to a halt. "Let's rest. I think we've gone far enough."

"There's a clearing," Silme said from in front of him. "With some downed trees to sit on."

Taziar glanced at Larson, apparently seeking confirmation or opinion, but Larson stared at his feet, avoiding Taziar's gaze. The Climber narrowed his eyes, studying Larson as if to read his silence. "Be right there," the smaller man told Silme. Shrugging, he pushed through a set of low branches to the clearing.

Larson ducked beneath the foliage, protecting Astryd from the whipping branches, and followed Taziar quietly.

Silme perched on a deadfall, one leg drawn to her chest, the other dangling over the leaf-strewn forest floor. Her hair fell about and into her face in a frizzy tangle, which did not in the least diminish her beauty. Taziar watched Larson's approach, gaze fixed on Astryd.

Larson entered the clearing slowly, shifted Astryd to his arms, and gently lowered her to the ground. For all her stillness, she felt warm and alive. Apparently, her limpness as she fell had protected her from injury in the same way a drunkard survives a car accident more often than his victim. This new line of thought made Larson bitter. He had lost his father to an inebriated driver, and his mother's subsequent financial hardship had forced Larson's sister Pam into a bad marriage and him to enlist for the war in Vietnam.

A faint crackle of leaves behind Larson sent him spinning into a crouch, sword drawn, gaze tearing through autumn-brown weeds. A bushy tail whisked to the opposite side of a broad oak, another squirrel close on its heels. *Calm, Al. Calm. Jumping at little, furry animals isn't going to help anyone.* He resheathed the sword.

Ignoring Larson, Taziar knelt beside Astryd, checking frantically for life signs, though her chest rose and fell in deep, sluggish breaths.

"Make her as comfortable as you can," Silme hitched forward on the deadfall. "She'll come around."

Taziar sat cross-legged, sliding his lap beneath Astryd's head to serve as a pillow. He stroked her short, feathered locks, brushing strands from her face, without bothering to question Silme's knowledge.

Larson scowled. Standing, he regarded Silme through the speckled shadows of the forest. "How do you know that?"

Silme shrugged. "Dragonrank mages have a visible measure of life energy, an aura that only other sorcerers can see. Astryd's has a bit of fraying around the edges, probably caused by the spell she tried to throw." Silme's gaze settled on Astryd's inert form.

"Life aura reflects a state of health, whether it's drained by spells, emotional states, injury, or illness. Other than the border, her aura looks bright."

Silme's calmness dispelled Larson's concern for Astryd, allowing frustration to flood in on him. Failure made him curt. "I thought we decided you were supposed to stay in Cullinsberg."

"You decided." Silme remained calm, driving Larson to fury. "I never agreed."

"You followed us, didn't you?" Larson did not pause for an answer. "You didn't say you'd follow us. Where I come from, that's agreement." It was a half-truth at best, but Larson did not consider his statement too carefully. None of his companions knew enough about twentieth century America to contradict him.

Taziar continued soothing Astryd, wisely avoiding the argument.

"Without my rocks, you would have been killed. I bought you the time to retreat."

Larson was shouting now. "If you hadn't come, I wouldn't have worried about retreating. I would have killed Bolverkr."

"Bolverkr would have killed you."

Though Silme spoke the truth, her words infuriated Larson. "I would have fought until one of us was dead, not worried about getting you and the baby safely away."

Silme's face reddened, echoing Larson's anger. "Nor, apparently, about leaving Shadow, Astryd, and me to face Bolverkr without you."

"Stop it!" Taziar screamed over the bickering. "We've got an enemy at our backs. We can handle him, but only if we work together."

Larson's rage died to annoyance. The hopelessness of the situation, Bolverkr's seemingly infinite power, and the destruction of Gaelinar's soul would not leave his thoughts long enough to dispel his irritability. "Christ, Shadow. I damn near cleaved the guy in half. Ten minutes later, he's fully healed, throwing magical grenades and directing lightning bolts like he was playing tiddledywinks. Surely he's healed the bumps and bruises from his fall by now. He can transport anywhere instantly. He has perfect access to our location through my thoughts. If he's not here now, slaughtering us like cattle, it's because he chooses not to be. How can we fight against that?''

Ignoring the sprinkling of English words in Larson's tirade, Taziar broke into hysterical laughter.

The humor was lost on Larson. ''What's so damned funny?''

''This list of doom from the one who just argued that he would have killed Bolverkr if Silme hadn't shown up.'' Taziar ran a finger along Astryd's closed eyelids. ''The same one, I might add, who killed Loki and helped destroy the Chaos-dragon that slaughtered the original Dragonrank Master and his followers. We can handle this. Everything is impossible until someone proves it otherwise. You know that.''

Larson listened dully. In the past, Taziar's enthusiasm and confidence had roused him from despair and rallied him to the most difficult of tasks. But this time, even the little thief's certainty could not penetrate the pall of dread hanging over Larson. Seeing no reason to puncture whatever morale his companions might still harbor, Larson forced a weak smile.

''I think, Allerum,'' Silme began, her gaze focused on a forested edge of the clearing, ''it might be best if you went home.''

Larson stared, so stunned it took several seconds to realize moisture glazed Silme's gray eyes. ''Home?'' He shifted to her side, reaching for her protectively. ''What do you mean by home? I haven't stopped traveling since I came to your world. Home's a series of forest floors, farm cottages, and primitive inns. I haven't had a home since I went to Vietnam. I . . .''

Silme dodged Larson's words and his embrace. ''That's exactly what I mean.''

Larson broke off, blinking. Comprehension seeped in slowly. ''What are you saying?''

Silme stared off into the woodlands, her back to her companions. ''When I talked to Bolverkr, he said something I can't get out of my mind.''

"What!" Larson's exclamation expressed startlement and disbelief that Silme would contemplate the opinions of an enemy, but Silme accepted it as a question.

"He said you were an anachronism. And an anathema."

Larson watched Silme's back, not certain what he was hearing. "Okay. I'll give you anachronism. That just means I'm in the wrong time, right? The other thing, I don't even know what it is."

"A cursed being," Taziar explained. "An anathema."

Larson whipped his attention to his small companion.

"You asked." Taziar shrugged, covering quickly, "Bolverkr was wrong, of course."

Silme ignored the exchange. "He said that something about your misplacement in time makes the natural forces of our worlds more sensitive to your interference. He said that, eventually, you would destroy it."

Tired of addressing Silme's back, Larson drew to her side, caught her arm, and turned her toward him. "Of course, you told him that was nonsense."

Silme returned his gaze, the first tears dripping from her eyes. "That's what I told him, but I'm not sure any more. How else can you explain one man, untrained in magic and barely versed in swordcraft, slaying a god, freeing a soul from Hel, and destroying a Chaos-dragon?"

Stunned, Larson scarcely found his voice. He recalled how each of those successes had cost him months of harried persecution, injury, and plaguing flashbacks. The first had claimed Silme's life, the second Gaelinar's hand and his morale, and the third the Kensei's life and nearly Taziar's and Larson's as well. "You were there the first time. I had help from one of the highest ranking sorceresses . . ." He gestured at Silme. ". . . also the world's best swordsman and at least one god."

"I explain those things," Taziar interrupted softly,

"the same way I explain one sapphire-rank Dragon-mage protecting the nine worlds from a diamond-rank master." He referred to Silme's dedication of her life and learning to shield innocents from her half brother's cruelties. "The same way I explain a single, tiny Climber breaking into the Dragonrank's stronghold and bypassing its defenses alone. Careful planning, competent execution, and, in Allerum's case, courageous fighting."

Silme's voice remained steady despite the tears. "No matter how you explain it, the fact remains. Until Allerum came to our world, the Balance simply was. We didn't have trouble with huge shifts tipping the world toward destruction."

Many thoughts converged on Larson. He wanted to scream in frustration, to remind Silme that he had not asked to come to her world. He wanted to tell her that the gods had dragged him from death because of a difficulty with the Balance, and the only solution had been to slide the Balance too far the opposite way. But his mind shifted to new and terrible thoughts. His love for Silme ached within him, tortured by a disapproval he dared not believe he had earned. His vision washed to the red blindness of a tracer round ignited too close. "This is crazy. There's no way back to my world. Hell, Loki said my world doesn't even exist any more!" Larson's grip tightened on Silme's arm. Receiving no answer, he finished his tirade. "Gary Mannix, the original Dragonrank Master, the one you call Geirmagnus. He came from a future even later than mine. He's the one who started this whole mess with the Balance in the first place. He discovered the Dragonrank mages and created the gods hoping they could find a way to take him back to his own time. He failed, damn it! How do you expect me to do it?"

Silme blinked, splashing tears from her lashes, and wiped away another glistening on her cheek. "I know you can get back. You took me there once."

Larson winced. In a time when Vidarr's only link with the world outside his sword-prison was Larson's thoughts, Silme had entered Larson's mind in order to confer with Vidarr. In the process, sorceress and silent god had accidentally sparked flashbacks of Vietnam so vivid they had become reality. Another time, Vidarr and Silme's half brother had battled in Larson's mind, instigating rapid-fire flashes of memory until, dizzied, sickened, and confused, Larson had clung to one, dashing the combatants into a wild, twentieth century firefight. "This is crazy! I didn't take you to 'Nam on purpose. I can't help it if I don't have mind barriers and the war drove me nuts. I didn't ask Freyr for my life. I only asked him to let me take lots of V.C. with me when I died."

Larson dropped logic for gut emotion. He slammed a fist into his palm. "Damn it, Silme. I served my time. I'm not going back to Nam. For God's sake, I'm dead there." Other thoughts converged on him, a chaotic jumble he had no way to interpret. *The future I once knew doesn't exist. I destroyed it.* Yet events had proven otherwise; some of the sojourns into memory had occurred after Loki's death. *I've been there. And, every time, I've brought others with me and back.* He recalled how Vidarr had taken a bullet from a V.C. rifle, and the wound had returned with him to Midgard.

The world of my future has to exist. Another idea followed naturally. *But maybe only in my mind.* That sparked a new train of thought. *If so, can I control it? Does that make me God?* The possibilities seemed endless, yet they were unsupported by facts. The only control Larson could recall having over the trips into memory was the ability to block the exit in his mind, preventing his companions from going home without his permission. And, though he always popped into the memory exactly as he recalled it, any events transpiring from that point seemed random, related to the actions of himself, his companions, and anyone else in the scene, rather than the events that had taken place the first time he had lived the situation.

The scope became too awesome for Larson to ponder. He had no choice but to assume his world still existed in some form, and that he could go there. He tried a different tack, no longer able to hold back his tears. "I love you, Silme. I once swore worlds would never keep us apart, and I rescued you from Hel to prove that. How could you suggest we part now?"

Silme buried her face in her palms.

Taziar claimed the argument, his voice calmly rational, unaffected by their recent battle, impending danger, and his concerns for Astryd. "Silme, I can't imagine why you'd trust the words of an enemy. But let's say Bolverkr spoke the truth, and Allerum has some mystical effect on the Balance. So what? That just means we need to be aware of it and use it well rather than foolishly."

Larson stared at Taziar, glad his small companion had a habit of cutting through the bullshit and approaching problems head on.

Taziar's features crinkled thoughtfully. "Allerum leaving can only make the rest of us that much weaker against Bolverkr. But you've given me another idea."

Now Silme also regarded Taziar.

"You've already proven you can take people from this world to yours. In fact, from what you've told me, you may *only* be able to go back when you *do* take someone with you."

Larson nodded encouragingly, eager to hear the rest of Taziar's idea.

"And Geirmagnus has shown that even the most powerful Dragonrank mages can't throw spells that bridge time. So, it follows that if you take us to your world, we're completely safe from Bolverkr. We can plan, prepare, perhaps gather weapons, all in relative safety."

Stunned by the idea, Larson took several seconds to discover its obvious flaws. "It won't work."

"Why not?" Silme asked.

Larson returned to the deadfall and sat. "A bunch of reasons. First, only sorcerers and gods can enter my mind. That means I can't take Shadow." He addressed Taziar directly. "You'd be stuck here to face Bolverkr alone."

Taziar's shoulders rose and fell in resigned acceptance.

"Second, the lapses into memory aren't something I control. They just happen when I'm stressed. I usually return to some horrible, traumatic place and time, too. Third, there's bombs, traps, V.C., and North Vietnam Army soldiers where I'd take you. Not to mention fire-breathing dragonlike things we call jets." Larson recalled how Silme had attacked a phantom with magics that had sent it exploding in a rain of twisted metal and turned Larson's own war buddies against them.

"Fourth, we have reason to believe my world has become nothing more than a figment of my imagination. And last, as far as I can tell, whenever I return to Nam, I'm thrown back into my other body. This . . ." He outlined his delicate elf form with both hands. ". . . stays here, unconscious. If it's killed . . ." He trailed off, lacking the knowledge to finish the sentence but naturally assuming the worst. The events in his memory seemed real enough, yet he could not discount the possibility that it all took place inside the brain of this elf body, that death for Allerum the elf meant death for Al Larson the man as well as anyone harbored in his thoughts. At best, he felt certain that death for his elf body meant he could never return to Midgard, trapped in the meaningless violence of the Vietnam conflict, forced to live in terror until the familiar death, riddled by V.C. assault rifles. *Or, perhaps Freyr will rescue me again, and I'll get caught in some asinine, Twilight Zone-ish time loop.*

Taziar's hands went still on Astryd's forehead while he considered Larson's words. "I'm sure you didn't spend your whole life in this Nam place. If you concentrate hard enough, I'm willing to bet you could take Silme and Astryd to a safe memory. It doesn't have to really exist. You'll be coming back eventually."

Larson waited, thin brows arched, hoping Taziar had the answer to his other points.

Taziar sighed, as if in answer. "As to leaving me and your body. Naturally, I'd protect both as best as I can.'' He hesitated, then, apparently seeing no way around the difficulties, he finished lamely. ''Fine. So it wasn't a perfect plan. At least keep it in mind if things get desperate.''

Larson banished the idea to the back of his thoughts. *I won't abandon Taziar or experiment with Silme's and Astryd's lives. Besides, dwelling on the thought will only give Bolverkr access to it.* Larson knew that because of his lack of mind barriers, sorcerers could read his superficial thoughts without his knowledge. To delve more deeply, though, required the reader to physically enter his mind. Larson had learned to detect and defend against presences and deeper probes, and he doubted Bolverkr would attempt such a thing, except as a full-scale attack.

Astryd's eyes fluttered open. Her body stiffened.

Taziar knelt, pressing a hand to her forehead to keep her from moving too quickly. ''Lie still. You're safe.''

Taziar's reassurance sounded ridiculous to Larson, and he bit his cheeks to keep from laughing in hysteria. *Safe, that is, except for one lunatic, all-powerful wizard out for our blood who could be anywhere preparing our doom.* He did not speak aloud.

''Bolverkr,'' Astryd managed.

''We ran,'' Taziar admitted. ''Silme . . .''

Larson tuned out the conversation, not wanting to be reminded of the rout and its consequences. Rising, he approached Silme, catching her in an embrace.

At first, Silme went rigid. Then, slowly, her arms circled him, and she pulled him closer.

''I'm sorry,'' Larson whispered into Silme's hair. ''I don't want to fight. I love you so much.''

Silme tilted her face toward his. Something flashed in the depths of her eyes, and Larson felt certain she would impart a message or distant thought of ultimate importance. ''I . . .'' she started and stopped. ''I . . .'' The look faded into the vast grayness of her eyes. ''. . . love you, too,'' she finished.

And though it did not seem like the urgent message she had needed to convey, right now, for Al Larson, it was enough.

* * *

That night, Silme awakened to the shrill of night insects and the unhurried, regular breaths of her companions. She was uncertain what had awakened her, aware only that it had happened abruptly, like a poke in the ribs by a sleeping companion. But Larson had rolled beyond reach, one hand clamped to the hilt of Taziar's sword, the other arm drapped across his face. Taziar and Astryd lay further away, curled together in slumber. The circle of wards Astryd had placed had dwindled to a pale ghost in the night. Moonlight flittered through the branches, diffusing night's ink to gray.

Needing to relieve her bladder, Silme rose with silent grace and pushed through Astryd's fading magic, suffering only a mild sting for her recklessness. Not wanting to wander too far from her friends, she wove between a clump of tightly-packed oaks to a narrow clearing. She fumbled with her dress.

Suddenly, light shattered the darkness.

Silme gasped, straggling backward. She crashed against the line of oaks hard enough to shoot pain along her spine.

A dark figure took shape, clearly outlined in brilliant white. She recognized Bolverkr at once, his eternal features becoming familiar beneath soft, blue-gray eyes. He kept his hands outstretched in a gesture of peace and parlay. His sorceries dispersed around him, plunging the woods back into night's gloom.

Blinded, Silme blinked aside afterimages, drawing breath to scream.

"Please, don't call out." Bolverkr's voice sounded gentle as wind. "I won't hurt you. I promise. We just need to talk."

Silme hesitated, lips still parted but no sound emerging. Usually, emotion tempered her logic only slightly, but now she found herself lost, unable to differentiate the two. She knew Bolverkr had drawn most of his images of her through his searches of Larson's emotions: a young, intense love blind to her flaws. Bolverkr had had the opportunity to kill her before and had chosen only to talk. *I'm in no danger, but if I draw my companions, Bolverkr may kill them. Maybe I can calm him, talk him out of this mindless vengeance.*

Silme stared at the tall, slender wizard, watched the wind feather his milk-white hair and send his brown cloak into a serene dance. His life aura hovered in a glow that dwarfed her own, though hers was vital and untapped and his still tarnished by the battle. Her mouth closed. Her thoughts drifted to a curiosity and hunger she could not deny. The Dragonrank school had taught her that mages were born with all the life energy they would ever possess, that strength came of honing skills until it took less internal chaos to cast any particular spell. Yet Bolverkr's power beckoned, teased her imagination until she needed to understand. Before she knew it, she had taken a step toward him.

Bolverkr smiled, revealing straight teeth. "Come with me. I told you before, there's enough for us both, and I'm willing to share."

Silme paused. It seemed so simple to follow, to forget the cares she had just left behind in the clearing. Yet something jarred.

"Come." Bolverkr stretched his hand toward her. "I offer power beyond anything you've known, mastery over wind, wave, and fire, the beauty of nature and her art. Why should one of your potential stay with companions so insignificant their presence or absence takes no accounting on the world's balance?"

Silme listened without trying to formulate a reply. She knew Bolverkr spoke the truth. Only Dragonrank sorcerers and gods wielded enough significance, whether for Law or Chaos, to seriously affect the Balance. Of her companions, only Astryd's demise would require compensation in the guise of equal deaths on the side of Chaos. And, at garnet rank, her life could be easily repaid. Still, Silme realized that, though accurate, Bolverkr's point carried no importance. "I've dedicated my life to protecting the innocent. Their effect on the Balance doesn't matter."

Bolverkr's eyebrows arched, smoothing some of the creases from his features. "Doesn't matter? But of course it matters, Silme. It's nature's way to destroy the weak and see that the strong live on to create a better, more vital and significant world. Food, time, and space are wasted on the weak. The mediocre drag us all under, prevent us from becoming the best we can. Come with me, Silme. We'll make the nine worlds perfect.''

Bolverkr's philosophy seemed vaguely familiar to Silme. She followed the memory to its source, the dark-skinned diamond-rank master who had been her half brother, Bramin. She recalled his wanton destruction and deadly rages, the dragons he called down upon villages on a whim. She remembered the great beasts swooping, gouting fire on innocent townsmen and their cottages, their screams wound through with Bramin's laughter.

Another image filled Silme's mind. She thought of the hovel that had served as her only home for ten years, then, later as a blessed vacation from her training at the Dragonrank school. But her last vision of the cottage pained. Her mother's broken body sprawled on the floor of the main room, her arms gashed from defending herself from her own son's knife. The corpse of Silme's younger brother dangled, decapitated, from the loft stairs. She had found her sister lifeless in her bed, and even the baby was not spared. Silme discovered her youngest sibling chopped in the cooking pot, as if prepared for some hideous stew. Every one had died at Bramin's hand to fulfill some ghastly, Chaos-inspired vengeance against Silme's interference, as if the dark sorcerer had forgotten this family had once nurtured him as well.

''Go away!'' Silme shrank from Bolverkr. ''Don't you know what Chaos does to people? It robs them of mercy, of kindness and forgiveness.''

Bolverkr dropped his hand. ''Chaos brings only vitality and power. You may choose to do as you wish with that power.''

Silme shook her head, aware her arguments would prove fruitless. The Chaos had poisoned Bolverkr beyond retrieval. *And my insistence, in the dream, that he surrender is the cause*. "Go away. I'm not interested in what you offer, and my friends never meant you any harm. Can't you just leave us alone?"

Bolverkr's cheeks turned scarlet, and his face lapsed into angry creases. "Your friends destroyed a legacy I spent my life building. They killed my wife and my unborn child, shredded my home, slaughtered every person I loved. That crime can only be paid in blood."

Silme bit her lip.

Bolverkr's patient tenderness vanished. "You, my dear Silme, have a choice. You know I can kill your so-called friends any time I choose. You can come with me, share my love and power, or you can die with them. That, my lady, would be a waste and a pity." Bolverkr turned away. A moment later, his magics crackled through the glade, trailing a wake of gray-white smoke. Bolverkr was gone.

Silme sagged to the ground, feeling spent and queasy, though her aura filled the clearing with a vibrant blue glow. She clutched the fetus to her protectively. Its aura hovered within her, more alert and vigorous than ever before. *It's so real, so alive. I can't let it die.* Yet, Silme knew Bolverkr had spoken the truth. *He could kill us at his leisure. Our only hope lies in my using my magic against Bolverkr. Even I'm not powerful enough to stand against him, but if we all work together, it just might be possible.* Silme let the thought trail, afraid to contemplate the possibilities and consequences. It had become her way to compute the odds, to determine even her most spontaneous courses of action by the probability of success and the way that harmed the fewest innocents. It had made her suggestions intelligent and reasonable, the kind that others accepted with due seriousness. Now, she felt muddled and confused, not wanting to assess Bolverkr's abilities because it might drag her morale deeper into the quagmire.

One course of action permeated Silme's thoughts. *I could take the Chaos Bolverkr offers, then turn that power against him while it's still renegade and not yet assimilated to me and the baby.* Logic interceded. *I tried that before, and it didn't work. Even infused slowly, the Chaos binds too quickly.* Silme recalled the contact she had created with Bolverkr, her intention then to take just enough Chaos to allow her to transport. But the smallest taste of that renegade power had made her crazy for more. Only her last rebelling spark of morality had allowed her to rechannel that Chaos to her rankstone. Its sheer volume had shattered her sapphire irrevocably, returning the Chaos to Bolverkr. *If I accept his gift of Chaos, it will destroy me. Our only chance is to fight with what we have.* Yet the thought of killing her baby seemed more evil and alien than attempting to tap Bolverkr's Chaos again.

Silme buried her face in her arms. *I can't tell the others about Bolverkr's visit. It would destroy them.* Silme justified her silence by recalling the dark atmosphere of depression that seemed to surround her friends since their defeat. *Nothing bad has come of it, no need for them to know.*

Deep within her, the Chaos that had become Silme's supported the decision.

CHAPTER 5:

Chaos Destruction

By foreign hands thy dying eyes were closed,
By foreign hands thy decent limbs composed,
By foreign hands thy humble grave adorned,
By strangers honored, and by strangers mourned!
  —Alexander Pope
    Elegy to the Memory of an Unfortunate Lady

Taziar Medakan threaded through the forest east of Cullinsberg, attuned to the nearly inaudible rustle of woodland creatures fleeing ahead and the louder sounds of his companions behind him. *They're right, of course. There's no need or reason to return to Cullinsberg. Ever.* Sorrow crushed in on him, heavy and densely suffocating. It was the second time he had run from his home city, a bounty on his head and grief filling his heart. Yet, before, he had always harbored a spark of hope that he would return, that the baron would forget the transgressions of one small thief for graver matters in the city of Cullinsberg. Now, a bleak sense of permanency hung over the exodus, like a lead weight dangling from Taziar's shoulders. It held the dark, unalterable hopelessness accompanying thoughts of death. The city of Taziar's birth, loves, hopes, and friendships had become a city of deaths, imprisonment, and torture. *It's over.* Taziar's perspective had always been one of beginnings, an acceptance of changes and hardships as challenges to be met with enthusiasm. But the baron's city of Cullinsberg had always remained his single anchoring focus, a place he knew by rote, a home that had outlasted his family.

Taziar pressed through a stand of pine, pausing to let his companions catch up. Silme came first, her mouth in a grim line that revealed thoughts as stormy as his own. Astryd followed, swept into the lengthy silence. Her shoulders sagged, she kept her gaze rolled toward the needle-covered ground, and she carried her garnet-tipped dragonstaff in a carelessly loose grip. Behind her, Larson stopped, drew the sword Taziar had given him, and examined the flat and edges with a scowl that appeared indelibly etched onto his features. It seemed to Taziar as if the elf would spend the rest of his life comparing a weapon Taziar had purchased from a roadside stand to the life-culminating labor of a Japanese swordsmith.

Guilt flickered through Taziar. *Here I am bemoaning the loss of a childhood village while my friends need comforting.* Repeatedly, Taziar's rallying speeches had kindled his friends to their best efforts, making the impossible seem merely difficult. But Taziar had played all his cards. His friends had grown numb to the reminders of past prowess and successes, and the rout at Bolverkr's castle cast a pall over every previous accomplishment. This time, even Taziar did not have the answers. *But I have to do something to raise my friends' spirits.*

Taziar considered, shoving aside his own sadness and discomfort for the cause of his friends' morale. He kept his voice cheerful and his tone optimistic. "You'll love Mittlerstadt. It's got the area's finest blacksmith, and the Thirsty Stallion makes a great meal, not to mention a decent glass of beer . . ." Taziar turned and pressed onward, threading through the trees, touting a village he had never visited with half-truths gleaned from friends or outright lies. His companions knew he had spent most of his life in Cullinsberg, yet they had no way of knowing he had never left its walls until after his twenty-first birthday, and then only with the baron's guardsmen at his heels. Aside from merchants and messengers, few people left the city's comforts for a cold, lonely ride through desolate woodlands.

Taziar glanced over his shoulder as he detoured around a tight grouping of trees with vine-choked lower branches. ". . . the typical friendly hospitality of a farm town . . . ." Taziar's words seemed to have little effect on his companions. Silme shuffled after him mechanically. Larson had sheathed the sword in order to facilitate movement through brush, but he kept his fist clutched to the hilt, as if to memorize it by feel. The flight of each songbird sent him skittering into a tense defense. Astryd kept her hands near her face, hiding her emotions from friends too absorbed with their own concerns to take notice of hers anyway.

The forest grew sparser. Ancient oaks and towering pines gave way to fragile, young locusts and poplars. Gradually, the trees disappeared, replaced by fields of broken, brown stalks and unrecognizable tangles of harvested vines. Taziar quieted, mulling new tactics to bolster confidence. Simple, happy conversation did not seem to be having a noticeable effect. Recently, humor seemed to enrage rather than soothe Silme; yet Taziar considered resorting to gibes and jokes because they seemed to improve Larson's mood, at least. The Climber had finally settled on a direct, confrontational approach when a subtle change in the patterns of the fields drew his attention.

Taziar discarded his current abstraction to study the area for the source of his discomfort. Behind him, the forest loomed. In front of him, the sun hung over lifeless fields, sprinkling golden highlights amid a flatland of brown earth and vegetation. In the distance, the village of Mittlerstadt huddled, a black spot on the horizon. Smoke twined from the town, the narrow stalks of gray diffusing among the clouds. *Cook fires*, Taziar guessed. His gait grew more cautious as he focused on his other senses. Wind ruffled the standing stalks, and Taziar sorted the shuffles of his companions' feet from habit. No other sound met his hearing. He would have expected to have disturbed red deer grazing the few dried grains missed at harvest or for some noises to drift over the open fields from the town, but the relative quiet did not seem significant enough to have caught his notice.

Still, Taziar's sense of alarm grew stronger as he dismissed potential causes, rather than bringing the reassurance he would have expected. He stopped, casting a sideways glance at his companions, not wanting to worry them with vague and nameless concerns. Silme drew up beside him. Astryd remained self-absorbed. Larson walked with stiff caution, eyes slitted and nostrils widened.

Cued by Larson's manner, Taziar sniffed the air, concentrating on the mingled odors that had grown familiar so gradually he had dismissed them. He discovered an acrid tinge too strong for hearths and a stench beneath it that he recognized as the root of his growing discomfort. He turned to face Larson and Astryd. "Do you smell . . .?" He broke off, not quite certain how to describe it.

"Death," Larson finished. "Yes. What. . . ?"

"Dragon!" Silme screamed.

Taziar whirled. A huge, green-black shape hurtled toward them from the village. Its leathery wings skimmed air, its scaled body rippled gracefully, and its mouth gaped open in a triangular head.

Silme's hand lashed upward. From instinct or concern, she was preparing to cast a spell.

The baby. "Silme, no!" Taziar sprang for Silme. He crashed into her side, dashing breath from her lungs in a frenzied shriek of broken spell words. They toppled in a snarl of limbs. Silme cursed. Something sharp slashed Taziar's cheek. Pain sapped his vision to white spots, and he recoiled, tearing himself away from Silme. Hand clenched to his face, Taziar rolled to a crouch. His sight cleared enough to show him Silme, now standing, with a scarlet-stained, utility knife in her fist. Blood trickled between Taziar's fingers.

She cut me. The realization seemed so alien, Taziar could only stare at Silme.

Silme glanced at the blade in her fist as if it belonged to a stranger. Her gaze whipped to Taziar, her expression mingling horror, desperation, and rage.

The exchange lasted only a second. Silme's motivations could wait. For now Taziar turned his attention to the more immediate danger. The dragon hovered in a nearly vertical position, its head reared back and its claws splayed. Another dragon shot toward it, copper-gold in the sunlight.

Two dragons. Fear clutched Taziar. He glanced at Larson who hunched in a perfect battle position, too far beneath the dragons to strike. Astryd knelt among the weeds, her eyes locked on the creatures.

Suddenly, the darker dragon's head lunged forward. Its jaw unhinged, and flame gouted from its mouth. The other dragon twisted, spiraling upward. But the blast caught it full in the chest. It screeched, the sound painful in Taziar's ears. Tongues of fire struck and bounced groundward. Larson sprang sideways, barely missed by a flame that singed the ground where he had stood. Sparks bounced from scales like armor, raining downward, fiery pinpoints that stung Taziar's skin. Astryd remained still.

Astryd. Understanding struck Taziar, making him feel foolish. *She called the yellow dragon, and she's directing its attack.*

The green-black dragon whipped after the gold. Now above the other, Astryd's creation straightened, then plunged for its foe like a living arrow. But the darker dragon changed its course, ripping to the left, then swerving directly toward Larson. Smoke billowed from its nostrils, followed by a spout of red-orange fire.

''Allerum!'' Taziar shouted.

The warning was unnecessary. Larson dove aside. Though spared the main blast, he did not move quickly enough. Cinders hissed against the back of his tunic, igniting to flames. He turned the leap into a wild, lurching roll, snuffing the fire against dirt and dry stems.

The copper-gold dragon plummeted, evening sunlight glazing its wings like molten fire. The dark one banked for another pass, dodging too late. The yellow dragon crashed into its side, digging golden claws into the base of a wing. The force of the attack sent the green-black dragon pitching toward the ground.

Larson leapt to his feet, charging the grounded beast. He slashed with enough force to overbalance himself. His blade sliced the opposite wing like paper.

The dragon screamed. Blood splattered over Larson, Astryd, and Taziar, and the great beast whirled on its attacker. Larson fought to change the direction of his momentum, but his foot mired on a dirt clod.

Weaponless, Taziar sprang for the dragon's head. His hip crashed into a scaled head immobile as granite, but one hand plunged into a moist eye. The beast roared. Its teeth clicked closed on empty air. Larson twisted out of its path.

Astryd's dragon circled, unable to strike against its enemy without endangering Larson and Taziar. Its bulk blotted the sun, thrusting the battle into swirling shadow. Blindly, the green-black dragon snapped at Taziar. Its bite fell short, but the force of the movement sent Taziar stumbling into a scaled shoulder. The great mouth twisted toward him, opened for another blast of fiery breath.

Pinned between the dragon's neck and foot, Taziar scrabbled for a hold on its leg. Blood slicked his fingers. The tips slipped from sticky scales. *It's got me.* Unable to climb, he hurled himself flat to the ground, hoping to avoid some of the flame, braced for pain.

A great shudder racked the beast, pinching Taziar's arm between its foot and shin. Then, the green-black dragon went limp. Its head flopped to the ground with an impact that shook the field. Its mangled wings sank, sending dust devils skittering across the dirt.

Taziar looked up. Larson's sword jutted from the corpse's opposite eye, buried nearly to the hilt. Heaving a relieved sigh, Taziar clambered over its muzzle.

Larson walked around the beast and offered a hand.

Taziar accepted, grasping Larson's wrist and using it to steady his ascent over the blood-wet scales. He dropped lightly to the ground. "Thanks."

Larson chuckled at the irony of being thanked for

the simple act of helping Taziar climb, after saving his life went unacknowledged. "Hey, pal, no problem. Any time you need a hand getting off a dead dragon, you just call me, okay?" He studied Taziar, and his smile wilted. Pulling a handkerchief from his pocket, he removed his waterskin and drenched the fabric. Replacing the skin, he dabbed at the gash on Taziar's cheek. "Jesus, how'd you get that?"

Astryd's dragon faded. The world seemed to brighten as evening light gaped through the place where it had hovered.

Taziar turned a glance toward Silme. She stood in the same spot where he had left her, though she no longer clutched her knife. She said nothing.

Taziar knew Silme must have injured him by accident. At the Dragonrank school, she had balanced her repertoire of magic toward defenses against her half brother's cruelties. One such spell allowed her to destroy dragons. *Apparently, she tried to cast it intuitively. Concerned for us, she forgot the baby. Then I dove on her unexpectedly, and she naturally defended herself.* Not wanting Silme to feel any worse than she already must, Taziar answered vaguely. "Just a war wound I picked up in the fight."

Larson examined the clean, straight cut doubtfully, but he did not challenge Taziar's claim. "Well, here. You hold pressure against it. I'm not your mother." He pressed the dampened cloth to the wound, waiting until Taziar raised his hand before letting go.

As Larson turned, Taziar assessed his companion. The elf's leather vest had absorbed most of the damage from the fire. A gap had burned into the center, the area around it darkly singed, and fingertip-sized holes lay scattered over the fabric of his tunic.

Larson ripped his sword from the dragon, using another handkerchief to clean the steel. "Can't believe I look and smell like I've spent a month in a downtown bar, and I didn't even get a damned cigarette."

Uncertain of Larson's reference, Taziar turned his attention to the sorceresses. Astryd and Silme still seemed tense, casting about near the woods as if searching for something.

Handkerchief still clamped to his cheek, Taziar approached Astryd. "What are you looking for?"

"Bolverkr." Astryd poked the brass-bound base of her staff at a clump of vines.

"What?" Taziar hoped he had misheard.

This time, Silme replied. "Bolverkr. We're watching for Bolverkr. Dragons aren't natural. They have to be created and controlled by sorcerers."

"Shit." Larson wandered over, still polishing the sword. "Are you sure? It doesn't make sense. If Bolverkr's here, what's he waiting for? He's got spells that can kill almost instantly. Why's he mucking around with dragons?"

Silme stiffened. "Come on. We'd better check the town." Whirling toward Mittlerstadt, she ran across the furrowed field.

The others caught up to Silme within a few strides. "What are you thinking?" Larson asked the question on all their minds.

Silme did not slow. "Against four people, especially ones who can fight, a dragon *doesn't* make sense. But against an entire town. . . ." She trailed off, the conclusion of her statement obvious.

Taziar cringed. "You think he may have attacked the townsfolk? But why?"

Larson clung to a previous unanswered question. "And, if Bolverkr's here, why hasn't he tried anything besides the dragon?"

"Why, why, why?" Silme flung back her head, setting her golden hair streaming. "How should I know? Do I look like Bolverkr's adviser to you?" She finished with a gasp, halting so suddenly, Taziar had to take a side step to keep from running into her.

Larson spun, and Taziar drew to Silme's side to see what had upset her. A twisted, male body lay in a pile of charred weeds, its clothing and much of its flesh seared away. Insects crawled over the remains.

Taziar's stomach lurched, and he turned away.

Astryd pointed toward the town. "Look!"

Glad of another place to turn his attention, Taziar glanced in the indicated direction. Heat haze shimmered around the dark hulk of Mittlerstadt. Taziar could now see that the trails of smoke came not from hearth fires, but from random locations around the streets. The cottages appeared as broken as the new-found corpse. "Oh, no."

Shivers racked Taziar, and fear froze him. Concerned for what he might find, his mind conjured a thousand excuses to avoid the town of Mittlerstadt. But he also knew he might find injured survivors needing aid.

Larson and Silme seemed unperturbed. Grabbing the corpse by its hands and feet, they hefted it and set it gently and neatly on the open ground. Familiar with Taziar's discomfort with killing and death, Larson pointed at the field. "Shadow, why don't you start digging and watch for Bolverkr. Silme and I can check for survivors and gather bodies for burial. Astryd, you see if you can find supplies in the town." Larson turned back to Taziar and offered the sword, hilt first. "If Bolverkr shows up, you'll need this. I'll get another."

Taziar accepted the sword reluctantly, aware Larson could find another weapon, though it would take some time and diligent searching. Farmers rarely had need of blades longer than a utility knife, and the ones who owned swords were usually veterans mustered by Cullinsberg's baron for the old Barbarian Wars. Guilt descended on Taziar at the thought that his friends would protect him from having to see the corpses, then send Astryd into the thick of the town. But, before he could protest, Astryd trotted off, followed by Silme and Larson. *It's probably for the best anyway. I'd rather I met Bolverkr alone than that Astryd did.*

Using the tip of his sword as a shovel, Taziar set to work.

Night descended over the gutted town of Mittlerstadt, plunging the world into new moon darkness. Unable to sleep, Silme chose first watch, lost in the arrhythmic harmony of insects as she sat guard over her sprawled companions. Silme recalled the havoc her half brother had wreaked across the towns of Norway, the trail of slaughter she had followed, the cries and pleas of the villagers, the skewed Dragonrank education she had chosen in order to balance Bramin's malice. *It begins again.* Yet Silme saw other things this time. Bolverkr's destruction seemed far more directed and thorough. He had not left a single survivor in the town of Mittlerstadt nor a bite of food or drop of water for Silme and her companions to find. He had even diverted the primitive sewage system directly into the river that supplied the town.

Silme's mind reconjured the images of corpses heaped in shallow graves and Taziar's hurried, mass eulogies. The Shadow Climber had cried unabashedly. Later, Astryd and Larson had joined his laments. But Silme had not shed a tear. She had seen innocents die too many times to mourn the loss of a few more strangers. And, this time, the sight of the scattered, half-charred corpses had raised emotions she'd never recognized before. She found a rhythm and beauty to nature's completed cycle: birth, life, and death. She saw artistry in the shattered and crumbled randomness of the city and its ghosts. The baby's life aura flickered within her, alternately invader and miracle.

Distantly, light sparked through the trees, a brilliant blast of triggered magics. A fox sprang to vivid relief. Caught suddenly in light, it froze, then twined back into gathered shadow.

Bolverkr's magic. Anger seethed through Silme, faded to concern, then died. She glanced at her companions. Larson slept tensely, curled like a fetus around his sword. Taziar lay on his back. Astryd sprawled nearby, her hand outflung near her dragonstaff and her head cradled on Taziar's thigh.

Silme looked back toward the light. It had withered to a fuzzy glow through branches. *This is a charade. My watch means nothing. Bolverkr could transport right next to us and kill at least one of us before the others came fully awake.* She rose, aware Bolverkr could have only one reason for making his presence known without attacking. *He wants to talk. And talking may be the only way to end this feud without bloodshed.*

Silme craned her neck, staring at her sleeping companions over one shoulder. Her conscience nudged her to awaken at least one, and deep down, she knew it was reckless to leave them unguarded. But another thought rose to smother the first. *No scavenger will harm them with so many corpses so shallowly buried. Our only enemy is Bolverkr, and I'll be watching him directly. They're tired and hungry. Better to let them sleep.* Again, Silme turned her attention on the hovering gleam visible beyond the forest's trunks. Without further debate, she slipped from the field and into the woodlands.

Bolverkr met Silme just beyond hearing range of her companions. He wore a shirt and breeches of matching tailored silk, black trimmed with blue. An azure cape lay, draped majestically over his narrow shoulders. Neatly combed, white hair fell to his collar. He looked more like a politician or a prince than a sorcerer hell-bent on bloody vengeance, and the tender glance he gave Silme completed the picture. "Hello," he said, with the bland affection of a friend seen only the previous day.

Silme frowned, not bothering to return the greeting.

"You've decided to join me?" Bolverkr did not wait for an answer to his question. He took a step toward her, reaching for the satin gold waves of her hair. "A wise choice. One you won't regret."

Silme sidled, avoiding Bolverkr's touch. "I came to talk." She added carefully in a voice designed to make her point clear without inciting, "Only to talk."

Bolverkr lowered his hand with a resigned shrug. "Very well. Talk." He leaned against a gnarled pine, watching Silme expectantly.

Having anticipated that Bolverkr would begin the conversation, Silme felt unprepared. She rose to the occasion, keeping accusation from her tone. "The dragon we met outside the town. . . .'' Silme paused to consider her wording.

Bolverkr smiled. "Pretty, wasn't he?"

Silme's hand curled at her side, a habit acquired when she used to carry a dragonstaff. Since her sapphire rankstone had exploded, she could no longer store spell energy and saw no reason to lug the container around. "So, I can, in fact, presume *you* sent the dragon after us."

"Do you know of any other Dragonrank mages this far south?" Bolverkr's pale eyes sparkled, and the grin remained. "Actually, though, I sent the creature after the village. You and the others arrived conveniently." He added quickly, "Though, of course, I kept it from hurting you."

"So you were there controlling it?" Though it seemed obvious, Silme asked anyway. Summonings had never become a part of her repertoire, but she knew from learning defenses against dragons that, once called, a dragon could be given a single command, such as to attack a specific individual, group, or village.

"Yes," Bolverkr admitted freely. "I was there."

Silme plucked at a fold in her dress. She met Bolverkr's gaze directly, gray eyes glaring into blue. "But when we killed your dragon, you didn't attack."

"Ah." Bolverkr chuckled, folding his arms across his chest. "So you noticed my gift to you."

"Gift?"

Bolverkr pushed off the pine trunk, straightening. "Freyr and the Fates threw you together with a group of fools, and your wonderful sense of loyalty makes you believe you need to protect them for eternity." He shrugged, his rugged, timeless face betraying no emotion.

A fox call whirred through the night, answered by a distant bark, like an echo.

Bolverkr continued, "No matter that these companions consist of an overprotected sorceress of insignificant level, a thief, and a crazed anachronism who, by all natural right, should be dead." Bolverkr crinkled his nose in disgust. "An elf, too. A magical creation of less consequence than the dragons you've killed as beasts."

"I love Allerum," Silme blurted. "And I care about my friends." Her words came without need for thought.

"Why?"

The question caught Silme off her guard. "What?"

"Why do you love Allerum? Why do you care about your friends?"

"I—" Silme considered. "I don't need a reason to love my husband or my friends."

"True." A puff of wind lifted Bolverkr's cloak, revealing silks that clearly outlined a slender but well-proportioned body. "But blind loyalty only works for lemmings. I would never fault anyone for dedicating himself to a cause he believes in. On the other hand, to devote your life and sacrifice a chance at happiness and total power for a love you can't justify is stupid and wasteful."

"Just because I can't justify my love to you doesn't mean it doesn't exist."

"Agreed," Bolverkr conceded. "But you should be able to justify it to yourself. When's the last time you took stock of your feelings? Do you really love these inferiors, or are you just reacting out of habit? Look deep inside yourself, Silme. I think your heart might tell you something different than your mind."

"I think not." Silme tried to redirect the conversation, but Bolverkr interrupted.

"How else can you explain knifing Taziar?"

Silme gasped, not wanting to be reminded of her blunder. She tried to believe she had reacted out of desperation, using the tenets gleaned from her travels with Kensei Gaelinar. Yet she could not forget the rage that had flashed through her at Taziar's interference. She could not escape the memory of a warm glow of self-righteous justice when the blade had struck home, though guilt had followed on its heels. "An accident," she grumbled vaguely. "A stupid accident."

Bolverkr smiled again, in amusement. He did not

have to say that the process of drawing a knife and cutting a friend was too complicated and deliberate to pass for accident. It was obvious. "Do as you will. In time, you'll realize what your heart already knows. The irrelevant companions you call friends have become an annoyance."

Silme folded her arms, stung to irritation. Recently, everyone and everything seemed to have become an annoyance, and she did feel as if she needed to sequence her priorities. Normally, the ability came naturally. Now, her wits constantly seemed in a scramble. Compulsive action had replaced her usually thoughtful, ordered plans.

Bolverkr's manner softened. "When that time comes, remember a sorcerer loves you and wants to share his power and his life with you. I'll be there." His voice faded to silence beneath the insect chorus. The fox calls became cyclical, the nearer more distant and the farther closer as the creatures sought one another in the darkness.

Bolverkr's sincerity touched Silme. Trying to read his deeper intentions, she met his gaze. Candor radiated from his eyes and expression, mature emotions that went far beyond Larson's adolescent passion. Her thoughts unwound like those of a stranger, detailing a life with Bolverkr and the Chaos he offered. Logic showed her a man of great consequence, powerfully tender as well as savagely vengeful. She knew he could understand her devotion to the highest causes and her frustration at having the same townsfolk she had rescued from Bamin's magic make signs of warding evil when they realized she was Dragonrank as well. He could teach her about things she never knew existed: the earliest years of the Dragonrank mages, spells her dedication to defense had forced her to forsake, the creation of gods and elves. And he could give her the power to practice them without draining out her life energy.

Silme's life aura gleamed, brighter than she ever remembered it in the past. Unaware of Bolverkr's methodical Chaos-transfer, she attributed its brilliance to the baby's linked aura and having gone longer than ever before without tapping life force. Still, beside Bolverkr's fiery glory, her aura was dwarfed like a lantern in sunlight. For a moment, Bolverkr's vast potential and the inherent common sense of their coupling took precedence over raw emotion. Then an image of Larson seeped into her thoughts, his angular features strangely handsome, his fragile frame and delicately-pointed ears belying a human mind weighted with morality and none of the elves' capriciousness. Yet, somehow, the virtues Silme had embraced since childhood seemed distant and insignificant, their importance erased by experience and time.

I love Allerum. Silme did not allow her thoughts to stray, grounding her reason on the single fact. To contemplate too long might throw her into a frenzy of ideas she did not understand. "Go away." Her words emerged softly and with too little punch to convince even herself of their sincerity.

Still, Bolverkr honored her request. Light cracked open the hovering darkness of moonless night, and the sorcerer disappeared, leaving a trailing pulse of oily smoke.

The forest seemed to close in on Silme. Suddenly wholly alone, battered from without and within, she began to cry.

CHAPTER 6:

Chaos' Massacre

Religion, blushing veils her sacred fires,
And unawares Morality expires
Nor public flame, nor private, dares to shine;
Nor human spark is left, nor glimpse divine!
Lo! thy dread empire Chaos! is restored:
Light dies before thy uncreating word;
Thy hand, great Anarch! lets the curtain fall,
And universal darkness buries all.
—Alexander Pope
Thoughts on Various Subjects

A gentle shake awakened Al Larson. He tensed, eyes flicking open to Astryd's tiny face and china doll features. Beyond her, darkness blurred the forest to hulking bands of black and gray. Silme curled some distance away. Larson could not see Taziar. Presumably, the Shadow Climber lay behind him.

My turn on watch. The constant click of insects and the bantered calls of foxes waxed from dismissed subconscious to wakeful background. Larson yawned, stretching to work the cramps from his muscles. He mouthed the word ''thanks,'' not wanting to awaken Silme and Taziar by speaking aloud. Silme always slept on the barest edge of awakening, and Taziar rested nearly as lightly.

Astryd shook her head. She gestured at Larson and herself, then pointed behind him into the woods.

Larson stiffened. His hand tightened on the sword hilt. Slowly he turned, seeing only a broad stretch of shadowed woodland. Taziar was nowhere in sight. "Where?" Larson started.

Astryd's fingers gouged Larson's arm in warning.

Breaking off, Larson turned back to Astryd, not understanding.

Astryd made a grabbing motion in front of her lips, a plea for silence. Again, she pointed deeper into the forest. Curving her fingers so the tips touched her thumb, she placed the hand by her mouth. Opening and closing her fingers rapidly, she simulated lips and the need to talk. Though crisp, her gestures lacked the urgency that would have cued Larson to danger.

Assuming Astryd wanted to converse in private, Larson nodded his understanding. He inclined his head toward Silme.

Astryd shook her head.

Larson bit his lip. The idea of leaving Silme asleep and alone pained him. He whispered, "We can't—"

Astryd clamped a hand to Larson's mouth, shaking her head more vigorously. She waited until he quieted before removing her hand.

Silme did not stir. The patterns of her breathing remained the same.

Turning, Astryd headed off into the forest, crooking a finger over her shoulder for Larson to follow.

Against his better judgment, Al Larson trailed Astryd through autumn-brown undergrowth encased in crumbled leaves. They veered between pine and around copses, ducking beneath a fallen, rotting trunk whose upper end had wedged against a neighbor. Slipping between a pair of narrow hickories, Larson discovered Taziar standing with his foot braced on a deadfall. Astryd sat on the downed trunk.

Larson crouched, his back against a towering oak, awaiting an explanation.

"I'm sorry to call you away in such a strange way." Astryd scuffed at a pile of pine needles. "I didn't want to wake Silme."

Larson frowned, acutely aware that they had not only not awakened Silme, but they had left her unprotected.

Astryd went straight to the point. "There's something wrong with Silme."

Freshly awakened from sleep and immediately reminded of his troubles, Larson did not try to hide his annoyance. "What cued you in? Her griping at Shadow or her suggesting I go back to hell?"

Astryd seemed to take no notice of Larson's sarcasm. "Neither." She looked up. "And both, I suppose. Do you remember how I linked my magic with Silme's so she could tap my life energy to transport without risking the baby?"

Larson nodded. At the time, he had lain unconscious and inches from death, but he saw no need for a detailed description of the process. "What of it?"

"It's a dangerous link, and not well understood. I think there's some . . . well . . . residual."

Taziar leaned forward, watching Astryd curiously. "What do you mean by residual?"

"It's hard to explain." Astryd kicked needles from one boot to the other. "It's as if there's an invisible, intangible thread tying her aura to mine. Every so often, a trickle of emotion slips through the contact."

Larson blinked, gathering his thoughts. Magic made little enough sense without complicating it with links and contacts. "So you can read her mind? And you see something bad?"

"No. That's not it at all." Astryd fidgeted, apparently having difficulty finding the words needed to describe a process she did not fully understand herself. "I'm not getting thoughts, just occasional glimpses of emotion. And I'm not trying to read them, either. They just sort of, well, slip through now and again." She sighed heavily, aware she still had not clarified the issue well enough. "I've tried tracing the thread to Silme by using a gentle probe. But she snapped closed the contact so violently, it hurt." Astryd winced at the memory. "Maybe she thought I was Bolverkr."

Taziar stepped behind Astryd and massaged her shoulders through the heavy fabric of her dress. "Don't you think you should discuss this with Silme?"

Astryd nodded, still looking at Larson. "I will. I

just haven't had a chance. Her mood . . .'' She trailed off. ''Her mood is why I wanted to talk with the two of you first.''

Larson raised his brows encouragingly.

''This may sound stupid.'' Astryd spoke slowly, as if considering each word. ''But she seems to feel as if she's being invaded. From within.''

Larson froze, the expression sounding familiar in his ears. Then, finding the proper memory, he laughed. ''You've never been pregnant, have you, Astryd?''

Taziar's fingers stilled on Astryd's shoulders.

''No,'' Astryd confessed. She regarded Larson more directly. ''And I'd venture to guess you haven't either.''

Taziar smiled.

Larson conceded the point. ''Do you have younger brothers and sisters?''

''Older,'' Astryd admitted. ''I'm the baby. Why?''

''I just remember when my mother was pregnant with my little brother. She used to call him 'that little alien in my stomach' and talk about how he danced on her bladder and sucked up artichokes.'' Remote images of his mother standing before the kitchen window warmed Larson's memory, sparking others. The details of his parents' Bronx home seemed faded, another man's life. Nearby, cranes banged and huffed, building city blocks of skyscrapers that would be called Co-op City. He remembered sneaking out at night with his best friend, Tom Jeffers, to clamber over the machinery and skeletal frames, while his brother collected sugar packets and near-empty paste tubes that the work crews had left behind.

Bitterness tinged the memory. Jeffers had died in Vietnam even before Larson had enlisted. Not wanting to contemplate his friend's death, Larson tore himself from reminiscing just in time to hear Astryd's question.

''Artichokes?''

Jarred back to the conversation, Larson nodded. ''My mother craved artichokes, white chocolate, and kosher dills all through the pregnancy. "And she never used to like pickles."

Astryd swiveled her gaze toward Taziar, and they both shrugged in ignorance.

Larson got to the point. "I'm just saying pregnant women do feel like there's an invader inside." He recalled his mother's temper flaring at the slightest provocation and his father cutting dinner table arguments short with a humble, "yes, dear." "And some of them get snappy and irritable, too. It's hormones." Now, Larson felt pleased Astryd had drawn him away to talk. It gave a name and explanation to Silme's raw-tempered, uncharacteristic behavior.

Several moments passed in silence before Larson noticed Astryd and Taziar were staring at him, apparently awaiting an explanation. He addressed the Shadow Climber. "You were a youngest child, too?"

"*Only* child." Taziar resumed his massage. "I've seen enough women with child to know some do act strangely. But what, exactly, is a hormone?"

The question reminded Larson of an ancient gag: "How do you make a hormone? Don't pay her." Having spent weeks recovering in Shylar's whorehouse, Larson found the joke appropriate, wishing the pun would translate into Old Scandinavian. *If it did, I could technically be the first person to ever tell it.* "Hormones are chemicals the body makes." He searched for a comparison his companions might understand. "It's like the excitement you have long after you've finished doing something stupid." Staring at Taziar, he smiled, "I mean, something *dangerous*."

"That's funny," Taziar said, though he did not smile.

"Anyway," Larson finished, "this hormone floats around in your blood, making you feel good. Pregnancy hormones make women weepy and testy."

"That doesn't seem fair," Astryd said.

Larson shrugged, not fully certain he had his facts correct, but aware it did not matter. "It evens out. Women make adrenaline, too. And men get violent and flaky around too much male hormones. They just don't get pregnant.''

Taziar fingered his cut cheek.

Astryd nodded. Her tension faded, and she seemed satisfied with Larson's explanation of Silme's behavior. ''Imagine how she must feel. All this hormony stuff poisoning her blood. Then she's got the baby to worry about. And every time we run into Bolverkr, she has to decide between killing her child and possibly letting her friends die.'' Astryd winced. ''Oh, poor Silme.''

Larson frowned, concerned with pressures of his own. The battle at Bolverkr's keep had left him feeling helpless and trivial, a man exposed to a thousand years of science yet unable to stand against a single, primitive man. *Gaelinar gave me his sword, the vehicle of his soul, because he believed I would take care of it. I failed him. I failed myself. And, now, my failure will kill my wife and child as well as my friends.* The image of Bolverkr collapsing, half-cleaved, to the ramparts filled Larson's memory. He swore. *I should never have turned my back on an enemy until I knew he was dead.* For now, Larson conveniently forgot that he had seen heart and lungs through a wound no man could have survived longer than a few seconds. *I can't believe I didn't lop off his head while I had the chance. That mistake may cost all our lives.*

Astryd rose. ''We need to let Silme know without doubt that we want her to save the baby over any of us. We need to rescue her from the choice.''

Taziar took Astryd's hand, his gaze on Larson. ''Good idea, but I think the approach is wrong. No matter what we say, Silme will put our lives before the unborn baby's. Our protests to the contrary would only make our sacrifice seem more noble; it would look as if we were more dedicated to her than she to us.''

Taziar's words confused Larson. Not wanting to sit through the justification again, he pressed for the solution. ''What do you think we should do?''

An updraft whipped through the pines, dropping a shower of needles onto Taziar and Astryd. Absently,

Taziar brushed needles from Astryd's hair. ''We need to show Silme some confidence, to make her truly believe we're capable of handling Bolverkr.''

Larson snorted.

Taziar raised his hand. ''Let me finish.''

Larson nodded grudgingly.

''If Silme thinks we can kill Bolverkr, she can stop worrying about us and focus on the baby. If one of us is slain then, it will seem like an error in logic. She'll have misjudged our competence rather than made a conscious choice to save the baby and let us die.''

Astryd shivered.

Larson had become accustomed to discussing his own death. Taziar seemed to speak of it openly enough, but Larson did not feel certain the Shadow Climber had fully considered the implications of his words. Astryd seemed all too aware of her mortality, enough to make her unpredictable in combat. Inwardly, Larson groaned. *We're facing the most dangerous enemy in the world, and our army consists of an incompetent twentieth century soldier, a witch in a hormonal storm, a midget adrenaline addict with few combat skills, and a sorceress' apprentice.* Despair winched tighter. ''You know, there is something else to consider.''

Apparently cued by an atypical soberness in Larson's tone, Astryd and Taziar regarded their companion intently.

''It's one thing for me to decide my baby takes precedence over my life. It's another for my friends to make the same sacrifice. Neither Silme nor I expect either of you to put the baby's life over your own. That would be unreasonable.'' Larson considered the situation from another perspective. ''Given a choice between rescuing Silme or the baby, I'd have to save Silme. I can hardly blame either of you for making the same decision about the one you love.''

Taziar neatly skirted the issue. ''No one has to die.''

Larson heaved a sigh. Taziar's eternal optimism in the face of hopeless odds had become familiar and annoying. ''And the world's oceans could dry up in seconds, leaving us an endless supply of fish. Bolverkr's not going to quit until he or we are dead.''

Taziar shook his head, tossing the needles from his hair and sending the sliding comma into his eyes. ''I know you're the soldier, and I'm just street scum.'' He used an English insult Larson had once hurled in anger. ''So correct me if I say something wrong.'' He combed black strands into place with his fingers. ''It seems to me that in battle there's rarely a clear-cut choice between one companion's life and another's. You attack the enemy and assist whoever needs help at the moment. I'm not planning to let Bolverkr place me in a situation where I have to choose between helping Astryd rather than Silme, or the baby rather than you. If it happens, there's likely to be too many extenuating circumstances for me to have made the decision in advance anyway.''

The simple logic of Taziar's statement struck Larson dumb. *He's absolutely right, and I should have thought of it first.* Despondency had colored his thoughts until they seemed a hopeless blur. *Bolverkr's got me shaken. I'm not thinking clearly.*

Astryd scratched a pine needle free of her collar. ''Silme might still have to make the decision to use magic to rescue one of us. For her, that's a likely and constant dilemma.''

Taziar turned the conversation full circle. ''Which is why we have to reassure and remind her of our competence. If she killed the baby out of necessity, to save one or all of us, it would be sad. If she killed the baby needlessly, out of doubt over our abilities, it would be a senseless tragedy.''

Now Taziar's explanation became perfectly obvious to Larson. ''Agreed. And as long as we're gathered here, we've got another problem to discuss.''

''Food,'' Astryd guessed.

Al Larson winced. He had hoped he would turn out to be the only one who had carried less than a day's provisions to Bolverkr's keep. ''I figured that, if we survived the fight, we'd go back to Cullinsberg to get

Silme, and we'd have a chance to pack rations then. I didn't expect her to follow us."

Taziar bobbed his head in understanding. "And why weigh ourselves down with gear when we had wards to avoid and a battle to win? I brought nothing but weapons and a change of clothes. Had to share Astryd's dinner tonight. At worst, I figured we'd buy food in Mittlerstadt."

"Shit." Larson's head began a dull, painful throb. "It's too cold for berries, and there's not a bow between us." He glanced at the sorceress. "Wait a second. Astryd, you've got to be able to make food or zap little animals or something."

"Make food?" Astryd stared, eyes wide with incredulity. "Dragonrank mages haven't been able to make objects out of nothing since they started tapping internal chaos sources. That was long before my birth."

Larson clamped the heel of one hand to his temple, trying to think through the headache. "For God's sake! You can make dragons out of nothing."

Astryd snorted in exasperation. "I've told you before. Dragons are the natural, material form of Chaos. All I have to do to summon a dragon is release some life energy. The hard part is controlling it."

"Damn it!" Frustration and pain made Larson curt. Suddenly, every wound he had taken seemed to spring to the forefront of his attention simultaneously. The burn from Bolverkr's ward stung. The impact of the sorcerer's spell had left a pounding bruise across Larson's chest, and his shoulder ached. "What about magical hunting?"

Astryd shook her head sadly. "If I could cast slaying spells, do you think Bolverkr would still be alive? I paralyzed someone once. It just about drained out my life energy, and that would kill me. At the least, I'd be unconscious and no use against Bolverkr. It's not worth the price for one rabbit."

Larson threw up his hands in frustration, and the abrupt gesture sparked pain through his injured shoulder. "Shit!" he cried again, this time in agony. "What the hell good is it to have a sorceress who can't cast spells?''

Taziar cut in. ''Allerum, back off. She knows what she's doing, and she's doing it the best she can. Don't blame Astryd for the laws of magic.''

Astryd closed her eyes but not quickly enough to hide the brimming tears.

Taziar caught Astryd to him, stroking her hair, her face buried in his tough, linen climbing shirt.

Remorse assailed Larson, compounding his irritation. ''Look, I'm sorry,'' he apologized with inappropriate gruffness. ''I'm just frustrated and upset. I didn't mean to take it out on Astryd.''

Astryd's back quivered.

Despite its seeming insincerity, Taziar accepted Larson's explanation. ''We're all on edge. But finding food is no big deal. There's another town about two days' travel from here. I've got money.''

''I'm sorry,'' Larson repeated, this time managing to soften his tone a bit. He knew he was acting viciously toward friends he had come to love like family. Al Larson realized the pressure had touched them all in ways it never had before. Despite her relative inexperience, Astryd had always proven strong and capable under fire; her crying seemed incongruous. Silme had turned into a creature Larson would just as soon avoid. Even Taziar, usually the honey-tongued arbitrator, had snapped at Larson's verbal attack on Astryd, compounding the offense. *Not that I blame him. It's just not like him.*

Larson bit his lip, aware this situation with Bolverkr went beyond any previous challenge. Always before, hope, enthusiasm and need had brought him through impossible tasks. And always before in the direst circumstances, he had clung to the knowledge that he was dead in Vietnam by all rights, that the time he had in Old Norway was borrowed. Now he had a wife and child to live for, friends whose company he wanted to enjoy for years to come. Yet Bolverkr chose his strategies well, destroying his enemies from within as well as without. All the wounds Larson had suffered seemed minimal, lost beneath a suffocating blanket of grief, fear, and impotent rage. *How can I fight an enemy I can't see, one who can pop in with deadly guerrilla tactics, then disappear before I can strike? How can I protect my wife, child, and friends against a sorcerer of nearly unlimited power? How can I hope to kill a man who can heal lethal wounds?*

Larson whirled, slamming his fist into an oak. The blow ached through his fingers, but he ignored the pain, pounding again and again until the bark scraped skin from his knuckles and he left bloody prints on the trunk. Turning, he headed back toward Silme, not bothering to see if his companions followed.

That morning, clouds pulsed a gray curtain across the sky. Once in place, they remained unmoving in a windless sky, as if they had come to stay forever. The trees formed black skeletons against the vast grayness of the heavens, their leaves and smaller branches fanning into an intertwining network.

Al Larson stared through the branches. His thoughts seemed as drab as the sky. The last of his rations sat like lead in his stomach, and he wished he had saved the food for a time when hunger might have made him less conscious of the stale rubberiness of the cheese. The meal had passed in silence. As they strapped on their packs and prepared to travel toward the nearest city, the only sound came from droplets pattering on colored clusters of leaves and needles. The rain seemed to have driven even the birds and insects to seek shelter.

As the day progressed, the rain pitched harder. Droplets slanted between gaps in the foliage, striking in icy pinpoints through Larson's tunic and breeks. His elf form made him impervious to cold, but the dampness and ceaseless rattle and ooze irritated him to a scowling quiet that warned his friends to let him keep his own company. Finally, fully soaked, Larson no longer cared about the rain. Then, as if on cue, it dropped to a trickle and the wind rose, cutting like daggers beneath his cloak. Concerned for Silme, Larson paused beneath a shielding tangle of branches, opening his pack to offer dry clothing.

At that moment, the clouds heaved rain with redoubled fury. Above Larson, a basket of leaves succumbed to the assault, spewing a gallon of stored water onto Larson's head. Water sloshed into his opened pack. Drenched, along with everything he owned, Larson swore until his voice cracked, then accidentally inhaled saliva and lapsed into a fit of coughing.

Larson caught his breath, glaring at his companions, daring any of them to laugh. But Silme had pressed ahead, apparently too preoccupied with her own worries to bother with Larson's. Astryd waited politely but did not make a move to help. Only Taziar thought to address the obvious concern. As Larson's last cough subsided, Taziar asked with sincere interest, "Can I help? Are you well?"

"Just . . ." Larson took a rattling gasp. ". . . fucking fine." Without bothering to check to see if any of his gear had escaped the soaking, he lashed the pack closed violently and headed after Silme.

Dark, rainy day became dark, rainy night. Images of Bolverkr chased Larson through his nightmares. Repeatedly, he awakened with his muscles so rigid they ached, and it took every relaxation technique he knew to settle back into restless, dream-haunted sleep. He spent his watch stiffly waiting, hearing enemies approaching in the rustle of the leaves and the constant pounding of the rain.

The storm continued into the next day and still showed no sign of abating. No one mentioned food. They all just hefted packs and headed deeper into the woodlands, brushing through branches that showered the next person in line. For a time, Taziar whistled a tune to the rhythm of the rain, but the condemning scowls of his companions silenced even the little Climber. Larson's belly felt pinched and empty. Hoping to forget the pain, he drew up beside Silme and gave her a heartfelt and encouraging squeeze.

Silme caught Larson by the wrist. Spinning, she

hurled his arm away. "I'm tired enough. Don't hang on me."

Stung by Silme's rebuff, Larson opened his mouth to protest. Then, recalling the decision to humor Silme, he lowered his head. "I'm sorry." As hard as he tried, he was unable to keep a twinge of defensiveness from entering his voice.

Silme did not seem to notice. She whirled with an aloof briskness that sent her hair whipping into Larson's face, then stomped off toward a break in the foliage.

Grumbling epithets about women and hormones, Larson followed. A hand clasped his shoulder.

Alert to the edge of paranoia, Larson spun, crouching, his sword half free before he identified the touch as Taziar's.

Taziar leapt backward, a look of surprise on his face and his hands hovering before him in a gesture of surrender.

Larson sheathed the sword. "Sorry. I'm a bit tense."

Taziar smiled, the expression misplaced in the gloom of the forest. "A bit tense?" He laughed. "A bit tense would be the fabric of Astryd's dress with a tall, fat man stuffed into it. You would qualify as a . . ." He borrowed an English idiom. ". . . coiled spring." He dropped to a rigid hunch, imitating Larson's startled defense.

Larson chuckled, the noise sounding eerily out of place in the crushing grayness and lingering silence. The need for a snappy comeback cracked the tension. "Yeah, well, you moved pretty quick yourself." He flexed to copy Taziar's harried retreat.

But before Larson could move, Silme reappeared through the brush. Her eyes were slitted and shadowed beneath drawn brows. Larson had seen that expression only once, on the face of a Cullinsbergen guardsman just before he and his companions had pounded Larson to oblivion.

"Don't start with the jokes," Silme's tone precluded argument. "This isn't the time or place, and I'm not in the mood. Now, Shadow, there's a road up ahead. You're the only one who knows the way. Will it take us to a town?''

Taziar darted past Larson, delivering a painless kick to the elf's shin as he passed.

Aware Taziar moved too gracefully for the kick to have been an accident, Larson made a playful grab for his companion. *You bastard.* His lunge fell short, but not far enough to escape Silme's notice.

Silme glared at the antics. Saying nothing, she stomped after Taziar.

Larson trailed them both. Taziar's banter had lifted the veil of depression briefly, but Silme's condemnation slammed it back into place. He could not recall pregnancy affecting his mother so early or so severely, though he had only been a child at the time. *And Mom didn't have death, Chaos, and starvation stalking her across the continent.* Still, one thing seemed clear. *I can't take seven months of this.*

A short brush through the foliage brought Larson to the packed earth pathway Silme had called a road. Exposed to two straight days of rain, the trail should have mired to mud. But the ground only looked damp, packed to stony hardness by years of foot, horse, and cart traffic. He was about to remark on his unusual finding when Taziar spoke, interrupting Larson's train of thought.

''This is the way,'' Taziar said with exaggerated enthusiasm.

Larson snorted, fairly sure Taziar had no more idea where he was going than anyone else. It only made sense that a well-traveled road would lead to civilization, and if Taziar knew the route, Larson doubted Silme would have needed to stumble upon the pathway. Larson kept these thoughts to himself, aware Taziar was doing his best to lift their spirits, a noble cause that Larson had already dismissed as hopeless. They all headed in the indicated direction. *Eastward,* Larson guessed, though two days without sun or starlight made navigation uncertain.

Taziar, Astryd, and Silme walked near the forested edges of the pathway, partially protected by an umbrella of interwoven branches. Already sodden and oblivious to cold, Larson varied his position, feeling most secure when slinking through the shadows of the trunks. As his companions again sank into the quagmire of their own personal contemplations, Larson fell prey to an oppressive paranoia. He saw flashes of Bolverkr behind every tree, heard the sorcerer's bootfalls between the patter of each raindrop, and nearly attacked a deer when it fled into his path, apparently spooked from sleep by something ahead. His sword wound up in his hand so often, he took to carrying it unsheathed. Oddities seized his attention. Though the rain never slackened, the roadway did not seem to absorb the water. Each new step brought Larson over earth scarcely damp, as if they traveled always in the rain's leading edge. The storm never passed them, and they seemed unable to move ahead of it.

Over time, the trees again thinned to first growth. Ropy brown vines and berryless copses strung between the trunks. Larson hacked through the brush with more force than necessary, gaining a perverse satisfaction from the slivers flying around his blade. Channeling his frustration into action felt good, easing cramps from his muscles and diverting tension from an unconscious tooth grinding that left his jaw aching.

Suddenly, Astryd screamed. "Look out! Look out! Look out!" Each repetition emerged at a higher pitch.

Confused by the vagueness of her warning, Larson dove forward and down. Astryd's shoulder crashed into his side, knocking him askew. He rolled to his feet awkwardly, sword readied, scanning the woodlands for danger like a cornered animal. "What is it? Where?"

Rising to one knee, Astryd pointed directly to the place Larson had nearly cleared.

Larson followed the direction of her finger, seeing nothing out of the ordinary.

"Spell," Astryd explained.

Clued, Larson stared beyond the spot. He could make out a colored pattern of interlocking glitters, silvered with clinging raindrops. "Bolverkr's?" The answer seemed so obvious as to make the question stupid.

Larson did not await a reply before asking. "But how could he know I'd step right there?" He inclined his head toward the ward.

"Hmmm." Taziar scratched his head in a gesture mocking deep thought. "How could Bolverkr know we'd take the natural extension of a road to the village. Hmmm." He looked up suddenly. "Maybe he read your—" He broke off abruptly, though not quickly enough to keep anyone from mentally finishing his sentence with the word "mind." "I didn't mean . . ." he started.

Larson waved Taziar silent, understanding that the Climber had intended his words as a joke, not to remind Larson of his inadequacy. Still, Larson could not keep bleak frustration from accompanying the thought. "You may think he's psychic. But I think he's fucking psycho."

"Bolverkr didn't need to know where you'd be walking. Look around." Astryd waved in a semicircle around the boundary where the woodland path met farm fields.

Larson examined the area from the corner of his eye. Now, he could discern several glints of magic in a random arrangement. Hunger goaded him to wonder why no forest animals had fallen prey to the trap. *More likely, Bolverkr cleared the bodies hoping we'd starve.*

"Look!" Taziar jabbed a finger toward the center of the field.

Larson obeyed. At the distant border of his vision, red and orange flickered through the dullness, and smoke wreathed upward. "The village?"

Astryd made a pained noise. "Thor! Not again."

As one, they sprinted toward the fire. Larson remained alert for glimpses of magic, harvested stalks rattling against his ankles and crunching beneath his boots. A mad dash brought them across the farmer's fields. There, a village smaller than Mittlerstadt lay in ruins. Burned and bloated bodies were scattered amid cottages pounded to rubble. Raindrops sizzled against dying clumps of flame.

Taziar froze. Astryd slammed the base of her staff

into the mud. Slowly, she slid down its length, collapsing in a heap at its base, her body racked with sobs. Taziar curled protectively around her, rocking soothingly, his own anguish clearly etched on his features.

Sadness enfolded Larson. But, more accustomed to senseless, wholesale slaughter, he maintained his composure.

Silme simply stared as if rooted. No emotion scored her expression. She might have been examining a Picasso in the New York Museum of Modern Art, studying lines and symmetry, seeking subtleties in tone and pattern.

"Silme?" Alarmed, Larson touched Silme's arm. She had always seemed so strong, he could not imagine her shattered by one setback. Still, they had all weathered so much in such a short space. *Everyone has a breaking point.*

Larson shook Silme's arm gently. "Silme?"

Silme's cheeks twitched. Her eyes closed deliberately, and she tightened the expression until creases ringed her nose. Then her lids flicked open, revealing turbulent, gray irises reflecting an internal struggle, a decision she could not quite reach.

Larson could only guess that she still wrestled with the choice between friends and baby. Pained by her sorrow, he swept her into a reassuring hug.

Silme did not return the embrace but neither did she pull away. She stood, stiff and silent in Larson's arms.

"I love you," he said.

Silme made no reply.

Larson pulled away. "You stay here with Astryd and Shadow. I'm going to look for food and a weapon for Shadow. If I can't find a sword this time, I'll get him an ax, a pick, a shovel. It doesn't matter." *Bolverkr's ass is mine.*

Taziar looked up. "I'll come with you."

"No." Larson rolled his gaze from Silme to Astryd, trying to indicate that they needed watching without offending them. Under ordinary circumstances, he would have chosen either sorceress to back him over any man he had ever met. But Astryd's inexperience seemed to have finally caught up with her, and Silme had become as unpredictable as death.

Apparently catching Larson's hint, Taziar returned to comforting Astryd.

Leaving his pack, Larson headed for the town proper. He discovered the first corpses at the edges of the village, a woman and three children, a bad beginning to a mission he would rather have forgotten. They lay half-buried beneath charred thatch and wood frame, eyes glazed, faces locked in terror. Steeling himself, Larson searched dispassionately, not allowing himself to speculate about their pasts or their shattered futures. They were dead and he was not. They no longer had need of food and weapons; his friends needed both.

As Larson leaned over the bodies, the strange, subtle odor of flayed muscle appeared beneath the stronger smells of blood and fire. Too familiar, it no longer bothered him. The recognition of Caucasian features, blue and green irises among the staring, sightless eyes pained more. He had known several Oriental friends before the war, and he had respected his Japanese swordmaster more than any man in his life. Still, the war had taught him to notice the differences between himself and enemies. The ruins reminded him of a walk with his buddies toward a town in the Mekong Delta, the shrill whine of phantom jets overhead, and the almost instantaneous explosion. Tight to the ground before he could recall moving, he had watched grass huts and villagers dissolve into a raging column of flame.

Now Larson wove quietly amidst tumbled stone, burning thatch, and twisted, leering corpses. Instead of the overwhelming gasoline reek of napalm, he knew the acrid smell of cleaner fires, damp earth, and death. In Vietnam, he could justify the devastation by concentrating on almond-shaped eyes, hair black as ink and sticky with blood, and olive-toned skin, ignoring the arms, legs, bodies, and heads, the hearts that once held hopes and dreams so like his own. Here in the tenth century, in a part of Europe Larson could only guess was Germany, he could no longer ground his sanity on the racial differences between himself and his enemies. His imagination reconstructed the scorched faces. Every young boy bore the features of his little brother Timmy. Each teenaged girl became his sister Pam. The adults resembled so many friends and relatives from his past, an endless parade of memory that haunted him until he no longer knew who he was mourning.

Overstimulated, Larson's mind numbed the sea of corpses and rubble to a blur, and he checked the bodies with the same indifference as he did the broken remains of their dwellings. Bolverkr had done his job as thoroughly as before. Larson uncovered rakes and hoes, myriad scraps of clothing, dolls with stuffing strewn across the wreckage like the organs of their young owners. He found the ruins of a healer's cottage, some of the vials of salve and powder still intact, useless to the dead. Yet Larson did not discover a single crust of bread. Stored foods had burnt to ash, along with their barrels. And though Larson found the remains of pastures, not one corpse belonged to an animal. Once again, Bolverkr had diverted the sewage into the fountain, but that seemed less of a problem. The constant rain provided a source of water. It held an odd, metallic taste Larson could not explain, but it quenched his thirst.

As the chaos around Larson grew familiar, the odors faded into background, and the vision of death lost its sting. Even the patter of rain seemed to disappear into a dark, empty vacuum of silence and apathy. Larson had seen enough death that the bodies no longer interested him, even as morbid curiosities. He already knew human liver looked the same color and texture as the dinner table liver he had refused as a child, that kidneys were shaped like kidney beans, and that medical science had a reason for calling brains "gray matter." Aside from checking for possessions and life signs, the bodies might have become mannequins for all they mattered to Larson; each funeral ground became just one more place to look for food and weaponry. The quiet grew peaceful beneath the rain's drumbeat, a welcome relief from Silme's nagging and the despondent, unnatural silences of his companions.

Larson's exploration did not go wholly unrewarded. He came away with a pocketful of copper coins, several crude knives, and scraps of cloth that could serve as bandages. A crevice in the road had gathered enough rain to allow him to fill a skin with muddy but untainted water. Pleased with these small gains, Larson pushed into a dwelling on the far edge of town that seemed to have been spared the worst of the dragon's attack.

A hole in the thatch roof supplied enough light for Larson to get a clear view of the furnishings. The loft had collapsed, filling the main room with splintered logs and mattress tickings. A table lay shattered beneath the rubble. In the corner, near the door, a body sprawled. Dark hair fell about shoulders well-muscled from a lifetime of farming. A thick back tapered to a narrow waist. A sword belt cinched crookedly around his girth, the empty, twisted leather of a sheath peeking from beneath one hip.

A sword. Excited by his discovery, Larson bounded toward the figure. As he approached, he could see bone jutting from a bloody hole in the man's thigh. A soft groan escaped the body.

Larson froze. *Alive?* It seemed only natural that someone might survive the carnage. Yet, after several hundred pulse checks, Larson had developed a healthy respect for Bolverkr's precision. He approached cautiously, not wanting to frighten the farmer. "I won't hurt you. My name's Al. I'm a friend." He used the language of Cullinsberg's barony.

The stranger responded with a moan. He remained still.

Larson approached and knelt at the man's side. He pressed his fingers to the corded neck, feeling a pulse thump solidly against his fingers. *Good. He's got a chance.* He glanced upward. *Must have taken a bad fall.* "What's your name?"

A long pause followed. The stranger took a shuddering breath. "Will-a-" He took another shallow gasp. "-perht." A thick dialect made it sound more like Wil-burt. "Leg broken. Hurts to breathe. Back. . ." He paused. "Not sure."

A medic in Vietnam had once taught Larson to misname the injured to keep them oriented and focused on something other than the pain. "Listen, Wolfgang. Just lie still. I'm going to get some help moving you."

"Willaperht," the man corrected.

Larson headed for the door. Reminded of Bolverkr's thoroughness, he paused. *How many chances am I going to get to find a sword? Willaperht can't use it for a while, and we're all safer if Shadow's armed as soon as possible.* "Hey, Wildwood, do you mind if I borrow your sword?"

"Willaperht. Don't know where it is."

Larson smiled, shaking his head. "That's all right. Don't bother to get up. I'll find it."

Willaperht moaned in anguish.

Larson returned to Willaperht's side, rubbing the man's shoulder comfortingly as he began his search. *Keep him distracted.* "You a soldier, Willy?"

This time, Willaperht did not bother to correct Larson. "Farmer. Taught myself sword to protect my family. My wife. . . ?"

Larson groped under the fallen rubble, seeing no sign of the sword. The sheath lay flaccid and empty on Willaperht's belt.

"My wife?" the farmer repeated.

It took Larson several seconds to realize Willaperht was asking a question. This did not seem the proper time to tell the injured man he was the town's only survivor. "I don't know. There're too many people, and they're all strangers to me. For now, let's just worry about you." Larson scowled, trying to decide where to look next.

Suddenly, from the opposite end of the cottage, light tore away the gloom. Fear slammed Larson. He dropped to his belly as if his legs had given out on him, then instantly realized that his trained reaction might cost him his life. He whirled, rising to a crouch. His sword whipped free.

Bolverkr stood on the opposite side of the cottage, leaning casually against the wall, one foot propped on the splintered remnants of the loft. "Looking for this, *Allerum?*" He raised a long sword, clutched in one fist.

Larson sprang. He covered the intervening space in a single leap and cut for Bolverkr's neck with all the power he could force into the stroke.

A hand's breadth in front of Bolverkr, Larson's blade rang against an invisible barrier. The unexpected impact staggered Larson. His fingers throbbed. The wound in his shoulder tore open, spilling blood.

Bolverkr remained calmly still, smiling.

Larson's pain transformed to rage. Howling, he slashed at the sorcerer again and again, his sword crashing repeatedly against defenses solid as a mountain.

Bolverkr waited with amused patience.

Larson's arms ached. He retreated, panting, studying Bolverkr with a glare of hatred. "Coward! I'm sick to death of your hit and run tactics. If you want a fight, let's fight. You and I. Right now. Weapon to weapon." He goaded Bolverkr, circling on the balls of his feet, anticipating a strike in anger.

Bolverkr watched Larson, a slight smile on his lips, like an adult watching someone else's child throw a tantrum. Abruptly, he lunged from the rubble.

Larson rushed forward to meet the attack. The invisible barrier caught him in the face. Pain flashed through his nose. The combined force of their charges sent him reeling. His foot came down on a broken table leg. He fell backward, twisting to avoid Willaperht, and came down hard on the farmer's wounded leg.

Willaperht screamed.

Larson cursed into the stone, cheeks stinging and ankle throbbing. Fist still tight around his sword hilt, he scurried to his feet, braced for Bolverkr's magic.

Larson expected a physical attack, so the probe Bolverkr jabbed into his mind caught him completely off guard. White hot agony speared his thoughts, scattering them, and bounced like echoes through his head. He heard himself scream as if from a great distance. Consciousness hovered, blackness pressing in from all sides.

"No!" Larson's voice emerged as a dull croak. Spots prickled and rang through his head, and it ached as if it might explode. *Wall. Got to build a wall.* The world faded around Larson as he threw his full concentration into the vision of a brick tower enclosing the intruder in his thoughts.

The pain subsided. Larson caught a bleary glance of the place where Bolverkr had stood, now empty. The distraction caused the walls to blur.

In Larson's mind, Bolverkr's laughter rang hollowly through the imagined tower.

Dizzied and sickened, Larson clawed through his pain for a coherent strategy. He knew from experience that Bolverkr could spark any memory Larson had inadvertently enclosed within the walls to a vividness that could incapacitate him. He steadied his consciousness, prepared for the inevitable cruel stab of remembrance, the waves of physical or emotional pain, the complete disruption of time, place, and person. *Only one thing to try.* Larson did not consider the tactic too carefully, aware he might falter. Bravely, he waited for his first flashing image of the Vietnam War, prepared to hurl every ounce of his concentration onto that moment, hoping to throw himself into flashback and drag Bolverkr with him. The other two times he had fallen through breeches in his memory, it had happened accidentally. Now, bolstered by Taziar's suggestions to try to enter his own world, he prepared to ground his reason on the hellish war that had driven him to madness. *All right, Bolverkr, let's see how you fare against AK-47s.*

"I've shattered real mind barriers." Though enmeshed in looping coils of Larson's thoughts and memories, Bolverkr fixed his attention on Larson's conjured walls. "Do you think your makeshift defenses can hold me?"

Cued by Bolverkr's words, Larson abandoned his idea. Even the diamond-rank master, Bramin, and the god, Vidarr, had found Larson's created walls too difficult to battle. Both had chosen to assault his memories instead, aware the walls came of Larson's thoughts, and a loss of concentration would cause his barriers to crumble.

Bolverkr snapped a wrist. Fire splashed the tower's wall, flinging burning sparks through Larson's mind. The brick shattered. Chunks of rock pounded Larson's thoughts like physical pain. He started to scream. Anguish pounded him to oblivion, cutting the sound midway. Larson collapsed into darkness.

Bolverkr extracted himself from the dark void of Larson's mind. The elf sprawled on a floor littered with chaotic jumbles of singed thatch, smashed beams and furniture, and fragmented stone. Still clutching Willaperht's sword, Bolverkr studied the base of Larson's skull. *So easy.* He raised the blade. But instead of Larson's neck, Bolverkr shoved it through Willaperht's.

The farmer tensed, shuddered once, then went still.

"You're spared this time," he told Larson's unconscious body. Bracing his foot on Willaperht's spine, Bolverkr withdrew the blade. "For Silme. Once she becomes mine, I'll kill your child. And when you have nothing left but your life, I'll take that, too."

Bolverkr turned, raising the sword. Willaperht's blood trickled down the steel onto the crossguard, striping Bolverkr's knuckles. He watched the scarlet rivulets fill irregularities in the knurling, a bright, beautiful contrast to the brown leather and silvered steel. "And you might as well have this." Bolverkr jammed the point between piled stones and twisted until the steel gave. The broken blade rattled into the crevice.

Bolverkr hurled the hilt at Larson's back. It struck a shoulder blade, sliding into a fold of the elf's cloak.

Blood washed from Willaperht's wound, staining Larson's sleeve.

Tapping an insignificant amount of life chaos, Bolverkr triggered an escape transport. White light filled the tiny cottage, then winked out, plummeting the two still forms into a wash of gray smoke.

CHAPTER 7:

Chaos of Thought and Passion

> Soldier, rest! thy warfare o'er,
> Sleep the sleep that knows no breaking
> Dream of battled fields no more,
> Days of danger, nights of waking.
> —Sir Walter Scott
> *The Lady of the Lake*

Al Larson sat beneath a patchwork canopy of branches, ignoring the ceaseless drip of rain, though a stream of droplets pattered on his head. Water plastered long, white-blond hair to his high-set cheekbones, revealing the delicate points of his ears. Yet despite the annoyance of rivulets running from his bangs into his eyes, he did not bother to find a drier seat. Despair rode him, familiar as a childhood playmate. And though his companions were around him, Larson might just as well have been alone. His thoughts carried him beyond the incomplete sanctity of the forest clearing to the tattered, charred corpses of innocents killed in his name, to the body of a young man named Willaperht who might still live if Larson had gone for help immediately rather than wasting time searching for a sword.

Larson buried his chin in his palms, swiveling his gaze to the right where Taziar practiced fighting maneuvers with a branch carved into a shaft. Astryd stood nearby, leaning against her garnet-tipped staff, calling inane suggestions that seemed to have little effect on Taziar's style. Though quick and graceful, Taziar's strokes lacked power. Accustomed to swords, he occasionally used thrusting gestures that, in combat, would accomplish nothing more than giving his enemy a chance to seize the weapon and disarm him. He also tended to lead with one side, as if the staff held an edge.

Larson turned away, discouraged by Taziar's lack of combat skill but unable to gather the momentum needed to teach. He had little enough training with any weapon other than single-edged sword, deer rifle, pistol, and M-16, just a natural eye for technique. And it was obvious Taziar had no technique at all.

Wind rattled through the trees, revealing endlessly gray sky through shifting gaps. A shower of leaf-held rain splashed down on Larson, unnoticed. In Vietnam, he had been told to befriend every companion, yet to hold each at a distance. Though his life might depend on any one of them, he could not afford to let their deaths cripple him. Then, he had tried this method with little success. Now, he found it even more difficult. Never before had his enemies slaughtered women and children as a personal affront to him. Never before did he have to weigh the lives of his beloved wife and forming child in the balance. The animallike cunning and stealth of the Viet Cong had turned his nights into frenzied firefights or left him curled, shivering despite the heat, sleeping on the heart-pounding, razor's edge of waking. Yet never before had Al Larson felt so helpless and openly flayed before an enemy. In Nam, youth, inexperience, and lack of responsibilities made him certain of his permanence. But now he was all too aware of his mortality. Silme and the baby gave that mortality meaning even as Bolverkr's easy victories tainted its significance.

A shadow fell over Larson. Chin sunk into his palms, he glanced up at Silme. The sorceress towered over him, her golden hair shimmering and her cheeks rosy despite the rain. Her pregnancy enhanced beauty Larson had already used as his definition for perfection. But the coldness in her gray eyes marred the effect.

Alerted to the possibility of an argument, Larson

lowered his gaze. His belly felt hollow. His conscience ached with the burden of hundreds of blameless deaths, all the murders committed in the name of keeping him from obtaining food or weaponry. Larson could not banish searing guilt and sorrow over the shattering of Gaelinar's sword, the "vehicle of the soul," though once the displaced American would have dismissed such a feeling as superstitious nonsense.

Taziar's staff crashed against an oak trunk used as a target.

"Why do you love me?" Silme's commanding tone turned an innocent question into a demand.

Larson did not bother to raise his head. "Silme, please. I need to be alone for a while."

Another crack sounded from Taziar's direction.

Silme shuffled her feet, kicking up soggy pine needles. "And I need to know why you love me."

Ire flashed through Larson. *Easy*, he cautioned himself. *She's going through a rough time, too. You promised to support her.* He kept his voice level, resorting to monotone to keep himself from provoking conflict. "I went to Hel to retrieve you from death. I blackmailed a god into telling me the secret to raising you. I bartered and fought with Hel's goddess and Hel's hound. With Gaelinar's help, I captured the Dragonrank sorceress who was Hel's guardian." Larson hesitated, mind suddenly filled with the battle. He and Kensei Gaelinar had fought the sorceress, Modgudr, on the bridge spanning the river, Gjoll. Modgudr had hidden behind a shielding spell, similar to the one Bolverkr had created in Willaperht's cottage. She had used the shield to defend against Gaelinar's strokes as well as to drive the Kensei toward Gjoll's fatal currents. *I struck her unexpectedly from behind, and my blow fell. Apparently, either the force field doesn't completely surround the mage or he can only use it to protect against enemies he sees.* A spark of hope flared, quickly dashed by Silme's next affront.

"I didn't ask *if* you love me. That's clear enough. I want to know why."

Taziar's staff drummed repeatedly against the oak.

Larson met Silme's gaze. The distance of his thoughts and the hostility in her expression unsettled him. He spoke from habit rather than his heart. "Because you're beautiful. You're the most beautiful woman I've ever met. I love you." He reached for her, urging her to sit beside him.

Silme back-stepped beyond Larson's reach. "So you love me just because of the way I look."

Realizing his mistake, Larson clarified. "No, not just because of the way you look."

"Then why?" Silme snapped. She folded her arms across her chest, glaring at Larson through narrowed eyes.

Frustration and the ludicrousness of Silme's behavior ignited Larson's anger again. "Cut it out, Silme. I know you're in a weird emotional state. But this isn't a goddamned quiz show, and I'm not in the mood. I've got more important things on my mind."

The noise of Taziar's striking staff disappeared.

The idea that he might have an audience further fueled Larson's annoyance.

Silme's cheeks flushed in scarlet contrast to the grim, white line of her lips. "There are things more important than our love? Is that what you're saying?"

"For the moment, yes." Larson leapt to his feet, control slipping. "Trying to keep my friends and family from starving to death or getting aced by some warped bastard of a warlock takes precedence over the exact reasons why I love my wife." He added with unconcealed sarcasm, "Is that okey-dokey with you?"

"No. That's not O-kee-doe-kee with me." Silme struggled with the slang, apparently guessing its intention from previous conversations. "If you loved me for legitimate reasons, you'd know why."

"That's nonsense!" Larson was shouting now. "That's not how love works. . . ."

"And if you really loved me, you'd go back to your own world."

The track of Larson's thoughts collapsed beneath him, and he found himself scrabbling for ideas as well as words. Rage inspired him. "Damn it, Silme! We're not talking about a subway ride here. I've crossed time once, and you've seen the results. Mythology as reality. Magic. We're supposed to be in historical ninth or tenth century Germany, for Christ's sake. You're not supposed to have elves or wizards or talking wolf-gods. You're not even supposed to have potatoes. Or a barony called Cullinsberg. And what the hell kind of a name is Tazz-ee-ar?''

''Hey!'' Taziar edged closer to the argument, Astryd at his heels. He spoke with a soft gentleness designed to soothe. ''It was my father's name, okey-dokey? Now why don't you two . . .''

Silme interrupted as if Taziar had not started. ''That damage has already been done. I'm trying to protect my world from more of your interference.''

''*My* interference!'' Larson balled his fists, looking for something safe to hit. ''I'm sick and tired of getting blamed for Freyr's magic. Despite what you think, shit happened before I arrived, and shit's still going to happen if I leave. I'm not taking the blame for every crummy, stupid, insignificant thing that goes wrong in this whole fucking world.''

Taziar caught Larson's forearm. ''Allerum, calm down.''

Larson jerked his arm free, sending Taziar stumbling sideways. Whirling, Larson slammed his fist into a tree trunk. Pain lanced through his fingers, and water showered his already sodden figure. ''I'm not going back to Nam.'' He punched the oak. ''I'm not going back to vicious enemies and ungrateful allies.'' He struck again. ''I'm not going to watch women and children dismembered in the name of peace.'' He buried his face in his sleeve, the blows becoming less violent and directed. ''I'm not going to live like a hunted animal, in constant fear.'' The significance of his words seeped through the hot blanket of anger. *What's the difference between Bolverkr and NVA artillery? Why should I care less about the scattered corpses in tenth century Germany than the scattered corpses in Saigon?* Madness descended upon him, stealing his vision and filling his ears with a wordless buzzing.

A comforting hand touched Larson's shoulder blade.

Larson shrank away. "Leave me alone. Just leave me the hell alone."

"Fine. I will." Silme's voice scarcely penetrated Larson's fog. "And don't try to follow me."

As Silme's looming presence disappeared, the air around Larson seemed to lighten.

Behind Larson, Astryd's voice settled to an accusing growl. "You know the state she's in. How could you upset her like that?"

Silence hovered. Larson kept his face hidden, his throbbing fist sagging at his side.

Astryd whirled, crashing through the brush, her steps rapidly growing more distant.

Larson waited, the persistent contact on his shoulder the only indication that Taziar had remained. Silent tears glided from Larson's eyes, mingling with the dripping rainwater.

"Allerum." Taziar's composure sounded out of place after the savagery of the argument and the wild chaos of Larson's emotions. "I'll talk to Silme. Will you be all right alone?"

Larson nodded slightly, wanting nothing more than the solace of being by himself. He fingered his hilt. Aware he should say something, he turned, but Taziar was already gone.

Alone. Larson could not shake the crushing feeling of abandonment. *Nothing left.* The idea of death no longer bothered him. It beckoned, welcoming. *But I'll be damned if I'll give that Dragonrank bastard the pleasure of becoming my executioner.* Larson's emotions flickered, flip-flopping him repeatedly from despair to rage. Finally, depression collapsed beneath wild, driving anger. *Bolverkr, I've played your game. Now it's time to use my baseball and my rules.*

Aware Bolverkr could read his thoughts, Larson let the events of the last few days cycle through his mind, fanning his frenzy with each pass. His actions became automatic, lacking the motivations and experience Bolverkr would need to understand them.

Larson returned to the decimated town, steeling himself against the sight of corpses his mind's defenses turned to statues. He worked mechanically, recalling the location of every tool from his recent, minute search of the damaged town.

First, Larson gathered clay crockery and metal cooking pots. Next, he returned to the pastures, scooping up heaps of nitrogen-rich soil. Burned timbers abounded in the dragon-decimated town. Larson collected a hefty pile along with dried twigs, branches, and intact timbers for fuel. He filled several pots with water from the contaminated river. Digging through the ruins of the healer's cottage, Larson uncovered his final ingredient, a single vial of yellow powder. Uncorked, it gave off the unmistakable, rotten egg odor of sulfur. He added a candle and some unraveled, linen thread to the pile.

Saltpeter, charcoal, and sulfur. Larson crowded his raw ingredients onto a space of ground on the boundary of what had once been a village. The formula was one Larson felt certain every man of his era learned as a toddler. *Gunpowder.* He surveyed the piled items, aware he needed one more thing. *A solid container that will allow pressure to build before shattering.* His gaze fell on a nearby corpse, and he hated the source that came naturally to his thoughts. *Bone.*

The idea of disarticulating human femurs made Larson queasy, dispelling some of the anger that had driven him for the past several minutes. The realization of what he planned to do struck him as hard as a physical blow. *Gunpowder.* Memory flooded his mind, of an early autumn day in tenth century Norway. Bramin crouched before Larson and Taziar, a rifle clutched in his grip. The gun had come from America in the late 1980s, brought by a one-way time traveler named Gary Mannix and called Geirmagnus, the first Dragonrank Master. But it was Larson's war memories that had taught Silme's half brother to wield the gun.

Larson's remembrance brought a vivid image of Taziar sprawled on the grass, gaping at a ragged hole in his thigh. The Climber's shocky-white face made a striking contrast to Bramin's inky skin and half dark elven features. The rifle barrel hovered, aimed at Larson's chest, and his own admonishment rang in his ears, bringing a measure of guilt. *Bramin, if you put guns into your world, you open the way for any weak coward to kill you before you see him coming. . . . Once you bring guns into your world, there is no more glory in war.*

The memory faded, leaving Larson awash in questions. He had intended his argument simply to distract Bramin, but the morality had seeped far deeper. Once having won the conflict, Larson had carried that rifle miles to Hvergelmir, the Helspring waterfall that destroys all things in its cascade. He had tossed the gun into the wild braid of waters, hoping to delay the invention to its appropriate time or later, symbolically annihilating his year in the Vietnam War as well.

Doubt assailed Larson. He thought of Silme and how pregnancy and the pressures of combat had wrung her to a cruel, sullen core. He considered Astryd. The less experienced sorceress had withdrawn into her loyalty to Silme, forgetting the debts she owed Taziar and Larson as well. Only the little Climber seemed unaffected by Bolverkr's constant threat. Taziar appeared more distressed by his companions' bickering than the fear of death.

Larson's fall from Bolverkr's wall filled his mind again. Repeatedly, he relived the crash of magics into his chest, the twisting stumble that had driven Gaelinar's blade into the granite, the resisting, reversed-direction force of Bolverkr's next spell striking the steel simultaneously. Then Larson's mind leapt forward to his mental battle in the farm town. Fresh rage burned through him. *It's time I started playing smart, not fair. Magic was discovered by a twentieth century parapsychologist named Gary Mannix. If Bolverkr can use post modern technology, then, damn it, so can I.*

Al Larson cast aside guilt and indecision almost as

quickly as they arose. *To use anything less than all the weapons I can create would be stupid. Bolverkr, let me introduce you to grenades.* Larson headed off to find suitable thighbones.

The sun swung westward, casting stripes through gaps in the clouds. Rain-smeared light settled over Al Larson where he hunched amid covered crocks, vials, and bones, extracting his third filtered crystallization of saltpeter. Firelight glazed the clearing to a hazy red. A pot dangled over the flames, heat waves dancing over a mixture of powder and boiling water. Larson's limbs had cramped hours ago, but, intent on his work, he did not notice the pain. Winding strips of cloth about his hands to protect them from the heat, he removed the pot from the fire, strained the contents through finely-woven cloth and divided the remaining saltpeter into crocks to cool and crystallize. He shook off the pot holders. Gathering thread and candle, he lit the wick from the flames, sat, and set to interweaving linen with wax.

A presence glided into Larson's brain.

Bolverkr. Larson went rigid, dropping the makeshift wick in order to channel his concentration to this new threat. Mental walls slammed into place, surrounding the intruder. *Damn! Just a few more minutes and I would have had a real weapon.* Frustrated and enraged by the interruption, Larson blasted notions at the being who had invaded his mind. *Bolverkr, you fucking, cheating coward! You want to fight, come on out and fight like a man. Sword to sword! Fist to fist! I'm sick of this mind game shit!*

No verbal answer followed, but the intruder radiated an aura of promised peace and friendship.

"Fuck it, Bolverkr." Larson sprang to his feet, dumping the partially melted candle from his lap. "How stupid do you think I am?" He tightened the conjured barriers. "I'm not going to fall for some ridiculous promise of parlay. Get the hell out here or I'm coming in after you."

I'm afraid that would be impossible. The soft reply whispered in Larson's mind.

Larson hesitated, recognizing the voice, yet not quite placing it, knowing for certain the intruder was not Bolverkr.

The other fell equally silent.

Expecting further explanation and a chance to identify the presence, Larson found the quiet unnerving. Still, the decision to speak as little as possible identified the being in a way his voice had not. *Vidarr?*

The presence strengthened, then returned to normal.

Driven to impatience by the morning's events and the effort of holding his mental barriers, Larson sighed loudly. "Can the crap, Vidarr. That emotion stuff may work for your god friends, but I'm just a regular guy. I need words. Okay?"

Vidarr's presence tingled with warning.

Larson granted no quarter. "What are you going to do? Kill me for asking you to communicate like a normal human being?"

I've told you before, just think what you wish to say. And I'm not a normal human being.

So I've noticed. Larson tried to keep insult and sarcasm from sweeping to the forefront of his consciousness along with the words. He dropped the mental walls. *Look, I don't mean to be disrespectful, but . . .*

. . . you are, Vidarr finished.

I don't mean to be disrespectful, Larson started again, *but I'm trying to fight Bolverkr, and I don't have time to waste discussing my bad attitude with a mute god. If you've come to help, I'm grateful. If not, I haven't got time for one-way chatter.*

I can't help you.

Then go away. Realizing that antagonizing a god, even one so familiar, might have consequences, Larson softened the command. *Please.* No longer needing to concentrate on holding walls, he sat, gathering the thread and wax.

Apology wove through Vidarr's words. *You have to understand. Bolverkr is the prime source of Chaos in this world. His death would affect the gods.*

Affect the gods? Affect the gods! Galled, Larson abandoned caution. He inhaled a sharp breath in a mock noise of horror, no longer trying to hold back the sarcasm. *Well, excuse me if my self-defense interferes with your comfort. Bolverkr's death may inconvenience the gods. My death would inconvenience me. As would the rape of my wife, the slaughter of my child, and the torture of my friends.*

It's not that simple.

No. Larson's fingers clenched around the wick. *I can see where a life of omnipotent idleness could get rough.*

Stop this nonsense, Allerum! Annoyance flowed freely from Vidarr. *I came to help. Don't incite me. You won't like the results.*

Anger churned inside Larson, driving him beyond fear of consequences or vague threats. *Wake up, Vidarr. You're a god of Law. There's nothing you can do to me that Bolverkr hasn't already considered. I've got nothing left to lose.*

Except Silme.

Suddenly attentive, Larson turned his focus fully inward. *What do you mean?*

Wake up, Allerum. Vidarr borrowed Larson's idiom. *Don't you see what Bolverkr's doing?*

If I could see Bolverkr, one of us would be dead by now. Not wanting to banter words, Larson clung to the point. *What does Bolverkr have to do with Silme?*

Vidarr's presence hovered, no emotion radiating from him. *I don't know for certain. You're the only one without mind barriers. I can't read anyone else's thoughts.*

THE POINT, VIDARR!

Vidarr cringed at the intensity and volume of Larson's mental reply. *Silme's acting wrong.*

Larson snorted. *Tell me something I don't know. This pregnancy's got her hormones in an upheaval.*

Her hor-, what?

The proximity of the name Silme and the syllable "hor" bothered Larson. He made a gesture of dismissal, though Vidarr could not see it from within his mind. *Never mind. This pregnancy and the pressure's made her crazy.*

Is that *what you think?*

Obviously. The implications of the question struck Larson. *Are you saying there's something else going on?*

You mean besides the fact that you're all acting bizarre and irritable?

Yeah. Besides that.

I recognize the influence of Chaos when I see it.

Frustration rattled through Larson. *You're not making any sense.*

I know Silme as well as I know my brothers. That woman you were traveling with may have looked like Silme and talked like Silme. But she's not acting like Silme. Vidarr shifted, carefully avoiding the tangled tapestry of Larson's memories. *Carrying a baby isn't enough to explain a drastic change in personality. I've seen Silme pressured before. I've known only a few, gods included, as graceful when stressed.*

Larson licked his lips, understanding the words but not quite able to form the conclusion. *Are you trying to say Bolverkr might have kidnapped Silme and replaced her with someone who looks like her?*

Amusement fluttered through Larson's brain. *Not a chance.*

I didn't think so.

Someone or something is intentionally driving a wedge between you and Silme. It seems only natural to blame Bolverkr. I don't know what he's doing, but I'm willing to gamble my immortality that he's doing something.

Larson suddenly felt cold. *Like what? What might he be doing? Give me some possibilities or examples.*

I can't.

The short fuse on Larson's temper flared again. *You can't? Or you won't?*

I can't, Vidarr repeated. *You know I'm not one of*

the gods who uses sorcery directly. I have to guess based on observation. From what I've seen, I can't think of anything Bolverkr could use to change a personality. Her mind barriers would stop him. It just doesn't make sense.

Gripping fear replaced Larson's anger. He recalled Silme's description of Bolverkr's follower. Apparently, Harriman had been a diplomat before Bolverkr's magic shattered his mind barriers, providing access for Bolverkr to manipulate Harriman's thoughts. Larson tried to put his concern into words.

Vidarr responded to the idea, without waiting for a coherent question. *No, Allerum. As far as I can tell, Silme's mind barriers remain intact.*

Relief rose, and hope followed. *Maybe one of the gods who does use magic might understand what's going on. Couldn't you ask?*

No. Vidarr fidgeted. His back struck a coil of thought, sparking the familiar and unique odor of damp, jungle clay.

Larson cringed, willing the god to remain still.

If the others knew I was here helping you, they'd chain me to a rock and beat me till I bled.

Larson found sympathy impossible. *If it makes you feel any better, I'd be happy to tell them you were no help at all.*

Very funny.

Larson picked up one of the hollowed thighbones and threaded the fuse through the tiny hole once served by a nutrient artery. Finished, he placed the bone aside and started on the next. *Seriously, if you're not allowed to help me because Bolverkr's death might affect the gods, and if just talking to me might cause them to hurt you, why are you here wasting my time?*

You want the truth?

It seems likely. I can make up my own lies.

The truth is, I don't know.

Larson smiled, certain he knew the justification. Vidarr had reasons to feel indebted to the man who had broken Loki's spell and freed Vidarr from a lengthy imprisonment in a sword. Vidarr's repayment, an attempt to stabilize Larson's mental state against reliving traumatic experiences in times of new stress, against wildly irrational startle responses, and against night terrors, had proven only partially successful. And Vidarr's coercing Larson to complete a second task against his will had shifted the balance of favors in Larson's direction.

Though Larson did not qualify in specific words, Vidarr caught the gist of his thoughts. *I'm a god. I owe you nothing.*

Larson struck home. *If you really believed that, you wouldn't be here.*

Sullen silence.

Larson continued positioning his wick.

Vidarr's brooding turned to thoughtful goodwill.

Refusing to acknowledge any nonverbal communication, Larson ignored the Silent God.

You're ungrateful, Vidarr said at length.

Oh. So the pot's calling the kettle black. Larson set aside the second bone. Fumbling the vial of sulfur from his pocket, he slid a pair of empty crocks toward him. *I rescued you from imprisonment, and how did you thank me? You sent me on a task you knew was impossible, lying to me along the way.*

I apologized.

Oh, well. That makes it okay, then. Angered anew by the memories, Larson dumped half of the yellow powder into each crock. He reached for the charcoal, bitterness oozing into his mental communication. *Kensei Gaelinar died for your brother. Spare me the "I'm a god, you're a measly mortal" speeches. I wielded you. That changes our relationship.* Larson measured out the charcoal, turning his thoughts momentarily to his work. *Four saltpeter to one charcoal to one sulfur.* He poured, returning to the conversation. *Don't get me wrong. I'd appreciate your company. If you've come to help, I'm grateful. Really. In fact, it hurts to think about such a thing, but your aid against Bolverkr might even put me in your debt again.*

Larson harvested the cooled crystals of saltpeter,

mixing them into the two crocks in the proper proportion. He continued. *But if you've only come to whine about how you can't help me because Bolverkr's death might affect the gods, you can leave now. Don't waste my time with excuses.*

Vidarr sighed, the sound echoing through Larson's head. *You don't understand. Bolverkr is ultrapowerful. The other gods have the right to kill me for interfering.*

Vidarr's words sparked an idea too intriguing for Larson to suppress. Aware Vidarr could read his motivations and not wanting to seem as if he was plotting, he sent the message in direct words. *You're a powerful being of Law. Perhaps your death could balance Bolverkr's?*

Stunned rage radiated from Vidarr. *Is that a threat?*

Just an observation. Larson turned his full concentration on Vidarr, alert for evidence of attack. *If I was scheming against you, why would I warn you? On the other hand, if the gods did kill you, I can't deny I'd use the opening in the Balance to slaughter Bolverkr.*

Vidarr's fury turned to calculated understanding. *Don't get too hooked on the idea. My death wouldn't open the Balance nearly enough to compensate for Bolverkr's death.*

The confession startled Larson. *You're saying Bolverkr's more powerful than you?*

Far more.

"Shit." Larson stirred his concoction methodically. *No wonder Bolverkr seems invincible. What would it take to balance him? Every god on Olympus?*

Olympus?

Larson scooped powder into one of the thighbones, packing it tightly. *Oops, wrong pantheon. Sorry. What's the name of the gods' world again?*

Asgard.

Yeah. That's it.

I can usually get that right.

Once powder filled the bone, Larson jammed a stone

into the opening, maneuvering until he felt certain he had a seal. *Sarcasm doesn't become you.*

Nor you, Vidarr replied. *But I've been putting up with yours since you got here.*

Touché.

What?

Never mind. Larson set to work on the second thigh-bone, mind racing. *Vidarr, I have an idea. You can't help me fight Bolverkr directly, right?* He did not wait for an answer. *Could you do something for me that wouldn't affect Bolverkr at all?*

Possibly. Guarded interest slipped from Vidarr.

Larson struggled with a second stone. *I'm hoping it won't happen. But if things get desperate, I promised Shadow I'd take Silme and Astryd to my world. If it comes to that, would you take care of my elf body here?*

A long silence followed. Not a trace of emotion tainted the pause.

Larson finished setting the second stone. He considered asking Vidarr the myriad questions that plagued him about reality and the existence of the world he once knew as the future. However, from past experience, he felt certain Vidarr would not have the answers. *Or if he does, I won't need to ask; he'll tell me.* Carefully, Larson rose, checking his pockets for a block of flint and his dagger. His heart pounded, revealing the trepidations he kept out of his thoughts.

Just as it seemed as if Vidarr had left without answering, the god's soft voice recurred. *Yes. I'll do this for you. I'll take care of your elf body if it becomes necessary.*

Larson read something discomforting beneath the god's promise. Before he could press the issue, Vidarr changed the subject.

What are those things you're working on? Lamps?

Just evening the odds a bit. Larson retrieved the bones from the ground. *Bolverkr's got magic I don't understand, and now I've got magic he won't understand.* He could not help adding to himself, *If we're*

*going to play without rules, we'll just see who fucking
loses.*

Vidarr's presence faded, leaving a final warning so
gently distant, Larson was uncertain it was intended
for him at all. *Let's just try to see to it we don't all
lose.*

CHAPTER 8:

Chaos-Controlled

Nature, with equal mind,
Sees all her sons at play;
Sees man control the wind,
The wind sweep man away.
—Matthew Arnold
Empedocles on Etna

The rain ceased with the same unnatural abruptness with which it had begun, settling the world into a deep silence that set Larson's every nerve jangling. Sitting in the gutted town, amid his gathered crocks and powders, he saw nothing move. No sound touched his senses, only a quiet, horrible certainty that something was about to happen. He crouched, clutching his makeshift bombs, feeling the drumming solo of his heartbeat against an otherwise overpowering stillness.

Suddenly, light snapped open the evening haze, silhouetting the ruins black against startling brilliance. A distant scream followed, mixing fear and rage.

Larson recognized the voice. *Astryd!* His breath seemed to freeze in his chest. He staggered to his feet, galloping from the village before he even realized he had moved. The clouds unraveled with abnormal speed. Twilight glared through, its grayness bright after days of veiled sun. The magical flash faded. As if it were a signal, a grotesque shadow blotted out his glimpse of sunlight.

Larson glanced upward as he ran, anguish clawing at him like a living thing. A dragon knifed through the air, its wings flapping whirlwinds through muddy fields. Its scales glinted gold in the sparse light of evening. Ignoring Larson, it speared over his head, veering south at a downward angle.

My friends are in trouble, forced to fight Bolverkr without me. How could I let that happen? Larson quickened his pace. Using the dragon as a guide, he sprinted, his momentum thrown so far forward he all but sprawled in the dirt. His hands clenched whitely about the gunpowder-filled bones.

The slap of the dragon's wings beat against Larson's ears. Beneath it, he heard Astryd's cry of outrage. Bolverkr's answer blurred to incomprehensibility, growing louder and clearer as Larson approached. ". . . helpless . . . to . . . dragon . . . down on me . . . ."

Larson darted over a rise, suddenly gaining a distant but perfect view of the battle. Near the forest's edge, Bolverkr stood on a ridge hedged by piled stones, his stance regally upright and unconcerned. Taziar hammered at the sorcerer with his staff; each blow fell short of its target. Behind Taziar, Astryd kept her gaze glued to the dragon. She made a stabbing gesture toward Bolverkr. Silme waited in a silent stillness, her lip blanched between her teeth, her features crinkled in confusion.

Silme! What has he done to Silme? Larson's instincts drove him to rush recklessly to Silme's defense. But common sense stopped him cold. *We'll win this by careful strategy or not at all.* Larson ducked behind a row of stones, forcing himself to think. *Bolverkr's shielded. I need to approach unseen or from behind to get through his magic barrier.*

Calm as a giant playing with children, Bolverkr ignored Taziar's attacks. The dragon screamed toward the sorcerer, obviously in Astryd's control.

Quietly, Larson crawled around a circling ledge of stone and brush, catching shifting glimpses of the combatants.

The dragon plummeted toward Bolverkr.

The sorcerer laughed. He made an abrupt chopping motion. Sparks sprayed from his fingertips, forming a gentle arc. The magics coalesced, exploding into a ball of white that streamed toward Astryd with all the inhuman speed of her dragon.

"No!" Too late, Taziar dove into the path of the spell. The magics shrieked over his head, slamming into Astryd's face. His staff crashed down on Bolverkr's invisible shield. The wood cracked, hurling splinters.

Astryd staggered and fell to one knee.

No longer controlled, the dragon spun crazily. Its form blurred to a pale outline, wavered as if to disappear. Then, gradually, it resolidified. Suddenly, it whirled toward Taziar.

Silme remained still, watching impassively.

Though driven to action, Larson forced himself to stay hidden. *No way to know if Bolverkr's shield can repel explosives. I can't attack until I'm behind him.* He quickened his crawl.

"See, Silme. I can kill your friends any time. Watch!" Bolverkr's words flowed past Larson unheard. Larson stared in horror as the great, golden beast dipped toward Taziar. The Climber ran in sharp patterns, but the dragon maneuvered with hawklike finesse. It sped downward. One black-nailed claw clouted Taziar's scalp, bowling him across stone and grass. The dragon backpedaled, leaping into the sky.

Bolverkr laughed again. "Still, I've got no reason to kill them. They're nothing to me. They can't hurt us. But Allerum is an anachronism. His influence will destroy our worlds! Will you pay for your love with the lives of gods and innocents?"

"But you destroy innocents, too." Silme's voice sounded strange, faltering.

Concerned for Taziar and intent on his own emplacement, Larson scarcely heard the exchange.

The dragon circled, swooping down on Astryd. Taziar screamed, darting toward the Dragonrank sorceress, the splayed remains of his staff still clamped in his fist.

"I destroyed two villages," Bolverkr confessed. "I killed those townsfolk so you might understand, so we might save the nine worlds. I killed two villages. Allerum's technology will kill thousands!''

The dragon hovered over Astryd. Her eyes went wide, wild, blue orbs of fear and desperation.

Silme rallied against Bolverkr. ''You're wrong,'' she shouted. ''Allerum doesn't want to harm anyone. He wouldn't use his knowledge to . . .''

Silme's defense was suffocated beneath Astryd's screeched spell words. Yellow light grew, outlining her tiny form. The dragon's mouth hinged open as it prepared to breathe its fire.

Too late! Though not yet behind Bolverkr, Larson lit the first wick, knowing the attack would reveal him, yet unwilling to let the dragon kill Astryd as the price for his positioning.

Taziar lunged. His wiry form arched through the air and thumped to a landing beside Astryd. He scrambled over her, shielding her with his body.

Caught by surprise, Astryd gasped. Her spell shattered, collapsing to harmless, fizzling pinpoints. The first tongue of flame issued from the dragon's mouth.

Larson hurled his makeshift bomb. The bone thudded against the scaled side. The dragon twisted as it gouted flame, its fires splashing slightly off target. ''Get out of the way!'' Larson warned his companions. ''Now!''

Taziar staggered a few steps, dragging Astryd, his clothes alight.

The Climber's movements seemed ponderous. Larson willed his friend to move faster.

The dragon hesitated.

The wick flame flickered, then seemed to disappear. Larson cursed his failure just as the bone exploded. Brown-white fragments pierced the reptilian hide. The beast roared, then winked out as if it had never existed. The blast's concussion slammed Taziar to the ground. He and Astryd lay still, flaccid as death, oblivious to the flames licking at their clothing.

Bolverkr whirled toward Larson, composure lost, shock and urgency etched clearly on his face. A blinding ball of light snapped to life in his fingers.

Larson fumbled with flint and steel, awkwardly igniting the other wick. *God, please let this penetrate his shield.* He drew back to throw even as Bolverkr's magics left his fingers, blazing a screaming, silver trail.

"No!" Silme did not move, yet a tendril of her consciousness stabbed into Larson's thoughts with enough force to incapacitate him. He collapsed, writhing in pain, blind to the spell that whizzed over his head. The bone tumbled from his grip, clicking against the flint and dagger as it fell. The clearing disappeared, replaced by another, more familiar battleground . . .

"Incoming!" The cry rang around Larson in a dozen different voices. "Incoming!" He woke in a cold sweat, rolling from bed to floor, painfully rigid and alert. Grabbing his M-16, he clutched it like a favorite doll, half-running, half-crawling for the exit of his wood-framed, bamboo hooch. One of his companions made a dive for the door at the same time. Struck in the ear by a flailing elbow, Larson tumbled into the oppressive, damp heat and darkness of the jungle night. Footsteps pounded around him. Guns coughed and chattered, muzzle flashes cutting the blackness in random spots, densest near the perimeter.

Tracers streaked the night red, and a mortar round thudded to earth, loud despite distance. Gunfire churned dirt that rattled from the tin-roofed shelters. Fear threatened to overwhelm Al Larson. The instinct to run nearly overpowered him, balanced only by the terrible realization that there was nowhere safe to go. He froze, watching illumination rounds glaring whitely, seeing dark forms running, rolling, and low-crawling on both sides of the coiled concertina wire perimeter.

"Mommy!" someone screamed in frantic, mindless agony. "Oh, Mommy, Mommy."

An explosion stifled the sound, close enough to rain dirt over Larson . . . .

* * *

. . . A curse reverberated through Larson's head in a foreign tongue he could not quite place, Silme's voice wildly out of place.

The fire support base wavered, smothered suddenly in darkness. The wet, closed heat snapped open to admit New Hampshire breezes. The gun clenched to his chest became a .30/.30 rifle; the white slashes across his vision transformed to the pond-reflected glimmer of dawn light through pine. The chaotic scramble of men vanished as abruptly as a cleaver cut, leaving a peace so complete Larson felt certain he had died.

Carl Larson's whisper rattled in his son's ear. "Al, ease up. Don't strangle the gun."

The voice seemed so familiar yet so wrong. *Dad's dead.* The thought intruded from a later, less innocent age. Panic descended upon Larson. He whirled, needing to see the father who had taught him to hunt deer, scarcely remembering to keep the barrel aimed at the ground.

The father watched his son impassively, eyes gray in the twilight. Shadows played across wide features, and he ran a meaty hand through close-cropped hair.

Rounder of face, eyes half-hidden beneath a blond mop, Larson studied his father as if for the first time. Every tautened nerve in his body screamed of danger and distortion. *Dad's dead. He's dead.* The paradox unsettled Larson. He dove for reality, grounding his sanity on a flash of memory. *Dragon! Taziar and Astryd need my help.*

An image of the golden-scaled beast filled Larson's mind. Still in his head, Silme shouted, pummeling his thoughts aside. The dragon shimmered and melted, replaced by a creature every bit as large. It stood on four legs, each one wide as a tree trunk. Plates rose rigidly from its back. But, unlike the graceful, slender-necked dragons, its triangular head jutted from a short bulbous neck, low to the ground. Larson recoiled, screaming. Around him, a crowd parted hurriedly, and a vast myriad of conversations and comments swallowed the noise. *It's just wax. A stegosaurus. '64 World's Fair.*

Even as Larson identified his surroundings, he was hurled into a savage vortex of memories. Bombarded by images, he lost all sense of place and time. Perceptions passed, too quickly for him to anchor his reason: turgid, ghost-white bodies muted to tight couples flinging their arms and hair in wild dances. Then his senses overturned beneath a pile of young male day campers. Flowers spun past, followed by a coffin. *Tom Jeffers' coffin.* Even as Larson identified it, his mind conjured its contents, though the closed casket ceremony had never forced him to recognize his friend. Soft, dark eyes bulged from a face half torn away, revealing bone streaked scarlet.

Grief struck Larson with a fullness that promised sanctuary. He lunged for its stability. Silme's scream slammed through his mind. He felt himself falling, spiraling through madness, clawing desperately for any reality. The collage of the past shattered. He jarred to a sudden halt, blinking to get his bearings . . .

A hearse zigzagged between tended plots, cars trailing it like links in a chain, distant but drawing closer. Al Larson leaned against a boulder in front of seemingly endless rows of headstones in lines as straight and proud as soldiers. Beside him, his younger brother, Timmy, huddled, clinging to Larson's T-shirt. Sandy hair framed brown eyes and a freckled face above a too-thin body. *Timmy.* Larson went motionless and silent, trying not to get too involved with the scene in case insanity closed in on him again.

But Timmy's grip felt warm through the cotton. Though quavering, his voice sounded near and real. "Why? Why did Daddy have to die? Why would he go to heaven and leave us?"

Larson forgot to breathe. The words he had meant to speak, that he *had* spoken the first time he lived this same incident vanished. Unable to gather the air needed for speech, Larson grabbed his brother in a crushing, welcoming embrace. "Timmy. God, Timmy."

The boy's arms looped around his brother, tightening.

Timmy's closeness soothed Larson. The sound of the child's heart remained a reassuring constant that precluded concern for groundings and other reality. *Timmy. It's really Timmy. If this is illusion, please, God, let it last.*

Suddenly, Timmy's grip went lax. He struggled. Bracing a hand on Larson's arm, he tried to push away.

Surprised and distressed by the change, Larson released his brother.

"Ow!" Timmy brushed at wrinkles, straightening the New York University symbol on the shirt Larson had gotten during his single semester. "Al, cut it out! Don't squish me."

Scarcely daring to believe excitement had caused him to brutalize his brother, Larson stared at his own muscular forearms in shocked disbelief. Accustomed to the slender appendages that matched his elf form, his weight-trained, human limbs appeared massive, strong as an ox's and nearly as awkward. His blue jeans felt comfortable compared to scratchy wool and homespun, the knees patched with sewn flowers. His black and white tennis shoes looked odd after months of leather boots. He raked back thick blond locks, missing the baby fine hair that had hung to his elven shoulders.

The funeral procession glided to a halt about two hundred yards to Larson's left, another family's problem on a neighboring plot.

Larson opened his mouth, but no words emerged. He had no idea where to start. *I've got Timmy back.* He recalled telling his brother about going to war, Vietnam's distant challenge as enticing as it was frightening, his optimism and youthful confidence not yet poisoned by reality. He remembered, too, the hollow glare of hatred in Timmy's eyes, the boy's refusal to say "good-bye" to his only brother. When Larson had stepped onto the bus that took him to his first army base, he left that silence unbroken, haunted by his brother's betrayal and hostility, feeling sorry for himself. Only much later did he come to realize the hurt he had inflicted on Timmy.

First Dad, then me. One by one, the child's loved ones abandoned him. *I have a chance to say something here and now, to make everything right for Timmy. How often in life do we get a second chance?* Caught up in the moment, other realities slipped from Larson's thoughts. For now, he forgot that he stood in a future he was destined to obliterate from existence, forgot that a semipermanent anchoring in the past meant that he had to have dragged a sorcerer with him to St. Raymond's Cemetery.

"Timmy." Larson put a hand on his brother's wrist, using the other to tousle the sandy hair. "Dad's death was a horrible accident. He didn't want to leave us. He didn't mean to leave us. He loved us dearly, the same way we loved him, and the same way I love you." The words would have been impossible for the nineteen-year-old Al Larson whose body huddled against a boulder in a graveyard. But the mentality that filled it now knew death as a personal enemy. He had tasted fear, been stung to action by desperation, and had slaughtered with his own hands. Still, the words came only with great difficulty. He agonized over each one, certain he could have chosen better ones, yet calmed by the realization that just talking was better than the way he had left Timmy the last time. Al Larson pressed his back against the boulder, now facing the funeral, his attention partially diverted by the procession.

The car doors opened. A couple emerged from the second vehicle, clinging to one another like lost children. Even from a distance, Larson guessed they were in their early forties, about his mother's age. And while he and Timmy mourned a father, these strangers were, undoubtedly, burying a son.

Timmy shifted closer to his brother.

"With Dad gone, Mom can't afford to take care of us all. I'm going to have to go to the war." The explanation pained Larson, trebling in difficulty as a huddled group of pallbearers hefted a flag-draped coffin. Muffled noises drifted to Larson's ears, the words a distorted mosaic of grief.

Larson wiped his palms on his jeans, fighting the denial that rose within him. *What if I'm here to stay? I'm not going back to war. They can't make me serve twice.* "It's not something I want to do. It's something I have to do. We don't have the money for me to go back to college. If I don't go voluntarily, the Army will drag me there. Understand, I want to stay with you. If it's at all possible, I'll be back in a year." Larson felt Timmy trembling against him and realized he was shaking at least as much. Unable to look at his brother, he watched as five men in army uniforms emerged from the next car in the procession, three carrying rifles. Mourners exited the remaining vehicles from both sides, forming a growing, dark cloud of suits and dresses.

Larson shivered, his thoughts sliding naturally to his own death in Vietnam. *Is this where they buried me?* Recalling his placement in time meant his human persona had another year to live, he amended. *Is this where they* will *bury me?* Memories surfaced, of the other members of his patrol killed, one by one, in the jungle depths, of his own crazed suicide run amid the blatter of enemy guns. *Missing in action, no doubt. Likely, they never found . . . will never find . . . the body. This body. My body.* Larson studied his jeans and sneaker clad form protectively. Suddenly fear nearly crippled him. *I'm going to die. I even know when. And how.* He clutched at the boulder, forcing aside the savage maelstrom of thought for Timmy's benefit. "I love you." He reached for the boy.

Timmy dodged so abruptly, he nearly fell from the boulder. "You're lying! Why are you lying?" he screamed in tearful hysteria.

Larson had never seen his brother so unhinged. "Timmy?"

Crying coarsened Timmy's voice. Sudden frenzied rage and fear turned it into a shrill parody. "You're going to die there! You're going to die in Vietnam, and you know it! You're lying! You already know you're going to die!''

"Timmy, quiet. Please." Larson glanced toward the funeral, relieved to find no one looking their way. Apparently, distance had obliterated Timmy's tirade. Still, Larson knew his brother well. This was not a simple childish outburst, grounded only on fear. The certainty in Timmy's voice was unmistakable. *He knows. How could he possibly know?* Only one source presented itself. *Someone entered his mind and told him. Some Dragonrank sorcerer. But who? And why?* Larson whirled. His father's headstone caught his eye, skewing his attention from his search just long enough for the words and dates to register:

R.I.P.
Carl Larson
Born: February 12, 1926
Died: May 5, 1968

Silme's voice broke the stillness, her presence confirming what Larson had already divined. "Allerum! You killed them!" She spoke in ancient Scandinavian, her tone combining fury and hatred, the accusation etched with venom.

Larson dropped to a crouch, scanning the rows of graves. Silme stared with narrowed eyes, one booted foot propped against a headstone. She wore the same red and gold robes as in tenth century Europe. Casually, she glanced at the funeral group behind her. Then, apparently finding them occupied and nonthreatening, she turned her full attention to Al and Tim Larson.

Timmy's fingers gouged Larson's shoulder, trembling.

Larson wanted to comfort his little brother but could not tear his gaze from Silme's aggressive stance. He used the same language. "What did you tell Timmy? Why would you torture a child?" Then, as Silme's words penetrated past his alarm for Timmy, he asked, "Killed who? What are you talking about?"

"Taz and Astryd," Silme hissed. "You killed them."

"No." Uncertainty took all vigor from Larson's denial. If his bone bomb had not killed Taziar and Astryd, it might have prevented them from escaping the dragon's flames. Urgency whipped through him. "Silme, we have to get back. We may still be able to save them." He glanced at Timmy, saw confusion and horror on the child's features. Yet Larson knew his responsibilities waited in tenth century Germany where his friends lay at the mercy of a Chaos-crazed sorcerer. *What's happened has happened. I can't change the past.* Realization struck. *Or can I?*

"You killed them." Silme lowered her foot. "And now I'm going to kill you."

"Kill me? Have you gone mad?" Ideas crawled through Larson's mind. He tried to stall, fighting a paralyzing wave of emotions. "Vidarr was right."

"Right about what?" Silme asked sullenly, despite herself. She had served the god faithfully for years, and, even now, paused long enough to hear him out.

Larson kept his gaze fixed on Silme, trying to read changes in her disposition. "He said you'd succumbed to Chaos. That Bolverkr had done something terrible to you."

Silme's expression became one of cruel amusement. "Bolverkr did nothing but open my eyes to the truth. He made me realize our marriage was based on desperation and convenience. And that you and Vidarr aren't worthy of my time."

Silme's words fell like a slap. *I can't believe I attributed her mood swings to the pregnancy. How stupid could I be?* Silme's loyalty to innocents and her religion had never fallen into question before. "Silme, what are you saying? Now you abuse children? You no longer believe in the god you've served for years. And you're going to kill your own husband and your baby? Can't you see how strange and ridiculous this is? Bolverkr's influenced you somehow. For God's sake, fight him! Remember who you were.''

The military men sorted themselves out from the cluster of relatives and friends. Larson envied their rifles, though surely they carried only blanks.

''I was a fool.'' Silme raised a hand in sudden threat. ''You're an anachronism and a menace to the Balance. And now, I destroy you.''

Larson shrank back against the stone, shielding Timmy. ''Wait, Silme! You can't cast spells. You'll kill the baby. It's your own flesh and blood.'' Larson groped around the boulder for a weapon, finding nothing. Once Silme called upon her life chaos, the baby would be killed; and, unless Larson moved quickly, he would die with it.

Timmy clutched at Larson.

Silme hesitated, but she did not lower her arm.

Larson measured the distance to her, saw the huge amount of ground he would need to cover faster than her spell, and knew despair. ''Silme, if you kill me, you have no way to get back to your own world.'' He mentally traced the route to the cemetery entrance, beyond the funeral party. *If I can get the bystanders between me and her, surely she won't cast.* He had to hope her long dedication to innocents would keep her from endangering them, even if her morality no longer did. *But how can I buy the time to run that far?* He continued, trying to distract her with speech until a coherent strategy formed. ''You're as much an anachronism here as I am there.'' Larson looped an arm around his brother, drawing the child closer. ''Will you have to destroy yourself?'' He lifted his pain-filled gaze to her eyes, seeing the perfect beauty that had stolen his love.

Again, Silme paused.

Behind her, three guns roared simultaneously, the first shot of the triple salute. Silme stiffened, spinning to face this new danger.

Now! Larson seized the opening. Shoving Timmy toward the procession, he sprang for Silme. He covered the distance between them in three running strides, raising his clasped hands to strike.

Silme whirled, back-stepping.

Larson tried to redirect his charge but momentum overbalanced him, and he sprawled to the ground at her feet. Scuttling backward, he tried to stand.

The toe of Silme's boot caught Larson square in the ribs, driving the breath from his lungs. She muttered the first harsh syllable of a spell word.

The second gunshot rang through the graveyard.

No! Ignoring his pain, Larson lunged, catching her foot as it retreated. He wrenched.

Silme's incantation broke to a gasp of enraged frustration. No light or sparks accompanied the change, no evidence that she had delved life energy for sorcery. She twisted, falling to her hands and knees. She fumbled for something in her cloak.

The third shot split the air. In its wake, Timmy called frantically, "Al! Al!"

Larson launched himself at Silme, wishing she had spent less time with his ronin swordmaster. "Run, Timmy. Get out of here. Go!"

Silme leapt for Larson at the same time. A glint of sunlight off metal in her fist warned him. Larson lurched sideways, grabbing for her wrist. His attack fell short, but the movement saved him. The knife sliced open a belt loop on his jeans, sparing his flesh. Her knee plunged into his thigh, missing his groin by inches.

Shit. Stunned by the ferocity of Silme's attack, Larson crouched. His fingers knotted, burrowing up handfuls of dirt. He could no longer doubt that she intended to kill him. Still, the idea of harming Silme seemed baser than the vilest evil. *But I don't need to hurt her. I only need time to run. And to think.*

Silme charged again, jabbing the knife expertly. Kensei Gaelinar had taught his lessons well.

Larson dodged, dropping his training for crude, street-fighting techniques. He ducked beneath Silme's guard, hurling both fistfuls of sand into her eyes.

Silme's aim went wild. She skittered backward, avoiding a blow that never came.

Larson did not press the attack, instead using the time gained to cover as much ground as possible. *She can't cast if she can't see.* He darted toward the funeral, and the exit, catching Timmy within four strides. He grabbed the child in mid-run.

Suddenly upended, Timmy yelped, then settled into Larson's arms like a giant rag doll.

Silme made a muffled noise of rage and pain.

Larson sprinted over tended grounds, skirting the funeral at the barest fringes of polite distance before using it as a shield. For now, all he could think about was rescuing Timmy and the baby, though other needs gnawed at the back of his mind.

Once Larson passed the funeral, the wrought iron fencing looked like black thread against the afternoon's silver; it funneled toward the central gate. Larson gained some solace from the realization that most of Silme's spells were defenses learned against Bramin's magic. Although Dragonrank mages could cast any spell, attempting one she had never tried before would cost vast quantities of life energy. And it would take longer and more acute concentration, not the sort of thing she would hurl in a wild situation or blindly. *I hope.* Larson repositioned Timmy over his shoulder, barely noticing the weight but needing to free his hands.

The gate loomed in Larson's vision. He charged for the opening and barreled through it. Setting Timmy down, he whirled, wasting time pulling the gates shut, hoping the technology of its latching would foil Silme, at least temporarily. As the gates creaked closed, too slowly, Larson slammed the bolt home.

"Who is she? What's going on? Why does she want to hurt us?" Timmy barraged his brother with questions.

"Later." Larson grabbed Timmy's hand, breaking back into a run that half-dragged his brother down the sidewalk. *If I stand still and look around, Silme can access my thoughts, locate us, and transport. We've got to keep moving.* Flipping Timmy back into his grip, Larson sprinted around smaller blocks toward the main highway and the hotel district. Cars whizzed along the roadways, seeming absurdly fast after more than a year spent among ox carts and horses.

Larson waited until a break appeared in the traffic, then darted into the street.

A canary yellow taxi careened around the corner, honking a continuous blast at Larson.

Larson came to an abrupt stop. Still in the car's path, he swung Timmy to safety.

The cab screeched to a halt inches away from Larson, horn blaring. The driver poked a darkly-bearded head through the window. "Are you deaf and blind or just stupid? I could have killed you!"

"I need a cab."

The driver glanced at the lit sign on the roof of his vehicle. "Well, surprise. You found one." He made a circular gesture, his smile softening his sarcasm. "Most of my fares come in by the door instead of the windshield."

A driver in a powder blue Dart behind the taxi leaned on his horn.

The cabby made an abrupt, obscene gesture through the window, and a line of vehicles squeezed around his taxi.

Seizing Timmy's hand, Larson sidled to the door, wrenched it open, and slid inside. Timmy took the seat beside him, then pulled the panel shut.

The cab threaded back into traffic.

Larson sank into a vinyl seat rank with cigarette smoke. He gasped for breath, only now realizing how much his lungs ached. His heart pained him, too. *I love Silme so much. How could I let this happen?* A worse thought filled his mind. *What if I have to hurt her?* Horror tightened its hold. *What if I have to kill her? Or she kills Timmy?*

Timmy touched his brother's hand in question.

The cabby cleared his throat. "You want to go any place in particular or just ride in circles?"

"Manhattan," Larson said at random. Shaken back

to reality, it occurred to him that he might have no money except rude gold and silver coins. He reached into his back pocket, reassured by the bulge of a wallet. Removing it, he flipped it open, discovering more than enough bills to afford the trip from the Bronx to anywhere in Manhattan. His driver's license met his gaze, and he thumbed it free. The smudged photo seemed familiar yet distantly alien, the man he used to be.

"You from I-o-way, kid?"

"What?" Drawn from his reverie, Larson looked up.

"Manhattan's a big town. You want to go any place in particular?"

Larson knew only that he had to keep moving, had to lead Silme away from his family's home in the Bronx village of Baychester. *She can read my thoughts. I can't even think about home or she'll find Mom and Pam. She might hurt them or use them to lure me into a trap.* "Broadway Theater." Feeling a strange need to explain his choice, he continued, "Every time one of my out of state relatives calls, they always tell me to give their regards to Broadway. This seems like as good a time as any." Hoping to confuse Silme, he filled his mind with images of Claremont Park, a broad square of Bronx greenery where he used to take Timmy when his brother was an infant while his mother and sister shopped at Sears.

"Yeah. Right." The cabby shrugged, and in the rearview mirror, Larson could see the man shaking his head.

Larson considered Claremont Park in rapt detail, purposefully diverting his thoughts from his family. Experience told him that sorcerers could only magically transport to places they had studied personally, but Astryd had once entered a prison she had seen only by accessing Larson's thoughts and looking through his eyes. Uncertain whether Silme could transport to a place Larson saw only in his memory, he repeatedly detailed the route from St. Raymond's Cemetery to Claremont Park. *Silme doesn't know about cars. She'll have to assume I walked. If I can get her to walk, too, it'll keep the baby alive a little longer.*

"Al, what's going on?" Timmy sounded frightened. "Why aren't we going home? How come I know you're going to die?" He huddled closer, his tears warm and wet on Larson's arm.

"Just a second, Timmy." Larson put his brother off a little longer, as a new idea disturbed him. *What if this is an alternate reality? The park I remember may not exist.* He addressed the cabby. "Driver, you familiar with Claremont Park?"

"Yeah, just took a couple of kids there this morning, in fact. Boy carrying this duct tape sword with a girl dressed like she come out of a fairy tale." The cabby shook his head at the memory. "There's some sort of group meeting there. Society for Creating Anarchy-ism or some such." He glanced back. "Why? You want to go there instead?"

"No," Larson said quickly, hoping he had not inflicted a Chaos-cursed sorceress on a crowd of college students. *I can't change focus now, or she'll know I'm diverting her. It's a big park. And I don't think she'll harm anyone if she doesn't find me there.* He turned his thoughts back to the route, keeping it always in a conscious pocket of memory.

"Al," Timmy whined.

Larson sighed heavily, aware his tale might better pass for an episode of Star Trek, yet knowing he had to tell the boy something. He wrapped his arm around the child. "Timmy, favorite brother of mine, you're not going to believe this . . . . ''

CHAPTER 9:

Chaos Transport

Nothing, I am sure, calls forth the
faculties so much as the being obliged
to struggle with the world.
—Mary Wallstonecraft
Thoughts on the Education of Daughters

Taziar Medakan jolted awake. He kept his eyes closed and, for a moment, he heard and felt nothing. Unable to remember where he was nor how he might have gotten there, he tried to orient in his mind. Instantly, agony hammered and squeezed him. His legs throbbed with bruises, his back stung from burns, and his wrists and ankles felt raw. A soft, unfamiliar cloak touched the damaged skin on his back through holes charred in the cloth of his climbing shirt. He discovered he was kneeling on stone, head sagged to his chest. It seemed an odd position for sleeping, but pain forestalled curiosity.

A voice tore open Taziar's dark void of pain. ''Answer me, bitch, or I'll tear open your throat and watch you bleed.''

A choked whimper followed, then Astryd replied, her tone weak and fearful but still vividly conveying frustration. ''I told you I don't know. I just don't know.''

Taziar's eyes snapped open. In the center of an unfamiliar room, Bolverkr supported Astryd with an arm wrapped across her abdomen. Her hands and feet were bound. The sorcerer's other arm looped around her neck, a dagger pressed tightly to her throat. Taziar knelt in a corner, opposite a heavy oak and brass door. Otherwise, the room stood empty.

Taziar lunged at Bolverkr, but his numbed legs did not obey him. The abrupt movement tore pain through his hands, and resistance jarred him backward. Only then did he realize ropes lashed his wrists so tightly that the hemp had abraded them raw. More rope encircled his ankles, tight enough to leave impressions in his boots, though the leather protected his skin. He howled. "Leave Astryd alone! Let her go!" He struggled madly. His efforts sprawled him to his side. He fought the ropes, pain flashing through him until it overcame vision and thought.

Bolverkr laughed. "So the little thief's awake. Things should get interesting now."

Taziar went still, curled against the pain. The ropes chewed into his flesh, and blood trickled across his palms. He rolled a sideways glance at Bolverkr. "Please. Let Astryd go. Free her, and I'll tell you anything you want to know." Briefly Taziar wondered why a sorcerer of such power chose to use brute force as a means of questioning. *And why doesn't Astryd leave magically?* Taziar knew most Dragonrank mages learned transport escapes early, and he had seen Astryd use spells to travel before.

Bolverkr's grip stiffened. The blade grazed Astryd's neck, but she did not seem to notice. Her expression combined desperation with defeat, and fatigue stole the sparkle from her eyes. Her usually feathered blonde locks now hung in limp, sweat-dampened bangs.

She's exhausted, her life energy wrung out. Taziar recalled hazy details of the battle, aware Astryd had spent her aura on a spell that his frantic dive to protect her had dispelled before she could finish its casting. *How ironic. I threw myself in front of her, ready to die to spare her. And she drained her life energy on a spell that was probably intended to protect me.* Answers wove through Taziar's anguish-fogged mind. He knew that, aside from Bolverkr, no Dragonrank mages held enough power to bring other people with them during transports. It would cost Astryd huge volumes of life energy to break Bolverkr's grip. Bolverkr would know that, too, and it explained why he had chosen a physical means of interrogation.

Bolverkr studied Taziar, a grim scowl tracing aged features. "Where did Silme and Allerum go?"

Taziar blinked, stunned by the question. A myriad of emotions swirled through his mind: relief that some of his companions had escaped safely, shock that Bolverkr could not locate the pair with his magic, and grinding terror that the sorcerer demanded information Taziar did not have. *When Bolverkr finds out I can't give him an answer, what will he do to Astryd?*

"Well?" Bolverkr said.

Stalling, Taziar licked his lips, glancing at Astryd's haggard face for some clue. Another thought dazed him deeper into silence. *Gods, what if she does have enough energy to transport but she doesn't want to leave me?* Astryd's obvious exhaustion precluded the possibility, but pain and concern stifled Taziar's ability to think clearly. He wanted to scream at her to save herself, to see to it that at least one of them survived the ordeal, but he needed to address Bolverkr's query first. He tried to sound matter-of-fact and unafraid. "When Astryd and I fell unconscious, Silme and Allerum were still fighting. Neither of us could know where they went."

Bolverkr tensed in rage. The blade bit into Astryd's flesh, and blood beaded down a line across her neck. "Where are they? Damn it, don't play games with me, or I'll hack your woman into pieces and feed them to you. You've got until I count to ten. One, two . . ."

"Wait!" Taziar screamed, needing time to think.

Bolverkr granted no quarter. ". . . three, four, five . . ."

"At least tell me enough to figure out what might have happened!" Taziar shouted over the next three numbers.

". . . nine. . . ." Apparently recognizing the merit of Taziar's question, Bolverkr dropped his count. "Fine. Silme disappeared without transporting. Allerum collapsed before my spell hit him, then disappeared before I could finish him. Now, *where did they go?"*

Taziar covered his joy at his companions' escape with a blank expression of confusion. As a child, he had won some of his food money by con man's tricks and feats of skill, including freeing himself from ropes. He plucked at Bolverkr's knots, drawing the sorcerer's attention away from the attempt by meeting his gaze. "Why don't you just use a locating spell?"

Bolverkr's blue eyes narrowed. "Of course, I tried a location triangle, you little bastard! It didn't work. I couldn't contact Allerum's mind either. It's as if they disappeared from the nine worlds. And *I want to know why!"*

Because they have *disappeared from our nine worlds.* The answer came easily to Taziar, based on his conversation with Larson after the attack on Bolverkr's keep, but he preferred to give the enemy as little information as possible. *Astryd was unconscious during that discussion. She probably really has no idea where they've gone.* "I can't tell you where Silme and Allerum went. I don't know."

"You don't?" Bolverkr's scowl disappeared, replaced by calculation. His grip on Astryd's abdomen loosened. "Strange coincidence. There are things I don't know either. Like mercy." He drove his fist into her gut.

Astryd stiffened, then sagged in Bolverkr's grip, fighting for breath. Panic scored her features.

Taziar cringed in sympathetic agony. The knots defied him. So far he had managed only to draw their opposite sides deeper into his flesh. "Stop! Bolverkr, please stop. Let her go, unharmed, and I'll tell you everything I know."

Sweat spangled Astryd's forehead. She gasped in several lungfuls of air.

"So you *do* know where they've gone?" A slight smile appeared on Bolverkr's face.

Taziar knew his own survival and Astryd's depended on Bolverkr's belief that the Climber had information. As his pain became more familiar, his mind was clearing, allowing logic to slip to the forefront. *If we convince him we know nothing, he'll kill us. If he thinks we've told all we know, he'll kill us. My life lasts only as long as my silence and only as long as my pleas of ignorance don't convince him.* Taziar had survived torture before, but this time Astryd's life and limbs hung in the balance as well. "Maybe I know where Allerum's gone. And Silme. Don't hurt Astryd. Free her, and I'll tell you what I know."

Bolverkr paused, apparently taking the deal under serious consideration. "That's fair. I have no feud with her. Fine, weasel. Talk." He stared at Taziar, aloofly menacing.

"Don't." Astryd wheezed, raising a glimmer of her usual emotional strength, now sapped by fatigue. "Don't tell him anything."

Taziar maneuvered back to a kneeling position, preferring to face Bolverkr as nearly upright as possible. "Let her go. Then I'll talk."

Bolverkr snorted. "First you say you know nothing. Then you say you know something. And I'm supposed to believe you when you say you'll talk? Without Astryd, what's to keep you from claiming you don't know anything after all?"

Taziar finally managed to work his smallest finger through one of the knots. "The same thing that will keep you from killing Astryd after I talk," Taziar admitted. "Nothing. But it's a lot more likely you can get me to talk than that I can get you to release Astryd. Let her go, and I promise to tell you where I believe Allerum and Silme have gone." Taziar did not bother to contemplate too long. He had no idea what he would tell Bolverkr, only that he needed to stall as long as possible in the hope that he could free himself or that Astryd would regain enough power to transport.

Bolverkr continued holding Astryd just as solidly. "But, you see, I'm not in a position where I have to bargain. I've agreed to let Astryd go when I could have simply promised to kill her quickly and without torture." No emotion radiated from Bolverkr. His expression went grave, matching the straightforward seriousness of his tone. "Here's the deal. There will be no other. I'm going to count to ten again. If you haven't told me everything about where Silme and Allerum are by that time, I'll cut off Astryd's head and throw it to you. Then I'll smash a gaping hole in your mind barriers and extract the information myself."

Taziar went rigid. Sweat trickled from every pore, and his mouth went so dry he doubted he could speak. His every instinct told him that Bolverkr would not threaten idly, and he knew the Dragonrank mage was capable of fulfilling his promise. The only being in history with enough power to rupture the natural mind barriers of any man, Bolverkr had gained his previous lackey, Harriman, by that method. Taziar picked more desperately at the knots. Their stiffness gave him almost no room to work, and his own blood slicked the coils, making a grip nearly impossible.

"One, two, three . . ."

Broken at last, Astryd began to cry.

". . . four, five . . ." The razor edge of knife blade turned the scrape at Astryd's throat into a welling line of blood. ". . . six . . ."

The ropes continued to defy Taziar. Hot tears of frustration blurred his vision. *Why does it matter whether I tell Bolverkr where I think they are? He can't get to them anyway.* A thought flitted past. *But if they went to Allerum's world, why did his elf body disappear?* Taziar discarded the latter question for more dire concerns.

". . . seven, eight. . . ."

Out of time. Fingers still entangled in the biting ropes, Taziar blurted, "They went to Allerum's world. Now let Astryd go."

"Allerum's world? What do you mean?" Bolverkr interrupted his count to ask.

Astryd shivered in his grip, her eyes clenched shut.

Taziar cleared his throat, speaking slowly, trying to use the opportunity to gain more time. "Well . . . um . . . you see. The truth is that I know that Allerum isn't really an elf. He—"

Bolverkr cut Taziar off. "I know all that! But he's

displaced in time. No one can transcend time. How could they get to Allerum's world?''

''Well,'' Taziar started again. He feigned a coughing fit.

Bolverkr shifted from foot to foot. His glare warned Taziar he would take little more of this stalling.

''Well, I don't really know. I mean, I'm no sorcerer. . . .'' Taziar trailed off, but Bolverkr was no longer listening.

The old sorcerer's eyes rolled back. His grip on Astryd's abdomen cinched, though the knife retreated slightly. His face lapsed into wrinkles.

''What's he doing?'' Taziar redoubled his efforts at the ropes with little more success.

''I don't know,'' Astryd whispered, her voice a pale ghost of its usual resonance.

Bolverkr appeared to pay no attention to the exchange, so Taziar took a chance. ''Listen, Astryd. Get yourself out of here. There's nothing you can do for me, except maybe to get some help.''

Astryd swallowed hard. ''I know. But I only have a shred of life energy left. It's all I can do to stay awake. Casting anything would be sure death.'' Her voice went tremulous. Just the effort of speaking drained her.

''Don't waste your power talking,'' Taziar said.

Astryd widened her eyes to indicate need. ''It'll be half a day or longer before I gain enough energy to do anything else, and you have to know this now. To take control of my dragon, Bolverkr broke into my mind barriers. . . .''

''Gods, no.''

Astryd continued, ''I don't believe he's manipulated anything yet, but he's got access. Don't trust me. If I start acting strangely, it means he's rearranged my thought processes. Whatever I might do, remember it's not really me. I love you so much.''

Taziar caught and held Astryd's urgent gaze. ''I love you, too.'' Still wrestling with his first knot, he turned his attention to Bolverkr. ''I'll get you out of this. You know I will.''

''I know,'' Astryd said, without a trace of doubt.

"Listen, though. The spell Bolverkr used against my barriers. It drained more life force than I would have believed anyone had. I'm not sure he's got enough left to do it again soon. Even if he does, I doubt he'd take a chance on letting his aura drop that low, especially when he doesn't know where his enemies are. I don't think he'll carry through on his threat to use the same spell on you."

Now you tell me. Taziar tried to think of soothing words, but, before he could speak them, he found Bolverkr returning his stare.

The Dragonrank mage's lips twitched into a frown of consideration.

"You promised to free Astryd," Taziar reminded.

"Yes, I did." Bolverkr spoke in a thoughtful monotone. "I lied. Are you surprised?" He did not give Taziar a chance to respond before addressing Astryd. "Silme once opened her mind barriers to me. I checked that link. It's not quite strong enough to let me transport to her. But she opened herself to you once, too. Didn't she?"

"No!" Astryd's denial came too quickly, and she huddled, looking even smaller.

"Let her go!" Taziar hurled himself at Bolverkr, no longer caring about his bonds. The ropes burned across flesh, and Taziar tumbled to the floor at Astryd's feet. Rolling, he rose to the most graceful crouch his tied ankles allowed. "Let her go! You promised to *let her go!*" Though Taziar knew appealing to Bolverkr's conscience would prove hopeless, desperation pressed him to try. "You said you had nothing against her."

"But I do have something against her." Bolverkr's voice went soft, his expression pensive yet amused. "It seems she has very poor taste in friends." Still clutching Astryd by the waist, he sheathed the dagger. Curving and opening the index finger of his now free hand, he gestured Taziar toward him.

Taziar hesitated. "What do you want from me?"

"Come here, and I'll bring you with us."

Taziar frowned, seeing no reason to trust Bolverkr's explanation. It seemed more likely that, once Taziar came within Bolverkr's reach, the sorcerer would kill him. *What possible reason would he have for bringing me along?*

"Come, now." This time, Bolverkr gestured with his entire hand, easily judging Taziar's reluctance. "If I wanted to kill you, I could do it from here. Bound, I doubt you could dodge my lightning."

Astryd remained still. Her eyes flickered from Bolverkr to Taziar.

Guessing Astryd was about to attempt escape, Taziar tried to seize Bolverkr's attention. "Why would you take me along? That doesn't make any sense." Taziar caught and held Bolverkr's gaze, not liking the idea of talking an enemy out of an action that would prolong his life, yet seeing the need to keep Bolverkr occupied.

Keen, blue eyes studied Taziar from features as craggy and timeless as stone. "I'm hardly obligated to reveal my motives to you." He sneered contemptuously. "But it's worth it if it'll make you cooperate. I don't like fighting on someone else's territory. Allerum may have the advantage of familiarity with place and time, but let's see him throw fire bones at me when I've got his closest friend tied at my side. We'll just call you indemnity against. . . ."

Astryd made a sudden, wild twist that broke Bolverkr's hold on her waist. She thrust a knee into his groin.

Bolverkr's expression flashed from derisive to pained. He swore, hunching and staggering backward.

Astryd lurched toward the door. The ropes around her ankles tripped her, and she sprawled on her face.

Equally crippled by his bonds, Taziar rolled toward her.

Bolverkr spoke a harsh, magical syllable, then broke into ugly laughter. Straightening, he trotted toward Taziar. "Astryd, you stupid bitch, don't you see? Run as far as you want, but you can't escape me. I can enter your mind from *anywhere*." His fingers closed on Taziar's arm.

Taziar stiffened, whirling toward Bolverkr, prepared to battle to the death to gain Astryd a few steps.

Long, slender fingers gouged through Taziar's sleeve. As the Climber launched himself at Bolverkr, the sorcerer shouted a stream of spell words as sharp as Larson's American curses. Something unseen slammed Taziar, and he spun into a dark, whirling vortex of magic. Dazed and dizzied, he clawed for focus. The ropes chafed, and Bolverkr's nails dug deeper into his flesh. Cut off from his other senses, Taziar focused on the pain. His being upended, suspended from any orientation to up or down, time or place. Only the pain remained constant.

Astryd's scream shattered the silent, lightless void, sounding muffled and far too close. Taziar's world flared open. He found himself amid neatly ordered stripes of harpstringlike thought pathways. Light flashed and sputtered across them. Bolverkr stood beside him, eyes darting as he searched for something.

"Astryd!" Taziar shouted in agony. "Where are you? Astryd!"

Ow! Stop shouting. It hurts. Astryd's words came at him from all directions with the deep, enthralling delivery of a god. Her fear was tangible.

Shocked silent, Taziar listened to the echoes of his own voice.

You're in my mind, Astryd explained. *Careful.*

Taziar had heard Astryd and Silme's descriptions of Larson's mind as a snarled tangle of thought and memory full of blind loops and frayed pathways. Astryd's mind seemed militarily well organized in comparison.

"This way." With magically enhanced strength, Bolverkr dragged Taziar around a woven tapestry of thought, toward a corner of Astryd's mind.

Taziar followed docilely, his bound ankles turning his gait into a shuffle. His thoughts raced in a wheel of futile plotting. Usually, delicate situations enhanced his clarity of mind. Now, ignorance left too many gaps for coherent, logical strategy. *How do I get out? How can I resist? If I fight, will I injure Astryd?*

Anchored on his dilemma and concerned for Astryd, Taziar never saw Bolverkr's foot lash toward him. The sorcerer's boot crashed against the side of Taziar's knee. Pain radiated through his leg. He toppled, his tied arms flailing uselessly for balance; he managed only to guide his fall so he landed on his shoulder rather than his head. The impact shuddered through Astryd's mind.

Astryd groaned.

Oblivious, Bolverkr planted his boot in the small of Taziar's back, pinning him to the floor. He raised a hand, chanting magical syllables.

A faint glow rose in the darkened corner of Astryd's mind. Gradually, it intensified, revealing a seemingly endless, thready corridor trailing off into black obscurity. "There," Bolverkr said in soft triumph.

Taziar wriggled, fighting the pressure of Bolverkr's foot.

Astryd's discomfort and uncertainty filled her mind in waves.

Again, Taziar entwined his fingers in the stiff tangle of ropes at his wrist, loosening a knot. *Got to get free. Got to do something. Anything. And fast.*

Bolverkr ground his heel into Taziar's spine to discourage struggling as well as to indicate his words were intended for the Climber. "I'm going to try to keep a solid grip on you. Understand this. If you fight your way free, you'll be lost outside the fabric of time. Dead. And no one, not the entire pantheon of gods, not every Dragonrank sorcerer who ever lived, could rescue you from oblivion."

Astryd added tremulously. *Shadow, nothing like this has ever been attempted before. I don't know for sure, but my training leads me to guess he's telling the truth. Be careful. I love you.* Sorrow permeated her words, pure and unfiltered by distance, facial expression or consideration. Her emotions came to Taziar directly from their source.

"I love you," he whispered, afraid to cause her anguish by talking too loudly. "I—"

Bolverkr seized Taziar's wrists and wrenched the little Climber to his feet. Pain cut the discussion short. Bolverkr raised his free hand.

A sensation of pins and needles tingled through Taziar, then exploded to a savage rush of magic. His being seemed to swell, pulsing until he thought his skin would tear open, spilling his insides through Astryd's mind. Then, suddenly, the force became external. He surged forward, whipping through a dark tunnel a thousand times faster than a hunter's arrow. Wind rushed past, icy and painful to his ears. He screamed. But he never heard the noise, as if it remained in place while he charged ever onward at a speed sound could never match.

As unnatural as the motion seemed, time accustomed Taziar to it enough to concentrate on other details. Bolverkr's grip remained tight enough to numb Taziar's forearm to the fingers. The sorcerer's closeness became a reassuring constant, despite its potential for evil. Glitters of magic popped and sputtered through the otherwise unbroken darkness, carrying an aura of Chaos-power Taziar knew originated from Bolverkr with a certainty far beyond common sense. Yet, soon, Taziar detected another presence amid the sorceries, an almost inaudible whisper entwined with the raging, near-omnipotent bellows of power issuing from Bolverkr. *Astryd.* Taziar twisted, seeking some tangible evidence of Astryd's presence.

Bolverkr's hold tightened convulsively.

Suddenly, Astryd's power guttered like a windswept candle flame. Panic spiked through Taziar, from an outside source that could only be Astryd, a terror so powerful and wholesome it scattered his wits. Taziar screamed, clawing blindly at Bolverkr.

The Dragonrank sorcerer swore, the sound piercing in Taziar's ear until the wind swirled it away. Bolverkr's other arm whipped around Taziar's waist, crushing the Climber against him.

The mind-shattering aura of terror snapped out, leaving no trace of Astryd's presence.

Astryd! Before Taziar could gather breath to scream again, he jolted to a sudden stop. Stunned by the impact, he scarcely noticed as his momentum resumed, this time, straight downward. Unconsciousness pressed at him. He tore at the rope, needing pain to revive himself. The knots gave, shearing skin from his hands with an agony that awakened but also incapacitated him.

Bolverkr shouted something incomprehensible, his rage, horror and desperation filling the darkness with the gripping, monster-sated reality of a child's nightmare. The certainty of death touched Taziar.

"No!" Bolverkr shouted, adding reckless courage to the boil of his projected emotion. Black nothingness snapped open, splintered to sudden light. Taziar landed on his feet with enough force to jar pain from soles to hips. He fell, rolling from habit, his hands free but smeared with blood, his lungs empty.

"Astryd?" Taziar said, his voice a choked hiss. Legs still tied, he slithered to a sitting position, gaze skimming wildly over his surroundings.

Taziar lay on a thick patch of grass behind a pair of tawny tents. Bolverkr crouched beside him, hands balled, tensed for action. In front of him, Silme stared, wide-eyed. The thud of steel on padding echoed from beyond the tents.

For several tense moments, nothing happened. Taziar gasped for breath, trying to assuage his throat and lungs before moving. His fingers edged toward the bindings on his ankles.

"Silme," Bolverkr said. A grin quivered across otherwise shaken features.

Silme glided toward Bolverkr tentatively. "How. . . ?" she started. "Why. . . ?" Then she hurled herself into his arms.

Shocked, Taziar watched the two embrace, certain Silme must be distracting Bolverkr to give her friend time to work his way free. He struggled with the ropes.

Distantly, steel chimed against steel. A crowd's roar followed.

Head cradled against Bolverkr's shoulder, Silme fixed her gaze directly on Taziar. "Taz! Put your hands on your head and leave them there, or I'll crush you like a gourd.''

Startled by Silme's unbridled hostility, Taziar obeyed.

Bolverkr released Silme, catching her hands. Though he addressed her, he watched Taziar. "Why did you come here?''

Silme shook back waves of golden hair. "When I saw Allerum using his technology against the dragon, I knew you'd been right about him all along. He didn't even care if he killed his own friends.'' She gestured at Taziar vaguely. "You got me thinking about how Allerum never belonged in our world. How he needed not just to die, since his soul might remain on one of our nine worlds. He needed to die in his own time.''

Taziar let one hand slide toward his neck. *This can't be real. Silme would never turn against us. Never. No body chemical in the world could make her do that.*

Silme glared in warning.

Taziar returned his hand.

Apparently satisfied, Silme continued. "Then I saw Allerum about to throw one of those . . .'' She crinkled her nose in disgust. ". . . things at you. I saw a way to stop him. Fast. I took it.''

Bolverkr smiled in hopeful triumph. "Allerum's dead, then, too?''

The same question plagued Taziar, but it was Bolverkr's use of the word "too'' that speared dread through him. He dared not make much of it yet, aware Silme would also want clarification. His chest squeezed closed, and breathing became a fully conscious process.

"No,'' Silme admitted calmly. "I acted on impulse. Allerum caught me unprepared. It's been a long time since I've used any spell, and I've never used many for attack.'' She paused thoughtfully, rubbing at her eyes, and Taziar saw her other hand flex around Bolverkr's fingers then loosen again. "From today, that's going to change.''

Beyond the tents, something thunked against hollow

metal, followed by smatterings of laughter and applause.

Finally, Silme anchored on the final word in Bolverkr's question. "Too? Where's Astryd?"

"Dead," Bolverkr confirmed matter-of-factly. "Drained out her life energy getting us here. Almost got us all trapped outside reality and time. . . ."

Taziar caught nothing more of Bolverkr's explanation. Grief snuffed his hearing to high-pitched ringing, and he saw Silme through a curtain of spots. Years of living on the streets had taught him to read motivations through expressions. He thought he saw a fleeting glimmer of horror on Silme's face, but it disappeared so quickly he could not tell whether her emotion or his imagination had conjured the image.

Astryd's dead. Astryd is dead! Without her corpse to confirm it, the certainty could not register. Taziar had suspected Astryd's death from the instant panic had overtaken her and her presence had disappeared from her own mind. So far, he had concentrated on his own peril, shoving the realization of Astryd's death from his mind, dismissing it as a misinterpretation of magical events he had no way of truly understanding. Now he could no longer deny it. *Astryd is dead. Her body is lost in the fabric of time. Bolverkr killed her, and I sat back and watched it happen.* His promise reverberated through his ears, a vow so easily shattered by circumstance. Repeatedly, he heard himself say, "I'll get you out of this. You know I will," followed by Astryd's confident "I know" in a voice he would never hear again. *Astryd.* He sank to the ground in a hopeless fit of apathy, not caring if Silme killed him for the transgression.

Gradually, Taziar's iron will kicked in, reminding him of responsibilities he needed to attend to before he could allow sorrow to paralyze him completely. *I can't surrender. There's too much at stake.* He listened to the indecipherable hubbub of voices beyond the tents, interspersed with the thump and chime of swords against padding or metal. *There's another world here, hordes of people helpless against Bol-*

verkr's magic and mental manipulations. If what Allerum has said is true, there're more innocents in New York City than in my entire world, and every one of them lacks the mind barriers to protect themselves from Bolverkr. Taziar shoved aside his own sense of loss for concern over the millions of people occupying Larson's era. *I can grieve later, but I'll dishonor Astryd's memory if I let sadness conquer me. For her and her causes, I have to fight.*

Despite his bold attempt to wad the realization of Astryd's death into the depths of remembrance, Taziar's will felt raw, his heart like a granite boulder in his chest. But the deafening ringing became familiar enough for him to listen through it, and Silme's muffled voice wafted to him.

". . . strangest thing. It seems to be some sort of fighting tournament. But their weapons are crude and unedged. Their style is ponderous. And I've never seen two soldiers battle so fairly. Not a single kick, no strikes to the head. It's weird.'' Silme shrugged, rolling her eyes at the oddity of it all. ''Their dress looks a lot like our own, though I've never seen such clean, tiny weave and straight stitching. I guess this is the rich side of the world.''

"Their army?'' Bolverkr guessed.

Silme frowned, shaking her head. ''No. I've seen war in Allerum's world. This just doesn't fit. From probing minds, I've gathered this is some sort of recreational group. Their language seems to be an unpolished derivative of several tongues, mixed with bizarre idioms and slang. I've been ignoring words and gathering meaning through light mind probes.''

Taziar curled like a fetus, pretending to be fully unmanned by grief, quietly inching his hands almost imperceptibly toward the ropes around his ankles.

This time, Silme did not seem to notice. ''This particular group calls themselves 'Sca' which seems to translate nearly into 'play group with imagination that supports anachronisms.' Something like that.''

Bolverkr's jaw fell, revealing a straight row of teeth.

"They have entire organizations to stand behind time traveling world wreckers?"

"I don't think so." Silme's gaze went solidly to Taziar, and she examined him with suspicion. "As far as I can tell, their mission isn't to protect anything. It seems to have more to do with recreating and romanticizing the past." Silme added pensively, "Our time. And later." Her tone softened, and uncertainty tainted her usual strident confidence. "We don't belong here."

Taziar froze.

"Yes." Bolverkr released Silme's hands. His arms dropped to his sides, fingers twitching with anticipation. "That's why we need to take care of our business and get out of here." He clasped his hands, as if to still them.

Silme turned her attention back to Bolverkr. "So you know a way to get us back?"

Bolverkr hesitated, apparently caught off guard by the question. His brow crinkled.

Taziar seized the moment to pull his hands to his lower legs.

"I came through Allerum's mind. That route won't exist any longer. You say you used a double link from our world to me. Now that we're both in the same place, we can't use that either, especially now that Astryd's dead."

"We'll find a way," Bolverkr said with the same vague assurance Taziar had used to comfort Astryd. "And even if we don't, why would it matter? There's no Balance to worry about, no other sorcerers or gods to stop us. Think of the possibilities, Silme. Two Dragonrank mages sharing ultimate authority in a world without mind barriers. I promised you power. I can deliver the world!"

The enormity of Bolverkr's suggestion struck Taziar. Horror filled him, quickly replaced by relief. *I know Silme too well. She'll never go along with such a thing. Whatever hold Bolverkr has over her, he'll lose from greed and arrogance.*

But Silme's smile revealed genuine pleasure. She

stood in rapt attention as Bolverkr rattled vivid descriptions of buildings crumbling to rubble, people fleeing in blind, bloody panic, and forests shattered to splintered, charred ruin.

And Taziar plucked at knots drawn to unbearable tightness by his struggles in Astryd's mind. Dried blood chipped from his fingers as he worked, trying not to draw attention.

Bolverkr finished with charged promises of a rulership too strong to challenge. "All I need, Silme, is a simple indication that you're truly on my side now. I need you to show that you've overcome this irrational love for a group of insignificant and ignorant strangers, something to seal the alliance."

Abruptly aware all eyes would fall on him, Taziar quit his attempts to free the ropes. He rolled his gaze to Bolverkr and Silme.

Silme's merciless, gray eyes met Taziar's stare without flinching. "If I killed Shadow. Would that be enough?"

Taziar's blood seemed to frost over in his veins. *Too slow again, Medakan. And now it's over.* His heart quickened to a flutter. Still, he could not quite comprehend the changes in Silme. *She wouldn't really kill me? Would she?*

The cold conviction of her expression told Taziar she would.

"Yes." Bolverkr grinned like a child with a rare but favorite treat. "Killing Taz Medakan would be enough. That was my reason for bringing him." He let the statement linger, giving Taziar plenty of time to understand the significance before letting him off the hook. "But with Astryd dead, I need the little weasel for barter against Allerum."

Taziar's heart rate slowed, though the knowledge that Bolverkr was about to suggest some equally evil course of action kept him from relaxing even slightly.

Silme, too, said nothing, apparently waiting for the other shoe to fall.

"Destroy Allerum's baby." Bolverkr said.

Silme hesitated, still unspeaking.

"It has no purpose anymore," the sorcerer continued, the words meaning more than Taziar could guess. "Evil spawns evil. Allerum's child has as much potential for evil as its father. Kill the baby, and it'll free you to use your magic the way nature intended. Later, we can make another."

A smile twitched across Silme's lips, looking foreign and cruel on beautiful features that had once represented beautiful morals as well. She glanced into the heavens, as if seeking divine guidance. Then her head sank to her chest. Her hands rose.

Spellbound, Taziar watched, fumbling blindly with his bonds at the same time. Finding the knot, he gouged at it with his nails.

A curtain of sparkling buttons wove into the air before Silme, interwoven with multicolored threads of enchantment. Each spot caught and reflected the evening light like a perfect diamond from the setting of a ring, a glittering funeral shroud for an infant who would never be born.

Bolverkr laughed, his joy triumphant, evil, and nearly tangible.

Sorrow tightened over Taziar. The death of the fetus saddened him, but the loss paled before the knowledge of Astryd's demise and Silme's betrayal. He plucked at the knot, not daring to contemplate too hard.

Suddenly, Silme's expression became pained. Her arms collapsed limply to her sides. The elegant curtain of magics dissolved to a gray net of outline, tarry smoke streaming from its remains. She gazed directly at Taziar, her eyes as wide as a frightened child's awakening from nightmare. Her lower lip uncurled, as if she wanted to speak but could not find the words. Her hands clenched at her lower abdomen. All color drained from her features, and she slumped to the ground.

Bolverkr's grin disappeared. He whirled to face Silme directly, his hands clamped to her arms. "Silme? What's happening?"

"Pain," she gasped, "The baby. Gods, it hurts." Her words garbled into a high-pitched whine of agony.

Taziar continued his struggle with the ropes. The knot inched open. He knew Bolverkr could see him; at any moment, his magics could tear through Taziar with the same quiet apathy as Silme had used to kill her own child.

But, fully absorbed in Silme, Bolverkr paid Taziar no heed. "Silme?" he said with alarm. He caught her close, harsh, magical syllables of healing rushing from his throat. As with Silme's spell, black chaos-smoke billowed from his sorceries, unlike anything Taziar had seen in his own world.

The knot fell free. Taziar's heart quickened.

Silme's breathing grew more comfortable. She kept her eyes closed against dispersing pain.

Swiftly, Taziar untangled the ropes from his ankles. He measured the distance to the tents, starting a cautious crawl. The dispersing smoke settled over him, bringing an alien sensation of hatred and cruelty, goading him to an evil so far beyond his nature it frightened him.

Bolverkr cried out, jerking away suddenly. "The Chaos I used for the spell. It's gone."

Silme's hands fell away from her abdomen. Still, she made no move to rise, and her voice retained the hesitant, breathy quality that comes with tears. "What do you mean, it's gone? Of course, it's gone. You used it."

"You don't understand." Bolverkr drew Silme closer.

Taziar ignored the corrupt stirrings within him, recognizing them as foreign rather than self, certain they came from the sorcerers. He felt the fog roll over him, heading toward the crowd beyond the tents.

Bolverkr continued, his voice growing more distant. "The Chaos I used is gone. Forever. I can tell I can't get it back."

From beyond the tents, steel crashed against steel. Someone screamed, followed by a collective gasp from the audience.

Realizing the noise would draw Bolverkr's attention, Taziar rose and ran.

From the unseen gathering, a strong male voice cried out a command. Then a string of familiar English swear words erupted from the ranks, followed by a heated argument Taziar could not decipher.

The Shadow Climber dodged between the tents. *The Chaos has touched them, too. Bolverkr's right. It's diffusing, fouling the air like a poison.*

Bolverkr howled a spell word. The snap of wood and the flutter of canvas filled Taziar's ears. The tent to his left collapsed, flames licking across the fabric. Taziar saw an open, grassy lot spotted with tents, pole shelters, and occasional young, spindly trees. A crowd of people surrounded a rectangle staked out with ropes and poles. The spectators wore an odd array of colors and clothing, some in belted silk dresses and tunics, others in crude sacks, and still more in strangely sewn fabrics Taziar did not recognize. Inside the rectangle, one man towered over another who knelt on one knee, looking dazed. Both wore thickly padded cloth, wound and tied around waist, chest, arms, and legs, partially hidden beneath hauberks of chain mail constructed of the most perfect rings Taziar had ever seen. The grounded man wore a hopelessly thin, steel helmet with a huge dent hammered into one side. Both held hilted sticks encased in a shiny, fabric-like substance.

Taziar took in the scene at a glance, more concerned with the wide open lot than with the crowd of screeching spectators. As every gaze whirled toward the mangled tent, Taziar plunged into the masses, at first hoping the sorcerers would hold their deadly spells around innocents, then cursing himself for the danger he placed these strangers in by making a ridiculous assumption not supported by facts. *Bolverkr's destroyed entire villages. Why would I think he would hesitate to murder a few bystanders?* More accustomed to guardsmen's tactics, Taziar had reacted from habit. *I have to get away from this crowd.*

Taziar floundered into a young blonde, her hair bunched into a long braid. She gave him a shove that sent him staggering into a hefty man. The collision jarred Taziar to his knees. Fleeing the ruined tent, a woman tripped over him, accidentally ramming a slippered foot into his ribs. Her consort's boot ground Taziar's hand into the dirt as he passed.

The pain scarcely registered beneath the throb of Taziar's bruises and the constant agony of his mangled wrists. Desperation and cordoned grief robbed all meaning from physical pain. As the throng parted, Taziar scrambled to his feet, racing toward the farther edge of the grassy lot, wishing for cover. He listened for Bolverkr's or Silme's voice beneath the mingled and unfamiliar language and accents of the crowd. No magical syllables touched his ears. No brilliant splashes of sorcery split the afternoon. A strange smell filled the air, the mingled reek of smoke, chemicals, and garbage, but Taziar did not find the ozone odor of killing spells.

Still, Taziar ran. Soon the cushion of grass was replaced by a tan walkway composed of perfect, giant squares of flat stone. A black ribbon of pathway stretched as far as Taziar could see, hedged by buildings taller than any mountain. People swarmed the lighter-colored walkways bordering the black surface, dressed in a wider variety of colors, patterns, and fabrics than Taziar had ever imagined.

But as varied as the clothing seemed, the spectrum of the human beings who wore them shocked Taziar far more. The split second glimpses he caught winding through the crowds were enough to reveal dark-skinned men and women with hair in tight curls or wild, bushlike arrangements. Some people waddled on legs thick as tree trunks, their bodies more bulbous than the richest royalty. These intermingled freely with others as skeletal as starving beggars. Most fell between the extremes. A curvaceous woman swayed her hips, each step flipping an indecently short skirt farther up her thigh. A willowy man in a loose-fitting shirt and sandals walked beside her, his honey-colored hair and beard dangling nearly to his navel.

Despite the teeming mass of people, Taziar never slowed. He wove and darted, ignoring the shouted warnings he did not understand and the muttered obscenities that he did. Most of the people parted around him. Those who stood firm or did not see him coming, he dodged. The buildings confused him. Lean, endless towers sandwiched squat hovels with grimy signs he could not read. To Taziar's left, a red light flashed. He skittered sideways, crashing into a stout woman so suddenly that she dropped an armload of packages. A bag tore, strewing gauzy fabric across the sidewalk.

"You clumsy idiot!" she shrieked, followed by an accusatory sentence Taziar did not understand.

Ignoring her, Taziar crouched, fixated on the light, expecting Bolverkr's attack. But the scarlet flashes simply outlined a series of runes on a building sign. Shortly, they disappeared and flashed on again.

The crowd parted around the heavy woman as she stuffed her purchases back into the ruined bag. Tossing a parting glare at Taziar, she huffed back down the street.

The pattern of the masses shifted slightly as it milled around Taziar where he stood, frozen in awed stillness. Now that the people had become more familiar, other sights and sounds broke through the hovering fog of grief and fear. Lights in red, green, yellow, and white flared and died throughout the city, some curled into letters, others in hovering dots suspended from wires or poles. An ear-splitting wail cut over the ceaseless hubbub of a thousand conversations. Slammed by a noise louder than anything he had ever heard, Taziar bolted in terror. Tearing through the crowd, he slid onto the darker roadway. Brakes squealed. A horn blasted. Something huge whipped by Taziar three times faster than the fleetest horse cart. Then a red metal vehicle fishtailed to an abrupt halt before him. The bumper smashed into Taziar's hip, hurling him to the roadway.

Dazed, Taziar skidded across macadam, the roadway chafing skin from his leg and side. His mind fogged. Agony and darkness closed in on him, and his thoughts churned madly.

"Oh, my God!" the driver shouted. His car door sprang open. The crowd converged on Taziar.

As the masses drew closer, panic assailed Taziar. Lurching to his feet, he sprinted the rest of the way across the street and darted across the walkway. Another high-pitched blare of noise slammed his hearing. Brakes screamed again, but this time, Taziar gained the sidewalk. Voices chased him.

Taziar fled in blind hysteria, unable to make sense of the sounds and sights around him, uncertain how to avoid the impossibly gigantic, metal objects that swooped down on him faster than he could see them coming. His world narrowed to a strip of vision surrounded by fabricated darkness. He flailed through the press of people, whipping across roads, between buildings and along alleyways with no knowledge of location or direction.

Finally, pain crushed in on Taziar. His legs ached. His lungs labored for every breath, lancing anguish through his ribs. His hip throbbed worse than any bruise he had gained in the battle. Deep in an alley, he pressed his back to a brick wall and slid slowly to the walkway. His vision returned, revealing darkness to his left and a sea of passing legs on the sidewalk to his right. Tears sprang to his eyes, and he did not bother to wipe them away. Gradually, grief stole all meaning from time, place, and pain, and Taziar surrendered to oblivion.

CHAPTER 10:

Chaos Coupled

He that wrestles with us strengthens our nerves
and sharpens our skill.
Our antagonist is our helper.
      —Edmund Burke
        Reflections on the Revolution in France

The yellow taxi threaded through afternoon traffic on
the Major Deegan Expressway. Jouncing with his
brother in the back seat, Al Larson studied the patterns
of cars, trucks, and buses, cringing each time the
cabby whipped into an opening scarcely large enough
for a pedestrian. The ceaseless rattle and bump of the
cab emphasized its speed until Larson felt like a hill-
billy locked in a phantom jet. He wished he had chosen a vehicle with working shocks as his reinitiation
to twentieth-century American technology.

''So.'' Timmy stared at Larson with a wide-eyed
innocence bordering on hero worship. ''That lady's a
witch who can read minds and make you think stuff
and use magic and junk like that?''

Phrased by a child, the explanation sounded like a
rambling rehash of a Disney animated feature. Larson
sighed. ''Sort of like that.'' Defining the present danger seemed enough for now. He had not attempted to
explain that he had died, then wound up in a warped,
mythological version of ancient Europe in the guise of
an elf. So far, Timmy seemed to have accepted his brother's story with guileless simplicity, and Larson did not
want to press the limits of even a child's credibility.

''Cool.'' Timmy bounced against the backrest, twisting to get a better view out the side window.

Still rattled by his run-in with Silme, Larson smiled at his brother's resilience. *One moment in a panicked frenzy, the next cool as a cucumber and ready to play cowboys and Indians with a Dragonrank mage.* His grin wilted. *Of course, it's all a game to Timmy. He trusts his big brother to keep him safe. And he has no way of knowing how dangerous Silme really is.*

Larson looped his arm protectively about Timmy. No longer directly threatened, he gathered enough composure to realize that the stakes had grown critical. *There's nothing I can do for Shadow and Astryd. If my bomb and the dragon didn't kill them, Bolverkr has had more than enough time to finish the deed.* Fighting down a wave of grief and guilt, he forced his thoughts to his present situation. *I love Silme. But I won't let her torture my family and friends or seven and a half million innocent people.* As readily as his morality rose to the challenge, doubt accompanied it. *I can't hurt Silme. Can I?* Larson wrestled with the dilemma, wishing he had paid more attention to Silme's descriptions of magic and Chaos as renegade or bonded to life energy. For now, it all seemed a blur.

Timmy's questions scarcely penetrated Al Larson's fog of emotion and speculation. ''How're you gonna get this witch? Does she make things disappear? Can she throw fire and make stuff dance and ride a broom?'' Timmy plunked back down onto the seat, studying Larson with sparkling brown eyes. ''When are we going home? I wish Dad was here. Dad would know what to do. . . .''

The word ''home'' triggered a new direction of thought. Larson waved his brother silent. ''Hush up, Timmy. I'm trying to think.'' *I have to keep Timmy and myself from concentrating on home and family. Otherwise, Silme can get that information from his mind.* Realization came with frightening intensity. *Shit. She might get it anyway. She can't delve too deeply into my thoughts because I know how to tell she's there and build defenses. But she could search*

Timmy's mind to its core. Larson went rigid. "Turn around!" he instructed the driver.

The cabby glanced at Larson over his shoulder. "You talking to me?"

Larson simulated a U-turn with his hand. "Turn around. Take us to Freedom Land."

The cabby blinked. "You want to go back to the Bronx?"

Through the windshield, Larson watched the taxi roar dangerously close to a silver sedan. He sucked in a sharp breath, slamming down his foot on an imaginary brake.

Calmly turning his gaze back to the road, the cabby slowed. "Hey, man. I'll take you wherever you want to go. But you probably ought to know Freedom Land closed down five-six years ago. They're building these new rent-controlled apartments. . . ."

". . . Co-op City," Larson finished. "Yes, I know. Take us there."

Timmy stared, silenced by the urgency in Larson's voice.

The cabby shrugged, tossing his blond head. "You're the boss. But, you know, you were only a few blocks from there when I picked you up." He flicked on the blinker, zipping across two lanes of traffic to an exit.

Someone leaned on a car horn.

Larson stiffened, watching the traffic miraculously part before them. "I changed my mind, all right?" he said between gritted teeth.

"Hey, no problem." The cabby sped down the ramp. "It's your bread, man." He met Larson's eyes in the rearview mirror. Then his gaze played over the reflection of honey-blond hair just long enough to annoy Larson's father, the sweat-dampened T-shirt, and patched blue jeans. The cabby's features squinted suspiciously. "Say, you ain't one of those hippy types that's gonna try to pay me with peace, love, and happiness, are ya, pal? 'Cause I ain't taking nothing but American dollars and cents."

"I've got money," Larson said quietly, wishing the

driver would keep his attention on the road. Just the normal highway speed made him nervous enough without the added concern about whether the cabby might cause a fifty car pileup. "If you take me to a drugstore on the way, I'll double your tip."

"You're the boss." The cabby maneuvered back onto the Major Deegan Expressway, now traveling northward.

Taziar Medakan awakened, sprawled alone in a dark alleyway. Afternoon light slanted between impossibly tall buildings, making Taziar realize that he had not slept long. His head pounded, making thought nearly impossible, overshadowing the grinding chorus of cuts, abrasions, and bruises. The gashes in his wrists had settled to a dull throb.

Taziar savored a moment of disorientation before reality intruded. Gradually he remembered deeper, more horrible pains. *Astryd and the baby are dead. Silme's joined Bolverkr. And I think I've found Karana's hell. What now?* Only one answer came. *I have to find Allerum.* Common sense seeped into thoughts nearly emptied by pain and panic. *Since Silme came here through Allerum's mind, they must have arrived together. She killed the baby in my presence. She couldn't have cast a transport spell until then or the baby would already have died. That means she didn't magically leave Allerum. He can't be far.* Ignorant of planes, subways, and automobiles, Taziar could not see the flaw in his logic. *If I search the city, I'm certain to find him.*

Buoyed by these new thoughts, Taziar tended to his disheveled appearance. First, he removed the cloak that Bolverkr had thrown over his damaged climbing garb, using brisk strokes and a bandage dampened in a puddle to scrub away the most obvious grass stains and dirt. He combed back sweat-plastered, black hair with his fingers. Spitting on his hands, he washed away dried blood, then drew down his sleeves to cover the gashes from the ropes. Rising, he brushed away dirt and flattened the wrinkles from his dark, linen shirt and britches. Then he donned the cloak, arranging it over the fire and road burns and belting it at the waist. The cloak hung to his ankles, the hem tattered into fringe, and he had to roll back the sleeves. But it did hide the worst of his injuries.

The normalcy of the routine soothed Taziar. Usually, panic was a stranger to him. The most dire circumstances only fueled his imagination, sending him into a flurry of thoughtful plotting. But Astryd's death unhinged him, and his new surroundings gave him nothing understandable or familiar on which to ground his reason. Cued to the reality of onrushing traffic, hordes of people, towering structures, and winking lights, Taziar's wits settled into a more manageable pattern.

Where do I start my search for Allerum? Taziar crept toward the mouth of the alleyway, reluctant to plunge back into the clustered human traffic. A wash of voices filled his ears. He had grown accustomed to the bizarre hubbub of English, an incomprehensible jumble of foreign words and accents that fused into a dull roar of background. One voice rose above the others, pitched grandly, apparently to draw attention. *Someone selling wares?* Taziar guessed, though his previous experience on New York City's sidewalks had revealed no street vendors.

Taziar poked his head around the corner.

An elderly woman shied from Taziar's sudden, partial emergence from an alleyway. Others glared, giving him a wide berth.

"Sorry," Taziar mumbled in his own language. Glancing along the sidewalk, he saw a small crowd gathered near the mouth of a parallel alley. At its center, a dynamic black monte shuffled a trio of playing cards folded into tents over a table constructed of cinder blocks and a board. A pimply white teenager stood on the opposite side of the table, garbed in a crisply neat, button-down shirt and dress trousers.

Drawn by the familiarity of a con game in a world that otherwise seemed hostile, Taziar crept closer, studying the scene through gaps in the gathering. The monte revealed the front of the cards with a showman's flourish: a red female with two heads and torsos, one upside down; and a not quite matched pair of black cards. One held a pattern of clovers in rows of two, the other a similar arrangement with single leaves. The monte flipped each card to its back. The reverse sides looked impossibly alike, a complicated series of blue circles, squares, and loops. Taziar watched as the black youth gathered the cards, two in one hand, one in the other, then tossed them back down in a different arrangement.

Though alert for sleights of hand and substitutions of cards, Taziar saw no trickery. The pock-faced player laid a handful of uniform, green papers on the table before the card Taziar knew was the red one.

The monte flicked the card to its opposite side, revealing the queen.

Applause splattered through the spectators. The winner shouted in excited triumph, drawing even more spectators.

The monte said something loudly that sent twitters of laughter through the crowd and included the words "son of a bitch." He drew a packet of folded, green papers from his pocket, counted off several bills and handed them to the player with a composure that could only have been rehearsed.

Taziar nodded sagely, guessing the setup. Obviously, the youths on either side of the table were working together. If so, Taziar knew the player's next move would be to feign difficulty finding enough money for his next attempt. He would talk one of the spectators into covering part or all of a huge bet, one he would promptly lose, along with the other man's contribution.

Despite language and technological barriers, other things seemed obvious. Apparently, this green paper possessed some value. It seemed odd to Taziar, but he accepted it with no way to question. Clearly, the object of the game was for the better to pick out the odd card based on watching the shuffle. The one card in three odds of selecting the correct card by random chance did not seem to bother the audience. By nature, people trusted their eyesight and ability to outwit scams as surely as the monte believed in his skill at deception.

As Taziar suspected, the pimple-faced teenager turned to a nearby man, speaking quickly and earnestly in low tones while the monte shifted from foot to foot with mock impatience. Taziar scanned the crowd for evidence of other shills. A petite brunette in an indecently short skirt watched with an expression and stance that revealed more than casual interest. From long practice, Taziar picked out the last two members of the monte's gang. A densely-muscled, black youth and a wiry Hispanic studied the proceedings with feigned indifference, occasionally measuring the crowd with glances. Of them all, Taziar felt most certain about the loyalties of his last find. The Hispanic teen carried a deck of cards in his jeans pocket, one back clearly visible above the stitched edge. The pattern matched the cards on the dealer's table.

As Taziar scrutinized the crowd, he also discovered a schemer unrelated to the gang. A nondescript, middle-aged man moved adeptly through the masses. Paunchy and balding, he was small, barely the height of an average woman, though he still towered nearly a full head over Taziar. Attracted by the same inconspicuousness that made the rest of the spectators ignore the stranger, Taziar watched him approach a jovial man clutching the hand of a young boy. As the thief maneuvered past the father, he deftly flicked a leather billfold from the father's back pocket. Stashing it in his own hip pocket, he barely paused before gliding toward his next victim.

Ordinarily, Taziar would have let the heist pass without comment or action. But the thief's bulging gut and carefully tailored clothes led Taziar to believe that he was not stealing from need. Drawn to the conclusion that father and son could make better use of the money, Taziar considered his options. *I have to find Allerum. Now isn't the time to get involved in conflicts that could get me into trouble.* Still, the simple challenge offered by the situation sent his heart into the familiar, calm cadence that preceded action. *I'll handle the bizarre things happening around me better if I'm composed. What could possibly lull me faster than the chance to match wits with a thief?* Decision made, Taziar closed on the pickpocket.

A collective sigh rose from the audience as the pimple-faced teen and his victim lost their money to the monte's sleight of hand.

While the crowd's attention was on the exchange of bills, the pickpocket swiped another wallet. Taziar moved simultaneously. Even as the thief stuffed the new cache into his pocket, Taziar relieved him of the father's wallet, along with a fat wad of loose bills.

Apparently oblivious, the pickpocket waded into the pedestrian traffic on the sidewalk and wandered out of sight.

A warm sense of accomplishment filled Taziar. Grinning, he approached the father and son, aware a slip now would turn a good deed into a fatal error. Briefly, he considered openly returning the man's property but discarded the idea as quickly. *Allerum said the people in his city tended to mistrust strangers. I've got no words to explain the truth if this man blames me for the theft.* Taziar held the wallet in his palm. To free his hands, he stuffed the additional, loose packet of bills into one of the inner pockets lining his shirt.

The father shifted for a better view. As Taziar slipped behind the man, the boy glanced around, a finger drilling into one nostril.

Taziar smiled at the child.

Apparently recognizing Taziar as a small adult rather than another child, the boy lost interest. He tugged at his father's sleeve.

The man looked down. A brief exchange followed from which Taziar managed to glean only a few prepositions and definite articles. The man hefted the boy, placing the child on his shoulders.

As the man moved, his attention fully focused on his son, Taziar tapped the wallet back into its proper pocket. The Climber hesitated, practiced at looking casual, aware a mad scramble from the site, though tempting, would draw attention. With appropriate nonchalance, he sauntered back into the milling crowd.

The ease of the maneuver disappointed Taziar, and he missed the exhilarating rush that usually accompanied danger. *Too simple. A blind beginner could have returned that purse.* He searched for a more interesting target. His gaze fell on the Hispanic member of the monte's gang. The deck of cards outlined against the hip pocket of his jeans beckoned, a challenge worthy of a master thief. Taziar took a step toward the stranger. Then, logic caught up with his runaway thoughts. *What am I doing? I've got two Chaos-warped sorcerers chasing me and a friend to locate. Why am I looking for more trouble?*

The answer came more easily than Taziar expected. Trapped in a world and time that seemed less ordered than Bolverkr's Chaos, Taziar was clinging to the only familiar situation he had found. The chance to match wits with future hustlers and thieves, sharks with years of others' experience to draw on, intrigued him; and the familiarity of the challenge soothed. Whatever technology the future brought, people apparently were still people, constantly seeking a fast and easy means to make their money. And it seemed there would always be other people willing to prey upon this basic flaw in human nature, sating the same flaw in themselves.

Now understanding his motivations, Taziar forced aside his curiosity. He turned to leave, tossing one last glance at the monte game. At the table, a small, oval-faced woman pulled a bill from her pocketbook.

Astryd! Taziar stared, not daring to question, afraid he might lose her again. *Astryd!* He shoved through the crowd, skidding to a stop beside her.

As Taziar drew up near the woman, he realized his mistake. She stood slightly shorter than he, but there all resemblance to Astryd ended. Dark hair fell to her shoulders. Her muddy-green eyes followed the monte's movements with a precision and concentration even Taziar's sudden appearance could not shake.

Hope vanished in an instant, dashed beneath a rush of disappointment. Unaccustomed to sudden, impetuous actions, Taziar froze, uncertain of his next move. Concerned that grief could shake his judgment so completely that he could mistake another woman for Astryd, he concentrated on the game, hoping to ground his sanity.

The monte talked continuously as he shuffled. Taziar managed to pluck a few catch phrases from the pitch, by their repetition, the resemblance to his own language, and Larson's hints. The phrase, "find the lady" seemed to recur with the greatest frequency.

The woman slapped her bill down before the center card.

The monte frowned, apparently displeased by the paltriness of her wager. He paused, as if waiting for her or someone else to increase the bet. When no one did, he revealed her chosen card as a black six. Collecting the money, he then showed her the queen as the leftmost card and another six on the right. He gathered the cards, a six tented in his left hand, the other six in his right with the queen beneath it. With a smooth, practiced sweep, he flicked the black card over the red and let it drop to the table. All eyes in the crowd then followed the displaced six as he rearranged them on the table.

Simple single substitution. Taziar assessed the method naturally, hardly daring to believe such an easy maneuver could fool a crowd. Yet he had already watched several people lose their money to it. Trained to observe every subtlety, he had no difficulty following the exchange. The queen sat in the middle, the decoy to her right.

The woman hesitated, her hand in her purse.

The monte continued his pitch, his words uninterpretable but his voice wheedling encouragements.

Taziar could not help liking this woman. He wanted to point out the correct card but realized she had no reason to trust him. *Besides, if it seems too easy, it probably is. I could be missing something, and I'd hate to steer her wrong.*

The woman sighed. She hauled a crumpled bill from her purse. Her hand hovered, her gaze shifting from card to card.

The crowd waited patiently, the monte less so. He said something that sent a ripple of laughter through the masses, making an undulating gesture with his hand to hurry the woman.

She placed the bill before the decoy.

The monte flipped it, revealing the six. He took her money then turned the other cards, gathering them for the next round.

The woman backed away, disappointment traced vividly across her features.

Before she could leave, Taziar touched her arm. He held up a finger, indicating she should wait, then closed in to win back her money, glad for the excuse to play.

The monte turned his attention to Taziar, gaze flicking over the dirty, overlarge cloak and the healing slash on his cheek.

Taziar plucked the stolen bankroll from his pocket.

Interest flashed across the monte's face, disappearing beneath a mask of professional indifference, but not quickly enough. Apparently, the sight of money allowed him to dismiss his player's battle-scarred appearance. The patter began again.

Taziar peeled through several, identical outer bills until he reached ones that looked like those the woman had played. He slipped two from the stack, then rifled through the others, gauging their value from the expressions on the faces of the monte's gang. Apparently, the pickpocket had arranged the wad with the least valuable bills outside in a gradual progression toward the center. Accustomed to rapid-fire assessments of objects and human reactions, Taziar noted that the two different types of outer bills, including the ones he had pulled out, had single digits in the corners. He found three types of double digit bills as well as four identical bills with triple digits. And the gang's interest told Taziar he carried enough money to mark him as a target.

The woman waited, watching.

The monte's patience seemed to have increased exponentially. He waited until Taziar looked up before launching into the usual shuffle and banter.

Taziar remained silent, easily following the original switch and the subsequent arrangement of the cards. The brunette in the miniskirt, whom Taziar had pegged as a gang member, drifted toward the game.

Not wanting to reveal himself as other than a curious passerby, Taziar hesitated, looking over the cards as if confused. He liked this woman who reminded him of Astryd and saw no reason to let her know he was as crooked as any monte. He dropped his two bills before the center card, trying to make the selection look casual and random.

Instantly, the long-legged brunette tossed a pair of double digit bills before the decoy card.

The monte looked at Taziar apologetically and said something the Shadow Climber guessed to mean that only one bet was allowed per round. The monte managed to indicate that, since both wagers were placed at once, he would have to accept the more valuable one. Returning Taziar's two fives, he concentrated on the female gang member's money instead.

Annoyance gripped Taziar, though he hid it behind a pall of bland disappointment. He doubted anyone else in the crowd recognized the woman as a shill, so he alone identified the scam. *There's no way to win this game. If the sleight of hand doesn't fool the player, he uses the gang to cheat.* In his youth as a con man, Taziar had always relied on complex, showy tricks, believing by audience deserved entertainment in exchange for their gold. When hunger drove him to simple trickery or thievery, he always played fairly, preying only on the rich and sharing his spoils. There was an honor even among swindlers; unwritten rules specified that if one con outwitted another's scam, the lesson learned outvalued the money lost. Now, suddenly, the stakes changed. The challenge escalated from a good deed designed to help a pretty woman to a temptation too difficult to resist. *There's got to be a way to win.* Reclaiming his bills, Taziar handed them to the woman he had mistaken for Astryd to replace the ones she had lost in the previous round.

Features twisted in confusion, the small woman tried to return the bills, speaking in sentences Taziar could only identify as questions.

Taziar shook his head, refusing the fives, then turned his attention back to the monte who was revealing the decoy as a six. The monte collected the brunette gang member's money as well as the cards, pausing only long enough to demonstrate that the central one was indeed the queen.

The monte gestured at Taziar with both hands, encouraging him to try again.

Taziar examined the youth more closely. His pants pockets bulged with money. He wore an open dress shirt over a white undershirt. His breast pocket contained a partially crushed box of white paper sticks, and the remainder of the deck of cards. He asked Taziar an uninterpretable question.

Taziar shrugged. "I don't understand your language," he said in the tongue of Cullinsberg's barony.

The wiry Hispanic gang member moved in. He leaned past Taziar, talking with the monte in low tones. As close as the youth stood, Taziar could scarcely hear him. Yet, coincidentally, he chose words Larson had taught Taziar. "The little guy's a foreigner."

The monte's reply emerged equally comprehensible and pitched too softly for the crowd to hear. "Who fucking cares? The ratty little dirtball's got money."

Taziar made no pretext of understanding. As the game ground to a halt, bystanders drifted away. The deck of cards in the Hispanic's pocket hovered, temptingly close to Taziar's reach. *I saw the rest of the leader's cards in his pocket. That can only mean this man carries an unrelated deck of his own.* Grasping the opportunity, Taziar calmly edged the cards from the teen's pocket and stashed them in his own.

A moment later, the gang member sidestepped, returning to his position. The monte spun the queen, face up, on the table. His speech became loud, slow and broken, addressed directly at Taziar. "You play?" He made grand gestures at the table. "You find the lady?"

Taziar drew the folded stack of bills from his pocket again. He glanced thoughtfully from the money to the cards.

The banter grew more urgent, the motions more beckoning. "Come on. It's fun. You'll . . ." The rest of his sentence was unfamiliar. ". . . find the lady." He tapped a fingertip on the red card and shouted something obviously for the benefit of the crowd, a showman to the core.

Apparently lured by high stakes, a new crowd formed. The youngsters Taziar had identified as gang members merged into the new group, and the pick-pocket returned as well.

Taziar nodded to indicate interest. Then he looked deep into the crowd, as if at someone. Raising a finger to indicate that he would return, he wove into the masses. Once beyond sight, he ducked into an alley-way. Behind him, he heard the din of conversation, pierced by the monte's charismatic baritone. Taziar heard something about a winner, knowing it had to be a member of the gang pretending to win in order to draw the attention of players who believed that if one person beat the odds, so could they.

Taziar flashed through the deck, studying the cards in the hazy light filtering into the alley. Plucking the queen of diamonds and a black six from the deck, he folded them into tents that matched the cards on the table. Shoving the remainder of the deck back into his pocket, he palmed the queen in his left hand, clutching the money in his right.

As Taziar worked his way back to the gaming table, the monte smiled in welcome. Unable to communicate with Taziar, he addressed the crowd in warm, conge-nial tones, turning the cards to reveal every face. The monte waited until Taziar stared at the cards. "Ready?" the black man said.

Taziar nodded.

The monte jumbled cards, talking the entire time.

Taziar ignored even those words he understood, following the double substitution as easily as he had the previous single exchanges. When the monte finished moving cards, Taziar knew the queen sat at the rightmost end of the table with the sixes central and to the left. Still clutching his own queen, Taziar opened the stack of bills and peeled from the middle, placing three hundreds in front of the center card. He let the fourth hundred slip from his fingers. It floated to the sidewalk.

Every eye followed the fluttering bill.

Taziar knelt to retrieve the fallen hundred dollar bill, dropping his left hand to the table as if to steady himself. With smooth and practiced dexterity, he replaced the central six with his queen. Now palming a six, he placed the last hundred with the others.

The monte grinned broadly. He tossed over the middle card, revealing Taziar's queen. "Sorry, sir. . . ." His smile wilted to a shocked grimace, and his words trailed into oblivion. The attention of every gang member riveted on the card, the diversion so engrossing that Taziar might as well have had a year to switch the monte's queen with the palmed six.

Gasps startled through the crowd, followed by a smattering of applause that strengthened and rose to cheers.

The monte flipped the rightmost card, revealing the replaced six. He stared. Then, regaining his composure, he huffed out a strained laugh. Plucking bills from his pocket, he flicked fifties and twenties onto Taziar's stack, the crowd loudly counting each bill with him.

As the monte tallied, he glanced meaningfully at the thickly-muscled gang member who had, so far, remained quiet and still. The large man's hand slid into his pocket. There was no mistaking the gesture. Taziar guessed that if he left without losing all the cash he had won, he would meet with a horrible accident in some alley.

As the last bill landed on the stack, Taziar reached for it.

The monte's hand touched his, pressing the money to the table. "Play some more?"

Taziar shook his head.

The monte's hand retreated, and Taziar put the bills in his pocket.

The monte asked another question, this one unfamiliar.

Again, Taziar shook his head, followed by a shrug to convey ignorance. He knew he was acting foolishly. He had no need for money. He could not even understand its relative value. But he cared little for the methods of this particular gang and felt certain he could find a more worthy cause.

Taziar also realized he would need a distraction if he wanted to leave the area alive. *As long as I stay in the crowd, I'm safe. If they threaten me here, I'm not only their last winner, I become their last player ever.* He put the extra queen into his pocket, retrieving the folded six from the purloined deck.

The largest gang member shifted his weight, casually watching Taziar.

Taziar remained near the table, feigning engrossment in the next player. His huge win had brought a surge of people who pressed eagerly toward the makeshift table, certain they could match the feats of an ignorant, little foreigner who could not even understand English. Each hoped to win large sums of money with minimal effort, and Taziar realized human nature would refill the gang's coffers, with overflow. *In that respect, I actually aided their scam.*

The monte returned to his pitch. He turned over the cards, mixing them, his usual prattle sounding like a thin, shaken whisper after his previous, strident bellows. As the last card fell, a heavyset man slapped down a fifty with such enthusiasm that he sent the cards scuttling. As the monte straightened them, Taziar siezed the moment to replace the queen with his six, leaving three black cards on the table and no red. Pocketing the second queen, Taziar turned, squeezing into the stream of sidewalk traffic. A casual glance over his shoulder revealed that the muscled hoodlum was following him. The wiry Hispanic teenager also disengaged from the crowd.

Taziar broke into a trot. A quick look backward showed him that his pursuer had quickened his pace as well.

Unaccustomed to the volume of traffic that filled New York City's streets, Taziar misjudged. The moment he took to check the hoodlum's position sent him careening into a slender redhead dressed in a multi-hued T-shirt, jeans nearly as tattered as Taziar's britches, and a string of beads. She fell with a gasp, flailing so wildly she took a nearby black businessman down with her. The man's foot crashed into Taziar's shin, sprawling him. A dive and twist saved Taziar from landing on the woman, but he hit the pavement instead. The passersby parted around the collision.

Taziar scrambled to his feet. The brawny hoodlum had almost closed the gap. The Hispanic youth was nowhere Taziar could see.

The familiar excitement of the chase made Taziar giddy. Suddenly, the strangeness of the city seemed to fade to insignificance. He might have been back in Cullinsberg, dodging through alleyways and scaling buildings with the guard force at his heels. The exotic city and its streets only added to the challenge. His grief disappeared, forgotten beneath more urgent need, and its release freed him to think logically. He felt joyful and unfettered for the first time in weeks, though he realized the youth might carry a gun or other un-guessable technology that would enable him to quickly end Taziar's life.

Taziar wove into a clustered knot of citizens on the edge of the sidewalk closest to the buildings. As they passed an alleyway, he glided inside, hoping to decoy the gang member into following the masses. Pigeons much like the ones in Cullinsberg fluttered skyward, their wing beats slapping echoes between the buildings; their cooing filled the alley. Metal ash cans and plastic bags lined the walls of the buildings.

Unfooled, the hoodlum whipped around the corner, now only a few arm's lengths behind Taziar. He growled a command, from which Taziar deciphered only the terminating swear word. A patterned sequence of whistles followed.

Taziar picked his way swiftly and carefully through the garbage. Recognizing the high-pitched noises as a signal, he suddenly wished he knew the exact location of the muscled teen's Hispanic companion. As Taziar moved, he eyeballed the walls on either side. Though well-mortared, the perfect bricks composing the walls would supply regular, if tiny, handholds.

The rumble of the crowds faded. A click reverberated through the alley, and a blade appeared, glinting in the gang member's hand. A new set of footsteps pattered from in front of Taziar. *That answers the question of where his friend went.* Taziar eased his back against the wall, fingers groping the brick for handholds, finding more than enough for a climb. Some distance directly above him, a metallic platform jutted from the building. Steps rose from it, zigzagging to several similar decks, each set a story higher than the previous one.

Now Taziar could see both youths, closing in on him from either side. Whirling, he fitted his fingers into miniscule ledges and clambered to the platform. Catching hold of the metal, he ducked through a space in the railing, landing lightly on the deck.

Beneath Taziar, the two gang members hesitated. The larger one swore, his tone mingling frustration and surprise. The Hispanic leapt to a trash can, using the height it gained him to catch the lowest rung of the fire escape. Carefully drawing himself up, he charged after Taziar. His companion followed, rattling the entire structure with his footfalls.

Taziar sprang back to the railing, aware a climb up the bricks, though taxing, would give him a more direct route to the rooftop. As the hoodlums charged toward him, he flattened to the side of the building and scrambled easily upward.

''Shit,'' the brawnier gang youth said, awe clearly

evident in the expletive. He continued to pound up the stairways.

"Look at the little son-of-a-bitch go." His sinewy companion seemed equally impressed. "How. . . ?"

The rest of the question blurred to nonsense in Taziar's ears. Still, their amazement made one thing clear. Apparently, despite the contrived regularity of handholds, climbing buildings was as unusual here as in his own time and city.

Catching the ledge, Taziar flung himself to the rooftop. Pigeons scattered, some taking to wing, others strutting beyond his reach, their heads bobbing crazily. A grimy metal box sat in a central position, spinning blades visible through its grates. To his left, a shack rose from the floor, latched by a rusted padlock.

Having gained several moments from his straighter climb, Taziar scuttled to the opposite side of the roof. As he passed the shack, a grinding, whirring noise erupted so suddenly that Taziar instinctively dodged.

His pursuers heaved to the rooftop behind him, panting, red-faced, and obviously annoyed.

Taziar gauged the distance to the neighboring building, and realized the strangeness and unusual height of the structures had caused him to miscalculate distances. The alley between this storefront and the next gaped like an open wound, too wide to jump even with a running start. Taziar looked down, measuring the distance to the alley below. His elevated position gave him a wide view of the street, including the location where the monte game had taken place. There, he could see a fight had broken out, presumably over the missing queen. People surged, a mad chaos of bodies. "Look!" Taziar said in accented English. He pointed.

The hoodlums closed, hunched and with wary deliberation. Taziar's effortless climb made it clear he was no normal immigrant. Either they worried that Taziar might have more unexpected tricks to use against them or, he hoped, they just wanted their money back without sending their victim tumbling to his death.

"Look!" Taziar said again, jabbing his finger toward the crowd. Having spent many of his early years in a gang, he understood the need for loyalty. *That card shuffler could be the only family these men have.* Desperate to communicate, he struggled with the language. "Summa bitch! Ex-kyuse-me." Running out of relevant expressions, he chose at random, trying to get his message across with wild gestures and a dire tone. "Buick. Follow that car!"

Apparently impressed by Taziar's urgency, if not his words, the robust youth took a careful glance over the edge. He remained partially twisted toward Taziar, as if concerned the Shadow Climber might rush him.

Taziar inched backward, away from the teenagers and the building's edge.

"Fuck!" the heavier hoodlum shouted. Ignoring Taziar, he charged back toward the fire escape, calling something sharply to his companion as he ran.

The wiry Hispanic studied Taziar for a moment. He pointed, addressing Taziar in a threatening manner before whirling to follow his friend.

Though unable to understand, Taziar guessed he had received a lecture on luck. He waited until both youngsters disappeared over the side before breaking into laughter. Moving back toward the edge, he tried to identify Al Larson in the milling crowds below him.

CHAPTER 11:

Chaos at the Tower

When bad men combine, the good must associate; else they will fall one by one, an unpitied sacrifice in a contemptible struggle.
> —Edmund Burke
> *Thoughts on the Cause of the Present Discontents*

Al Larson hated himself for an evil he saw no way to avoid. Crouched against the Jeffers' wooden house, he watched flames of gold and red engulf the dwelling he had called home for more than fifteen years. Heat blackened white-painted shingles. Yellow trim disappeared beneath fire that crackled and capered like demons. And Al Larson lamented that, if the war had taught him nothing else, it had shown him how to build a successful pyre, to overcome the protestations of his conscience, and to destroy even those things he loved.

Timmy clutched his older brother's waist, tears rolling down cherubic cheeks.

Though concerned for the child, Larson kept his eyes locked on the burning house. Soon, neighbors would mobilize. Someone would call the fire department, and Larson knew he and Timmy had best disappear long before that happened. Still, he waited, wanting to make certain his mother and sister escaped unharmed.

Timmy said nothing. He did not question Larson's wisdom.

But Larson was questioning enough for both of them. *What am I doing? What the hell am I doing? There has to be another way to protect Mom and Pam.*

Larson sighed, knowing the luxury of time might have given him a better strategy, but he had been unable to conjure one from the swirl of thoughts and emotions besieging him. *Silme never met Mom or Pam, so she can't enter their minds to find them. But she could use Timmy's thoughts or mine to locate this house. I had no choice. I have to force the women to leave until this is settled, to move someplace without Timmy or me knowing where.* The rationalization did not quiet his guilt. *One more crisis. Just what Mom and Pam needed. First Dad's death, then Timmy's and my disappearance. And now I'm burning down my own goddamned house.*

The wind shifted, funneling ash and smoke into Larson's lungs. He coughed. *I've waited long enough. Perhaps too long.* Grabbing Timmy, he followed a line of trees toward the road.

A screen door slammed. Someone screamed, and the village of Baychester awakened sluggishly to danger.

Larson broke into a run, hoping no one had spotted him. *Please let Mom and Pam get out safely. Please, God, let them not be home.* Larson had never thought much of religion; his jokingly forsaking Christianity for the warlike Norse pantheon just before his death in Vietnam had resulted in his being dragged into ancient history. But now he could not stop himself from appealing to a higher source.

Lawns and rows of closely-placed houses disappeared behind Larson and Timmy, replaced by streets. The wail of a siren floated over the village like an accusing scream. Every instinct told Larson to stay, to check on his mother's and sister's safety and keep looters from pillaging his family's belongings, the familiar, beloved objects that were all that remained of Carl Larson and the house in Baychester. But Al Larson knew he could not afford to see his family; to give Silme even a distant glimpse of his mother's current looks or plans would be folly. He believed the Dragonrank sorceress could glean some details from his or Timmy's memories, but he hoped those would prove distant enough that they would only allow her to recognize the women if she found them by random chance. *In a city this size. Think of the odds.*

Now outside the village, Larson slowed, not wanting his haste to draw attention. To get hauled in by the police, even just for questioning, meant remaining in one place long enough for Silme to locate him. *Sure suicide.* It also brought the possibility of being forced to confront his mother. Releasing Timmy's hand, Larson kept his pace brisk, trying for an air of casual disinterest with little success. He could only hope the oddities of New York City would keep Silme busy until he could devise a coherent strategy against her.

Larson's walk brought him to the enormous tract of dirt that had once been Freedom Land and would soon become Co-op City. Bulldozers and cranes huffed over the single street, adding beams to a towering skeleton of steel that, when finished, would loom over the double-story dwellings in Baychester. Construction workers scurried around the machinery, their white undershirts dampened in wide, semicircular patches at the neck and armpits. One lounged near the marked perimeter of the hard hat area, munching an apple and sipping coffee from a styrofoam cup. A radio near his feet blasted the news through a wash of static.

As Larson passed by, one of the other workers approached the man on break and flopped down beside him.

Timmy gasped for air.

Larson paused, giving the boy a chance to catch his breath.

The new worker removed his yellow hard hat to rub sweat from his forehead with the back of his hand. "What's the word on that lady jumper?"

The first worker spoke around a mouthful of apple. "Don't think it's a lady anymore. They're saying it's a real small guy now. And he ain't maybe jumping. Actually climbed higher, straight up the goddamned wall."

The other man grunted, scratching at a hairy beer gut beneath his shirt. "Little guy in black and gray crawling up a building? Gotta be a publicity stunt. Some company's showing off new mountain climbing gear or looking for free advertising."

Larson froze, images of Taziar rising to his mind, though he knew it was impossible. Still, he eavesdropped, aware that with a Dragonrank sorceress loose in the city, he had to pay attention to any reports of weird happenings.

The first man shrugged. "Yeah, well. That was my thought, too, man. But if they're looking for publicity, why's he climbing Sears and Roebuck? Why not the Empire State Building or some real skyscraper in Manhattan? Besides, they're sayin' now they don't think he understands English. Jabbered back at them in some sort of French or German. What kind of advertising you going to get when the guy can't even say nothing about no product?"

A short silence fell. Larson ran their conversation repeatedly through his mind, unable to shake the certainty. *A little man who doesn't speak English climbing a twelve-story building. Who the hell else could it be?*

"So, you hear anything from your son?"

"Not since last week when they moved him to Mai Lai. . . ."

Larson pressed on, concerned for the climber and not wanting to hear war tales. "Come on." Seizing Timmy's hand, he rushed the child across the lot, fumbling in his pocket for a dime. Near St. Raymond's Parish Cemetery, where the population clustered, he had had no difficulty finding an independent cab. Here, in this section of town empty except for construction, he would need to call for a ride.

Timmy stumbled.

Larson stopped, reached to carry the child, and caught his first clear glimpse of his brother's features since burning down the house. Tears glazed the freckled, doll-like face. His brown eyes looked hollow and haunted.

Larson had seen the same expression in the visage of a Vietnamese girl after one of his companions raped and killed her mother. He shivered, barraged with pain. Then, he had walked away, sickened. And although he had not participated, his failure to put an end to the torture made him equally guilty by his conscience's judgment. Since that first time, he had seen the hopeless agony of surrender in the eyes of too many children, had watched innocence die in the split second it took for a blow or bullet to slaughter loved ones, had wondered what the future held for those children and their morality. The comparison ached through him. *Not Timmy. Please, not Timmy.*

Larson hated the idea of stopping long enough to give Silme a transport site or of delaying his aid to a man who might be Taziar, but both seemed preferable to letting Timmy succumb to despair. He knelt, catching Timmy's forearms, losing himself in the child's eyes.

"I want to go home." Timmy burst into sobs. "I want to be with Mommy and Pam. And Dad. I want to go home."

Larson clutched Timmy to his chest, waiting for the child to calm down enough to understand his words. Timmy's grip went convulsively tight around his brother.

Larson whispered soothingly, despising each second that ticked by, yet understanding the need.

The child's hold loosened, but his face remained buried in Larson's T-shirt.

Larson stroked his brother's sandy locks. "Timmy, do you trust me?"

Timmy's head bobbed beneath Larson's hand.

"I had to burn the house. The witch can read our minds because she's met us. I had to get Mom and Pam to leave so we don't know where they are. Do you understand that?"

Timmy hesitated. His voice was muffled almost to incomprehensibility, but Larson managed to catch the main idea. The boy wanted to know why Larson had not simply told the women to relocate.

Larson chewed his lip, trying to decide how to explain. He pictured himself attempting to talk his mother and sister into abandoning their home. *Well, you see, Mom, there's this sorceress who followed me from ancient Norway. I'm an elf there, you see.* He shook his head, on the verge of hysterical laughter. *They'd think Dad's death drove me over the edge. They'd probably have me committed, and Silme would have all the time in the world to identify them.* "Listen, Timmy. You're just going to have to believe me. That was the only way to keep Mom and Pam safe."

Timmy nodded again, still clinging.

"This is kind of like the first ten minutes of a 'Mission: Impossible' episode. Lots of bad things are going to happen over the next few hours or days. *If we last that long.* He kept the thought to himself. "Silme's got magic bombs and bazookas and dragons and whatnot. I may have to find a gun and shoot her." Larson shivered at the thought. "Peo-ple. . . ." His voice cracked, and he paused to gather his composure before continuing. *It won't help Timmy if I get overwrought.* "People may die. Even me."

Timmy looked up, a grimace of horror covering his features.

Larson wanted to support Timmy, but lies and false reassurances would only lead to later betrayals. "If that happens, I want you to run to the nearest policeman as fast as you can. Can you handle that?"

Timmy lowered and raised his head once in an uncertain nod. "I don't want you to die. Are you going to die?"

"I don't want to die, either. I'm going to do everything I can to keep that from happening. But I brought Silme here. She's my responsibility." He tousled Timmy's bangs. "We can't go back to Mom and Pam until Silme's taken care of." *I wish I could have gotten Timmy elsewhere, too.* Larson shook his head in frustration. *But Silme's already entered his mind once. She can find him anywhere.* Only one solution came to the forefront of his thoughts. "Timmy, I can try to get the police to put you in protective custody." *God only knows what I'd say. In their place, I sure as hell wouldn't believe my story.*

Timmy went rigid. "I want to stay with you."

Larson considered, understanding the child's motives. Having lost his father, sister, and mother, he was clinging desperately to his only remaining family member, the brother he had always emulated as the ideal of masculine cool. "All right. Fine. But there's going to have to be some rules."

Timmy whipped his head up and down in a frenzied promise.

"First, you have to trust me. Bad things are going to happen. No matter what, you have to believe I'm doing my best to be the good guy. Second, if I'm killed, you run. Third, you have to do whatever I tell you, no matter how weird it sounds." Larson rose. Placing an arm across Timmy's shoulders, he steered the boy across the lot. "I love you, you little turd."

Timmy stuck out his lip. The hunted look disappeared from his features. "Yah. You big jerk." He ducked under Larson's hold.

"Creep," Larson returned, flipping Timmy's hair into his eyes.

"Dumbhead." Timmy shook his locks back.

"Jerkface."

"Retard."

Larson laughed, hardly daring to believe he had discussed his death only three breaths back, and now he was exchanging insults with an eight-year-old. He took Timmy's hand as they came to the lot's end and crossed the street toward the supermarket. "Listen, this guy who's climbing the building. If it's who I think it is, you'll like him. He's kind of an Errol Flynn type."

"Earl who?"

"Robin Hood." Larson pulled open one of the glass doors. He ushered Timmy through, then followed the boy inside. "You remember that movie where the guy steals from the rich and gives to the poor."

Timmy danced in a circle, waving an imaginary

weapon. "You mean he's real fast and jumps around and people can't catch him and he fights good with a sword?"

"Not exactly." Larson approached the pay telephone, grabbing the book dangling from its chain. Only then did it strike him how near Timmy's description had actually come to the truth. "But real close." Larson flipped through the yellow pages to the Taxicab section, seeing no reason to tell Timmy that his older brother could beat Taziar in any sword spar, even with one hand tied behind his back.

Finding a number, Larson dropped his dime into the slot and dialed.

When Larson's cab approached the corner of Webster and Fordham, they discovered a snarl of traffic behind a milling horde of gawking pedestrians. Patting Timmy's knee reassuringly, Larson leaned over the seat to address the driver. "I'm going to get out here. Take my brother to Marion and 193rd and wait there with the meter running. I'll be back."

Timmy opened his mouth to protest, but Larson cut him short.

"I'll return as soon as I can. Hopefully with Taz. Remember what I told you about listening to me." Freeing his wallet from his pants pocket, Larson fished through the bill section, finding only a ten and four ones remaining. Though only two dollars and change showed on the meter, he handed over the ten. Then he opened the door and charged out onto the sidewalk.

Behind him, the cab backed into the jam.

Larson hated leaving Timmy with no protection other than a strange cabby, yet he knew the boy's presence would make rescuing Taziar even more impossible than it already seemed. *If it's even Shadow doing the climbing. This is crazy. There's no possible way he could have gotten here.* Still, the description fit too well. Despite logic's contradiction, Larson's intuition told him the climber could be no one else.

The crowd pressed in on Larson. Panic clutched

him, with a claustrophobia he had never experienced before Vietnam. Every instinct told him to flee, and the resolve he raised to combat impulse also brought determined rage. He elbowed through the masses, ignoring curses, shouts, and jabs.

A man grabbed Larson by the front of his shirt. Larson glared into a pair of eyes recessed in a fat, red face. The stranger's gaze traveled up Larson's brawny, six foot frame to his hard, ice-blue eyes. Backing down, the man faded into the crowd.

Larson scarcely hesitated. He rushed and shoved the spectators, clearing a path like a bulldozer through a herd of sheep. He saw police and fire vehicles and the flashing lights of Emergency Rescue Teams. Uniformed men perched atop the cars with binoculars. Police on foot or horseback cordoned the sidewalk, some ushering people leaving the building to safety beyond the barricades. A patrol supervisor with a bullhorn peered upward, his head cocked, listening to the radio at his belt. Other officers waited nearby. One elderly man in civilian clothes talked urgently with the supervisor.

Larson glanced upward. Men hung out most of the fifth floor windows, hurriedly trying to assemble a net. Several stories above them, a lone figure clung to the bricks with one hand. He used the other to shield his eyes from the sun as he scanned the crowd.

"Jump!" someone yelled nearby, his voice snapping clear over the hubbub. "Jump!"

Larson was seized by a sudden urge to rip out the stranger's lungs without benefit of anesthesia. Instead, he rammed through the crowd with a violence and determination that many cursed but no one challenged.

As Larson reached the edge of the cordoned boundary, Taziar Medakan's familiar voice wafted from beneath a blast of radio static. A louder voice followed in a Brooklyn accent so thick it sounded like a parody. "Did the translator get that, Captain?"

The supervisor glanced at the aging civilian, who

wrung his manicured hands. "It's gibberish. The accent's German, but the words don't mean a damned thing."

"Gibberish my ass!" Larson shouted. "I heard him clear as day."

The translator and the supervisor whirled. The elderly man flushed. The policeman looked skeptical and frustrated, but hopeful.

"Listen, young man." The translator jabbed a finger at Larson. "I speak six languages. . . ."

Larson ignored the translator, locking an urgent, sincere expression on his face and addressing the policeman directly. "The jumper said 'I'm sorry . . .'" He left out the expletive. "'. . . but I don't speak your language.'"

The translator snorted.

The supervisor shifted from foot to foot. A tense, crowd-drawing situation always dragged out the crazies, and he had to suspect Larson was fabricating. Yet the police officer seemed near his wits' end. "What language is he speaking?"

Larson opened his mouth, instantly realizing archaic German would not work for an answer. Inadvertently, he hesitated just long enough to put his integrity into question. "He's speaking perfect Perkanian."

"Perkanian?" The translator threw up his hands. "What kind of nonsense. . . ? There's no place called . . ."

"Perkania." Larson continued to hold the policeman's gaze, trying to sound confident and matter-of-fact. "It's a tiny country near Estonia." The lie came easily.

Another policeman trotted to the supervisor's side. "Captain, I've got Bellevue on the line."

The captain waved his subordinate silent, but the translator seized the moment. "Captain, this man is wasting your time. Anyone could make up what the jumper might have said. And there's no country called Perkania."

Larson could no longer control his temper. "Look,"

he snapped. "If you never learned your geography, that's your own fucking problem. There's a man up there who might slip and fall twelve stories if we don't get him down. If you can't talk him in, then move your fat butt aside and let someone do it who can." Larson softened his tone, his focus returning to the captain. "May I try, sir?" He extended a hand for the radio.

Taziar's voice crackled through the static again. "I'm looking for an elf named Allerum, or rather a man named Allerum."

Oh, my God. Realization smacked Larson. *He climbed the freaking building hoping to pick me out of seven and a half million people.* Larson choked back a laugh, turning it into a feigned sneeze. In tenth century Germany, the strategy made sense. *From the roof of the tallest building in Cullinsberg, Shadow could probably view his city end to end.*

Taziar hesitated in frustration, then finished in English so heavily accented, Larson felt certain he alone recognized the words. "Team player. Buddy Allerum. Stupid son of a bitch."

Larson thumbed the button. "Shadow," he said in the tongue of Cullinsberg's barony. "It's me. Allerum."

"Mardain's mercy." Taziar swung around so suddenly, the crowd loosed a collective gasp. "How come I can hear you, but I can't see you? Where are you?"

"I'm on the ground. I'll explain later."

"I'm coming down."

"No, wait. Stay there. Whatever you do, don't move."

The supervisor made a gesture of impatience. "What's he saying?"

Larson addressed Taziar first. "Hang on, buddy." He turned to the policeman, suddenly recognizing the unintentional pun of his own words. He returned to English, knowing he could not relay the actual conversation without cornering himself into an unbelievable story. *I've got to get Shadow down and out of here without committing either of us to the loony bin.* "He said his name is Taz, and he has some demands. First, he wants me up there to talk to him directly. Through the window."

The supervisor frowned. "Are you willing to do that?"

"Yes. Of course. A man's life is at stake." Larson handed back the radio, then ducked beneath the barricade.

The translator waved his hands wildly. "I can't believe you're wasting time with this imposter."

The Brooklyn accent came over the radio again. "Captain?"

"Hang on Dixson," the patrol supervisor said. He looked at Larson. "What's your name, kid?"

"Al," Larson started. Then, recognizing the danger of his mother hearing his name on television or radio news, he caught himself. "Smith. Al Smith." *Oh, good going, Larson. Why didn't you just say John Doe?* He changed the subject immediately. "And if it'll make him feel better . . ." He jerked a thumb at the translator. ". . . I can prove I'm really talking with this climber." He reached for the speaker again.

The captain passed the radio.

Larson thumbed it on. "Dixson?"

"Yeah."

"I'm going to tell your jumper to nod twice. Tell us when he does."

"All right."

Larson switched to archaic, dialectal German. "Shadow, listen. You can't come down because the place is crawling with . . ." The word "police" had no translation, so Larson used the closest one he could find. ". . . city guardsmen. Climbing buildings is illegal here. They'll arrest you if you come down. Don't do anything elusive, or I'll never find you again. Just hold tight, and I'll be up to get you." *Somehow.* "Now, don't ask any questions. Just nod your head two times."

"He's nodding," Dixson confirmed. "Twice."

The translator fell silent, utterly speechless.

"Come on." The captain placed an arm around Larson's shoulders and steered him across the concrete. "You got any experience talking down jumpers?"

None whatsoever, but I won't need any. Larson thought it better to lie. "Used to work a suicide hot line in high school."

The patrol supervisor glanced upward, past Taziar's clinging form, and silently mouthed, "Praise the Lord."

A trio of uniformed policemen herded a dozen gawking office personnel out the front door; they filed through the cordoned area and into the crowd. While the supervisor waited for them to pass, Larson took a closer look at his surroundings. The ropes, barricades, and emergency vehicles formed a semicircle extending from the front of the building, directly beneath Taziar. The danger area included a single street around which mounted police diverted traffic. The back exit and at least one side door remained clear for shoppers to enter and leave Sears and Roebuck.

The patrol supervisor waved at a group of uniformed officers. "McCloskey. Johnston."

A husky, middle-aged redhead and a willowy brunet disengaged from the others and obediently trotted over.

The captain took the two aside, talking in hushed tones.

Unable to hear the conversation, Larson continued to study the area. Cops and emergency personnel scurried in efficient patterns, exchanging-messages and controlling the crowd with masterful cooperation. Taziar clung at the level of the tenth floor, his attention now turned toward the window. Apparently, he was staring at the policeman called Dixson.

"Mr. Smith." The redhead touched Larson's arm. His tone made it clear he had tried to get Larson's attention at least once before.

Larson glanced up into a wide face with friendly, blue eyes.

"Mr. Smith, we're going to accompany you upstairs

to talk to the jumper and to help you decide what to say." The redhead smiled, gesturing Larson through the door ahead of him. "Don't worry. You're not alone."

That's what worries me. Larson smiled nervously.

The policemen near the door moved aside to let Larson and his escort through it.

"Just call me Al." Larson entered the building and waited for the officers to take the lead. His thoughts were spinning, and he saw no reason to further complicate the matter by needing to learn a new name. *I had enough trouble remembering to answer to Allerum. And that starts with Al.*

The door opened onto a squat entryway. Ahead, another set of steel-framed, glass doors led into the main store. To the left, a pair of elevators graced the wall. Directly opposite loomed a dark, metal door with a "1" stenciled on it in white paint.

Larson followed the policemen through the lobby to the elevator bank.

The redhead framed a wipe-lipped smile. "John McCloskey," he said. "The quiet guy is Phil Johnston."

"Ha ha." Johnston punched the "up" elevator button. Resting a hand against the frame of the leftmost elevator, he turned to face Larson and McCloskey.

Larson watched the milling shoppers in Sears and Roebuck.

"What language did you say this jumper was speaking?" Johnston asked.

Larson drew a blank. The invented country near Estonia seemed to have disappeared from his mind as quickly as it had come. "What language is he speaking?" He stalled. "Um, he's speaking, um. . . ."

The door ground open, revealing a drab, two-toned car and a row of black push buttons. Johnston stepped inside, trailed by Larson and McCloskey. The door rattled shut.

The seconds of reprieve gave Larson the time he

needed to untangle his lies. "Perkanian." *That's it.* "He's speaking Perkanian."

Johnston pressed "10." "Never heard of it."

"Small country." Larson shrugged.

McCloskey kept his chin tilted upward, watching the floor numbers light on the overhead monitor. "Not to be a wise guy or nothing, Al. But Perkanian doesn't strike me as the type of language they teach in high school."

Larson sighed, trying to concentrate on his next move and bothered by the need to make petty conversation. "My grandparents came from Perkania." *Or Queens. One of the two.* "They used to talk Perkanian with my old man when they didn't want me to understand what they were talking about. Things like sex and Christmas presents. Stuff like that. I've got a thing for picking up languages." The ad-lib seemed plausible, and Larson impressed himself with his own quick alibi. Then another thought made him frown. *Great. I'm becoming a good liar. Something to be proud of.*

"Yeah?" McCloskey glanced away from the advancing numbers to look at Larson. "I had enough trouble just getting past 'Oy Maddamoysal.' " His Bronx accent mangled the French.

It took Larson a moment to decipher. "I think you mean 'Oui, Mademoiselle.' " Larson developed a sudden appreciation for freshman French. "I've got some advice for you, McCloskey. If you ever go to France, don't go alone."

The officers chuckled.

Larson stared at his feet, aware he had to get Taziar down without turning him over to the police, his head empty of ideas. It was too late for truth. Even if he could have convinced the police about a Chaos-crazed sorceress and a thief from ancient Germany, he would first have to admit to creating Perkania and using an alias. *Knowing I lied once, why would they believe me? At best, they'd haul us both into the station. Or Bellevue. And every second Silme has to accustom herself to the city, locate us and plot, the more dangerous she becomes.* Larson shook his head, panicky about the only solution that sprang to mind. *We've got to escape cleanly and quickly. Which means I have to ditch the escort.*

The elevator pinged, slowing before it ground to a halt. Still uncertain, but aware he had to make a fast decision, Larson ushered the policemen ahead of him.

They stepped into the hallway.

Larson followed, taking an instant to get his bearings. Across from the elevators, the stairwell was marked with a painted "10." The hallway led off to the left and right, broken only by doors, a water fountain, and the occasional recessed fire extinguishers. From his memory of Taziar's position, Larson guessed Dixson and his team were stationed down the left hallway and inside one of the front offices.

As if to confirm Larson's guess, McCloskey and Johnston turned left.

Here goes nothing. Calling on his boxing and martial arts training, Larson slammed the side of his hand into the back of McCloskey's neck.

The redhead toppled without a sound.

Johnston whirled. "What the. . . ?"

Larson plunged a fist into Johnston's face.

The cop crumpled, crashing awkwardly to the corridor.

Shit. Larson nursed his knuckles, cursing himself, and hating what urgency had forced him to do. Whirling, he ran to the stairwell, aware his attack would only buy him a few minutes. Shoving through the door, he took the concrete steps two at a time. *I punched out a pair of cops. If Nam and Gaelinar taught me nothing else, they made me one hell of a dirty fighter. I can't believe I sucker-punched a cop.* Oddly, his attack against New York City's finest raised more doubt and guilt than shooting soldiers in the jungle or slaughtering guardsmen in Cullinsberg's streets. There was something sacred, something magically innocent about the world of his childhood, a memory-protected sanctuary from the hard, cold realities thrust at him since the day his plane had touched down in Vietnam. Still, for all its familiarity, New York City had changed. The events that had once composed his life faded to trivia beneath the atrocities of war and the threat of a Dragonrank mage. Even with live mythology, dragons and wizards, the warped ancient Europe he'd just come from seemed less of a fantasy world than the New York City he used to know.

At the next landing, Larson burst through the door. He raced down the left hallway, nearly trampling a young secretary juggling three styrofoam cups. She gasped, dodging so abruptly she sent coffee sloshing over herself and Larson.

Without wasting time on apologies, Larson sprinted past. Finding an office he believed was directly above Taziar, he shoved through the door without knocking. He found himself facing a wide, wooden desk with a matching leather chair. There was no one in the room. *Thank God.* Larson careened around the desk to the window beyond it. He slammed his hands against the frame. The window jolted ajar, one pane shattering beneath the blow. Larson crammed his head through the opening just in time to see glass rain down on Taziar. *Shit. Still don't know my own strength.* Larson ducked back inside hating the seconds lost but knowing the sprinkle of glass on pavement would draw every eye. He counted to himself, wasting a full twenty seconds for the shards to land and the crowd to glance up, see no one, and refocus on Taziar.

Larson eased the window farther open, poked his face through it, and glanced downward. He caught a solid glimpse of Taziar's black mop of hair and small, callused hands. The Climber gripped the bricks with a lax ease. "Shadow," Larson whispered.

Taziar did not move.

Larson raised his voice slightly. "Shadow."

Taziar looked up, staring blankly.

Expecting a welcoming grin and not receiving so much as a glimmer of recognition from his friend, Larson hesitated. Then he remembered how different he looked from the tall, skinny elf Taziar Medakan had come to know. "It's Allerum." He gestured Taziar to him.

The Shadow Climber remained still, clearly doubtful.

Those cops will be awake and alerting everyone any moment. Larson's patience evaporated. "Taz, you stupid little bastard! Get the hell up here!"

Apparently, the words and voice were enough identification for Taziar. He scrambled to the ledge.

Larson retreated, leaving Taziar space to clamber inside.

Taziar leapt lightly to the floor, studying this friend in the body of a stranger. "Allerum, you've changed."

"Hurry!" Larson whirled, charging for the door. His hip struck a corner of the desk, jarring pain through his leg and knocking the desk askew. Papers scattered to the floor, spiraling in the breeze from the window. "We've got to get out of here, and we can't get grabbed."

"Relax." Taziar caught up to Larson at the door. "I do this for a living, remember?"

Larson grabbed Taziar by the arms. "No, listen. You don't understand. I don't do this climb, dodge, and leap around buildings thing. If we get separated, we'll never find each other again."

"It's not a problem."

Larson blinked, stunned. "There's seven and a half million people in New York. Finding one would be like finding a needle in a haystack. A *big* haystack."

"I found you this time, didn't I?"

Larson groaned, unwilling to go into a long explanation now. "Luck. If we get separated, I'll meet you. . . ." He trailed off, realizing he could never explain city blocks and taxicabs in a reasonable amount of time. "Never mind. Just stay with me." Releasing Taziar, he pulled open the door, emerging into an empty hallway. Contradicting his last command, he raised a hand to still Taziar. "Wait right here. I need to check something." Larson crept down the hallway to the right, retracing his earlier route.

Seconds ticked by in silence while Larson's mind raced, trying to relate the corridors to his memory of the building's outside.

Suddenly, pounding footsteps echoed from the stairwell. The elevator whirred. Its display clicked from "3" to "4."

Here they come. Larson spun back toward Taziar. Even as he moved, an ear-piercing hiss split the air, followed by a crash that shook the hallway.

Larson's heart leapt. He dove for cover, rolling flat against the wall.

A fire extinguisher rocked hollowly on the floor. A pool of white powder settled around Taziar's feet. Dust swam crazily through air.

The stairwell door clicked.

"What are you doing? What the hell are you doing?" Larson ran. Grabbing Taziar as he passed, he bolted up the corridor, skidding around a corner into a perpendicular hallway.

"This way!" someone shouted. Footfalls thudded through the hall they had just left.

"What . . . were you doing?" Larson whispered as he ran.

"Just looking for something to help us get away." Taziar kept pace, his arm mashed in Larson's desperate grasp.

"That wasn't it. That only works on fires." Larson careened around the next corner, coming suddenly upon a second bank of elevators. He hammered at the down button. The numbers changed with maddening slowness. The footsteps drew closer.

Larson slammed the button repeatedly with his fist. "You better know this. Silme's trying to kill me."

Taziar studied the chemical residue on his hand. "I know. I saw her league with Bolverkr."

"Bolverkr? Oh, shit! He's here, too?" Suddenly, running from the cops seemed a miniscule annoyance.

The pursuit grew louder. Larson could pick out at least six separate sets of footsteps. *Damn it! That elevator's going to get here just in time for them to use it. Nice work, Larson.* "Come on." He charged for the stairwell, turning the knob with one hand while his shoulder struck the door at a dead run.

The panel swung open, revealing concrete steps. Larson shoved Taziar, sending the Climber hurtling down the stairs, the little man's agility all that saved him from a fatal fall. Not bothering to silence the door, Larson plunged after his companion. "Move! Move! Move!"

Taziar and Larson whipped headlong down several flights. On the seventh floor landing, Larson ripped open the metal door. "Follow me." Surging through, he fled back in the direction they had come, now four floors lower.

As they whipped around the corner, Larson and Taziar discovered a cluster of four milling, chatting office personnel in the center of the corridor.

Larson did not slow.

The group scattered to the walls. Larson raced through, Taziar swerving between the people behind him. "Excuse me," he said in heavily accented English.

Without looking back, Larson tore around the next corner. Finding the stairwell across from the elevators that he and his police escort had used, he again hit the door, running and turning the knob simultaneously. Taziar balked, apparently not wanting to get thrown down the steps again. But this time, Larson did not hesitate. He galloped down the concrete steps, hearing no sound beneath the slap of his own sneakers, yet certain Taziar had followed.

As Larson rounded the third floor landing, he heard the click of a door opening below. *Uh-oh!* Leaping the last half flight to the landing, he ripped open the door and exited onto the second floor. Finding the corridor empty, he waited for Taziar to dart in, then took the time to ease the door closed quietly. *Letting them know our location after all that maneuvering would be stupid.*

Taziar waited, breathing softly but deeply.

Larson realized he was panting and tried to control

each breath. He made a throwing motion to indicate the need to travel up the corridor and back around the first corner. There, he knew from his memory of Sears and Roebuck, they would find a set of escalators. *Hopefully unguarded.* Larson shook his head, aware New York City's police force would mobilize swiftly. *But it's only been a few minutes since I punched the cops. Most of what's out there is rescue forces and crowd controllers. They had no reason to expect violence, especially from a translator.* Larson headed for the corner at a brisk walk.

"What now?" Taziar said in the barony's tongue, pawing his hair from his eyes and pulling his cloak more securely over his mangled climbing outfit.

Larson answered in the same language. "We're going to join the crowd in the shop. Try to blend in as best as you can, but be ready to turn and leave if the area's crawling with . . . city guardsmen. Follow my lead."

Braced for action, Larson started around the corner. The area opened into a central lobby with soda and candy machines. Several people lounged on chairs arranged in clusters, smoking, talking, and eating. They paid no heed as Taziar and Larson walked past and onto the down escalator.

Taziar stared at his feet, hands well away from the conveyor belt railings.

"It's an escalator," Larson explained, gaze playing over the people in the store below, trying to pick out police officers. "Careful when we get to the bottom. The steps sort of disappear, and you have to watch your balance."

Taziar cast his glance to the bottom of the flight. "Are we safe now?"

"I wish." Larson searched his memory for the location of the men's rest room. *I need a secure place to think.* "We've got to get out of the building, at least. Even then, they'll hunt us all over the city."

"Mardain," Taziar muttered a curt blasphemy. "I never would have guessed climbing was that serious an offense."

Larson flushed, anticipating the end of the escalator ride, still seeing no policemen in the store. "Climbing's not that serious. Just a city ordinance thing. A misdemeanor probably." He stepped down, turning to help Taziar do the same.

But the Climber took the sudden flattening of the mechanical steps in stride.

"Unfortunately, assault and battery is a felony. It's me they'll mostly be chasing." Through the doorway to the main entryway, Larson could see milling policemen. He slipped through the aisles in the opposite direction. "All right, we have to sneak out of here without being seen. Or at least without being recognized."

Taziar gawked at the rows and shelves of merchandise.

"Most of them won't know you." Larson thought aloud. "Some of them had binoculars. But most of those people were probably the fire rescue crew, not cops."

Taziar shrugged. "I'm not understanding you."

Larson switched to the barony's tongue. "I'm just saying you were too high for many of the city guards to get a good look at you. You might be able to walk out right under their noses." Larson studied Taziar doubtfully. "If you weren't wearing that burned, shredded, crudely-sewn, centuries out of date, black outfit that practically has 'weirdo' stitched in neon."

Taziar fell easily into Larson's sarcastic rhythm. "Oh, well. Excuse me for not dressing for the occasion. What is the proper attire for being attacked by a dragon, hit by an exploding bone, tortured, and flung through time?"

Larson continued toward the rest room.

Taziar asked the obvious. "Why don't we just change clothes?"

"Don't be ridiculous." Larson discarded the idea, threading through the sporting goods section. "I'm a foot taller than you and twice your weight. We couldn't switch."

"Switch? Who said anything about switch?" Taziar

stared at the equipment, gaze sweeping up to the fluorescent lighting. "Now, I admit I'm a bit confused about your customs, but I do know what to do in a shop. I saw some racks back there that looked like clothes. Why not buy some?"

Larson sighed. "I've got this odd, moral thing about limiting myself to one felony a day. I'm not stealing, and the four dollars in my pocket would barely buy a decent T-shirt."

"I have money."

"You don't understand. The gold and silver you're carrying would probably bring decent money from a coin collector. Here in Sears, they're worse than useless. They'd draw attention."

"Will this?" Taziar displayed a fat roll of bills that stopped Larson in his tracks.

"Where did you get that?"

"I—" Taziar started.

Larson pocketed the money and waved Taziar quiet. "Don't tell me. I'm sure I don't want to know." He led the smaller man around the end of the row and down a short corridor to the men's room. They pushed inside.

Six porcelain urinals lined the walls, and three stalls filled the area beyond them. Sinks and a paper towel dispenser jutted from the opposite wall. A man used the farthest urinal.

Taziar watched with unabashed wonder.

The stranger looked over casually, then glared at the little Climber.

Larson smacked Taziar's shoulder with the back of his hand. "Don't stare. It's impolite." He motioned to a corner.

Taziar wandered to the indicated location. "I'm sorry. I just never saw a man piss in a fountain before."

Larson shook his head in frustration. "I'll explain later. For right now, you stay in one of those with the door closed." He inclined his head toward a stall. "I'll be back. *Please* don't start any trouble."

The New Yorker zipped his pants, throwing Larson and Taziar a hostile glance before leaving.

Probably thinks we're gay. Too harried to see the humor in the situation, Larson headed back into the store without bothering to see if Taziar had obeyed.

CHAPTER 12:

Chaos Hunted

Behold! human beings living in an underground den. . . . Like ourselves . . . they see only their own shadows, or the shadows of one another, which the fire throws on the opposite wall of the cave.

—Plato
The Republic

The taxicab crawled through rush hour traffic, cutting through cracks and openings so tiny that Al Larson felt like a thread poked repeatedly and recklessly through the eye of a needle. Timmy sat at Larson's right. To his left, Taziar Medakan plucked at his own blue jeans, toying with the first zipper he had ever seen. He also wore a black and gray shirt and a Dodger's cap pulled low over his eyes. Wisps of sable hair poked from beneath the brim, making him look as much like a child as Timmy.

Taziar's disguise, in addition to timing and luck, had gotten them past the police, but Larson knew they had not seen the last of New York's finest. *They'll forgive Shadow. Climbing a building, though stupid, seems harmless. But I laid out two cops, and cops protect their own.* Larson accepted the thought philosophically, without need for judgment. In Vietnam, if someone, even another American, had assaulted his companions, he also would have sought revenge. And the police had the law on their side as well. *After I tried to convince Taziar that cops are friends, unlike Cullinsberg's cruel, thrill-seeking murderers on the take, he may get a stunning example of police brutality.*

Timmy leaned across Larson, studying Taziar with shameless forthrightness. "This is Robin Hood?" He sounded skeptical.

Larson pushed his thoughts aside. "His name's Taz, Timmy."

Taziar looked up, leaving the zipper in its closed position. At the least, he seemed to have guessed its use and the proper location for social dignity. "How do you say 'Shadow' in your language?"

Larson pronounced the word for Taziar. It sounded vaguely similar to its ancient German equivalent.

Taziar nodded. "Just wanted to make sure it didn't come out like 'cow dung' or 'idiot' or some swear word. Tell your brother he can call me . . ." He used his best English. ". . . Shadow."

Larson relayed the message.

"This is the Grand Concourse," the cabby said.

Larson located the subway sign and its corresponding concrete steps dragging downward into darkness. "Pull over if you can."

The driver complied, double parking against a row of cars. Behind him, a horn blared, followed by a linear symphony of honks that stretched down the roadway.

Ignoring the noise, Larson ushered his companions onto the sidewalk. Once out of the taxi, he leaned against the driver's window, drew a twenty from his pocket and handed it to the cabby.

The cabby accepted it, his brow furrowed. The previous ten more than covered the fare.

"You keep that. Forget where you took us, and I'll give you another." Larson dangled a twenty between his thumb and first finger.

The man smiled, revealing tobacco-stained teeth. "Make it two, and I never saw any of you in my life."

Larson passed a pair of twenties to the grinning cabby, then joined his companions. "Come on."

Taziar and Timmy spoke simultaneously, their languages markedly different, but their words nearly identical. "Where are we going?"

The taxicab pulled back out into traffic. A single horn wailed, then the noise level died to the normal rush hour hubbub.

Taziar relaxed visibly.

"Subway," Larson said to Timmy. He switched to the barony tongue. "We need a safe place to talk, someplace Silme and Bolverkr won't be able to recognize in a location spell. Down those steps we'll find row after row of connected cars that all look essentially the same. They're moving, too, so by the time the sorcerers could locate us and transport, we'd be elsewhere." He continued toward the steps as he talked. "It's just a temporary solution. We can hardly live on the subway, but it should give us a safe place to exchange information and plan strategy."

Taziar nodded, his gaze flicking among automobiles, buildings, and the hordes of people.

Timmy tugged at his brother's shirt. "It took all those funny words just to say 'subway' to him?"

"Huh?" Larson turned to Timmy, realizing his explanation to Taziar had taken far longer than his answer to Timmy. "They don't have subways where Shadow comes from." *Or three quarters of the things you use every day.* Larson trotted down the steps. "I had to explain it to him."

At the bottom of the flight, Larson pulled out two singles.

Timmy continued to watch Taziar. "When's he going to do something like Robin Hood?"

"Oh, for God's sake."

Apparently recognizing annoyance in Larson's tone, if not his words, Taziar questioned. "What's the matter now?"

"I made the mistake of telling Timmy you're quick and agile. He keeps watching for you to do something . . ." He tried to put the swashbuckler image into words.

". . . quick and agile?" Taziar supplied.

"Right." Larson waved Taziar and Timmy aside.

"Wait here and don't move. I need to get us through the turnstile." He added swiftly, "Legally."

Larson walked to the back of the fast moving line. Purchasing three tokens, he returned to find Taziar juggling eight gold barony ducats to Timmy's evident amusement. A small crowd had gathered.

Larson sprang to Taziar's side, snatching a coin out of the air. "What the hell are you doing?"

Taziar caught the other ducats easily, amidst a spattering of applause. "Being quick and agile. For Timmy."

"Well, cut it out." Larson separated bills in his pocket. "The last thing we need now is attention. And don't be flashing money around." Unobtrusively, he handed Taziar a generous third of the currency. "Speaking of which, in case we get separated, you should have some of this."

The cash disappeared in Taziar's grip.

Larson pressed bills into Timmy's hand. "Here. Put this in your pocket and keep it there. It should get you anywhere in case of emergency. Hopefully, you won't need it, but it's not worth taking chances." Without awaiting a reply, he headed for the turnstile. Placing a token in the slot, he passed through, turned and dropped in tokens for Timmy and Taziar. They joined the milling crowd on the platform.

In the pit, subway rails gleamed like stiff, silver snakes. A wall separated the southbound tracks from the northbound side. Businesspeople slouched near where they knew the cars would stop. Others sat on benches evenly spaced against the outer wall that separated the platform from the token booth and stairs. A concession stand interrupted the array of seats.

Larson addressed his brother. "We may be riding all night or longer. I'm going to get some survival gear. If the train comes, don't get on until I'm back. Then, help Shadow. Remember, he's never seen a subway before."

"Okay." Timmy's face twisted in concentration as he prepared for his job with appropriate seriousness.

Trotting to the booth, Larson purchased several

comic books, two dozen packages of crackers and candy and three cups of soda. As he turned, a line of subway cars pulled to the platform, brakes squealing. The familiar, metallic oil odor blasted through the air.

People funneled onto already packed cars, grabbing handholds on the poles edging each rattan seat. Larson grabbed his change and raced on board. Taziar followed hesitantly, Timmy urging him onward.

The doors hissed closed.

"Hang on tight," Larson warned. Hands full, he braced himself by looping a foot around a chair leg.

The car accelerated with a halting spasm. Caught by surprise, Taziar jolted into a businessman in front of him, saved from a fall only by his natural grace.

The stranger turned to glare. Then, apparently mistaking Taziar for a child, he smiled indulgently instead.

"Excuse me, sir," Taziar managed in passable English.

The car clacked and rattled over the tracks. As its movement stabilized, Larson passed the sodas to Timmy and Taziar.

Taziar released the pole, staring into his drink doubtfully.

"Sweet beer," Larson explained. "With a lot more fizz and none of the kick. Drink slowly until you get used to it. And, for God's sake, don't spill it on anyone." The subway slowed gradually. "Hang on. There's going to be another hard shock. In fact, we'll be starting and stopping over and over again."

Taziar curled the fingers of his free hand around the pole, this time taking the jerky movements in stride.

The doors wrenched open, and people filed off or on.

"What are you guys talking about?" Timmy asked.

The car started again with another lurch, sloshing cola down the front of Taziar's shirt.

"Timmy," Larson shouted over the rumble of conversations and the squeal of metal wheels against track. "Shadow and I need to talk for a while. Here." He handed over the comic books. "Whenever a seat frees up, take it and read." He turned back to Taziar. "Now, tell me how you got here." He sipped at his drink.

Over the next half hour, Taziar described the sequence of events from the time he had awakened until Silme's decision to slay the baby.

Larson listened with rapt attention and empathy. The deaths of Astryd and the baby tore at his heart, a single, paired grief he did not try to separate. "I'm sorry, Taz. I'm so sorry." The words seemed inadequate. The tears that sprang to his eyes added the sincerity his words could not. He crushed the paper cup in frustration, the only gesture he dared in the crowded car.

Taziar said nothing. He looked away.

Dozens of stops came and went while both men regained their composure. The silence that hung between them seemed so much more meaningful that it overpowered the continuous, surflike roar of half-heard conversations. People loaded and unloaded, the ratio of standing to sitting passengers becoming more equal by tedious increments.

Gradually, Larson shoved aside grief, aware it could wait. For now, plotting had to take precedence. "Did you get any feel for Bolverkr's and Silme's plans."

"Just that they wanted to slaughter us." Taziar glanced up, eyes bloodshot and shadowed by the brim of his cap. The harsh, German accent sounded ridiculous issuing from this boyish figure.

Larson snickered, barely catching himself before hysterical laughter overtook him.

"Oh, and the usual posturing men do when they want to impress a woman. Bolverkr promised Silme the world."

Larson frowned, staring at the scratched, green walls of the car. "Unfortunately, Bolverkr's powerful enough that he might be able to give it to her."

"I'm not so sure."

The subway ground to another halt. Larson watched people file through the single sliding door to the platform. This time, only three people replaced the exiting crowd. "What do you mean? Vidarr said Bolverkr's even more powerful than the gods."

"In our world, true." Taziar apparently meant "our" to refer to Bolverkr, Silme, and himself. "But when Bolverkr threw that spell, he said something about the Chaos he used never coming back."

The doors closed, and the train continued. Larson stared at Taziar. "What does that mean?"

"I'm not sure." Taziar no longer needed to hold the pole. He finished the last sip of soda and clung to the paper cup as if it was the finest mug. "From what I saw, I'd guess the rules are different here. The Chaos they threw into their spells dispersed, though not without consequence. I felt its evil wash through me. Then it passed over a group of passersby, sending them into a wild argument."

Larson made a vague noise of consideration.

"It seems to me as if every spell drains Chaos permanently, releasing it into the surroundings."

"Chaos is life energy," Larson recalled aloud.

"Right."

"So every spell Bolverkr throws not only makes him weaker magically but physically. Each loss of Chaos takes him one step closer to death."

"Presumably."

A horrible idea followed naturally. "And Silme, too."

"Presumably," Taziar repeated with less vigor. He went quiet a moment, then raised a loophole. "Assuming Chaos and life force are linked in your world the same as in mine." He threw the question back to Larson. "Are they?"

Larson snorted. "How would I know? Sorcerers don't exist here as far as I know. At least, they didn't before Bolverkr and Silme."

At the next stop, Timmy managed to find a seat on the far side of a row, near a window that overlooked the central wall between tracks.

Taziar worked with the available information. "We can't fight Bolverkr at his current power. That's clear enough. The best strategy seems obvious to me. The more spells he casts and the stronger those spells are, the more equal the fight becomes. If we can survive his magic long enough, he'll eventually weaken enough for us to best him.''

Larson said nothing, his thoughts still on Silme.

''At least we know he won't waste his spells. As for Silme, Bolverkr must have found a way to channel Chaos to her. Immediately after she cast that spell and lost some Chaos, there was a moment before pain set in when her loyalties seemed to shift back to me, as if the Chaos lost some of its influence over her.''

Hope thrilled through Larson. ''You mean if we can drain enough Chaos from Silme . . .'' He trailed off, letting Taziar finish the sentence.

Taziar obliged. ''. . . we may get her back. Yes. I think it's possible. That is, so long as Bolverkr doesn't keep replacing the Chaos she loses.''

For the first time in weeks, Larson's spirits lifted. The odds had gone from hopeless to vaguely possible, and, for now, that seemed more than enough.

Afternoon passed to evening on New York's Independent Line. As rush hour dispersed to quieter times, Larson, Taziar, and Timmy found seats together. Timmy slept, his sandy head propped against the window. Beside him, Taziar munched at a peanut butter cracker, occasionally adding inspiration to the clouded phantom plans taking shape in Larson's mind. The general strategy seemed obvious, guerrilla attacks that drained Bolverkr's Chaos followed by sudden retreats. However, the practical mechanics of such a scheme eluded Larson. And Taziar's ignorance of the city made his input little more than useless.

Larson glanced around the subway car, at the double row of parallel seats and the aisle between them. A stout, dark-haired man sat in the last seat of the opposite row beside a curvaceous, but moon-faced, bleached blonde in a fur coat. She wore a large diamond on her left hand. In front of the couple, three teenagers discussed rock and roll, dressed in tie-dyed T-shirts and bell-bottom jeans with fringe. Six businessmen in suits reposed in various locations around the car. Two women in gray skirts and suit coats sat, chatting softly together.

The subway ground to another stop, the halt and start up having grown so familiar in the last few hours that Larson no longer noticed it. But, this time, the three men who boarded drew his attention. They wore matching black T-shirts displaying rearing cobras and tucked into grimy jeans. One, tanned and blond, wore a leather jacket that fell to his knees, and Larson could tell the youth carried something beneath its folds. The jacketed stranger walked to the door between their car and the one ahead of it, steadying himself against the door frame. The largest of the three braced himself between the seat directly in front of Larson and its neighbor. He was a dark-haired, scar-faced man a few years older than Larson and obviously the leader of the trio. The last, a redhead, took a position at the back of the car.

The door slid shut. The subway lurched.

As if it were a signal, the blond at the front whipped a sawed-off shotgun from beneath his coat. Scarface raised a .45 Colt army sidearm, and the redhead drew a .38 special. "Don't scream," the leader said. "Do what I say, and no one gets hurt." All three moved as lightly as cats, covering every person in the car. They had the routine down well.

Larson stiffened.

The leader grabbed one of the teenagers by a tie-dyed sleeve and shoved a plastic drawstring bag into the youth's quivering hand. "Go around the car. I want wallets and jewelry. I don't want trouble."

The car went deathly still. Larson could hear his heart hammering, and the almost inaudible sound of the shotgun's safety clicking off. *No big deal. It's just money. One blast from that 12 gauge will blow us all to kingdom come.* He bit his lip, recalling how safe the subways had always seemed before Vietnam, wondering if this could be part of the spreading effects from Bolverkr's and Silme's Chaos.

The teenager obeyed, opening the bag for a businessman on Larson's side of the car. The people in the seats in front of Larson, Taziar, and Timmy gave up their possessions without hesitation, keeping their heads low and their movements nonthreatening.

Concerned for Taziar's ignorance and his tendency to embrace challenges and fight injustice, Larson whispered. "Give them your money. Don't start any trouble."

"Shut up!" The leader swung around, the .45 aimed at Larson's head. "Say another word and I'll blow you away!"

Larson went silent, gaze locked on the man's hands.

The teen with the bag waited until the gun retreated before shuffling between the scar-faced hoodlum and Larson.

Larson dumped his money, watch, and wallet into the bag, relieved to see his friend and brother surrender their bills also. *It's not worth dying over.*

No longer the direct focus of the leader's attention, Larson took a surreptitious glance around the car. Several people seemed rattled, shivering or clinging with white knuckles to the seat backs. One of the businessmen kept a hand clenched across his mouth. The bleached blond sat still as a statue, but her fiancé's gaze kept rolling between the gunmen. His hands twitched, and his arms tensed and loosened.

Larson willed the man still. *Don't be a hero, you dumb ass. You'll get us all killed.*

Timmy curled like a fetus against the window. Taziar remained still, following Larson's lead.

The shotgun and .38 special remained leveled and steady. The bagman finished Larson's row and started toward the couple.

Larson mentally prepared himself for trouble, careful to give no outward sign of his tension. The man dropped his wallet into the bag, the natural action soothing Larson's raw-edged nerves. Then the man stopped.

The teen took a hesitant step forward.

"Watch and ring, too." The leader swung his .45 toward the hefty man.

With a twisted glare, the man removed and tossed

in his watch. "The ring doesn't come off." He indicated the diamond on his fiancée's hand.

Larson suppressed a groan.

"The ring, too!" Scarface said. "Now!"

The tension in the car increased visibly. Tears coursed down the face of one of the well-dressed women.

"Look," the man said. "It's too tight. It doesn't come off."

Don't do it, man. Don't do it. Larson tried to send a mental message.

The teen looked nervously between the guns.

The leader made a subtle gesture with his head, addressing the hippie with the bag. "Take the ring off her finger. I don't care if you have to take the fucking finger with it!"

The teen reached toward the woman, Outraged, the hefty man sprang to his feet.

The .45 blasted, its roar deafening, sending Larson's ears into aching ringing. The hefty man collapsed back into his seat, his pale eyes staring.

The bleached blonde gasped. Scream after scream shuddered from her throat.

"Shut up!" The gun swung toward her. "Shut the hell up!" The leader's hand tensed.

Larson sprang. He slammed one arm around the leader's throat, the other groping for the gun. Cartilage cracked beneath Larson's wrist. The gun fired, and the bullet went wild, punching a hole in the ceiling. Screams echoed through the car. Larson wrenched the .45 from the leader's hand.

The shotgun. Using the gasping leader as a shield, Larson whirled and fired. The bullet tore through the blond hoodlum's chest, driving him into the door frame. Larson spun again, his mind blandly registering that his prisoner was no longer struggling.

The redhead had a perfect bead on Larson. For an instant, he hesitated. Then, apparently realizing the leader Larson was using as a shield was already dead, the redhead pulled the trigger.

The subway car jolted to a sudden stop.

The redhead stumbled. His shot pinged through a metal pole, winging one of the businessmen, who shrieked. Larson returned fire as the car's momentum shifted backward. His slug blasted a hole in the hoodlum's head.

Terrified screams ripped from half a dozen throats. Other passengers dove for cover beneath the seats. The doors jogged open.

The noise drew Larson. Every combat instinct aroused, he swung the gun toward the sound, still clutching the leader's corpse.

A half dozen men in uniforms graced the platform, pistols drawn. "Put down the gun! Now!"

Larson hesitated less than a second. Before he could think to lower his weapon, a bullet tore through his upper left arm. Pain shocked through him. His legs seemed to give out, and he collapsed to the floor, his right hand clinging naturally to the wound, his vision a swirl of scarlet.

"Al!" Timmy's hysterical cry sounded thousands of miles away.

A louder voice filled Larson's ringing ears. "Roll over." Someone kicked him. "Roll over now!"

An alarm shrilled through the subway car. Footsteps pounded around Larson. Voices, high-pitched and frenzied, cut through Larson's fog, their words meaningless. He looked up to a gun clenched in two white fists the barrel pointed at his head. "Roll over!"

Guarding his injured shoulder, Larson scrambled until he lay facedown on the dirty, tile floor.

"Al! Al! Leave him alone! Leave my brother alone!" Timmy's shrieks emerged, recognizable over the confusion of words and noises.

"Put your right arm behind you," the commanding voice instructed.

Larson moved his hand to the small of his back. Immediately, a man's weight dropped onto his spine. A metal cuff slapped around his wrist. A sweaty hand seized his injured arm, jerking it behind him with an abruptness that stabbed agony through his wound. He loosed a sharp moan.

The cop snorted, snapping the second handcuff into place. "Yeah, I feel sorry for you, punk. Get up." He yanked Larson to his feet. "You're under arrest. You have the right to remain silent . . . ."

The policeman's words registered only as a familiar rhythm from every television cop show Larson had ever seen. His world buckled and spun. He caught a bleary, shock-glazed glance at the other passengers, huddled in a corner, ringed by Transit Authorities, and all talking at once. One policeman clutched Timmy, who clawed and kicked in the uniformed arms.

After a while, the subway sputtered and sped away. The four corpses lay heaped on the concrete. The handful of recently alighted passengers formed a gawking semicircle on the platform. Larson did not see Taziar among the others.

Despite multiple simultaneous conversations, Larson picked one of the softer ones from the clamor. ". . . found the shotgun and a .38. We searched the whole car. No sign of the gun he was holding. Finally just had to let the train go . . . ."

"Timmy," Larson gasped. "He's only eight. He thinks policemen are his friends . . . ."

"Shut up!" The policeman snarled in Larson's face. He broke off his reading of the rights. "You should have thought of that before you started killing people." His tone reverted to its gruff monotone. "You have the right to an attorney . . . ."

Larson went silent, catching another piece of the conversation on which he had been eavesdropping. ". . . Check the kid first. Sometimes these guys'll hand off their weapons to a child, thinking we won't think to search 'em. Then . . ." He broke off abruptly. "Hey!" He ran toward the tracks. "Hey, you! Stop!"

Every head whipped toward the tracks. Larson caught a glimpse of a pale form dashing through the pit. *Shadow!*

The conclusion to Larson's rights was obscured by a warning shout. "Halt! Police! Halt, or we'll shoot!"

Larson gasped.

A grumble emerged, barely audible beneath the wild

cacophony of shouts and suggestions. "Speak for yourself, Murph. I ain't shooting no little kid."—

"He doesn't speak English!" Larson screamed.

The policeman at Larson's side yanked at the cuffs, shooting pain through his injured arm. The agony went deep, the incessant, screaming grind of a toothache.

Larson finished despite the pain. "He's scared. Please, don't shoot him. Please. Please don't shoot." Fear for Taziar brought tears to Larson's eyes. He had only known the Shadow Climber a few months, yet the image of the thief's tiny body bleeding on the rails, crushed beneath the metal wheels like a crow-picked road kill made him grief-crazy in a way even his unborn baby's death had not.

"Hey," Someone shouted. "Don't touch that. . . ."

Third rail. Larson cringed as his mind finished the sentence for him. *It'll fry him. I have to warn him. In his language.* "Shadow, don't touch the steel—"

"Shut up!" The man who had handcuffed Larson lashed a hand across his face.

The blow staggered Larson. He fell to his knees, dizziness crushing his world to a gray blank. He tried to catch his balance, the natural movements seeming slowed and outside reality. He collapsed to the concrete, feeling no pain.

Timmy screamed.

"Shit," someone unidentifiable said. Gasps shuddered through the crowd.

A closer voice addressed the cop standing over Larson. "Easy on that guy, Gaets. That woman says he saved her life. Jumped the punk that shot her boyfriend."

Gaets grunted, the sound uninterpretable without the accompanying facial expression.

Larson rolled, fighting for understanding. Awareness returned in a rush, unconsciousness fading behind him in a crackle of pinpoints and sparks. "Timmy," he managed. "Timmy, don't fight. I'm all right. Do whatever they say."

A subway screeched to a halt on the opposite track.

Larson's mind kicked into overdrive. His glance toward the rail pit had revealed that this was one of the many stations without a wall separating the inbound and outbound trains. *That means Shadow might have run onto the other track! Right under the wheels of that subway.* "Shadow," he said hoarsely. "Is Shadow okay?"

"He got away," Timmy answered excitedly from across the platform. "He runned and leaped and climbed right up the wall. Just like Robin Hood."

Larson never remembered Robin Hood dodging through subway pits. Relief flooded him. *At least one thing went right.*

Gaets helped Larson to his feet, his grip still firm, but his manner gentler.

"Meat wagon's on the way. Think we should get this kid to a hospital, too?"

"Naw," Gaets replied. "It's a clean shot through the arm. We've already lost one possible accomplice. I say we get him down to the station, ASAP."

Gaets nudged Larson toward the stairway, the Transit Authority clearing a pathway through the spectators.

Several other policemen joined the group clustered around Larson.

"What kind of story you getting?" Gaets asked one of the newcomers.

"Most of them didn't see nothing. A few willing to come in and give a statement, though they each saw something different. The blonde lady seems to have the most coherent story, when she's not crying hysterically. The little boy says he's this guy's brother." He pointed at Larson. "At least two witnesses are saying this guy killed one of the gunmen with his bare hands."

"Shit," one said.

Docilely, Larson let himself be led away, adding nothing to the exchange. Knowing Taziar had escaped alive freed his mind to concentrate on other matters, and the policeman's description struck home. *I did kill someone with my bare hands.* He felt no remorse for the slaying. *The man was a murderer. If I hadn't taken him, he would have become a mass murderer, if he wasn't already.* But Gaelinar's lessons had penetrated deep. *I killed him accidentally, because I don't know my own body and my own strength well enough. I lost control. And, without control of myself, I have nothing.* A sudden thought shivered terror through him. *What if I hit those cops back at Sears harder than I intended, too? What if I'm a cop-killer?*

Larson's insides felt as if they had melted within him, and self-loathing hammered at the back of his mind. Torn by emotional pain, the physical ramifications seeped into his thoughts more slowly. His taste of brutality had, so far, been mild, a slap on the wrist compared to the broken skulls reported during protests and college campus demonstrations. *If I killed either of those cops, I'll never make it to trial.* And the most frightening thing of all was that Larson knew from his war experience that, if he was the policeman and someone else Al Larson, he would stand back and let his companions beat the cop-killer to death.

CHAPTER 13:

Chaos Justice

At the height of their madness
The night winds pause
Recollecting themselves;
But no lull in these wars.
—Herman Melville
The Armies of the Wilderness

Taziar Medakan huddled against the wall of a building just beyond the subway station, muddled by the flashing lights and the sudden blatters of sound, metallic voices surrounded by fizzles and crackles. Ignorance made a plan of action impossible, yet Larson's descriptions and his own scant experience gave him a few usable facts. *The guards caught Allerum and Timmy, presumably to torture them in some dungeon. This time, Allerum can't find me. He says the city's too big to search, and with those car vehicles, they could take him far away and anywhere. I've got to find Allerum again. And, this time, I can't let him out of my sight.*

Taziar sighed, ignoring the myriad aches of abrasions and bruises, hoping he had chosen the correct location from which to observe. His position in the building's shadow gave him a clear view of both inbound and outbound subway exits, and he hoped that would prove enough. Except for the trains, Taziar had seen no other ways to leave the station. *And, if the guards planned to use the underground vehicles, why did they make everybody leave the car?* Taziar sighed again, certain he was overlooking something. It seemed to be taking far too long for the city guards to pound Larson and Timmy unconscious and drag them from the concrete bowels of New York City. *There's just too much I don't understand.*

Still, Taziar had some tricks of his own. Gingerly, he touched the .45 in his pocket. Having seen the damage the pistol could create, he held a healthy respect for the weapon. The observation had given him a reasonable idea of which end the projectiles came from, though he had little grasp of the mechanisms and procedures involved in activating it. Once, in ancient Norway, Silme's half brother had shot Taziar, but the time-displaced rifle bore little resemblance to the dense chunk of carbon steel he now carried.

Taziar jabbed his fingers into his jeans' pocket, patting the crumpled wad of currency, his other ace in the hole. On the train, he had pretended to shuffle the bills into the gunmen's bag, palming more than twice as many as he dropped. It had proven easier than the trick he had used against the monte gang. Cards needed to remain crisp, while paper money wadded into neat balls that could be straightened. Taziar frowned. Larson's casual folding of the bills had led him to believe creases and rumples did not deflate their value. Now, he hoped he would not need to test that theory.

A chunky, middle-aged woman sat on a bench across the street from the subway and the blinking bank of police cars. Her cheeks looked flushed, her lips unnaturally red. Thin, black lines circled her eyes. Her lashes seemed impossibly long, curving around lids discolored blue. Despite the need to plan, Taziar could not help staring. *Did she paint dyes on her face? Or was she just normally ugly?*

Before Taziar could answer the question, even in his own mind, several members of the town guard emerged from the subway. Others followed, Larson between them, his hands manacled behind him. Still more guards appeared. They headed toward the row of flashing cars.

Taziar flattened to the stone, certain of only one thing. *If they ride away in those vehicles, I'll never find Allerum again.* He watched, heart pounding, as the uniformed men ushered Larson into the back seat of one of the squad cars.

Desperate for a solution, Taziar glanced around. A taxicab turned the corner, identical to the one he, Timmy, and Larson had used to escape the Sears building. The woman rose to greet it, and the cab decelerated.

The squad car doors slammed. The guardsmen climbed into the front seat, then closed their doors, too. The vehicle hummed to life.

Taziar recalled a day in another world. Larson's sarcasm came back to him verbatim, though riddled with English phrases: "You're all set if you ever want to take a transcontinental cab ride in an American made car." Waiting until the policemen were all involved with Larson and one another, Taziar darted across the street to the taxicab. Seizing a rear car handle, he worked the mechanism. The door swung open.

Taziar sprang into the back seat just as the woman edged in from the other side. He pulled his door closed.

The woman stared, blinking her color-enhanced eyes repeatedly. Then her face lapsed into angry creases, and she shouted at Taziar, waving her arms wildly. Not a single word was comprehensible.

The first police car roared away from the curb. The others began to follow.

Taziar ignored the woman, leaning forward. A man stared bank from the driver's seat, his olive-skinned face fuzzed with three days' growth of beard. He waved a hand, calling calmly over the woman's tirade.

The car with Larson in it glided down the roadway.

Taziar chose the only universal language he knew. Digging into his pocket, he emerged with a random handful of currency and hurled it into the front seat. Ones, twenties, and fifties fluttered, churning through the air, then fell to the vinyl. "Follow that car!" he screamed in his best English. He jabbed a finger at the squad car. "Follow that *damned* car!"

The woman lapsed into shocked silence.

A sparkle appeared in the cabby's eyes as he stared at the money. "You want me to chase down a police car?"

The squad car turned a corner.

Taziar could not catch all the cabby's words, but he recognized police as the term Larson used for guards. "Police. Yeah. Follow that car!" He crooked his finger to indicate the turn. "Okeydokey?"

The driver glanced at the money strewn across his seat. "Sure. Okeydokey, man. You got it." He addressed the woman.

She shouted something back at him, flinging her arms frantically.

The cabby spoke, his voice becoming menacing.

The woman pursed her lips, then clambered back outside. She slammed the door hard enough to shake the entire vehicle.

The taxicab maneuvered into the road on the trail of the squad cars.

A short circuit in the overhead socket caused the light bulb to flicker and sputter, dancing shadows over the four men in the police interrogation room. Seated in a folding chair, Al Larson kept his right hand clamped over the hastily bandaged gunshot wound in his shoulder. Across a metal and wooden table, a white-haired detective named Harrison tented his fingers over a sheaf of papers. A telephone graced the corner near his left elbow, and he sat in a cushioned swivel chair that seemed far more comfortable than the seats of Larson and his two police escorts.

At least they took off the handcuffs. Larson knotted his free hand, keeping it draped in his lap. *I hope that means they're willing to listen.*

"What's your name, kid?" Detective Harrison asked, staring at the papers as if to read and talk at the same time.

Larson presumed they had recovered his wallet from the subway. If so, lying could only get him deeper into trouble. "Larson."

The detective glanced over at one of the officers who nodded almost imperceptibly.

Satisfied, Harrison looked back at his papers. "First name?"

"Al," Larson said.

"Al?" The detective shuffled a page from the stack. "Al, what?"

"Al, *sir.*" Larson supplied naturally.

Detective Harrison looked directly at Larson for the first time. He squinted, apparently trying to read his captive's intentions. Then, satisfied Larson was not trying to sound intentionally flippant, he clarified. "No, I meant Al-*len*, Al-*bert*, Al-*exander?*"

"Just Al, sir."

A thoughtful silence fell. Harrison looked at the officer. This time, the patrolman shrugged.

Larson felt a need to clarify. "My father didn't like nicknames. He thought people should be named what they're called. Hence my sister Pam, not Pamela, and my brother Tim, not Timothy." He added quickly, "Though we do call Tim, 'Timmy.' "

"Right." Detective Harrison flipped the paper across the desk. "If you're going to answer any more questions, you'll have to sign this first."

The page slid in front of Larson. Reaching out, he straightened it. A quick glance revealed it as a waiver, stating his constitutional rights. At the bottom, he was given the option of whether to sign it, thus proving he understood that he did not have to submit to questioning and had chosen to do so willingly.

Harrison offered a black ballpoint.

Taking it, Larson signed. He passed pen and waiver back to the detective.

"You can read, I presume, Mr. Larson?"

"Yes, sir." Larson said.

"You understand you are still under arrest. Nothing you say is going to change that. Even in extenuating circumstances, we can't . . . um . . . 'unarrest' you until the District Attorney asks for a dismissal. You will go to jail until your appearance before a magistrate."

Larson bit his lip, not liking the sound of the detective's explanation. "I'm willing to cooperate any way I can." *Anything else would be folly, an admission of guilt. Right now, that's the last thing I need.*

"Very well, Mr. Larson. Your story of what happened this evening on the subway." Harrison pocketed the pen and swept the waiver aside. He made a broad gesture indicating Larson should begin.

Al Larson launched into his tale, starting with the moment the gunmen entered the train and ending with his arrest. He avoided all mention of Taziar or of their original purpose for taking the subway. He kept his tone casual, not daring to overplay his hand in the rescue of innocent passengers.

As he spoke the last word, the interview room fell back into an unnerving hush. The patrol officer nearest the door fidgeted, chewing at a thumbnail. The other watched Larson.

Detective Harrison leaned forward, fingers laced on the tabletop. "Mr. Larson, how many shots did you fire?"

"Two, sir."

"And are you aware where each of those bullets went?"

"Yes, sir." Larson wondered where the line of questioning was leading.

"Mr. Larson." A hard edge entered Harrison's tone. He met and held Larson's gaze. "Are you also aware we took four corpses off that train?"

"It doesn't surprise me," Larson admitted. He added belatedly, "Sir."

The detective's cheek twitched, and Larson guessed he had come to a significant question. "Mr. Larson, how many of those men did you kill?"

"Three, I think, sir."

"Three men, Mr. Larson. With two bullets."

"Right."

"How do you explain that?" Detective Harrison leaned back into his chair, his hands still threaded and clenched.

Larson blinked, unable to guess what Harrison

wanted. "I already told you the story. I accidentally crushed one guy's windpipe." Once spoken, the words sounded bad, and Larson felt the need to add, "While wrestling free a gun he was using to shoot down passengers."

The light splayed shadows over Harrison's face, making him look camouflage-painted. "How exactly, Mr. Larson, does one *accidentally* crush a man's windpipe?"

Oh, for Christ's sake. The repetition and unwarranted suspicion wore at Larson's patience. His shoulder ached, and his head throbbed. Every wasted second pulsed at his sensitivities. *Surely Silme and Bolverkr have located us by now. I hope Timmy's okay. And Shadow.* "Look, Detective Harrison. I was scared. Things happened fast. Innocents were getting killed. I did what I thought was right. Stress can do some pretty impressive things to the human body, especially when loved ones are in danger. My baby brother was in that subway."

The patrolmen exchanged knowing glances. Detective Harrison frowned. "We'll get back to your brother in a moment, Mr. Larson. I admit, I've heard of mothers lifting cars off their children. But panic doesn't turn a nineteen-year-old college student into a crack marksmen. Mr. Larson, where did you learn to shoot?"

You've obviously managed to obtain some information about me already. You tell me. Larson choked back the words but did not manage to fully contain his sarcasm. "I was trained in the 101st anti-squirrel division."

Harrison's frown deepened. His knuckles blanched. "What are you saying, Mr. Larson?"

"I'm a hunter." Larson wrestled down his temper, aware angering policemen could only hurt his case. "My father's taken me to New Hampshire every deer season since I was legal to hold a gun."

"You hunted game with a handgun?"

"Of course not." Larson glanced between the uniformed officers, hoping to get some support against this lunacy. But the patrolmen kept their expressions unreadable. "But a gun is a gun. Once you've learned to quick-draw a rifle on a distant, moving target, how much training does it take to pull a trigger?"

"Mr. Larson, you want me to believe you've never handled a handgun? Yet you fired only two shots, one through a man's heart and the other through a man's brain. Two bullets. Two perfect, lethal shots. How do you explain that, Mr. Larson?"

Impressed with his own targeting, Larson took a moment to respond. When he did, it sounded lame. "Luck?"

Harrison jerked his head forward, flinging his face completely into darkness. "Luck, Mr. Larson? Is that the best you can do? Do you expect me to believe you attacked a gang of gunmen, unarmed, fired two shots and killed three people without any training except matching wits with Thumper and Bambi?"

Larson's control broke. "Damn it, Detective Harrison. I'm not trying to 'get you to believe' anything. I'm just telling the goddamned truth. What you choose to believe is your own business." Fuming, he could not help adding, "And can the 'Mr. Larson' stuff. I know my name." He clutched the arms of the chair, tensed to rise.

Detective Harrison retreated. The light strengthened, revealing flushed cheeks and narrowed eyes. "Mr. Larson, stay seated or we'll have to cuff you again. And please calm down. I'm just trying to put the stories together."

Larson remained rigid. "There must have been a dozen witnesses. Surely they've told you the same thing I did."

"There's a blonde woman who claims you saved her life," Harrison admitted. "There's others who give a story similar to yours."

Larson said nothing, waiting for the other shoe to fall.

"Some are saying you were part of the gang. At least one claims you boarded the subway with the gunmen."

"That's ludicrous!" Larson burrowed his nails into the chair seat. "Timmy and I were on that train for hours." As soon as Larson spoke the words, he realized his mistake.

"For hours, Mr. Larson? For hours?" Harrison stared without blinking. "Do you realize how weird that is? What were you doing on the subway for hours?"

Larson shrugged. Finding no ready answer, he invented a lame one. "Cheap amusement. My little brother digs trains, okay?"

"Ah, back to your brother." Harrison unclasped his hands, removed the pen from his pocket, and twiddled it. "To hear him tell it, you're a cross between Elliot Ness and God Almighty. The kid needs to get away from the TV set. He kept babbling about witches and Robin Hood."

Larson groaned. "What happens now?"

"Well, I've still got some details to work out." Harrison flipped the pen, catching it by the cap. "I know you have an accomplice who made a break for it. We think he took the gun. That's suspicious." He stared at Larson.

Larson saw no need to answer a statement. *How the hell am I going to explain Shadow?* A more bewildering thought struck home. *His climbing Sears and Roebuck made the news. Surely, if we discuss the little sewer rat for long, they'll connect this incident with the other. And my ass is toast.*

Harrison continued. "If I can get enough answers to satisfy me, I'll get you to the night court magistrate for an initial appearance tonight. Judge Stoffer's fair. If we decide it's self-defense, he might let you off on your own recognizance. If we decide it's manslaughter, he'll probably have you post bond. But if we draw up a first-degree murder charge, you're in jail till the trial."

Larson stiffened further, aware his life, his friends', and seven and a half million strangers' might depend on how well he answered Harrison's questions.

Apparently misinterpreting Larson's discomfort,

Harrison softened. "Don't get too hyped up. You may never hit lockup. I'm guessing it'll be a lesser charge. If Stoffer's got a full docket, he might well clear it by giving you a choice between jail and the army."

Larson felt as if an iced dagger had been thrust between his ribs.

The detective continued, apparently missing Larson's sudden, deadly-coiled stillness. "I mean, war's hell, but it's better than a jail cell. As easily as you shot those punks and as little remorse as you've shown, I can't imagine you're a Conscientious Ob . . ."

Roused from his initial shock, Larson sprang to his feet. "No!" His fist crashed against the desktop. "I'm not going to Vietnam." The telephone jumped, its bell clanging dully. "I'm not going back to Nam!"

As suddenly, light blasted through the interrogation room, aching through Larson's eyes. Shadows spun, then fled like spiders. The patrol officers dove behind the desk, while the detective froze in blind confusion. In between Harrison and Larson, Silme and Bolverkr appeared in a misty wash of smoke.

Bolverkr's arm arched. Lightning flashed down from the ceiling, striking the chair where Larson had sat a moment before. The seat splintered. The metal glowed, then warped into a twisted outline of legs and frame.

Bolverkr swore. He whirled toward Larson.

An officer peered over the desk, his handgun aimed at Bolverkr. "Police! Stand where you are!"

Larson snatched up another chair.

Gleaming strands of magic formed between Bolverkr's hands.

Larson ducked, hurling the chair at the sorcerer. Wood shattered against an invisible shield, but the impact drove barrier and Dragonrank mage a step backward. The spell misfired to glittering slivers in his hand.

A gun roared as Larson leapt for the door. Without bothering to see the consequences, he seized the handle and wrenched.

Bolverkr cursed. "Don't waste spells."

A probe speared through Larson's mind with an abruptness that sent him sprawling through the doorway. Silme's voice filled his head. "You're dead now, Allerum. You're dead." Her presence slammed into his skull.

Desperately, Larson threw up a mental wall. Magic crashed against the conjured barrier. For an instant, the imagined bricks wavered. Then the spell exploded to sparks, scattering in a backlash that again lit the room like day.

Silme screamed.

Larson staggered to his feet, taking in the outer room at a glance. Policemen huddled behind overturned desks and chairs, guns drawn. The precinct lockup facility contained a single drunkard who cowered in its farthest corner. Still dazed by Silme's attack and weakened by his wound, Larson lurched against the bars, seizing the cold metal to steady himself.

"Don't move!" one of the cops hollered. "Don't anybody move."

Ignoring the warning, Larson whirled. Bolverkr was now only a few steps away from him.

"Shit!" Larson tried to dodge the sorcerer's charge, but Bolverkr's shield slammed into his gut, driving him back against the bars. His skull banged into the steel. Consciousness receded before a rush of rising darkness. Larson struggled in blind panic.

Bolverkr pressed in, his shield crushing Larson against the cage. The bars branded impressions into Larson's back, the pressure on his ribs quickly growing unbearable. He tried to drop to the floor, but Bolverkr pinned him like a moth beneath a cat's paw. All breath was compressed from his lungs. His head felt as if it would rupture between the bars. Air-starved, Larson felt the darkness deepen, scarcely noticing Silme's frantic search through his mind. His near unconsciousness gave her nothing concrete to manipulate.

Silme retreated. A moment later, a bullet bounced from Bolverkr's shield, inches from Larson's head. Realization penetrated Larson's numb and dizzied mind. *Silme's taken control of a cop. She's making him fire at me.* Larson rallied. Bracing against the bars, he tried to fling Bolverkr backward.

Pain shuddered through Larson's body. His empty lungs forced him to gasp in wild, uncontrollable bursts.

Another gunshot sounded. Then another.

Two more bullets ricocheted from Bolverkr's magics. Then a slug passed through the unprotected back of his shield, tearing a line along his side.

Bolverkr shrieked in anguish. His face a scarlet mask of fury, he whirled toward the policemen, sorceries snapping between his fingers.

The pressure on Larson disappeared. He sucked a dire lungful of air, then leapt for the sorcerer's unshielded back.

Fire erupted from Bolverkr's fingers, a storm of savage flame as ugly as his rage swirled through with black smoke. Furniture and men disappeared, boiled away in the rush of magics. Stunned by the sudden loss of a huge volume of Chaos, Bolverkr pitched a step backward.

Abruptly closer to his target than anticipated, Larson struck Bolverkr's back with his forearms instead of his fists.

Without bothering to assess the threat behind him. Bolverkr grabbed Silme and waved an arm. The air snapped open, swallowing the mages, leaving only an oily smoke that paled against the streaming, tarry residue of Bolverkr's magical fire.

The room fell horribly quiet. Lacy black smoke veiled Larson's vision. Evil drummed at his sensibilities, goading him to vengeance and violence. For an instant, the idea seized him to find the startled survivors and slaughter them one by one. But morality rose to beat the thought aside. *It's Chaos. It's the damned Chaos.* He coughed, choking on smoke and the dusty heat of cinders. *Got to get out of here while it's still possible.* He dropped, crawling to the front door.

Larson had just reached the panel when a sound clicked through the smoky darkness. A hand reached out of nowhere and wrapped around his neck. A gun's barrel gouged into his temple.

Larson froze, heart thumping. "Don't shoot," he rasped. "Please, don't shoot."

No reply. The gun remained in place.

Slowly, without threat, Larson rolled his eyes to a soot- and sweat-streaked face. Hazel eyes stared wildly back at him from beneath a patrolman's cap.

"Easy." Larson spoke soothingly, resorting to horror film clichés to make his point. "That smoke is a . . . an evil being possessing you. Think about what you're doing. Think, buddy, think!"

The arm tightened around Larson's throat. The gun dug into his scalp.

Larson's mind raced. *Gotta fight.* He gritted his teeth. *But I can't outmaneuver a bullet.*

The officer tensed suddenly.

Understanding flashed through Larson's mind. *He's going to shoot me whether I move or not.* Without time for strategy, he let his body go limp, collapsing suddenly to the ground.

The gun blast shattered Larson's hearing. Pain tore through his scalp.

Shot in the head. He shot me in the goddamned head. I'm dead. Larson rolled onto concrete, the paradox of his movement reviving a survival instinct that seemed ridiculous and impossible.

The gun roared again, the sound muffled to Larson's near-deafened ears. Chips of floor tile stung his arm and face.

Catching a moving, sideways glimpse of the officer's legs, Larson dove for them. His shoulder crashed against a knee. His fingers curled around a shin, yanking.

The cop tumbled, his gun careening into the raging inferno behind them. He clawed for Larson, driving an elbow into his face.

Larson fought through pain. Sweat trickled into his eyes, thickened with blood. Half-blinded, he wrapped his fingers around the officer's neck, driving his thumbs into the man's windpipe.

Now the policeman's struggles became more violent and less directed. He heaved at Larson's chest, arching to get his feet beneath him.

Larson released his choke hold with one hand. He drove his fist into the other man's forehead. The officer's head slammed against tile, and he went limp beneath Larson.

Larson clambered to his feet, not daring to check for a pulse. Sound filtered back to his ears, the whoosh of passing traffic and the distant blast of a car horn. He wiped his eyes with the back of his hand, smearing blood across his brow. Snatching the unconscious officer's hat, he ducked through the door. Once outside, he prodded the wound in his scalp with a finger. The touch hurt, and sweat stung the wound; but he felt certain the bullet had only grazed him.

Stars winked down at Larson through a thin blanket of smog, broken in patches by the New York skyline. A stubby yard of grass surrounded the three-story precinct, interrupted by a concrete path leading from the front door to a sidewalk parallel to the street. Another stripe of tree-lined yard separated the walk from the road.

Though tainted with factory contaminants, the cool, crisp air seemed a welcome relief after the heated smoke and rank discharge of Chaos. Still, the change in atmosphere came with a suddenness Larson's lungs could not accept. He coughed twice, then doubled over into a racking fit.

A hand dropped to Larson's shoulder.

Gripped by sudden panic, Larson whirled, striking at the presence. His arm swirled through air. The abruptness of his movement sent him into another bout of coughing. "Still a little excitable, I see." Taziar crouched just beyond Larson's reach, near the building's corner.

"Shit." Larson managed between coughs, his voice strained. "Don't sneak up on me." He loosed another series of rasping coughs. "I might hurt you."

Taziar's blue eyes caught the light from an upper

window, twinkling with childish mischief. "You'd never catch me." He handed Larson a bandage from his jeans pocket.

Larson ignored the crack, his voice wheezy. "Silme and Bolverkr were here." Meticulously, he mopped blood and sweat from his forehead before twisting the strip of cloth into a tight knot around his head, staunching the bleeding. Covering it with the policeman's cap, he scooted around the corner of the building. The pain in his head had nearly disappeared, but the arm wound still throbbed with a deep, dull agony, sapping him of strength.

"Obviously they were here. The air is foul with Chaos. I hope that means you forced them to cast some draining spells."

Larson replied in a voice more closely approximating his normal one. "I don't know that I can take all the credit. But Bolverkr cast the most spectacular spell I've ever seen." Larson exhaled through pursed lips. "I'm glad he didn't use that against us at his castle." He considered aloud. "I wonder why not?"

Taziar shrugged. "Hard to say. Guess it's the same reason a soldier doesn't always use the best maneuver in a fight. He didn't think of it under pressure. Remember, too, he was crazed then. Or maybe he didn't want to waste the life energy."

"Doesn't make a difference." Larson dismissed the question for more urgent matters. "In the future, we need to be prepared for fire. That was the spell, some sort of wave of flame. And we need to find Timmy. Fast."

"I know. . . ."

"Let's go." Larson started along the building, uncertain where to begin his search.

"Wait." Taziar caught Larson's forearm.

Larson shook free. "You don't understand. We need to move quickly. For all I know, Timmy might be within the area of the fire."

"He's not."

Larson turned.

"You didn't let me finish." Taziar drew up beside

Larson. "I was trying to say, 'I know where Timmy is.' I got here shortly after you did. What do you think I've been doing all evening?"

"What?"

Taziar paused, apparently surprised by the question. "I just told you. Looking for Timmy. And you, too." He smiled. "I started high and worked down. Timmy's on the second floor. He's fine. For you, I just followed the fighting noises." He brushed aside the hem of his shirt, revealing the Colt .45. "Oh, and here. Can you use this?" He pulled the pistol from his belt, clutching it upside down with a finger looped behind the trigger and the barrel facing his own abdomen.

Larson winced. "Better than you can, I'm sure." He took the gun, pausing to check the cartridge. *Four shots left*. He chambered the gun, placing it in the cocked and locked position for hip defense. He tucked it into his waistband, disliking the cold touch of carbon steel against his skin. "Now tell me about Timmy." He placed his back to the wall, crouched in the shadow of the precinct building.

"He's on the second floor in a room." Taziar rubbed his side, looking relieved to have disposed of the gun. "There's a woman with him."

"A policewoman?"

Taziar's eyes widened. "You have female city guards?"

"A few." Larson rearranged the gun to a more comfortable position. *Bleeding, armed, and wearing a cop cap. We've got to keep out of sight. This would be impossible to explain.*

"I don't know. How do you tell?"

"A uniform? A gun?"

Taziar's mouth formed a grim line. "I didn't see either."

"Go on."

"There's a man who enters and leaves at intervals. He does have a uniform. Gun, too, I think."

Larson frowned. "How did you see all this?"

"Through the window. The rooms to either side have windows, too."

"Open window or closed?"

Taziar did not hesitate. "Half opened. The rooms to either side are empty. All three rooms lead to the same hallway. There're long bars along the hall ceiling that make light. The rooms are lit by flasks hanging from a metal stalk."

Fluorescent and overhead lighting. Larson chuckled inwardly at Taziar's focus on the technologies he could not understand. "You did your homework."

"Excuse me?"

"You did a good job scouting the area." Larson rephrased his comment in words Taziar could comprehend.

"Thank you." Taziar accepted the compliment offhandedly. "It's what I do. Remember? It's kind of nice not to get scolded about it for a change." A slight smile and a friendly gaze stole all bitterness from the comment."

Larson grunted. "Yeah. Well, I guess sneaking off half-cocked has its place. Though remind me to tell you about third rails sometime." He changed the subject. "Let's get moving. Where is this room Timmy's in anyway?"

Taziar inclined his head, indicating the back of the precinct.

Larson inched toward the corner. "Listen, you've been up there clambering around already, right?"

Taziar followed closely. He made no verbal reply.

Larson swiveled his neck to look over his shoulder, catching the end of Taziar's affirmative nod. "You think it's climbable?"

Taziar stared. He imitated the tone Larson used when voicing sarcasm. "No. It's impossible. I made up that whole story about Timmy and the rooms."

Larson loosed a snorting laugh, only then realizing how silly his question must have seemed to a man who had scaled a skyscraper. "No. I meant do you think I could climb it."

Taziar studied Larson's sturdy, human frame. "I

haven't seen you in this form all that much. I'd guess you could.''

"Good. Let's go.'' Larson continued around the building, Taziar behind him. "I have an idea.''

CHAPTER 14:

Chaos Stand

One God, one Law, one element,
And one far-off divine event,
To which the whole creation moves.
—Alfred, Lord Tennyson
In Memoriam, Conclusion

Still wearing the policeman's cap, Al Larson crept over checkered patterns of black and white tile and around the simple furnishings of the police office, cautious as a thief. A metal desk was set near one corner, lusterless despite the glow from the overhead lighting. Mismatched chairs formed a semicircle around the front of the desk, with one chair on rollers behind it. A telephone graced the right corner of the desktop, amid framed pictures and lopsided stacks of paper. Exhaustion rode Larson. Despite Taziar's boost, the single-story climb had made his injured arm ache, and only concern for Timmy's safety kept him alert despite fatigue and pain.

The now-open window that Larson had used as his entrance riffled air through the office. Directly across the room, the door stood ajar.

A sudden gust of wind whipped through the confines. The door flapped opened, then thrashed back toward its closed position.

Realizing the panel would bang against its frame, Larson sprang to quiet it. He skidded across the room, just in time to shove his fingers between jamb and door. The wood bruised his knuckles painfully, and he sublimated the urge to scream with a string of mental swear words. Catching the knob with his other hand, he levered the door off his fingers without opening it.

Footfalls rang from the hallway beyond.

Larson froze, hand straying to the Colt .45 sidearm. He hoped he would not need to use it for anything worse than intimidation. *I can't leave Timmy. My brother's life is worth too much, and it's obvious the cops can't protect him against Bolverkr and Silme.*

The footsteps tracked past Larson's door and on to the next, the room where Timmy waited with a female stranger. The hall went silent as the walker paused before the door. Hinges creaked, then the door clicked closed without latching.

Larson peeked out into the hallway. Doors interrupted the walls on both sides, the one to Timmy's room resting, unlatched, against its jamb. No living creature moved through the corridor. Apparently, most of the men had run to the defense of their colleagues downstairs. *Which means anyone left up here's going to be trigger-twitchy as hell.* The .45 slipped naturally into his fist.

Quickly, Larson exited his room, twisting the knob and closing it silently behind him. Two strides brought him to the room in which Taziar had seen Timmy.

A gruff, male voice wafted through the crack. ". . . tracked down your mother. She was looking for you. Real worried. She's coming to get you. . . ."

The news shocked Larson. *Oh, no. Why did we have to hear that? Now we know where Mom will be at a given time. And Silme will probably search Timmy's mind for the information.* The concern that he had burned down his home for no good reason wrestled with the need for his full concentration.

Timmy's alto lilted through the door. "But Al said we shouldn't be with her now. That we shouldn't know where she's at."

The man snorted. "Your brother slaughtered—"

The woman interrupted. "Timmy, I'm sure Al had a good reason for giving you that advice. But things are different now. You understand. Don't you want to go home with your mother?"

Timmy gave no verbal reply, but Larson guessed the boy must have nodded, because no one pressed him further.

"Your mother's staying with. . . ." the man started.

Recognizing the danger of learning that piece of information, Larson grasped the knob and pounded on the door. "There's violence in the main office! We need every man!" He ran farther down the hallway, hammering on the next door as if to relay the same message in a linear pattern of urgency. Then, he darted quietly to a position on the farther side of the door to Timmy's room, back flattened to the wall.

A moment later, the door creaked partway open. A slender policeman appeared in the doorway, leading with his handgun. He faced the direction Larson had taken, decoyed by footfalls and unaware that Larson now stood behind him. Seeing no one, he started to turn.

Swinging his gun, Larson clouted the policeman against the temple, remembering, at the last moment, to pull the blow. *Tired as I am, I'm still stronger than I'm used to.* The cop's .38 clattered to the floor. He crumpled into Larson's arms.

Though small, the senseless man felt like a lead weight in Larson's crippled grip. Prodding the door open with his knee, he dragged the man back into the room, aiming the .45 from beneath one sagging armpit.

Timmy hunched in a plush chair. A plump, handsome woman in her thirties sat beside him. *A social worker,* Larson guessed. Beyond them, the window edged open silently, as if of its own accord.

The woman gasped, gaze locked on the gun. Timmy went still, eyes wide, utterly speechless.

"Freeze! Hands up!" Larson tried to sound desperate, but his tone emerged more tired than anything else. He dropped the policeman; the still form flopped to the floor.

Taziar clambered through the window. With the woman and Timmy focusing their attention on Larson's weapon, the Shadow Climber went unnoticed.

Larson kept his eyes on the woman, watching the remainder of the room only through peripheral vision.

The social worker's mouth opened.

Afraid she might scream, Larson pointed the .45 directly at her chest. "Lady, shut up. You scream, I kill you. And don't move, please." Larson kept the gun in place, using neither it nor his hand to gesture. *Please? Did I just say please?* The incongruity of the propriety struck him. *Wouldn't want to be impolite while threatening her life.*

The social worker raised her arms, glancing protectively at Timmy, fear etched like a grisly mask across her features.

Just inside the doorway, Larson pinned the policeman's .38 beneath his shoe and dragged it into the room. He kicked the door closed behind him, then, circumventing the woman, used the ball of his foot to send the gun skittering across the room to Taziar. "Cover her," he said in English for the woman's benefit, aware his other-world companion would have no idea what he meant. He adopted a perfect Weaver stance.

The woman twisted her head toward Taziar. She started to shake. Timmy opened his mouth, presumably to greet his brother.

Before he could speak, Taziar clamped a hand over Timmy's lips. He spun the boy, gesturing him to silence before removing the restraining hand. Catching Timmy's wrist, Taziar led the child to a position beside the window. Releasing his hold, the Climber picked up the gun.

"Please," the social worker said soothingly, voice faltering, tears glazing her eyes and her face drained of color. "Don't hurt the boy."

"Just stay quiet and still, and we won't hurt anyone." Larson switched to the barony tongue to address Taziar. "Keep the thing pointed at her and pretend you know what you're doing."

Taziar positioned himself between Timmy and the social worker, the gun leveled in both hands, finger well back from the trigger, his posture a poor imitation of Larson's earlier pose. He only succeeded in looking as if he wanted the Police Special as far away from himself as possible.

It'll have to do. Larson jammed the .45 back into his pocket, aware that, to a person on the wrong end of a gun, even a .22 seemed like a naval cannon, no matter how incompetent the wielder. He glanced at the policeman. *We have to work fast, before this guy wakes up.* Kneeling, he set to work stripping the man of shirt and undershirt.

Abruptly, the radio at the policeman's belt crackled. A voice emerged, uninterpretable beneath the static.

Startled, Larson jumped, naturally bringing the .45 up to cover his only threat.

The woman shuddered back into the chair, biting off a scream midway through, then clamping a hand over her mouth to stifle the sound. Timmy's head flicked repeatedly from her to Taziar to Larson.

The policeman on the floor groaned.

Larson swore. Seeing that Taziar still held the woman captive, he returned his own gun to his pants and set to work knotting the clothing together. The need for speed made him feel slow and clumsy. *Can't afford to hit this guy again. I don't want to kill him.* Finishing the tie, he bounded across the room to Timmy's side, hoping the other men in the precinct were too involved with the fires to hear or answer the broken scream.

"Go! Out!" Larson commanded Taziar in his language. Without waiting to see if the Climber obeyed, he turned to the social worker. "Give me your jacket."

"W–what?"

"Give me the damn jacket now! Move!" Larson made a threatening gesture with a muscled arm, not wanting to waste the time to draw his gun again. The need for action so soon after his gunshot wound was making him nauseated and dizzy.

The woman removed her pants suit jacket in nervous, jerky motions that, to Larson's heightened senses, seemed to progress in slow motion. She hurled the polyester jacket toward him.

The policeman stiffened, eyes fluttering open.

Larson snatched the garment from midair, the brisk gesture aching through his shoulder. Hastily attaching the jacket to the shirts, he grabbed Timmy and laced the string of clothing through the boy's belt. Taziar was nowhere to be seen.

"Hey!" The cop scrambled to an awkward crouch. Then, apparently realizing Larson had a gun and he did not, he fast-crawled behind a chair.

Seizing both ends of his makeshift rope, Larson eased Timmy to the windowsill. "Careful," he whispered through gritted teeth. "You'll be all right. Shadow'll be there to catch you." He forced his thoughts away from Taziar's slight stature. *A guy who climbs buildings with stolen objects and no support has to be strong, no matter how small.* Scrambling onto the ledge, he lowered the boy as far as possible before letting go. Whirling, Larson prepared to climb.

"Hey!" the policeman shouted again. "You! Freeze!" Footfalls thumped across the floor toward Larson. The social worker screamed, long, loud, and unstifled.

Larson skittered down the wall, the effort of supporting his weight tearing at the wound in his shoulder. Halfway down, his strength gave out. He plummeted, the penetrating, driving ache in his arm overwhelming his other senses. He did not feel Taziar's steadying hands, helping him through an instinctive roll. The pain of impact brought tears to his eyes. The police cap tumbled from his head, revealing the bloody headband.

Timmy made a high-pitched noise of distress.

Al Larson managed to stagger to his feet. As he rose, he found himself staring into Taziar Medakan's face. Timmy stood, watching in horror.

"Quick." The Shadow Climber said. He crammed his Dodger's cap on Larson's head. Too tight, it squeezed the wound, but the pain seemed minimal compared with the deeper ache of his shoulder.

Bulling through agony with will alone, Larson grabbed Timmy with his good arm and swung the boy to his uninjured shoulder. "Hang on. We're out of here." He ran. Scarcely able to see through the darkness, Larson kept to the grass, tracing brightly lit sidewalks. Though he could not see or hear Taziar, he trusted that his companion sprinted along beside him.

From his perch, Timmy prattled excitedly. "He is Robin Hood. Shadow really *is* Robin Hood. You should have seen him crawl all over the wall. Outta sight! Did you really point a gun at that lady? I can't believe the way you decked out that cop." He made several sound effects to mimic punches.

Larson let Timmy ramble on, afraid to let his last words to his brother become "shut up." *Silme and Bolverkr will return and soon. There's nothing left but to make a stand, someplace where no more innocents can get injured.* Larson gritted his teeth until his jaw hurt nearly as much as his arm. *We're going to need food. And ammunition.* He channeled his mind to practical issues, aware he could never hope to defeat two high-ranking Dragonrank sorcerers. *God, I hope Shadow's swiped some cash from somewhere. What a time for shopping.* If he had felt any less battered and harried, he might have found the observation funny. He clutched Taziar's cap to his head with his free hand. *Can't afford to lose the hat. Dirt won't bother anyone, and half the young adult population in New York wears clothing as tattered as mine. But blood's gonna draw attention.*

Larson shifted to a more sobering thought. *There's got to be a way to keep Timmy safe.* He drew a blank, and his attempts tore memory to the forefront. He could not help but recall the last time he had dealt with a loved one Timmy's age, a half-breed, bumbling boy named Brendor who had served as Silme's apprentice. He recalled leaving the child with Silme's friends in a village, hoping to keep Brendor secure until they defeated Bramin and returned for the child.

The remembrances came, rapid-fire, between each of Larson's running steps and panting breaths. Vivid as yesterday, he saw Brendor's savage rush, felt the boy crush him to the ground with magically enhanced strength. He relived the brilliant yellow spears of Silme's sorcery as they tore through the last remnants of Brendor, a corpse killed and animated by Bramin.

Silme can track Timmy through his mind. As dangerous as it seems, Timmy is safer with me. Larson put the thought of his mother heading toward the station from his mind. *We'll just have to start the battle before Mom arrives. And hope Silme and Bolverkr take the bait.*

Larson and Taziar ran on.

Cobwebs choked the abandoned warehouse on 6th Street, dividing its single room into triangles with gossamer walls. Al Larson crouched on a floor thick with dust and the scattered, unidentifiable shards that had fallen from objects long ago moved. Timmy huddled in a corner, his grime-smeared features angelic in sleep. Taziar sat beside a fire extinguisher and behind the bags of rations they had bought with what little of his money remained. He chewed on a ham and cheese sandwich, pausing after every bite to stare at the unfamiliar arrangement of meat and bread. He offered the next taste to Larson.

Larson shook his head, frowning. He knew he should eat, yet he dared not do so. Anxiety kept hunger at bay, and he felt certain he could not keep food down for long. Images of Silme paraded through his mind: the smile that seemed to touch deep into his soul, her warm, silky skin pressed up against him in desire, the soft look in her gray eyes when he made a comment only she could understand. His mind seemed incapable of capturing her beauty; every glance he took showed facets he had forgotten, the perfect shape of her features, the cascade of golden hair, the firm, slender curves he could never tire of seeing. Thoughts of her brought a whirlwind of grief and hope. *We can get her back. We have to be able to free her from Chaos.* He could not abandon that hope, yet reality intruded. *I have to fight against her. I might have to kill her.* His hand fell on the .45. It felt heavy and dragging, out of place at his side. "I can't do it."

Taziar looked up. "Excuse me?"

"I can't hurt Silme. I just can't."

Taziar set his sandwich on the bag of canned goods and jerky sticks. "I know. That's why you need to focus your attention on Bolverkr. I'll handle Silme."

Doubt assailed Larson. "Handle her? What does that mean, handle her? Kill her?"

Taziar scooted around to face Larson, sitting cross-legged, the fire extinguisher against his knee. "If that's what it takes, yes." He brushed away the comma of hair that continually slipped down his forehead. Though routine, the gesture seemed contrived, not quite hiding his nervousness.

Larson knew just the idea of killing anyone sickened Taziar, that the little Climber tended to freeze in combat, even when his life or his friends' lives lay in the balance. Still, Larson's love for Silme drove him to discard this knowledge and assume the worst. "I know she may have to die. I've accepted that. But you won't kill her if you see another way?"

Taziar said nothing.

Larson's concern quadrupled in an instant. "Right?"

Taziar brushed crumbs from his lap.

"Answer me, damn it!"

Larson's shout awakened Timmy. The boy opened one eye, then rolled over and relaxed again.

"Allerum," Taziar said mildly. "It is fair to assume I have a plan. Silme and Bolverkr can read your mind. Therefore, if I told you anything, I'd be an idiot." He shrugged. "Despite Bolverkr's opinion, I'm not an idiot."

"But . . ." Larson started. He stopped, uncertain what to say. If he needed to steal an elephant from seven hundred armed guards on the topmost floor of the Empire State Building, he would consult Taziar. But for combat strategy, Taziar's eye for guesswork and detail had proven worse than blind in the past. Still, Taziar had made an effective point. The best plot in the world became far more dangerous than the lousiest once it fell into enemy hands. "At least tell me what you want with that?'' He pointed to the fire extinguisher that Taziar had pilfered on the way out of the grocery store.

''Sure.'' Taziar patted the canister, his fingers thudding hollowly against it. ''You told me it fights fires.''

''Right,'' Larson agreed.

''And you told me Bolverkr has a spectacular fire spell that we should prepare against.''

''Ri–ight.'' Larson blinked, the pieces falling together slowly. ''You brought it to put out Bolverkr's fire spell?''

''Ri–ight,'' Taziar imitated Larson's thoughtful stretching of the syllable.

Larson closed his eyes, his fingers on the blood-smeared headband, shaking his head at the craziness of the idea. ''Shadow, if Bolverkr hits us with that spell, we'll be cooked before you could even think to use the extinguisher.''

''Maybe.'' Taziar shrugged. ''Maybe not. No one's supposed to be able to dodge those magical lightning flashes either, but I've done it several times.''

Larson pursed his lips in consideration. He recognized his challenging and irritation as a reaction to fear for Silme. Once identified, he could not disperse it, but he did find it easier to think around the concern. ''Actually, that's not a bad idea. From what I remember from Silme and Astryd talking, Dragonrank magic doesn't work all that well against nonmagical objects and beings, like us. If there was a spell that could shatter a man's heart instantly or could heat the air around us all to a bazillion degrees or could create a giant blend-o-matic, I'm sure Bolverkr would have used it against us already. I've seen single spells destroy dragons and 'living corpses,' but the worst I've experienced is a spell that paralyzed me and the lightning that missed you.''

Taziar retrieved his sandwich, not bothering to voice the obvious. They both remembered how Bramin's paralyzing spell had once left Larson helpless, that Bramin would have stabbed Larson to death if not for Taziar's unexpected interference. Both knew Taziar had dodged the lightning with a skill and speed Larson could never hope to match. Even then, the concussion had left the little Climber unconscious on Bolverkr's ramparts.

Larson's words died to hopeless silence.

"We can handle this," Taziar said with cheerful certainty. "Remember, as powerful as he seems, Bolverkr's Chaos isn't infinite. If it was, he could make up any spell he wanted, even that blend-o-whatever-you said. The bulk of Silme's power comes from him, so, in that respect, her presence weakens him. They can throw twice as many spells against us at once, but with Bolverkr's Chaos-energy curtailed by the sharing and by whatever he's lost permanently in your world, he's not likely to try some newly invented, complicated, mass-slaughtering spell."

Larson considered, but took little comfort from Taziar's explanation. *Right. So all we have to worry about is being burned, electrocuted, mentally tortured, chased by a dragon, or paralyzed, unable to move but fully aware of our defenselessness. Great. How comforting.*

Taziar took another bite of sandwich, ignoring Larson's turmoil. He chewed carefully, then swallowed before speaking. "I was thinking. Since I didn't save enough money to buy more bullets, would it help if you kept this?" He held out the policeman's gun, casually pointing the barrel toward Larson.

Having been taught since childhood to treat every gun as if it were loaded and lacking a safety, Larson cringed out of the line of fire. "Careful with that!"

Taziar lowered the weapon.

"You want me to hold both guns?" Larson knew it made more sense to spread their fire, yet he had no time for a crash course in marksmanship. He realized a quick and dirty "aim and shoot" technique would only take a few minutes to explain to Taziar; but, with himself, Silme, and Timmy in the room, wild shooting would prove far more dangerous than none at all. "All right." Larson took the second gun. "But what will you use for a weapon?"

"This." Taziar pulled out his utility knife. "And this." He patted the fire extinguisher. "I'm not much good with any weapon. If you're capable enough with yours, I shouldn't need one. I've seen and felt what guns can do."

"Not against Bolverkr." Another wave of frustration struck Larson. "Those magical shields of his deflect bullets, too. And I'm not shooting Silme unless I have to."

"Nor would I expect you to. I don't want to harm Silme, either." Taziar looked away, his food forgotten.

Only then it occurred to Larson how callous his attitude must seem. *Here I am going on about how I don't want to hurt Silme, even though she was indirectly the cause of Astryd's death. He understands how I feel about Silme. He's not going to do anything foolish. And he cares for her, too.* "Look, Shadow. I'm sorry. I'm just sick and tired, frustrated, annoyed . . ." He paused, hardly daring to admit it to himself. ". . . and scared. I'm also damned scared."

"Good," Taziar said.

"Yeah. What's so good about it?"

"It's just good to see something normal in all this chaos. Now get some sleep."

"Sleep?" The suggestion startled Larson. "How am I supposed to sleep?"

"I don't know, but you can't afford not to." Taziar glanced at Timmy. "We can't go to Bolverkr. We have to wait until he comes to us. If I were him, I'd be thrilled to know my opponents had decided to exhaust themselves by staying awake forever. So I figured we'd work shifts, one of us up during the day, the other at night. There'll be some overlap for exchanging ideas." He waved at the darkening confines of the warehouse. "I'm guessing I'm more used to a night schedule than you. Besides, you're more injured. So you sleep now."

"Here." Larson rummaged through the bags, emerging with a flashlight and a package of batteries. Placing the batteries into the stem, he switched on the light and handed it to Taziar. "Not the best lantern in the world, but it'll have to do."

Taziar accepted the flashlight, staring at it curiously.

Larson crawled over to Timmy. Catching a shoulder, he shook the boy.

"Hmmn?" Timmy rolled toward Larson.

"Timmy, sorry to wake you, but this is important."

"Uhn-huhn." Timmy sighed, opening one eye reluctantly.

Certain Timmy was awake enough to hear, Larson continued. "At any time, the witch and an evil sorcerer named Bolverkr may appear here. No matter what happens, I want you to stay in this corner and away from the fight. Do you understand that?"

"Uhn-huh."

"Don't do anything else unless I tell you to. Or unless I'm killed. Then, you run away. Got that?"

"Uhn-huh."

Larson frowned, believing Timmy had received the message, but wishing he could make sure. "All right, go back to sleep."

"Okay," the boy murmured.

Larson moved away, hoping a sudden spell against him would not strike Timmy as well. He curled against the wall, barraged by worries and tension. His muscles cramped. He closed his eyes against a burning discomfort, certain he would never fall asleep. Yet fatigue overtook him in minutes.

Larson awakened to Taziar's warning shout. Instantly alert, he sprang to a crouch, and his eyes snapped open to blinding light. A grim sense of evil engulfed him, and he caught a dull, retinal impression of a brilliant flash against the painful glare. Taziar crashed against him, bowling him into a concrete corner that bruised his leg and sent pain shocking through his wounded shoulder. Something struck the stone where he had lain. Electricity raised the hair along the back of his neck, and a thunderstorm odor permeated the air.

A second later, Taziar's weight disappeared. Again,

Larson leapt to a crouch, blinking wildly as the flare of magics faded to a darkness pierced only by the flashlight's beam on the floor. Taziar had scuttled along the wall, and was now several feet from Larson. The Shadow Climber clutched the fire extinguisher as if it were a baby. Bolverkr's dark form towered in the room's center. Silme stood some distance behind him, her arm flexed in menace, her fingers clenched around a glowing sphere of readied sorcery.

Larson seized the .45, firing a quick-draw hip shot. The bullet struck Bolverkr's shield, whining off into the darkness. Impact staggered the Dragonrank sorcerer back a step, and Larson stole the second it gained him to dart around for Bolverkr's unshielded back.

"Al!" Timmy shouted from the corner, now behind Larson. "Watch out! The witch!"

Larson ducked as he fired. His shot pinged off at an angle, defining the edge of Bolverkr's shield.

A deafening hiss reverberated through the room so abruptly that even Larson jumped, though this time he recognized the sound of the fire extinguisher.

Silme screamed. Her spell splintered to glimmering fragments around her. White powder coated her dress.

Apparently equally startled, Bolverkr ripped both his arms downward. Magic pulsed through the room, chokingly thick with Chaos smoke, and he disappeared.

"Bolverkr!" Silme shouted, suddenly without an ally. Gathering her composure, she began another spell.

Larson spun crazily, trying to relocate Bolverkr. *Only two bullets left in this gun. Got to make them count.* He felt for the .38 and found it tucked in his belt, its presence reassuring.

Awkwardly, Taziar backed away from Silme, still gripping the fire extinguisher.

Light tented between Silme's fingertips, chaotic as a spider's web, its glow intensifying with each new strand. Suddenly, she tensed.

Again, the fire extinguisher boomed, blasting some of its contents over Silme.

For the second time, Silme's unfinished spell fizzled to harmless sparks. "You little bastard!" she shrieked. "You *insect!*" She began to charge Taziar, then retreated, hurriedly forming another spell. Chaos in the form of tarry smoke undulated from her, gorging the room with a foul-smelling, translucent mist.

Bolverkr! Where the fuck is Bolverkr? Larson wished his eyes could adjust fully to the wavering darkness, afraid to concentrate on Silme for fear of missing Bolverkr. *Shadow knows what he's doing.* Taziar's plan seemed clear now. *He's trying to force her to keep casting, to drain enough Chaos for her identity to come through.* Larson tried not to contemplate the situation too hard. *Guess this is where we find out whether Chaos and life energy are the same thing here.*

"Allerum!" Taziar screamed. "Behind you!"

Even as the warning came, Larson heard rushing footfalls at his back. *Bolverkr!* He whirled, firing as he moved.

But the person who charged was not a sorcerer hellbent on vengeance, just a boy under his influence. The bullet tore through Timmy's abdomen. He collapsed, screaming in agony and terror.

Timmy. A thousand emotions paralyzed Larson. The .45 fell from his fingers, the sound of its landing lost beneath another blast from the extinguisher. Larson could not know that Bolverkr had drawn illusions in his brother's mind, warping Larson's form to look like Bolverkr's own. Nor could he know that Bolverkr had imitated Al Larson's voice, desperately commanding the boy to battle. Larson knew only that he had sent his eight-year-old brother into an unbearable anguish that could only end in death.

"Timmy." Larson's voice rose to a hysterical shriek. "Timmy! Timmy!"

Behind Larson, light flared and snapped, slashing ricocheting bands through the confines of the warehouse.

Larson could not gather enough interest to turn, but his instincts betrayed him. He spun, apathy transforming the movement to an awkward stumbling. Silme's magic silhouetted Taziar in blue, revealing an expression of stark realization through air smoky as a barroom's.

Suddenly, the Shadow Climber collapsed. The fire extinguisher crashed down on his abdomen, driving breath between clenched teeth. The magics faded to a sultry afterimage. He lay still, eyes open and staring, blood trickling from the corner of his mouth.

Timmy's screams fell silent.

Larson's muscles all seemed to give out at once. He dropped to his knees, no longer caring whether he lived or died. Tears streamed from his eyes, and he crawled toward the still form of his brother, dragging himself with an effort that seemed heroic. He reached for a pulse. His hand hovered over the boy's neck, the ragged, scarlet hole in Timmy's shirt mesmerizing him, a solid fact in his consciousness that he tried to drive away but could not. He willed his hand forward. It disobeyed him, hanging in midair like a thing disconnected. Until Larson touched Timmy, he could presume the boy lived.

Even as Larson waited, poised between fantasy and knowledge, a grimmer reality intruded. *Silme's still alive. And she's planning to destroy my world.* His hand retreated from Timmy, closing over the Police Special instead. *My best friend is dead. My brother is dead. And I'm dead, too. But I'm going to take my enemies with me.* Slowly, he twisted, raising the gun.

Haze swirled through the warehouse, turning Silme into distant shadow. She stood over Taziar, her expression as blank as the Climber's. She did not seem to notice the threat behind her.

Larson drew a perfect bead on Silme's spine at the level of her chest. His hand tensed. The gun trembled in his grip. Despite all that had happened, he could still feel her warmth against him, still remember the concerns of the world that she repeatedly, unselfishly took upon herself. *She's not Silme anymore. She's the Chaos-warped stranger who killed Taziar.* Rage rose in Larson like fire, and he gathered the courage to shoot.

Suddenly, shadows leapt, broken like glass, as light erupted in the middle of the room. Bolverkr appeared between Larson and Silme, black smoke trailing from his figure.

Aim destroyed, Larson pulled his shot. He whipped the gun toward Bolverkr.

The Dragonrank mage laughed. Sorcery glazed eddying mist, and the air seemed as tense and impending as a predator coiled to spring. A ball of white-hot magics flared into his hands with the suddenness of a gas jet.

Larson fired. The shot struck Bolverkr's shield at the level of his heart, then bounced into the shadows. Chaos-smoke leeched from Bolverkr's spell. He tensed to throw, then went suddenly rigid. Light danced and died in his grip. He whirled toward Silme, the threat behind him abruptly forgotten. "Bitch! What are you doing? What the hell are you doing?" He used a commanding tone, yet a hint of frenzy betrayed him.

His back. No shield. Even as Larson reaimed, Bolverkr lurched out of the firing line. Smoke boiled from him.

"The power is mine," Silme chanted, invisible in the thick wash of dispersing Chaos. "You gave it to me. It's mine!" Her voice was almost unrecognizable. *"And I want it all!"*

Dense as grease, the Chaos-smoke roiled through the room. Larson's lungs ached, and his eyes burned. The air became rancid, suffocating him toward the brink of unconsciousness. He sank to the floor. The world blurred to two dark figures who pirouetted like dancers or like demons capering through the ruins of hell.

"Silme, I said I'd share. There's enough for us both." Bolverkr pitched backward with an abruptness that all but sprawled him over Larson.

Silme's answer was a shriek that combined pain and fury. "It's mine! All mine! Give it to me!"

Larson scrambled for consciousness, desperate to gather the shards of his composure. Dizziness battered him, upending him through a smoky swirl of vertigo.

They're fighting through the link. They're battling over the same ugly, evil Chaos that turned Bolverkr into a monster and Silme into an enemy. With effort, Larson raked his limbs toward him, trying to regain enough balance to rise, forcing his focus to his own snarl of pain and grief. The handle of the pistol gouged his palm. He forced memory for a solid grounding. *Timmy's dying.* The thought flooded Larson with grief, numbing him. The gun slipped from quivering fingers.

Silme and Bolverkr tore back and forth, limbs jerking as if in a seizure. Though no physical blows fell, sweat sheened their hands and faces, haloing features strained with mental effort. The smoke thickened.

Timmy . . . is . . . dying. Larson gritted his teeth, demanding a rage that would not come. His vision all but disappeared beneath the hovering blanket of Chaos darkness. *His killer is here. I can avenge him.* A dribble of anger suffused Larson, crushed by a voice from within. *You, Al Larson, you are Timmy's slayer.* And the swirling Chaos dragged satisfaction into the thought. *Slaughter. Destruction. Chaos ruin.*

Larson fought the battering tide of Chaos' smoke. Again, he raised the gun. But the darkness slammed his sight to nothing. Even movement was lost, and only the muffled exchange of the Dragonrank mages' curses told Larson the battle continued.

But, where his own efforts to spark fury had failed, the strain of fighting Chaos succeeded. Larson surged to his feet, the gun clamped in both fists, desperately scanning the fog for his target. *Bolverkr. You're going to die, you son of a bitch.* Larson stumbled toward the noises of the war.

Even as Larson moved, Bolverkr jerked backward with the sudden triumph of a tug of war.

Silme gasped in frustration.

Larson sprang for the sorcerer. The gun's barrel drove against the back of Bolverkr's skull. And Larson pulled the trigger in a red fog of anger. "Die, you bastard!"

An explosion rang through the room. Bolverkr toppled, Larson atop him, his body twisted, but the gun still clamped to the Dragonrank mage's head.

Silme screamed. Slammed suddenly with all the remaining Chaos, she crumpled.

"Let's see you heal this." Larson fired at Bolverkr again, point-blank. Blood splattered Larson's face. The Chaos seethed around him like a living thing. Perceptions struck him, distant and not his own. He knew a familiar war in Vietnam, escalating, fed by Chaos from another era. He saw trains and subway cars scrawled black with graffiti, children with knives battling in alleyways and concrete parks, intolerance of skin color, ideas, and religion sparking to a violence justified by warped, self-righteous moralities, a New York Larson no longer knew as home. The gun spoke repeatedly, until it dry fired, its wielder's finger still spasming on the trigger.

Now, the anger Larson had needed for action became a curse. He slammed the gun down on the remains of Bolverkr's head. Bone gashed his palm, and impact resonated through his fingers. Torn from his hands by force, the gun bounced into the darkness.

Chaos. Larson staggered to his feet, nudging through anger for a semblance of sanity and self. *Silme has it all. It'll warp her like Bolverkr. There's no choice any longer. I have to kill her.* Rationality seeped through, bringing an important memory. *The .45. There's still one bullet left.*

Dropping back to his hands and knees, Larson fished through the darkness, scarcely noticing that the blackness had died back to an opaque haze and he could breath more freely. A glint of metal met his gaze, and he crept toward it. His hand closed over the .45.

Larson could again discern shapes through the haze of Chaos. All four bodies lay still, Timmy at one end of the room, Taziar at the other, Silme and Bolverkr between them. Larson crept to Silme's side. The Chaos smoke grew progressively lighter, and it seemed to take Larson's fury with it. The emotion unraveled, leaving nothing in its place.

Now beside Silme, Larson crouched at her head.

Tentatively, he extended a finger, tracing a winding highlight through the gold of her hair. Even sweat-slicked and clammy, she seemed the epitome of beauty, her warmth so real and alive. "I love you, Silme," he said, the words deafening in the silence. "I love you so much. And I'm sorry." He pressed the gun against her temple, wishing he had just one more bullet. One more bullet. For himself.

A perception touched Larson's consciousness, an alien idea that took the form of concept rather than words. *Don't do it, Allerum. It's not necessary.* The presence did not actually call him by a name. Rather, it seemed to appeal to the portion of his being that had been an elf in Midgard.

Startled, Larson glanced around. The darkness had faded to a maddeningly shifting gray. All the bodies lay where he had left them, but a new figure stood near the door. He towered over Larson, easily eight feet tall. White hair hung around comely features, and the gray eyes held the color and timelessness of mountains. Divinity fairly radiated from the being, a depth of sensation Larson had not known, even in the presence of Norway's gods.

Larson blinked. *I've finally gone irreversibly over the edge.* He drew some comfort from the thought. *At least the pain will be gone. Thank God for small favors.*

You're welcome, the other sent, again in concepts. Though voiceless, Larson discovered something familiar in the tone.

"Vidarr?" Larson shook his head, knowing he must be mistaken. If this was Vidarr, he had aged a thousand years. *Aged a thousand years? Christ, could this be a future Vidarr?*

Vidarr confirmed the identification.

"But you're . . ." Larson started. "How could . . ." The theological implications became too staggering, and philosophy seemed far too secondary to discuss when Silme's life hung in the balance. "What did you mean when you implied Silme's death wasn't necessary?"

Vidarr responded in the same complex, nonverbal manner. *Chaos doesn't bind or assimilate in your world. It only goads.* He waved a hand through the air, as if gathering something, and the room brightened again. *When Silme cast the spell that paralyzed Taziar, she lost enough of her bound Chaos to release her from its influence. She went after Bolverkr's power not because she wanted it, but to save you from his spells.*

"Oh, no." Larson dropped the gun and hugged Silme to him, stroking the damp locks. "Is she going to be okay?"

She was knocked unconscious by the sheer volume of Chaos she pulled to herself. She's starting to come around now.

Larson drew Silme closer. "What about Timmy? Is he. . . ?" He let the question hang.

He's alive. The concept of a tenuous link to life came clearly with the words. *For now. So is Taziar. But say good-bye. Neither will survive more than a few minutes longer.*

Silme trembled in Larson's arms, her lids flickering. "Can't you do something for them? You must be able to do something?"

I could, Vidarr admitted. *But I won't. If I've learned nothing else over the last ten centuries, it's not to interfere. You mortals make your own histories and cause your own ends.*

"Cut it out!" Frustration drove Larson to shout. "Don't give me that Silent God and noninterference bullshit! I know you too well."

You don't know me at all. Not anymore.

"Damn it!" Larson could almost feel the seconds ticking away, stealing his brother's final breath. "I don't have time for this. You want me to beg. Fine, I'll beg. Please, Vidarr, save my brother and my friend. We'll discuss the implications later. You can always change your mind and kill them again. I'll do anything! Anything, Vidarr."

I'm sorry. There was no trace of compromise.

You bastard! Hot tears entered Larson's eyes, and it

was all he could do to keep from rushing Vidarr. "You have to do something!"

On the contrary. I don't have to do anything at all. Except return this Chaos. Vidarr arched his arm once more. *And take Bolverkr's body and Silme back where they belong.*

"Take Silme? You're going to take Silme, too?" Terror battered at Larson's remaining reason. "You're going to leave me with nothing?" Another thought surfaced, without Vidarr's input. "Or will I simply die in Vietnam, never rescued by Freyr?"

All that has gone before has gone before. Your history from this moment is open. You have to chart your own waters.

This time, the concepts seemed more vague. "Chart my own waters? What the hell is that supposed to mean? You're starting to sound like Gaelinar." Larson imitated his swordmaster; hysteria allowed him to joke about the Kensei for the first time since his death. "Ah so, hero. It's not the weapon that cuts, it's the intention of the wielder." He returned to his normal voice. "I'm having enough trouble keeping my sanity. Damn it, use a language I can understand!"

Vidarr remained patient. *Just as alternate events have occurred since you returned to the graveyard, so will they continue. No mortal should know when he's going to die. From now on, whatever happens happens, unrelated to the future you remember.*

Silme sat up, clutching at Larson's hand.

Larson glanced at her, and her smile sparked hope. "You're saying I can make my own choices."

Correct.

"Then I choose to return to Midgard with Silme."

You can't.

"Why not?"

I destroyed your elf body.

"What!" Larson's voice roared through the room. He leapt to his feet. "You promised to protect it! You lied! You fucking traitor! How could you swear to protect it then destroy it? I thought gods didn't lie."

I didn't lie. I promised only to take care of the body

as I saw fit. Vidarr ignored the advancing human. *I saw fit to destroy it.*

"You arrogant son-of-a. . . ."

God, Vidarr finished, this time in straight words. *I'm a god. And the son of a god. Don't ever forget that.* He switched back to instant conceptualizations. *Now let me explain.*

Silme drifted toward Taziar's still form, as if in a trance.

Vidarr continued. *When Bolverkr left our world, it was instantly hurled too far in the direction of Law. Only one of two things could happen: either the world could shatter into nothingness, or we had to kill several powerful, Lawful creatures quickly. Our world had only one group of beings powerful enough to balance Bolverkr's disappearance.*

"Gods," Larson said, the word as much an expletive as an answer.

Ragnarok. The fated war that destroyed the gods. All but one god. Me. One God. Your God, Allerum.

"No." Larson rallied for a last, desperate protest. "No. My God is merciful. You're mean, spiteful, and deceitful. Like Bolverkr, you would take everything I love from me. But, in one way, you're worse. Bolverkr had the decency to claim my life as well, but you're stupid enough to believe I would draw solace from living on, haunted by my brother's slaying, and the loss of my best friend, my baby, and my wife."

Check the Bible, Allerum. Your God is no stranger to meanness or spite.

Larson fell into a deep, mournful silence. There was nothing left to live for, and nothing left to say.

Silme cleared her throat. "My Lord, may I speak?"

Of course.

Silme used the edge of her skirt to wipe the blood from Taziar's cheek. The expression on her face mixed grief and guilt. "There's no Balance in this world of Allerum's. Is that correct?"

Correct.

"Well, since this is supposedly a future time from

mine, I have to assume my absence hasn't caused Midgard to collapse."

Actually, even after Ragnarok, the world remains dangerously tipped toward Law. It is only because I return this mass of Chaos to the past that the world still exists.

Silme rolled the fire extinguisher from Taziar, her voice level. "Since you've gathered the dispersed Chaos, can I assume the Chaos you take back doesn't necessarily need to be bound to any individual?"

Correct. You're asking if I can take the Chaos you wield and leave you behind.

Silme nodded.

Larson held his breath. His heart pounded, but he dared not raise too much hope for fear it would come crashing down around him again.

That would require you to cast out every bit of Chaos you hold. You would no longer be a sorceress, Silme. You would be trapped in a world whose language you don't speak and whose technology you don't understand. Is that what you want?

"No," Silme admitted.

Larson lowered his head.

"I want Allerum. I love him. He's made sacrifices for me, and now it's time for me to make a few for him. I have no reason to return to Midgard. My family's dead. My loved ones are here. And I'm not stupid. If I return to Midgard with as much Chaos as I carry now, I'll become as corrupted and terrible as my brother ever was. But if you take my Chaos unbound, you can distribute it more evenly. No individual needs to be wholly evil."

A silence followed Silme's speech. To Larson, it seemed to last an eternity.

At last, Vidarr replied. *Very well. You can stay, on the condition that you drain yourself of all Chaos before leaving this room. Once I gather that Chaos, you will never see or hear from me again. You must accept the consequences of your decision and your actions, and they are yours to suffer.*

"I do," Silme said, certainly unaware of the irony

in her choice of phrase. She glanced from Taziar to Timmy, a worried frown creasing her features. "And I think I know exactly what to do with all this magic."

Larson recalled how Bolverkr had used his sorcery to heal his own fatal wound. For the first time in as long as he could remember, Al Larson smiled.

EPILOGUE

Al Larson perched on the edge of his hotel bed, staring at the clock's hash marks of hands and numbers glowing through the darkness. *One in the afternoon.* Larson estimated he had been awake for thirty hours.

After Silme had healed Timmy and Taziar, they had all headed back to the police station. Larson had sent Silme and Timmy with his mother and sister, to an uncle's house in New Jersey. Then, the most intense questioning in Larson's life had begun.

Policemen from two precincts had fired challenges at Al Larson until exhaustion rode them all. Seven separate interpreters had failed to find a means to communicate with Taziar. The police had forced Larson to relay multiple, complex commands to the Climber before reluctantly accepting that Taziar's language was, in fact, a language, and allowing Larson to do the translating.

Larson smiled weakly at the remembrance, not quite distant enough to find it humorous yet. He glanced over to the other bed. Taziar slept, curled beneath the bedspread, looking as fragile and insubstantial as a battered child. It had seemed easier for Larson to answer those questions the cops had aimed at the Shadow Climber. So, instead of translating, Larson had used the exchanges in barony tongue to explain the progress of the questioning, then he'd given the police the best and most consistent responses he could muster. Once, to lighten the mood, he had told Taziar a joke. That technique backfired when Taziar could not hold back a chuckle at what should have been a gruelingly serious query.

By the end of the precinct night shift, everyone appeared to have tired of the whole affair, eager to finish as soon as possible. The witnesses to the subway crime corroborated Larson's story, hailing him as a hero. From then on, the cops' manner softened. They became more willing to give Larson the benefit of the doubt on other matters as well. The murder and resisting arrest charges were dismissed. A kidnapping case dissolved when Mrs. Larson failed to press charges against her son or Taziar. And, with their own officers babbling about sorcerers and evil possessions, the precinct glossed over Larson's earlier escape.

Now, immersed in memory, Larson drew a knee to his chest. With the shades drawn and the lights turned off, the hotel furnishings looked like ghostly black silhouettes in the darkness. He had brought Taziar here, too tired to make the longer drive to New Jersey until after a rest. Still, something nagged at the edges of Larson's consciousness. Some small thing he had placed on hold kept sleep at bay.

Larson sighed, searching his memory. Some of the other charges had proven more difficult to dodge. His previously clean police record, a semester of college and a history of participation in high school athletics had helped emphasize his upstanding image. To his surprise, the two officers he had attacked in Sears and Roebuck dropped the assault charges. McCloskey apparently believed Larson's story: that he tripped over the elevator door slot and accidentally knocked the shambling redhead unconscious. Though more skeptical, Johnston grunted when Larson said he had then panicked and hit his other escort. Still, the quieter policeman did not push the issue either.

Larson stretched his legs, jabbing his hands into his jeans' pockets. A crumpled envelope met his touch, and he pulled it free. His mother had handed it to him just before the questioning, without explanation, and he had promptly forgotten it in the confusion. He held the envelope in both hands, certain it was the object that bothered him and believing, without the need to look, that it held bad news. He folded it, delaying, letting his thoughts wander back to the ordeal in the police station.

Avoiding the miscellaneous weapons charges had required more finesse. Larson had claimed Bolverkr as a stranger who had been chasing him for some time, demanding money and threatening his life; in the process, Larson implied that Carl Larson might have gotten himself indebted to a mob-tied loan shark. And, though he knew he should try to avoid bitterness, Larson could not help feeling a modicum of satisfaction that his story might cast suspicion on the drunken driver who had killed his father. A roomful of officers confirmed Larson's understatement that Bolverkr was dangerous and eager to murder, and that affirmation led naturally to the gunfight in the 6th Street warehouse.

Perhaps because of the confusion and swirling fog of Chaos, most of the officers who had survived Bolverkr's and Silme's attack remembered the Dragonrank sorcerer's accomplice as a man. In the end, Larson claimed that Bolverkr had lured him, Timmy, and Taziar to the warehouse where the sorcerer attacked and wounded them. Larson confessed to having shot Bolverkr, aware the police would uncover bullets as well as traces of Taziar's, Timmy's, and Bolverkr's blood, though they could never find the body.

Larson sighed more deeply, clenching the letter in both hands, listening to the rustle of stiff paper bending in his grip. It was not over yet. He knew the police would be sorting questions and answers for a long time, that he would still go to trial, perhaps even serve some time in jail. Still, when it was all over, he had reached the hotel room in reasonably good spirits, despite exhaustion. He had Silme, Taziar, and his family, far more than he had a right to expect. *I'm surrounded by people I love and who love me. For the first time in more than a year, my life is on the right track. Aside from Astryd and my father, I have everything. What more could I ask for?*

Buoyed by the thought, Larson rose and crept to the window. Pulling one curtain a few inches aside, he let the exposed beam of sunlight fall across the paper in his hands. Without glancing at the return address, he drew the letter free. He read only one word, the first: "Greetings. . . ."

Larson stood frozen for a full minute. His gaze locked on the word, and he was unable to continue.

Gradually, helplessness suffused Larson. *Greetings.* He wadded the letter in his fist, his mood shattered. *Greetings. And welcome to your new future, Al Larson.* He hurled the letter across the room, watched it bounce from door to lamp to television before landing at the foot of Taziar's bed. *Greetings. Welcome back to Vietnam.* He held his breath for a moment, as if the mere act of tossing the letter away might make it disappear, along with everything for which it stood. *Back to shallow graves and body counts. Back to maggots and leeches, the constant odor of excrement and death. Back to sleepless nights and desperate days, warm blood, the screams of the injured and fear hovering always like a too familiar friend.*

A million possibilities came to Larson's mind at once, each crazier than the one before. He sorted and discarded every one. *This is no dream. If I ignore it, the government won't just forget about it. And I'm not running.* Grief turned to frustration then flared to rage. *Finally, things were going right.* He slammed his hand against the window hard enough to rattle the pane. *And now, NOW, I'm going to die.* "Damn it." His fist crashed against the glass again. "Damn it, damn it, *damn it!*" He shouted, emphasizing each word with another blow to the window. With the last strike, the glass exploded, raining shards to the street below with a musical sprinkle of sound.

"Allerum, calm down." Taziar's voice wafted from behind Larson. "What's wrong with you?"

Larson whirled.

The little Climber watched him through widened, concerned eyes, keeping the bed safely between them.

Anger waned beneath an onrush of self-pity. Larson

stared at his hand, rivulets of his own blood twining between his fingers. "I've been drafted." The words sounded strange, impossible. "I've been fucking drafted."

Taziar said nothing, not understanding the English word.

Larson did not bother to explain. "Last time, I only enlisted this week. I knew they'd have to draft me this time. I figured I had a year, at least. I can't believe this is happening. Just when I thought things were working out."

Apparently, Taziar put the pieces together. "Don't panic, Allerum. You told me Vidarr said this would be a different future. Maybe this time things will go better."

"Better?" Larson shouted. "Better! The only way it could be better is if I'd die in my first firefight instead of a month shy of leaving hell. We're talking about Nam, Shadow. Viet-fucking-nam. The place that drove me mad, stole every shred of compassion I ever had, then took my life as an afterthought!"

Taziar crawled across the bed to Larson's side. "Calm down. We'll work this out."

"No." Larson sat on the edge of the bed, feeling weak and rubbery in the wake of his fury. His head sank to his chest. Blood seeped into the coverlet, unnoticed. "The first time, I had all my wits about me and I still died. I've been getting flashes of war memory in your world. What's going to happen when I'm back, stressed by similar circumstances to the ones that caused the insanity?" Larson did not wait for Taziar to respond to a mostly rhetorical question. "I'll get confused, maybe panic. I'll get not just myself but every member of my platoon killed. And, if I survive, and any of them do, too, they'd be stupid not to shoot me dead."

Taziar placed a hand on Larson's shoulder. "You're saying you're a danger to the other soldiers."

"Yeah. That's what I'm saying."

"Maybe if you explained that? Maybe they wouldn't want you?"

"How could I possibly explain?"

"The way you just did to me," Taziar suggested with simple logic.

Larson placed his chin into cupped palms. "It won't work. They'll have no record of me enlisting or going to Vietnam. They'll think I'm just scared, just like everyone else." He looked up. "Shadow, I believe in fighting for my country. I really do. But, damn it, I've already served my time, and no one should have to go through hell twice. I may inhabit the same body, but I'm not the same person I was. I can't be."

Taziar rubbed Larson's shoulder reassuringly. "What if I went with you?"

"What?" Larson raised his head, twisting to confront Taziar directly.

Taziar withdrew, sitting cross-legged on the coverlet. "What if I went with you? I can keep you on task. I think we work pretty well together. We've handled Bramin and Fenrir and Bolverkr. . . ."

"Whoa, Taz! I'm not talking about a romp in the park or protecting loved ones from crazed enemies. I'm talking about running around in a steamy, smelly jungle, killing guys you don't know, kids in their early teens. Meanwhile, they're sneaking around slaughtering you and your buddies."

Taziar hesitated, an unnameable emotion sparking in his usually friendly eyes, now reddened and swollen from a previous session of crying. "You do what you have to do."

There was a determined tinge to Taziar's voice that shocked Larson past anger and exhaustion to rationality. "First of all, the army would never let you in. Even if we could forge the paperwork to make you a citizen, you couldn't pass the height and weight requirements. Second, even if we joined together, they'd separate us right after Basic. And, third, it's not like you to give up on a problem this way." Larson remembered how he had felt when he believed he had to kill Silme, how he had wished for the means to take his own life as well. "You once told me how you became reckless right after your father was hanged as a way to avoid confronting problems, and that after his murderer's death you learned to love action for its own sake. Well, if you're thinking of running off and getting killed so you don't have to mourn Astryd, you'd better think again. You're going to stay here, live, and suffer grief like the rest of us!''

Taziar recoiled, startled. Slowly, a lopsided grin wriggled across his features. ''Well, I see your point. Wouldn't want death to go cheating me out of a good cry.'' The smile became more natural. ''But I'm worried about you. There's got to be a way to get you out of this war.''

Larson shrugged, becoming calmer and more fatalistic himself. ''Maybe this is the best thing. I mean, the future I remember didn't actually happen. It's my duty as much as anyone else's to fight this war.'' He spoke easily, hiding a stifling fear and hatred from Taziar.

''What about putting your buddies in danger?'' Taziar reminded.

'Yeah. There's still that.''

Silence followed. Blood soaked into the flowered pattern of the coverlet.

''What are you going to do?'' Taziar asked at length.

''I think,'' Larson said carefully, ''I'm going to take your advice. For once, I'm going to tell the truth. And see where it gets me.''

Two months later, Larson sat on a rigid, wooden bench, dressing amid a swarm of inductees. A familiar day of examinations, paperwork, and questioning had passed in a dark blur of depression. The room hummed with conversations, none of which Larson heard. And, even the sound of his own name did not disrupt the mechanical donning of his jeans.

''Larson! Al!'' A voice boomed again, louder, now directly behind him.

Startled, Larson jumped, diving to safety behind the bench. He peered over the edge, his heart pounding, strangers' laughter echoing around him.

A tall, muscular man stared at him impassively,

hands clenched to hips. Young men in various stages of dress chuckled merrily until a gesture from the newcomer silenced them.

Larson flushed and rose. "You scared me, sir," he said by way of apology, clutching a hand to his chest.

Some of the inductees snickered, but the man ignored them as well as Larson's comment. "You're Larson, I presume?"

Larson nodded.

"Come with me." Without further explanation, he exited the dressing room.

Hurriedly, Larson buttoned and zippered his fly, grabbing his shoes without bothering to put them on. He trotted after the burly man who was now most of the way down a long hall. Even as Larson watched, the other man turned a corner.

Larson had to trot to keep up with the man's huge strides. He caught up halfway down the next hallway. *What's going on? Why was I singled out?* He glanced over his shoulder to affirm that no one had followed. By the time he looked back, the larger man had whipped around another bend in the corridor.

Larson raced around the corner so quickly, he nearly banged into the stranger's back. "Where are we going?" he asked.

"Here." The man stopped, pointing at a plain, wooden door.

Larson halted beside him.

"Well, go ahead, Larson. Go on in."

Larson caught the knob, uncertain what to expect. His mind conjured a thousand impossible explanations, from a horror film version of hell to a Twilight Zonish image of other worlds. *This is insane. Vidarr said he wouldn't interfere, and I believe that. They singled me out for a logical, routine reason.* Larson twisted and pushed.

The door swung open to reveal a squat office painted olive drab. A paunchy, balding man sat behind a government-issue desk. Wire-rimmed glasses perched on an amicable face. A handful of manila folders and a pen covered the desk's surface. One file lay open.

Mine, Larson guessed. A lone, wooden chair faced the desk.

The door closed behind Larson. The man behind the desk picked up the pen and twirled it between his fingers. "Al Larson?"

"Yes, sir." Larson listened to his escort's footsteps retreating down the corridor.

"I'm Dr. Millson. I'm a psychiatrist." He paused, studying Larson for a reaction.

Larson narrowed his eyes in confusion. He set his shoes on the floor by his chair.

"Do you know why you're here?"

"Yes, sir," Larson said. "I'm being inducted into the United State Army."

"How does that make you feel?"

Larson shrugged, too uncomfortable and puzzled to give an emotional response. "I had already enlisted before my draft letter came," he said vaguely, not wholly certain whether he spoke the truth.

Dr. Millson sat back, still playing with the pen, seeming a bit disconcerted himself. "When I asked about knowing why you're here, I meant 'do you know why you're here *in my office* at this time?' "

"No, sir." Larson sank deeper into confusion. *I haven't done anything weird that I know about.*

"Do you remember taking a written test for us?"

Larson nodded. "Sure."

Millson leaned forward, pencil still weaving between his fingers. "Al, what was your state of mind at that time?"

Larson shrugged, trying to remember if he had written anything bizarre. "Regular, I guess, sir. Why?"

In characteristic fashion, the psychiatrist threw the question back. "Why do you think, Al?"

"I honestly don't know." Larson guessed some of his responses seemed unusual for a man of his age, either due to his experiences or his grief for Astryd, the baby, and his father. "I didn't get called before a psychiatrist the last time I was inducted." He looked up, soberly awaiting Millson's response to his reference, remembering his promise to tell the truth.

Millson's gaze fell to the file. His eyes rolled back up to meet Larson's. "You've been inducted before?"

Larson kept his tone level, allowing no emotion to leach through. "Of course. I spent almost a year in Vietnam."

The pen stopped moving, then dropped to the paper. Millson scribbled something. "When was this?"

"November 16, 1968 through September 8, 1969."

Millson glanced up, a frown-scoring his features. "Are you sure of those dates, Al?"

"Yes, sir. Particularly the second one. That was the day I died."

Millson put the pen aside and leaned forward, his chin on his hands, his full concentration focused on Larson. "Do you know today's date?"

Larson nodded, still keeping his expression rigid and unreadable. "Yes, sir, I do. August 3, 1968."

"Doesn't something strike you as odd in the comparison of those dates?"

"Yes, sir. It's because I wound up in a sort of time loop."

"A time loop, Al?"

"Yes, sir."

"Tell me more." Millson looked openly skeptical.

Larson ignored Millson's manner. He explained with the composed matter-of-factness that could only accompany truth. "The Norse god, Freyr, rescued me from death and put me into another body. An elf's body." He added, "Mine was pretty torn up, I guess."

Millson retrieved his pen. "And why do you think this god . . ." He paused, squinting over the rim of his glasses. ". . . Fred, was it?"

"Freyr." Larson restored the name, adding its Old Norse inflection.

"Why did Freyr do this favor for you?"

Larson met Millson's gaze without flinching. "It was hardly a favor. Freyr needed a man from our century because we don't have mind barriers and the people in his time do. He needed someone to wield a sword that could only communicate with an unshielded mind."

"I see." A light seemed to dawn behind Millson's dark eyes. He wound the pen between his fingers again. "Al, has anything like this ever happened to you before?"

"Of course not."

"Do you ever hear voices in your head?"

"Well, yes, sir," Larson admitted. "But only when there's a sorcerer or god who wants to talk to me."

"And what do these sorcerers and gods say to you?"

Larson shrugged. "It depends on the sorcerer or god. Bramin and the Fenris Wolf mostly just threatened. Sometimes, they forced me to remember things from the war."

"The Vietnam War."

"Right."

"What about Freyr?"

Larson continued, still holding his voice to a monotone. "Freyr stayed sort of aloof. Vidarr. . . ." He clarified, "That was the sword. See, he was a god, too." He considered. "Still is. Anyway, Vidarr used to argue with me a lot, though he always meant well. He thought I was too sarcastic."

The speed of the pen increased, lashing between the stubby fingers like the tail of a riled cat. Millson sighed into a long silence. "Al, tell me. Who's the president of the United States?"

"Lyndon Baines Johnson. At least until September."

"And before him?"

"Kennedy."

"And before him?"

"Eisenhower. Dwight."

Millson frowned, apparently not receiving the responses he expected. "Classic," he muttered.

Larson said nothing, not daring to believe other men might have told Dr. Millson stories about dying, Old Norway, and gods. A strange thought struck him. *Perhaps my return has changed history as well as the future. Maybe I got those presidents wrong.* Suddenly, he needed to know. "Did I make a mistake?"

"Huh?"

"The presidents. Did I miss one?"

"Oh." Millson seemed startled by the question. "No. No. Your *memory* works just fine. No evidence of an organic brain lesion."

Larson blinked, uncertain what to make of the statement. By declaring one aspect of Larson's mental functioning normal, he seemed to imply others were faulty. *Not surprising after the story I just told.* "Is that good?"

"Well, yes. Of course." Millson set aside the pen. "Al, have you ever been hospitalized for mental illness?"

"No." The psychiatrist's intention came through clearly. "Are you suggesting I should be?"

Millson dodged the question. He gathered the papers on his desk, shoving them into the manila envelope. "You stay here. I'll be back shortly." He scurried out of the office with little decorum, as if he needed to put distance between himself and Larson.

Al Larson folded his hands in his lap. And waited.

Silme met Al Larson at the outer door, looking stunningly beautiful in curve-hugging blue jeans and a T-shirt that left little to the imagination. The comparison to the conservative, loose-fitting garments she had worn in Old Norway staggered Larson. He stared, studying the golden waves of hair, his eyes tracking down breasts and thighs with a pleasure that almost allowed him to forget a day of needles, doctors' cold hands, and corridors full of young men in their underwear.

"Gosh," Larson said at last. He tried to say more, but was overcome by incoherent stammering.

Silme laughed. She caught his hand, leading him onto the sidewalk. "So how did it go?" She used English, colored with her melodious accent.

"They didn't take me." Larson placed an arm around Silme's narrow waist. "They did recommend a good psychiatrist, though." He waited. Although Silme could no longer cast spells, she had retained her ability to explore superficial thoughts, a process that had never cost her life energy in the past. Now she was using the procedure to help her learn English, slang and connotation as well as denotation.

"They think you're crazy?" Silme tested her newly gained knowledge.

"Right."

"You're not going to see the doctor. Are you?"

Larson retrieved the psychiatrist's card from his pocket. "Actually, I was thinking I might." He corrected quickly, "Not because I'm insane for talking to sorceresses and gods, though. I'm just thinking he might be able to help with the war memories."

"I hope so," Silme said. "You know, I love you."

"I love you, too." Larson gave Silme a vigorous hug. "And you know why?"

Silme embraced him with nearly as much force. "No, why?"

"No reason at all. Does that bother you?"

Silme hesitated, her grip loosening. Then she laughed. "Not this time. Not in the least."

Larson released Silme, taking her hand and continuing the walk along the roadway. Now, fully drawn into his joy, the induction process faded, allowing other thoughts to intrude. "Shadow didn't feel up to coming along?" Astryd's death had taken its toll on the little Climber. And, though understandable, it hurt Larson to see the friend who had kept his spirits through so much pain now fade into a quagmire of despair no one could broach. Over the last two months, Taziar had made obvious and conscious efforts not to inflict his grief on anyone else, even those who had known Astryd and shared his sorrow. He had even learned some new English phrases.

Silme stopped at a four-way intersection, waiting for the walk sign to light, watching the cars trickle past. "Shadow came along. He's just down the road here, helping a woman who locked her keys in the. . . ." Silme trailed off, apparently trying to remember the correct English word.

"Car?" Larson supplied.

People joined Larson and Silme in clusters of two and three, gathering to wait for the light.

"Correct." Silme pointed to a row of cars parked along the curb ahead. "He's right there."

Larson craned his neck around the crowd. Taziar crouched on the hood of a red Mustang, concentrating on some unrecognizable object in his hand. He wore a black dress shirt tucked into pants equally dark, looking like a tiny but dashing villain. A woman leaned against the bumper, watching him intently. She was small. Larson guessed she would stand only a few inches taller than Taziar. Copper highlights wound through sandy curls, defying the current long, straight style. Her body went against the trend as well, stocky and muscled like an athlete's, squarish in an era of tall, willowy women.

The walk sign lit, and Larson and Silme crossed with the group. Apprehension struck Larson. *Shadow doesn't know a damned thing about modern locks. What if he breaks something?*

As if to enhance Larson's concern, a policeman wandered over to the car just as Larson and Silme arrived. The remainder of the crowd passed with no more than a disinterested glimpse.

Taziar looked up. "How'd it go?" he asked in barony tongue.

Closer, Larson identified the object in Taziar's hand as a piece of wood carved to the shape of a key. The Climber clutched tiny tools, using them to scrape shavings from the wood.

"Fine," Larson said. "They didn't take me."

"Great!" Taziar said with genuine enthusiasm, before returning to his work. "Perfect."

The officer peered over Larson's shoulder. "What's he doing?"

The woman poked a finger at the Mustang's driver's window, a fingernail clicking against the glass. "I locked my keys inside. There."

Larson looked in the indicated direction. A ring with three keys lay on the seat, frustratingly beyond the locked doors and closed windows.

The woman's freckled face turned from the policeman to Taziar and back. "He's making a temporary
key, I think."

The policeman snorted. "That's stupid. It's not going to work."

Larson nodded, echoing the sentiment.

Taziar sprang from the hood to the ground. "Excuse
me," he said in English, pushing past Larson and the
officer. "May I, Claire?" He turned his attention to
the woman, awaiting permission.

Claire nodded. "Can't hurt. Give it a try."

Taziar placed the makeshift key in the lock. To Larson's surprise, it fit, though when Taziar twisted, nothing happened.

The policeman rolled his eyes.

Larson sighed, sympathizing with his friend's failure.

Taziar put a bit more pressure on the key, then
whipped it free. Seizing the handle, he opened the
door, ushering Claire inside.

An expression of delight crossed Claire's features in
direct contrast to the policeman's shocked stare. Claire
snatched up her keys. "Thanks, Taz. Thank you so
much."

The policeman took the wooden key from Taziar,
examined the complex series of serrations from all
sides, then returned it to Claire. "I wouldn't have believed it," he muttered. Shaking his head, he continued on his way.

Larson squeezed Silme's hand.

"Taz, hold on just a minute, would you?" Without
awaiting a response, she turned her back, rummaging
through her purse. Shortly, she spun around to face
Taziar again. She handed him a folded ten dollar bill,
then climbed into the car and settled into the driver's
seat. She started the engine, then rolled down her window. "Bye! And thanks again." With a final wave,
she pulled onto the road and roared away.

Taziar watched the car glide into city traffic,
smoothing the bill between his fingers.

Noticing something unusual, Larson reached for the ten. "Can I see that?"

Taziar relinquished it without looking.

Larson studied the bill, discovering numbers hastily scrawled across Alexander Hamilton. "I think she liked you."

Taziar turned. "What do you mean?"

"She left you her telephone number." Larson indicated the handwritten numbers. "Apparently, she wants to see you again."

Taziar made a noncommittal noise. At length, he smiled.

Larson handed back the bill. "At least, you seem to have found your calling. Carving out a working key. I'm impressed." It occurred to Larson just how versatile his companion's skills were. *Even without an education, he could become almost anything. A circus acrobat, a locksmith, a stunt man.* He smiled. *Even a jockey.*

"Just one thing," Taziar said.

Larson nodded, prepared for a discussion on telephones and twentieth century dating practices and, thus, wholly unprepared for Taziar's question.

"What's this for?" Taziar balanced the policeman's badge on his palm.

Startled speechless, Larson stared, his smile wilting. "I don't believe you did that."

Silme lowered her head, apparently trying to glean the implications from Larson's most shallow thoughts.

"You know I'll give it back."

"I don't believe you did that." Larson found himself unable to find other words, though his mind did conjure the perfect want ad: *For sale: Small, agile lunatic. Slightly used. Guaranteed never a dull moment.*

Taziar met Larson's consternation with laughter. He whirled with a dancer's grace, taking in the skyscrapers, lights, and human and vehicular traffic. "I think I love New York."

Silme chuckled.

Larson knew the year would bring its trials: teaching two other-world companions English, turning them into American citizens, convincing his family he should marry a woman he seemed to have known only a few days. Yet, in the wake of all that had happened, those issues seemed trivial. He joined the laughter, wholeheartedly, though he knew it was aimed at him.

Taziar's mirth died away. Larson followed his gaze to a familiar, rocket-shaped building, the tallest in the world, its spire visible through the smog. The expression of determination on the Shadow Climber's face looked frighteningly unconstrained.

Taziar will get along in this endless, concrete playground. Let's just hope New York City can survive Taziar Medakan. "Come on." Larson grabbed Taziar's arm, offering his other hand to Silme. "Let's go home."

According to Norse Mythology, the end of their religious pantheon would come in the form of a great war, the Ragnarok. The gods' enemies would gain access to Asgard via a rainbow bridge called the Bifrost. One god, Heimdallr, was charged with preventing the giants and Hel's hordes from crossing the Bifrost Bridge. Therefore, Heimdallr's responsibility was to guard the Bifrost in order to prevent Ragnarok and assure that the Norse gods survived and reigned for eternity.

Any organization dedicated to recreating the Old Norse age and beliefs, perhaps a subgroup of the Society for Creative Anachronism, could thus be said to have taken over Heimdallr's job as "Guardian of the Bifrost."

—Astryd Larson,
newsletter
August 1991

DAW

An Exciting New Fantasy Talent!

Mickey Zucker Reichert

THE BIFROST GUARDIANS

☐ **GODSLAYER: Book 1** (UE2372—$3.95)

Snatched from the midst of a Vietnam battlefield, Al Larson is hurled through time and space into the body of an elvish warrior to stand against Loki in the combat with Chaos.

☐ **SHADOW CLIMBER: Book 2** (UE2284—$3.50)

Here is the unforgettable tale of the thief-hero Taziar Shadow Climber and his quest for vengeance against his father's slayer. Together with the barbarian lord Moonbear, he will face all comers in a world where death waits one swordstroke or evil enchantment away!

☐ **DRAGONRANK MASTER: Book 3** (UE2366—$4.50)

United at last, the characters from *Godslayer* and those from *Shadow Climber* join in a climactic conflict between the forces of Chaos and Order, forced to fight their way from the legendary world of elves, gods, and magic to the bloody battlefields of Vietnam, and back again.

☐ **SHADOW'S REALM: Book 4** (UE2419—$4.50)

They had killed the Chaos Dragon, and, in so doing, released a force against which all their spells and swords might prove useless—a primal power which now sought to destroy them—and their entire world.

DAW

A Superstar in the DAW Firmament!
Mercedes Lackey

☐ **BY THE SWORD** (UE2463—$4.95)

Granddaughter of the sorceress Kethry, could she master her own powers and save her world from the evils of a mage-backed war?

THE LAST HERALD-MAGE

Vanyel, last of the legendary Herald-Mages of Valdemar, faces a desperate struggle to master his wild talents—talents which, untrained, could endanger all Valdemar. . . .

☐ **MAGIC'S PAWN: Book 1**	(UE2352—$4.50)
☐ **MAGIC'S PROMISE: Book 2**	(UE2401—$4.50)
☐ **MAGIC'S PRICE: Book 3**	(UE2426—$4.50)

VOWS AND HONOR

Tarma and Kethry . . . swordswoman and mage . . . united by the will of the Goddess—and a sworn blood-oath to avenge not only the wrongs done to them but to all womankind!

☐ **THE OATHBOUND: Book 1**	(UE2285—$4.95)
☐ **OATHBREAKERS: Book 2**	(UE2319—$4.95)

THE HERALDS OF VALDEMAR

Chosen by a mysterious equine Companion, young Talia is awakened to her special mind powers. But will her powers, courage, and skill be enough to save the realm from the sorcerous doom that is reaching out to engulf it?

☐ **ARROWS OF THE QUEEN: Book 1**	(UE2378—$3.95)
☐ **ARROW'S FLIGHT: Book 2**	(UE2377—$3.95)
☐ **ARROW'S FALL: Book 3**	(UE2400—$3.95)

PENGUIN USA
P.O. Box 999, Bergenfield, New Jersey 07621

Please send me the DAW BOOKS I have checked above. I am enclosing $________ (check or money order—no currency or C.O.D.'s). Please include the list price plus $1.00 per order to cover handling costs. Prices and numbers are subject to change without notice. (Prices slightly higher in Canada.)

Name ____

Address ____

City _____________________ State __________ Zip __________

Please allow 4-6 weeks for delivery.

Once they'd ordered—why wasn't he surprised that she drank plain black coffee rather than a frothy cappuccino?—they found a quiet table.

Close up, Dominic could see that her eyes weren't quite the piercing ice-blue he'd always thought they were; the edge of her irises were almost navy. In other circumstances, and if she were any other woman, he'd admit to the attraction and maybe ask her out to dinner. But this was Catriona Findlay, the one *solicitor* who intimidated most of the *lawyers* he knew. The woman's mind was like a steel trap. She didn't suffer fools at all, let alone gladly.

So instead, he waited for her to start the conversation.

"Thank you again for agreeing to meet me," she said.

As openings went, it was polite enough. But he'd noticed the fleeting expression in her eyes that said she really didn't want to be having this conversation.

Curiouser and curiouser, he thought. "You said half an hour," he mused, doing his best to look casual but watching her very closely indeed.

"Yes. So I'll cut to the chase," she said, and took a deep breath. "Will you marry me?"

What?

Dear Reader,

I love friends-to-lovers books—so I thought I'd write something different with a rivals-to-lovers book.

Catriona and Dominic think they dislike each other. They're rivals, and she thinks he's a smug mansplainer, while he thinks she's cold and sharp. One of them is going to be the next new partner in the legal firm where they work, and they're both determined to get it!

When Catriona has to get married to inherit the family home—to save it rather than for greed!—the only one she can turn to is Dominic. Their deal means he'll get the partnership and can support his family. They both think they're getting the business deal they want—until they spend time together and realize that maybe they got the wrong idea about each other...

I hope you enjoy their journey!

With love,

Kate Hardy